# Hard Men
## to Kill

# Hard Men to Kill

## WILLIAM W. JOHNSTONE

### AND J.A. JOHNSTONE

**PINNACLE BOOKS**
Kensington Publishing Corp.
kensingtonbooks.com

PINNACLE BOOKS are published by

Kensington Publishing Corp.
900 Third Avenue
New York, NY 10022

PUBLISHER'S NOTE: Following the death of William W. Johnstone, the Johnstone family is working with a carefully selected writer to organize and complete Mr. Johnstone's outlines and many unfinished manuscripts to create additional novels in all of his series like The Last Gunfighter, Mountain Man, and Eagles, among others. This novel was inspired by Mr. Johnstone's superb storytelling.

All Kensington titles, imprints, and distributed lines are available at special quantity discounts for bulk purchases for sales promotion, premiums, fund-raising, and educational or institutional use.

Special book excerpts or customized printings can also be created to fit specific needs. For details, write or phone the office of the Kensington Sales Manager: Kensington Publishing Corp., 900 Third Avenue, New York, NY 10022. Attn. Sales Department. Phone: 1-800-221-2647.

PINNACLE BOOKS, the Pinnacle logo, and the WWJ steer head logo Reg. U.S. Pat. & TM Off.

First Printing: April 2025
ISBN-13: 978-0-7860-5161-8
ISBN-13: 978-0-7860-5162-5 (eBook)

10 9 8 7 6 5 4 3 2 1

Printed in the United States of America

# CHAPTER 1

"Give us the money." Clement leaned forward, square jaw jutting out belligerently. His gnarled hands curled into fists the size of ham hocks. The muscles in his forearms tensed, threatening to rip his soiled denim shirt. He gritted his teeth and then tossed his head like a fiery stallion getting ready to buck. Long blond hair flew back.

His hard gray eyes bored into the banker's rheumy blue ones, but the portly man refused to flinch. He leaned forward and braced himself on his desk.

"You do not deserve a dime, Mister Clement. Not a single, solitary penny. As long as I am president, you shall not get it from this bank."

"I can take it." Clem's voice rasped with menace.

"We have guards. In the lobby. They are watching you right now. Make a move to harm me and, I swear, they will fill you so full of holes there won't be five pounds of your bellicose manner left to bury." He cleared his throat. "I might add that your grave will be in the potter's field since you can't afford even a simple burial."

"He's an Elk," Charlie Dawson said uneasily. He had listened to the men insult each other and now they moved on to outright threats of bodily harm. "The order will see that he gets a decent burial."

"You, too, Mister Dawson? Will they bury you, as well?" The banker settled back and tented his fingers atop his bulging belly. "Leave. Both of you. My patience has worn out."

"You can't take what my partner says too seriously, Mister Norton. It's just that Clem here's all excited. We found the biggest, best vein of gold in the whole of California, and it's just waiting to be dug out. We need supplies so we can get it pulled out of the Betty Sue. There's enough blasting powder, but we can use supplies. To eat."

"Food," growled Clem, not budging an inch from his crouch of looming halfway across the banker's desk.

"You should have left him buried in the mine," Norton said. "You're reasonable. Him," he said, sniffing pompously as he looked down his bulbous nose at the two miners, "he needs to be taught manners."

"Clem, go on and wait outside. I can handle this," Charlie said. He felt a tad uneasy now. The banker had pushed too hard. Clem neared the end of his fuse and was about ready to explode like a keg of Giant Powder.

Clem reared up to his almost six-foot height and glared. He spun about, growled like an angry wolf, and stalked out. The two guards in the lobby watched him with some trepidation, hands resting on their holstered six-shooters. They breathed a sigh of relief when the trouble Clem promised left, slamming the door behind him.

"Now, Mister Norton, how about—?"

"You owe money all over town. The general store. Jones won't give you another loan. Sam, over at the Blue Spruce Saloon, won't even stand you a round of drinks. Not a drop of that panther piss he calls beer. No, Mister Dawson, you have drained this entire lake we so fondly call Potluck of money. There is not a drop to be had. None." Norton pointed a stubby finger at the door. "Get out. Now."

Charlie Dawson reared back and looked over his shoulder. Both guards looked more comfortable throwing him out than they had his partner. He was solid enough and his hands were powerful from swinging a pick all day. He was four inches shorter than Clem, but his shoulders were broader and his chest thicker. And they had no idea how fast he was with the Walker Colt tucked into his waistband.

He pushed his flat-brimmed hat back on his forehead enough to let a lock of brown hair pop out. If ever a man looked ready for a fight, it was him.

Charlie stood and glared at the banker.

"You're making a big mistake. The Betty Sue Mine is going to produce the most gold California's seen since the Rush of '49. That's twenty years, Mister Norton, twenty years. It's time for the next big strike, and we're it. The Betty Sue's going to produce more gold than you will ever be able to lift with those fancy manicured hands of yours. This bank could have been part of it. Your stockholders will look back on this day and wonder what kind of banker you were to pass up this golden opportunity. I'll say it again. Golden!"

"Leave. Now." Norton jabbed his finger several times in the direction of the door.

Charlie left, giving the two guards a baleful look. He stepped out into the Northern California sun. His partner leaned against the brick building, smoking a cheroot. The puffs of smoke rose and disappeared in the gentle breeze blowing off the mountains where their mine stood waiting silently for them to become millionaires.

"No luck?"

"You know he turned us down," Charlie said glumly. "We're going to need a new pick. I broke our old one. And some food . . ."

"I can hunt. I'm a better shot 'n you."

"We'll need ammunition. All I've got is in the cylinder." He touched the Colt in his waistband.

"Not much better," Clem said. He drew the Army Colt he carried at his right hip. "Maybe two more cylinders. No more."

"Twenty rounds or so between us. You'll have to make every shot count, and there won't be any chance of bringing down a deer for some venison stew, not with a pistol shot. The Winchester's out of ammo."

Charlie hitched up his britches.

"All this means is that we've got a lot of work ahead of us, and our bellies are going to rumble a mite." Charlie wanted to say more but had nothing more to add to detailing their problems.

"Mine already thinks my throat's been slit." Clem finished his smoke and went to his swayback nag. He stepped up and waited silently for his partner.

"We'll show everyone in Potluck. We'll show

Norton and Jonesy and Sam and every last one of them when we strike it big. We'll buy the saloon and the general store and . . . and . . . the bank!"

Clem shrugged and turned his horse's face toward the road leading from town. Charlie dug his heels into his scrawny horse's flanks, wondering how horse stew tasted.

"Ready to blast," Clem bellowed.

"Go on, then. I'm already halfway out of the mine." Charlie Dawson stopped and waited. There was something Clem was holding back. "You need a lucifer? Use the flame on the candle."

"Ran out of matches a couple days back."

"So what is it? Spit it out."

"This is the last of our blasting powder. We might try blasting somewhere else. This don't look like we're blasting into the mother lode. Looks like quartz but I'm not even seeing fool's gold."

"The rock's fine," Charlie protested. "All we need to do is clear it out to get to the mother lode." He fell silent for a moment. "You're saying there isn't any gold?"

"Ain't seen a single flake. This isn't blue dirt. We're wasting our powder." He looked around. "Betty Sue's sucking the life from us."

"The mine's got plenty of gold. I feel it."

"The assay doesn't say it."

"You know the assayer wouldn't give us the report. I feel it in my bones that the report was a good one."

"He wouldn't give us the report because we couldn't pay for it."

"Then you don't know what it said. I'm beginning to think you're turning into a chicken, Clem. We've been together going on two years, and this is the first time I've seen you so negative."

Clem ran his callused finger around in the borehole tamped with blasting powder. He pulled it out and looked at the black grains clinging to his skin.

"It'll be a waste. There's no gold here."

"Betty Sue'd never lie to us. You said so yourself!"

"That was six months ago."

"Look. Look at this spot! It's gleaming with quartz. There's gold behind this patch and—"

The clatter of horses' hooves caused Charlie to fall silent. Clem moved beside him and whispered, "You got your gun?"

"It's in the cabin."

"Mine, too." Clem picked up a pry bar and started for the mouth of the mine. Charlie followed close behind carrying their single good pickax.

The day's fading sunlight blinded him. Charlie squinted as he made out four riders. Three remained mounted. Their leader strutted over and stopped a few paces away, his hand resting on his holstered six-gun.

"Good," he said. "You gents are already leaving."

"What do you want, Jimmy Norton? Did your pa get tired of you stinking up the bank so he sent you into the countryside to air out?"

"You talk big, Dawson. Do your jawing somewhere

else. I got papers." He held his coat open. A sheaf of folded documents caused an inner pocket to bulge.

"What are they?" Clem tapped the pry bar against his left palm. Every time he dropped it caused a sound like a gunshot. Two of the mounted men flinched at the noise. The third went for his six-shooter.

"Whoa there, Fredricks," Norton said, holding up his hand. "There's no call to cut down these two. They're just leaving. And shooting them'd be a waste of lead."

"Get your mangy carcass off our land," Charlie said. He stepped closer, readying the pick.

"You stay where you are. I got papers. This here mine's changed hands. You got foreclosed on for not paying taxes. When I heard that, I put up the money outta my own pocket to buy the Betty Sue." Norton spat. "That's a lousy name. I'm calling this here claim the Gold King Mine."

"Taxes?" Clem pushed past his partner. "We don't have to pay taxes for another eight months."

"It was an early assessment, and you missed the deadline. Not that you deadbeats coulda paid, even in a thousand years." Norton drew his six-shooter when Clem took another menacing step forward. "You back off or I swear, I'll gun you down."

"You have to give us a notice," Charlie said. "Nobody told us squat."

"Consider yourselves served," Norton said, yanking the sheaf of papers from his pocket. He thrust them at Charlie.

"We'll get a lawyer to fight this," Charlie said,

glancing over the top page. A few sheets fluttered down. Clem picked them up and looked at them.

"You don't have money to patch a leaky bucket. Get off the land right now." He snatched the papers from Charlie. "Get off *my* land, you deadbeats."

The metallic click as pistols cocked caused Charlie to reach out to restrain his partner. Clem had a way of flying off the handle. He never said much, but his fists often did. Matched against four armed and angry men was a sure way to get ventilated.

"Let us get our bedrolls from the cabin."

"Go on," Jimmy Norton said.

The mounted man called out a warning, but it was too late. Both Clem and Charlie used their weapons to whack at Norton and the other two. Their horses reared and fought them. The solitary mounted man tried to shoot, but his horse bucked.

The two miners raced for their cabin. Clem kicked in the door, not bothering to push it open. He dived for their pistols hanging on a peg by the door. Charlie fielded his and swung around, blazing away.

His first shot caught Jimmy Norton in the gut. The man staggered away, clutching his belly.

Huge chunks of wooden wall began filling the air. The other three fired wildly. The flying splinters made Charlie and Clem duck low. They pressed against an overturned table that gave hardly more protection than the thin cabin walls.

"We're in a world of trouble now," Charlie said.

Clem held up the papers Norton had dropped and

started to pass them to his partner. A new fusillade tore through, causing him to stuff the papers into his waistband. He spun and fired through the door. His lead caused some consternation. Another of their attackers yelped in pain.

"We don't have much ammunition. I'm about out. What about you?"

Clem shook his head.

Then their troubles multiplied. A piece of roof fell in. Charlie looked up and saw flames spreading around the hole.

"They're burning us out!"

The entire cabin exploded in a fireball.

# CHAPTER 2

"This way!" Clem rolled away from the table and kicked like a mule. A section of the back wall blasted outward, already on fire.

Charlie wasn't going to argue. The roof was collapsing overhead, showering burning fragments all around. He rolled and rolled again, colliding with his partner. For a moment they lay in a pile, gasping. Smoke billowed out, filling their lungs. Both coughed. Eyes watering, they made their way from the cabin.

Charlie began swatting out embers that threatened to set fire to his clothes. Beside him, Clem rolled over and over in the dirt to accomplish the same end. They sat upright when bullets began kicking up tiny dust devils around them. The fire hadn't ended the assault. Norton and his cronies had come around the cabin and spotted them.

Clem steadied his Army Colt against his upraised knee and fired.

A loud screech rewarded his marksmanship.

"He shot me!" Jimmy Norton cried. "Help me. Help me!"

Charlie couldn't see Norton through the smoke gusting from the cabin, but he homed in on the voice. He emptied his Colt in that direction. New cries of anguish greeted him.

"Not Norton," Clem said.

"At least one of his henchmen. Maybe two." Charlie clicked the trigger a couple more times. "I'm out of bullets."

"Me, too."

The two got to their feet and staggered as their cabin roof collapsed fully, sending out more waves of flame and heat and smoke. Using this as a cover, they got to the shed used as a stable. They saddled their horses, tucked whatever lay around into their saddlebags, and mounted.

Just outside the shed, they saw two of Norton's gang tending the other two. From where they sat astride their horses, they couldn't make out who was shot or how badly.

"Let's ride," Charlie said. "There's nothing we can do here."

Clem led the way from the now smoldering ruins of the cabin. In minutes, the trail curled around the mountain and led down to a small river flowing along the floor of the valley that led to Potluck. They rode in silence until they reached the outskirts of town. It took the better part of three hours to reach their destination. For all the gunplay and arson at the Betty Sue Mine, the town stretched out all quiet, even peaceful.

"What do you think we ought to do?" Charlie asked. "Go to Marshal Thompson?"

"He's banker Norton's brother-in-law."

"I don't even know who the sheriff is, much less where he hangs his hat."

"Whoever he is, he's out serving process. That's the only way he gets paid." Clem shrugged. "It don't matter. He wouldn't cross the local marshal, no matter what."

"We can't let Jimmy Norton steal our mine."

"He dropped this. Norton did." Clem held out the two sheets he had picked up when Norton declared himself to be owner of the Betty Sue.

"There's something wrong here, Clem. This is our assay report."

"The one we couldn't pay to see."

"Norton got it and it doesn't make a lick of sense. It says the gold content of the ore we turned in for assay is . . ."

"Danged near zero," Clem finished.

Charlie scowled. "So why'd Norton want to run us off if the mine's not worth the powder it'd take to blow up?" He read down the first page. "There's nothing in the rock. Not a speck of gold."

"Not worth throwing the assay sample through Jones Mercantile's plate glass window," Clem said. He looked at the merchant's store. The owner stood in the doorway, glaring at the two miners.

"There's more on the second page." Charlie started to read when a loud shout caused him to look up. The page got away from him, but Clem snatched it in midair.

He tucked the pages away in his vest pocket. With his partner, he twisted around to face Marshal Thompson.

The lawman bustled down the street, his bowed legs working as fast as he could without falling over.

"You, two. Climb on down from them horses. I got a bone to pick with you."

Clem and Charlie exchanged a glance. Without a word, they wheeled their horses around and galloped away. The law dog shouted after them. Then came an errant bullet that missed by a country mile. When they reached the town limits, they slowed to give their horses a breather.

"It doesn't look as if we're welcomed with open arms in Potluck."

"Not any longer," Clem said.

"What are we going to do? We owe 'bout everyone, and the marshal isn't inclined to listen to us. Not if he takes a potshot at us just for coming to town."

"Ride." Clem sucked on his teeth for a minute, then said, "A long ways away."

"Sacramento?"

"Too close," Clem decided.

"San Francisco? We haven't been there in a spell. It's big enough a town to get lost in."

"We need to get lost fast." Clem jerked his thumb over his shoulder.

"A posse! Marshal Thompson's got a posse coming after us!"

"There's no chance to outrun them, not on these nags." Clem patted his horse's neck. The mare turned a large brown eye in his direction as if taking offense at being called a plug.

"I've got an idea. Follow me."

"Why not? You can't get us into worse trouble than we're in."

Charlie Dawson grumbled at that as he guided his horse off the road and down a steep incline to the river that ran past Potluck. The horses splashed in the fetlock-deep water. He headed back up the stream rather than away. He hoped the posse would think he and Clem wanted to escape by going north away from town. The deep stream curled back and ran past Potluck, just a few yards from buildings in a few places.

They splashed along until they passed the town and the stream turned into steeper going. He kept up the diversion until his horse began to stumble from the effort of fighting both the increasing elevation and the rapidly flowing water. Charlie cut away from the stream and worked his way into a stand of pines. Weaving about to confuse the trail, he rode deeper into the woods until he knew his horse had reached the end of its strength. He dropped to the ground and waited for his partner to catch up.

Clem had taken a different route to keep from creating a noticeable trail where they left the stream. He finally rode up from higher on the hillside. A quick kick to get his leg over the saddle and he jumped to the ground. His swayback horse was in better condition than Charlie's, but not by much.

"We can't hide out here forever," Charlie said, "but we can rest and let the posse chase its tail around.

Knowing the kind of men Marshal Thompson recruited, they'll get real thirsty fast and head on back to a saloon to brag on how they chased down two desperadoes and run us plumb out of the county."

Clem snorted in contempt.

"Why'd you think the marshal came after us so quick?"

"We rode in. Jimmy Norton didn't. That'd mean we done the slimy snake in," Clem said.

Charlie sank down, back to a sap-sticky tree trunk. He was too tired to care.

"What'll we do in San Francisco? If you remember the last time we were there, it's a goddanged expensive town. We don't have a dime between us."

"Not so. I've got two nickels." Clem pulled them out of the watch pocket on his jeans and held them in the palm of his hand.

"So we can buy a beer apiece. I could use a brew right now."

"You weren't just flapping your gums. Things cost a lot more in San Francisco. Maybe we could split one."

"I know you. You'd drink the mug danged near dry before you gave me a turn."

"My money."

"Our money. We're partners." Before Charlie went on with his notion of how partners shared everything, the sound of riders approaching through the forest brought him up short. Clem had already heard and reached for his gun. He relaxed when he remembered his six-gun was as empty as a banker's promise.

Darkness hid them as two riders passed by not ten yards away.

"Ain't got no reason to think they came this way. We'll never get a share of the reward."

"We won't get shot at neither," replied his companion. "Those are dangerous owlhoots."

"They only shot up Jimmy Norton. He's gonna live, the doc said."

"He's too cussed to die. Him and his old man. They'd steal pennies off a dead man's eyes."

"And you wouldn't?"

"It'd be more money 'n we're likely to make from wanderin' around blindly in this danged forest."

The two riders drew rein. Cloaked in shadow, they were hidden. If Charlie and Clem hadn't heard their approach, they wouldn't have known the posse members were anywhere near.

Clem nudged his partner. He went to his horse and pulled off the lariat. He played it out into a loop and spun it expertly. With silent steps, he went to where the two deputized townsmen sat on their horses. Charlie grabbed his rope and followed. He wished they'd had a chance to discuss this. Clem had an impulsive streak that got them into trouble.

Ahead a lucifer flared. For a few seconds, he saw the eerie visage of the man lighting his cigarette. Then only the glowing coal showed in the twilight.

"We need to claim part of the reward when the marshal runs them two down. Do you know them?"

The other rider puffed on his cigarette. The pungent smoke drifted through the still forest.

"I think so. They have a mine up on the mountain above town. Never talked with either of them varmints. I think—"

He never finished his thought. Clem's rope sailed through the air and neatly dropped around his target's shoulders. A quick yank on the lariat sent the man flying through the air. He landed on the pine needle forest carpet with a dull thud. Charlie threw his loop. The rope missed and fell in front of the other rider.

The rope hadn't secured his target, but it did spook the horse. It reared and threw the rider to the ground. He landed flat on his back. Charlie heard the air gust from the man's lungs. He pulled in his rope and threw a quick hitch around the gasping man's boots. When the man sat up, Charlie finished the job, a double loop around the shoulders, and then finished with the man's hands.

He plucked a Smith & Wesson from the man's holster, cocked the six-gun, and pointed it at his captive.

"I'll shoot you if you make even a tiny peep."

"Do that and you'll have the rest of the posse on your neck!"

"Won't matter to you. You'll be dead."

Charlie's logic convinced his prisoner to stay quiet. Behind him, Clem spun another couple loops around the other downed posse member.

He held up the man's pistol for his partner to see.

"We've got guns again," he said.

"What do we do with them? I don't want to waste ammo shooting them. We can string 'em up, I suppose."

"Yup."

"Wait, you can't do that. We don't even know you.

We can tell the marshal we never caught a glimpse of you. Right, Flaco? Right?"

The man Clem had tied up grunted in agreement. Clem had taken the man's bandanna and gagged him with it.

"It would be a waste of rope, too," Charlie said, enjoying being in charge for a moment. He whipped off his captive's bandanna and quickly gagged him with it. He dragged his prisoner to where Clem secured the other man to a tree. The two were bound and gagged side by side.

They bucked and strained but the ropes were tied too well.

Charlie stepped back and looked at their handiwork. "Where'd you learn to throw a lariat like that?"

"Worked as a cowboy," Clem said.

"You never said anything about that." There wasn't very much he knew of his partner's life before they teamed up. "Around here?"

"Texas. He was easier to rope than a longhorn." Clem prodded his captive with the toe of his boot.

"We've got two more horses, guns, and from the look of their saddlebags, enough to keep us on the trail for a week."

He and Clem stared at each other. A slow smile came to Clem's lips.

"It'll be enough to let us ride to . . . San Francisco."

"Yeah," Charlie agreed, seeing what his partner did. "It'll get us to San Francisco. Do they have any money we can spend by the Golden Gate?"

He and Clem rifled the men's pockets. They left

watches but found almost two dollars in small change. They split it between them.

"It hardly seems fair," Charlie said. "You've got ten cents more 'n me now."

Clem fumbled in his jeans watch pocket and pulled out a nickel. He silently handed it over. Charlie hesitated, then took it.

"Partners," he said.

"Partners." Clem turned and mounted the nearest horse in their new remuda. With two horses each, they could make better time, riding until their mount tired, then switching to their own horses. It'd have to do to keep them ahead of the posse.

Charlie fetched their mounts, took his seat on the new horse, and said loudly, "Let's head for San Francisco!"

They rode off. Toward San Francisco. They had given the two the idea when they mentioned the city to throw the posse off their trail. What better place to go than where Marshal Thompson was least likely to track them?

# CHAPTER 3

"Charlie Dawson looked over his shoulder every minute or two. He knew the quotation about wicked men fleeing when no one chased after them. But they had dodged tight knots of riders more than once in the week it took to reach San Francisco Bay. Those might have been posses after them, or simply travelers going about other business. No matter which it was, he was glad to be in sight of the tall-masted ships harbored in the Bay. He and Clem had come straight down the middle of the state and finally reached the eastern side of the Bay.

"Is it worth the money to take a ferry across to San Francisco, or should we ride for another couple days and go around the southern end?"

Clem grunted. His partner wasn't sure what that meant. They had the money taken from the two from the posse and nothing more. The food they'd stolen was about gone. Being on the eastern side of San Francisco Bay wasn't a problem when they had nowhere to go and no place to be.

He still preferred being in the city itself. Over the years, he had drifted through San Francisco enough to have an idea where things were and something about the people living there—and those just passing through. All were a tough, hard bunch. That meant opportunity.

But to do what?

He and Clem were miners. At least that was the way he thought of himself. He wasn't sure about his partner after seeing how easily he roped the man outside of Potluck. Somewhere, somehow, Clem had learned enough to become a passable cowboy. No matter how Charlie hinted that his partner should tell what other skills he had accumulated in his travels before they teamed up, Clem had remained tight-lipped. Try as he might to find what other skills he had brought only grunts in reply or Clem stayed mum, not even bothering to acknowledge questions.

He was the same as he'd been since Charlie met him. He wasn't even sure what his partner's name was. Clement. A last name or a first? Calling him Clem suited him just fine. But was that because he was hog-tied to a name he didn't like, and he did like Clement and Clem? Charlie had no idea.

"Take a ferry," Clem said unexpectedly. "I've ridden long enough."

"To the ferry it is," Charlie said. He was happy to let someone else make the decision. Riding around the Bay meant they'd have to spend some money to buy food, anyway. The money for a ferry had to be less than what they'd spend. More than that, he was wearing the seat of his pants paper-thin from spending so much time in the saddle.

A smile curled his lips, just for a moment, as he remembered the last time he'd seen Marshal Thompson back in Potluck. The law dog had hurried toward them, bowed legs letting a whole lot of sunlight pass between his thighs. Charlie felt another day's hard ride would turn him into a copy of the lawman, at least as far as his legs went.

They reached the dock area and boarded a ferry crossing to the Embarcadero on the San Francisco side. The broad-beamed boat rocked more than Charlie preferred. He was a landlubber through and through. By the time they reached San Francisco, his belly wanted to upchuck what little he had eaten. The horses hadn't been happy with the journey, either. They led the mounts to dry land and were set upon immediately by a half dozen men waving fistfuls of greenbacks and yelling over each other.

"They want to buy the horses and tack," Charlie said softly. "We need the money. It's not like we need extra horses in town."

Their next problem was deciding which horses to sell. The old nags they'd owned when working the mine had seen better days, but the notion of getting rid of horses they'd stolen appealed more. While there was little chance anyone recognized the brands, Charlie decided to play it safe. Clem had no opinion.

"We'll get more money for them, too," Charlie rationalized.

"Good sale, here's fifty dollars for the pair," one

dealer in horseflesh cried. He shoved the sheaf of bills under Charlie's nose.

"Why are there so many anxious buyers?" he asked.

"There's always a shortage of horses in town, especially saddle horses. The ones that don't get sold for riding end up pulling trolley cars. You want to sell the other two?" The horse trader looked over the remaining horses. "They'll make someone a meal or two. Even if they're a bit tough to chew."

Charlie handed over the reins and snatched the greenbacks from the man's hands while he told him no deal on the remaining two horses. The man started to dicker.

Charlie pushed past the man, who quickly moved to another rider disembarking from the ferry. Getting away from the docks area made for more peace and quiet, though the bustle of a big city already wore on Charlie's nerves. Bells clanged and people shouted and the rattle of steel on steel as trolleys were pulled down broad streets made him jumpy.

As they walked from the Ferry Building, he counted out half the money and passed it to Clem, who stuffed it into his pocket without counting.

"I might have miscounted. You should make sure you got your due," Charlie said.

"Did you shortchange me?"

"No, but—"

"Then there's no need to count it. You're my partner. You wouldn't cheat me." Clem strode off, tugging on his horse's reins. Charlie hurried after him.

They moved away from Union Square and headed

north toward the Barbary Coast stretching along the Bay all the way to the Golden Gate. It was a rougher section of town, but they had enjoyed a few weeks there right after they'd become partners. The drinks were watered but cheaper than at the Palace or the Bella Union Melodeon. And finding somewhere safe enough to sleep was at the top of Charlie's mind. Flophouses sold a bed for a quarter a night. They had plenty of money now, so they had weeks of hunting before they had to get a job, but he wanted to see what was available in the way of a job.

Stable hands were always in demand. Since they both carried six-shooters, jobs as bank guards or couriers were possible. All it took was waiting for the right situation. Selling the other two horses gave them the luxury of not having to rush into something that wasn't suitable.

After all, they were landowners, even if the Betty Sue was a worthless hole in the ground and Jimmy Norton claimed that taxes hadn't been paid. Not one in a hundred of the men crowded around the docks owned more than what they wore on their backs. That made Charlie a little bit cocky, even if the Potluck banker's son had stolen the mine out from under them.

"We'll have another mine one day," Charlie said softly. "It'll produce so much gold it'll take an entire mule train to pull the wagon."

"Mines are hard work." Clem pointed to a saloon. "Let's get a drink and find a poker game. Gambling's easier than swinging a pick."

"I'd lose my shirt. I never figure the odds right. Maybe faro . . ."

"That's for suckers. I dealt blackjack and five-card stud for six months over in Virginia City."

"You did?" ·

Again he was puzzled at Clem's checkered background. The man had done about everything and not once in two years had he spoken of anything but mining.

"I can wet my whistle," Charlie allowed. He hitched up his pants, settled the Colt in his waistband, and headed for a likely-looking gin mill. Outside he looked around skeptically. The way shadows moved warned that men intended to steal their horses the minute they went into the saloon. Charlie actually considered leading his horse inside. Some customers did that, but no one appreciated it.

"That one," Clem said. "Give him a dollar to watch our horses."

"Why him?" Charlie looked over the down-and-out lowlife his partner had singled out.

"He's honest. He stays bought."

"How can you know that?" Charlie was talking to Clem's back. His partner had passed over the reins to his mare and went into the dive. Charlie negotiated the deal with the layabout and then, with some trepidation, went into the smoke-filled saloon.

Clem had already settled into a chair at a table with four others. He had his share of their money in front of him after a single hand. Charlie watched the other men in the game and picked out which two were in cahoots. They worked to bamboozle the others, including Clem.

Charlie poked his partner to let him know, but Clem motioned him away.

Charlie worried about losing half their money straightaway but went to the bar. He considered shots of whiskey but settled for beer. It was bitter and caused his lips to pucker. In all his born days, he'd never tasted anything better. The brew erased the trail dust in his mouth and burned away the cottony, sticky gum that had formed from not having much to drink, even water.

They had ridden hard and fast and not taken enough time to rest along the way. Coming into a saloon, even this low-life drinking emporium, now felt like a vacation.

He downed the beer and ordered another. He braced both elbows on the stained bar and looked around the room. The half dozen customers who weren't seated at the poker table with Clem were mostly drunk or so close to it they were propped up by walls and tables.

This was the kind of place he missed. Being a prospector and then a miner had kept him away from the benefits of civilization. A long draft on the beer and he was ready for a third. To his surprise, he felt a bit woozy.

"Vice requires practice," he told the barkeep. "That's strong beer you serve."

The bartender only grunted and took his money. Charlie worked on this one more slowly. He blinked to focus his eyes. Clem had managed to accumulate a stack of paper money in front of him on the table.

The two cardsharps cheated openly now, and Clem still won.

"You're mighty lucky," one gambler said.

"First time that's happened in a month of Sundays," Clem said. He riffled through the money in front of him. It was more than he'd ever seen come out of the Betty Sue Mine.

"I got the feeling you're not the yokel you look," the gambler said. "You must be one of them high-stakes fancy cardsharps that spend all their time up at the Union Club. You're used to high stakes from the look of it. A steady hand, a cool eye. Yes, sir, you're a professional gambler, and I was taken in by your slick style."

"Nothing of the sort," Clem said.

"You about cleaned me out, all 'cept for this twenty-dollar gold piece." The gambler spun the small, glittery coin around and then slammed it down on the table with the flat of his hand. "One draw of the cards, high card wins."

"Your gold piece against my paper money?" Clem asked.

"Seems fair. Paper money's not worth its face value. But gold? Now, gold is gold just about everywhere. You don't need to go to a bank to get their notes."

"These are genuine greenbacks," Clem said. "Issued by the Federals."

"That does make them worth more, I reckon. A *little* more." The gambler spun the coin on the table. It made a delightful ringing sound when it finally toppled over. "But they're not precious metal. Nothing is, 'cept real gold."

"I shuffle," Clem said.

The gambler pushed the deck across the table so Clem could give the deck a lengthy shuffle.

Charlie watched. His vision blurred a little. When his partner returned the deck to the center of the table where the gambler picked it up, he blinked. The gambler slid a card onto the bottom of the deck.

"Clem, he—" Charlie grunted when he felt the hard barrel of a pistol shoved into his back. The barkeep stood right behind him, the butt of the six-gun resting on the bar.

Clem cut the deck and came off with a king. The gambler slid the card off the bottom of the deck.

"Ace of spades. You lose."

"Clem, he—" That was as far as Charlie got before the bartender slugged him. He crumpled to the floor. He was aware of the gambler and his partner talking in the far distance. Footsteps. His partner's boots stopped inches from his nose.

"Passed out from too much booze," the bartender said. Clem replied but the words jumbled and echoed strangely.

Charlie blinked hard to clear his vision. Clem got his arm around his shoulders and half lifted him. This was the signal for the gambler to hightail it out the door. Charlie tried pointing but his hand shook too much.

"Drugged me. He cheated." His voice sounded thready and weak.

Charlie landed hard on his back when Clem dropped him to race after the gambler. It might have been an hour or a second he lay there. He wasn't sure how much time passed since the world spun in wild, crazy circles. After an hour or a couple seconds, Clem returned and hoisted him to his feet.

He felt strong enough to take a step. With his partner's help, he took one step, then another, and another. Outside in a cold San Francisco night filled with salt air and rotting fish, he came to his senses as surely as someone holding smelling salts under his nose.

Before he got out a word, Clem said, "They stole our horses and gear."

# CHAPTER 4

"The bartender drugged me," Charlie Dawson complained. "I'm going to settle his hash." He touched the Colt shoved into his waistband. Clem's strong hand on his arm held him back. He looked angrily at his partner. "He's in cahoots with the gambler. And whoever stole our horses!"

"Likely," Clem said. "But what are you going to do? Shoot him?"

"Make him give it all back!"

Clem's grip tightened. Charlie tried to pull free, but his head still spun and occasional blurry patches made the world fuzzier than it was. He finally relented.

"He'll deny it. I don't know why he didn't give me enough knockout drops to lay me out flat. I'm just a tad woozy."

"Your cooking."

"What are you going on about? What's my cooking got to do with anything?"

"You have a gut of pure iron to tolerate the beans you fix. You can digest rat poison after getting used to it."

"My victuals aren't that bad." He tried to face down his partner, then burst out laughing. "Maybe you're right. But what's your excuse? I tried to warn you the gambler slid a card off the bottom of the deck."

"He was good. I didn't see and I was watching real close."

"Real close," Charlie muttered. He looked around at where they had walked—stumbled. The Goat and Compass had the look of a real dive. In the back of his mind, he remembered this was a hangout for the leader of the Sydney Ducks. Not the kind of place for anyone not in the vicious gang. But he found it almost impossible to keep a train of thought running. Another drink would do him. If it didn't have knockout drops in it.

They were in a Barbary Coast bar. Men walked in and stumbled out. Ladies of the night rustled some cash from the pockets of the ones not able to tolerate their booze—or knockout drops. Outright robbery went on in the middle of the street and the occasional splashing sounds from the Bay warned that some victims got tossed into the water.

The "specials" patrolled in packs of three or four. Their blue wool coats were moth-eaten, but the badges pinned to their chests were shined so bright they looked like tiny suns reflecting the gaslight. Every last man wore a six-gun slung at his hip and carried a weighted sap or long nightstick capable of breaking a skull open with one whack.

"I can tell them," Charlie said, watching a pack of the patrolling coppers march past. He wasn't sure if he felt insulted. None of the policemen gave him or Clem a second look in spite of how they looked. They weren't dangerous enough. Or pitiful enough.

"You know they're in the pay of the saloon owners. Annoy them and end up in jail."

Charlie sagged. His partner was right. He had been mining too long and had forgotten how things worked in the big city. But things here weren't much different from Potluck. The banker's son stole their mine without so much as a fare-thee-well. The marshal took his marching orders from the banker. Along the Barbary Coast, things were more honest, if that was the word. Crooks were open and corruption rotted the innards of the community. The gangs controlled everything with an iron hand, just as the Tongs ran things over in Chinatown.

"All open for everyone to see," he said to himself.

"I lost all my money. What do you have left?"

"Most from the sale of the horses. Twenty dollars or thereabouts. We won't starve."

"Unless we get robbed." Clem touched the Army Colt at his side to show he wasn't going to allow that.

"Buying back the horses we sold's not possible. We should hunt for the thieves who stole the ones we kept."

"And our gear." Clem dropped to hands and knees and crawled around where they'd tethered their horses. Like a small child, he followed the tracks, then got to his feet and pointed.

"They went that way?" Charlie made sure the pistol in his waistband came free easily. Catching the hammer on his clothing when he needed firepower meant death. He didn't cotton to the idea of being killed and his body tossed in the Bay for the fishes.

For the sharks.

He remembered watching the fins cutting through the dark water from when he and Clem had spent a few weeks here before heading north to Potluck to find their fortune in those already petered-out gold fields.

"There's a stable," Clem said. "Trail goes straight to it."

Charlie slid his six-shooter free and held it at his side. He stopped in the door leading into the stables. A dozen stalls were all filled. Standing on tiptoe, he got a look at most of the horses. He entered to check the last four stalls.

He turned to stone when he heard the metallic click of a hammer cocking.

"You lookin' to leave a horse, I can oblige. You lookin' to steal a horse, and I can oblige you that, too. With both barrels of this here shotgun."

He turned slowly. An old man with wattles that bobbed every time he swallowed stood in an empty stall. He was an old geezer, but the shotgun never wavered. The twin barrels looked like railroad tunnels as they lifted slightly to point directly at Charlie's face.

"Looking for my horse. It got itself stolen an hour back."

"No stole horses in this here livery stable. Get your carcass out. I don't like nobody makin' false accusations. This here's an honest establishment."

Charlie took the chance to examine the horses he hadn't seen before. His heart sank. Neither his nor Clem's mount was here.

"You have any other horses?"

"Clear out. I'm giving you to the count of three. One, two—" The old man stopped counting suddenly.

He slowly lowered his shotgun. Clem had drawn a bead on the man's head.

"You can't steal none of these horses. I pay for protection. The specials'll have you strung up to a lamppost before you get a block. I pay 'em enough for that kind of protection."

"It won't matter a lick to you if my partner puts a bullet through your skull," Charlie said. He waved Clem back. "The horses aren't here."

"They were brought here. The tracks say so."

"He must have sold them already. Isn't that true?"

"Yeah, I . . ." The stableman clamped his mouth shut.

Charlie lifted his six-gun and cocked it. He walked slowly toward the man.

"Who bought the horses? I can count, too. And when I get to three, your brains'll be splattered all over the wall."

"Who knows what he calls himself? I never heard his name, anyway. The color of his money's always good. He pays in specie."

"How much?" Clem asked.

"That's not important," Charlie said. "Where do we find him?"

"There's a corral down toward the Embarcadero. He wears a red silk cravat with a shiny headlight diamond in it."

Clem and Charlie exchanged a glance. This was the man who had bought their other horses.

"Much obliged," Charlie said, backing away.

"I want the money," Clem said.

This was a sticking point for the livery stable owner.

From the set of his jaw and the way his shoulders bunched up, he'd die before he turned over one red cent.

"Let's go fetch our horses," Charlie said. He herded Clem in front of him. When they were outside, they heard a steady stream of curses that turned the air blue. The stable hand wasn't pleased at all that he had been caught so easily.

The aspersions he cast on Charlie's parents, brothers, and sisters almost made him go back in to settle the score. Clem stopped him.

"You don't have any sisters and your ma died twenty years back."

"Longer," Charlie said. "I hardly knew her. I wasn't even ten when she died of scarlet fever."

"Don't get het up over insults like that. They don't mean a thing."

Charlie stared at his partner. They'd worked shoulder to shoulder for two years, and he hardly knew the man. Clement. Clem. That was a sign he should have asked more questions, not that Clem would have answered.

Clem hardly seemed steamed about losing his money to the gambler or their horses to a thief. If anything, he came alive. Trouble was on the way and he relished it.

They trooped along the shoreline until they spotted the Ferry Building. Not far from it were a dozen different corrals along Montgomery Street.

"If we split up, we can check the horses that much faster," Charlie suggested.

"Stick together. Watch each other's back."

"I suppose you're right. Anyone who runs stolen horses has to be on guard all the time."

"He had two bodyguards when we docked this afternoon."

"He did?" Charlie's eyebrows arched. He hadn't noticed anyone but the horse trader. Being too anxious to get into the city—and to swill a beer or two—had made him careless. He wondered that Clem hadn't been thoughtless.

They slowly circled each corral. When they reached the third one, they attracted unwanted attention. Two men with rifles atop a shed nudged each other and then slid to the ground.

"What'll we do?" Charlie asked.

"Lie."

The guards trooped over and kept their rifles pointed at the ground under the two men's feet. A quick move would level those deadly firearms and fill Clem and Charlie with more lead than they could tolerate.

"What're you doin' pokin' 'round here?" The guard spat. His eyes never left the two interlopers.

"We're in the market for horses," Clem said.

"Come around in the morning. Mister Sarkasian don't show up 'til ten."

"Yeah," said the other guard. "He likes to sleep late."

"The first ferry doesn't come over from Oakland 'til then," the first guard said, giving his partner a deep scowl for making fun of their boss. "That's when he buys and sells." He squinted and stepped closer. "You two came over this afternoon 'nd sold him horses. You lookin' to steal 'em back?"

Both guards' rifles lifted.

"Nothing of the sort. We need . . . we need more horses."

They all turned when the sound of a horse's hooves drowned out the sort of slapping of waves against the shore. A man astride a large black stallion galloped off.

"That's a mighty fine horse. How much?"

"Ain't your concern. He's been sold."

"We'd like to buy horses that look that fine," Charlie said. "Mister Sark—" He stumbled on the name.

"Sarkasian, and you do that. Come around tomorrow when he's here. Now you two get on out of here. It'd be a pity to frighten the horses."

"We wouldn't . . ." Charlie's words trailed off. They meant they didn't want to frighten the horses by gunning down two nosy miners. "In the morning. See you then. And Mister . . ."

"Sarkasian," supplied a guard.

Charlie and Clem tried not to run off. They sauntered away until they turned the corner and were hidden from the guards' line of fire. They pressed themselves against a brick wall. Charlie was sweating. Clem looked as if he was out for an evening stroll.

"I didn't see our horses in any of the corrals, but I wasn't able to get much of a look at the farthest pens."

"We can sneak a look if we go down a couple blocks," Clem said.

"Those two are alert now. If they spot us, they'll shoot."

"We shoot back."

The matter-of-fact way Clem spoke made Charlie uneasy. He'd get them into a gunfight yet.

"We keep our eyes peeled. We don't poke them like caged wildcats."

They made their way along Montgomery Street, dodging the bustling evening traffic. When they'd gone far enough, they cut back toward the Bay and the corrals. Ahead of them lay the three corrals they hadn't gotten a good look at before.

Edging closer, they got as close as they could without revealing themselves if the guards had returned to their post atop the shed. That had been chosen as a lookout because it gave them a clear shot from the nearest to the farthest corral, should anyone be foolish enough to try a little horse-rustling.

"I don't see anything," Clem said.

"I don't either," Charlie replied. Then he froze. Behind him, he heard a six-gun cock. Whoever held the pistol was close to panting, as if from exhaustion. Charlie had seen a man who made his first kill pant like that.

"Get your hands in the air where I can see them. Do it or I shoot!"

Charlie's hands shot up. Clem was slower to obey. But he did, much to Charlie's relief.

# CHAPTER 5

"You got it all wrong, mister," Charlie said. "We're not trying to steal those horses. We're hunting for some that got stolen."

"You're bounty hunters?"

"Not exactly," Charlie said. "We find lost things and return them to their owners."

"That's like a bounty hunter," the man said. He pursed his lips and nodded slowly as he thought on the matter. "You any good at finding things?"

"Yup." Clem turned and faced their assailant.

Charlie joined his partner, keeping his hands in the air. Clem was more relaxed about it and held his hand just over his holster, ready to draw. With the man behind them already drawing a bead, he'd never clear leather. Charlie swallowed. If his partner made a move, he'd have to go for his six-gun. In the past week, he'd shot more men than he ever had in his life. Jimmy Norton had deserved it. This man would, too, because he intended to shoot them in the back.

Or did he?

"Do you need something that's lost to get itself

found? We can do that," Charlie said. He lowered his hands, expecting a slug to rip through him. It didn't happen.

"My horse. A thoroughbred. It was stolen this afternoon. It's worth a thousand dollars. More when I put him out to stud, but that'll be a while. I want to ride him. I look like a king on that horse."

"That black stallion? About fifteen hands high?" Clem stepped closer to the man.

"You saw him? You saw Black Knight?" The man moved so that the street lamp lit up his worried face. Shadows across his high cheekbones turned him gaunt. Deep-set eyes glowed in the dark.

The man was well-dressed. Charlie guessed what had been spent on the coat and trousers and vest would keep him in victuals for a couple months. Longer. A cravat was held by a small ruby stickpin. As he moved, he showed that the small pistol clutched in his hand usually rode in a shoulder rig. The tailoring of his fine coat was such that the gun would be hidden until it was needed. Shoes so highly polished they reflected like mirrors finished off the portrait of a wealthy man who was worried about a thief.

"Reckon we did," Clem said. "What's it worth to you getting the horse back?"

"I paid thousands for Black Knight."

"We wouldn't ask that much," Charlie said hastily, before Clem demanded an equal payment. "Two hundred. We'll return your horse for two hundred dollars."

"In gold," Clem added.

"How long before you can do the job? Who stole

him? I don't care what you do to the thief. I want my horse back."

"We won't turn the thief over to the police, but we can get the horse."

"Whoever did this is the worst kind of thief. He deserves to be hanged. That's what they do to horse thieves, but it won't matter if you return Black Knight."

"We'll need some money to loosen some tongues, if you know what I mean," Charlie said.

"Bribes? Well, yes. Let me see what I have." He fumbled in a vest pocket and brought out four silver dollars and a few dimes. He held it out, then drew back. "You're not going to take the money and vanish, are you?"

"Sir, me and my associate, Mister Clement here, are honest men. We give you our word we'll do everything possible." Charlie took the money once more offered, then added a business card to the pile of change. He squinted as he read the card in the dim light.

"Lester Lecroix, Esq. I am one of the best lawyers in San Francisco. Some might say that I am the best." He cleared his throat and tried to look modest. He failed.

"Wouldn't cross a lawyer, no, sir," Charlie said. "You know the law inside and out."

"Why not go to the police?" Clem asked. "A man like you's got friends there, in the police."

"They are a corrupt organization, and I often find myself defending men they have falsely accused. They are not on the side of the law, as I see it. Some are worse than the felons I defend in court."

"Do you think one of them stole Black Knight?"

Charlie craned his neck around, trying to remember which corral they had seen the man take the midnight black stallion out of. He mapped out the street where the stallion had trotted, as proud as a king.

As noble as a Black Knight.

"I wouldn't put it past them. My horse was stabled at the foot of Russian Hill. How a thief spirited Knight away is beyond me. The stableboy claims he had nothing to do with it."

"You believe him?"

"I do," Lecroix said with some reluctance. "His father and his father before him have all served my family dutifully and well since we came from France fifty years ago."

"You have other servants?" Clem asked.

"Of course, don't be ridiculous. But they are all loyal, too."

Charlie pursed his lips and asked, "Do you know anyone named Sarkasian?"

It was as if he had stuck Lecroix with a pin. He sputtered a moment, then finally composed himself.

"How do you know about him? I can't discuss a client. Unless . . ."

"You know where he hangs his hat?" Clem asked. "We don't need to know what your business with him is."

"He's a respectable man of affairs. He owns several millinery stores and a taxi service."

"Does he deal in leather goods? Saddles and the like?" Charlie felt his heart racing now.

"I suppose. I had no call to delve that deeply into his business dealings. He needed some advice on an investment, that's all." Lecroix tucked his pistol back into his shoulder holster. "Do you suspect him? If you do, I swear I'll see him in prison!"

"We have to get on the trail before it turns cold," Charlie said. "We can collect our money at your office. When we return your horse."

"Why, yes, that's fine," Lecroix said. He seemed flustered.

"I got a question," Clem piped up. "Why'd you come poking around down here?"

"I've asked everyone I come across if they've seen Black Knight. A ruffian of my acquaintance at the Bella Union claimed to have seen my horse being led in this direction. It was a long shot, I know, and he is a shifty man, but it was possible. That particular theater is only a few blocks from where the horse is stabled."

"Let us get to work," Charlie said. "We'll get back to you as quick as a fox."

"But we don't stink like a fox," Clem added.

Lecroix looked at them askance, then left, mumbling to himself. When he was out of earshot, Charlie turned to his partner and said, "You thinking what I am? That Sarkasian saw the horse and had someone steal it? Then it was put in his corral?"

"Until he came to ride it off," Clem finished. He looked down the street where the man they'd seen had ridden the black stallion.

"This might be an easy two hundred dollars."

"We need a job. Finding things might be what we do best."

Charlie didn't add, "Whatever we do best, it's not mining."

Side by side, they set out to track down the black stallion and its rider.

"It's good that we found where the horseflesh peddler lived. If we asked just one more person, they'd've called the police." Charlie saw the small stable at the rear of a fancy house that made even the ones on Russian Hill and Nob Hill look cheap. "Who'd have thought buying and selling horses from people on the ferry was this profitable."

"That and a taxi service and stores," said Clem, "and outright horse-rustling."

"He must have seen Lecroix on Black Knight and taken a fancy to the horse."

"The lawyer might have charged him too much, and this is the horse trader's way of evening the score."

"He's got a guard at the back gate. Getting the horse isn't an easy chore," Charlie said. He sucked on his teeth as he thought about the situation. A plan slowly formed. "We divert the guard, get him away from his post. Then we take the horse."

"Let's shoot him."

"The guard?" Charlie was outraged. "We can't kill him in cold blood."

"He's wearing iron. That makes him fair game."

"No!" Charlie looked at his partner, wondering if he

was joshing. As far as he could tell, Clem meant it. He'd walk up to the guard, gun him down, and then steal back the horse.

"I'm better with horses than you. Go around the carriage house and start a fire."

"Burn it down?"

Charlie worried that they were drawing attention in this neighborhood. They weren't dressed to the nines like most everyone riding past, many of them in fancy carriages. Thievery paid better than being a down-and-out miner.

"Do it," he said. "Hurry up." He hitched up his pants and settled the six-gun in his waistband. Pulling his coat around his body did little to hide the weapon. The coat was threadbare and a size too small. If he tugged hard, he could button it in front, but if he did, a button might pop off if he breathed too hard.

Clem stormed off. He caught the guard's attention, but the man was too smart to be lured away. He kept an eagle eye on Clem until he disappeared around the carriage house. Charlie walked slowly toward the corral. The main house was some distance away. Nobody watched from the second story. He walked faster when he caught sight of the first wisps of greasy, black smoke rising from the back of the carriage house.

The guard's nose wrinkled. He caught the scent of burning brush. He let out a yell and raced off to put out the fire. Charlie hoped the shout hadn't alerted other guards. Sarkasian kept a small army around him, if the guards at the ferry docks and the corrals there were an indication.

Charlie recoiled when the carriage house caught fire. Huge gouts of flame licked at the sky. Billows of black smoke laid down a choking fog that forced the guard back a few steps. He lifted his arm and breathed through the bend of his elbow to renew his advance.

The horses in the corral began to rear and paw the air as the fire raged. Charlie cursed his bad luck. He hadn't thought the horses would get all riled up. He just hadn't thought. A better plan would have helped him out. With more courage than good sense, he climbed the fence rails and balanced on the top. When Black Knight stamped past, he jumped. The momentum carried him over the horse's back. Charlie grabbed the straining equine neck with both arms and fought to keep his seat.

"Whoa, boy, settle down," he tried to soothe. The horse had none of it. Its powerful kicks almost threw him off. He clung on for dear life.

Another horse lashed out with its front hooves and knocked the latch off the gate. In a thunderous stampede, the horses galloped away, snorting in fear. Black Knight joined them. Charlie tried to change direction and found the horse was too strong. Without a bridle and bit, the stallion was wild and free of any rider's control.

Content to just stay astride the straining horse, Charlie let Black Knight run. It turned back into town. More than one pedestrian saw the headlong rush. One or two shouted at him for riding so dangerously. Just getting away from the horse thief's corral was good enough for Charlie. After almost ten minutes of frantic gallop, the powerful stallion began to falter. Its flanks

were covered with lather and its eyes were still wide
with fear. But when he felt Black Knight weakening,
Charlie was better able to steer the horse northward
toward its old stable.

To his surprise, another rider trotted up beside him.
Clem sat on another horse from the remuda.

"How'd you get away?" Charlie called.

"Picked a good one, let her run," Clem replied.

"Sarkasian will have his men scouring the town for
us. We have to get back to Lecroix right away or—"

Charlie fell silent when Clem pointed. Black Knight
headed directly for home. If the stallion had been exhausted from its earlier frantic run, sight of a familiar
stall renewed its energy. Again Charlie grabbed the
muscled neck to keep from being tossed off. The horse
bolted into the stable and slowed to go into a stall better
outfitted than most of the places Charlie had slept at any
time in his life.

Black Knight stood patiently, sides heaving, waiting
for the groom to rush out to tend it.

Charlie backed from the stable on shaky legs. He
wasn't much of a horseman and that had been one
hellacious ride across town. When he turned, he almost
bumped into Lecroix. The man grinned from ear to ear.
He grabbed Charlie's hand and pumped hard, like he
had to get well water up from a hundred feet below.

"You're a man of your word. I didn't think you'd do
it. You returned my precious Black Knight to me!"

"Groom's working on the stallion now," Clem said.
He stood a few feet away, holding the reins of the horse
he'd taken from the corral. Charlie wanted to ask how

his partner had harnessed the horse, but that was a minor mystery.

"Jed's a good groom. He'll check out Knight. He will," Lecroix said. The man started to leave. Charlie reached out and grabbed the man's sleeve to hold him back.

"You promised us two hundred dollars if we found your stallion and brought him back. There he is, all safe and sound."

"I did, didn't I? We never had a written contract, but a man's word is his bond. You fulfilled your duties well. Can I do less?" Lecroix fished out a bulging leather wallet from an inner coat pocket and began counting out greenbacks.

"You said gold." Clem looked belligerent. He thrust out his chin and lifted fists halfway to his chest, as if ready to engage in fisticuffs to get their due.

"That's all right," Charlie interrupted. "We'll take paper money. We have to be on our way, and I'm sure rustling up so much in gold would take even a fine gentleman like you some time."

Lecroix hardly heard. He finished counting out the money and held it out. Charlie grabbed it before Clem.

"Thank you, sir. If you have anything else you want us to find, we're in the business. Of finding lost objects. Or stolen horses."

"I'll keep you in mind," Lecroix said, starting to push past Clem.

"Here," Clem said. He passed over the reins to Lecroix. "This horse is part of the deal."

"Why, yes, whatever you say." Lecroix signaled. A

youngster of ten or twelve rushed over and took the reins. He led the horse into the stables. Lecroix was too mesmerized with his thoroughbred Black Knight to pay attention to anything else happening around him.

Charlie saw they had been dismissed. He tucked the money into his coat pocket.

"That went well," he said.

Clem nodded.

They walked away. Charlie had a question on the tip of his tongue. He finally spit it out.

"Why'd you give him the horse you rode?"

"Black Knight was his. We returned it. The other horse was stolen. I'm not a horse thief."

Charlie tried to find fault with his partner's logic and couldn't. They went off to find a new saloon to celebrate. The first one they'd picked hadn't been too lucky for them, even if it had launched them on a new business.

# CHAPTER 6

"That looks a likely place to dip our beaks," Charlie said. The bar had been built at the very end of Meiggs Wharf. The icy San Francisco Bay water lapped at the pilings under their feet so hard it sent curtains of foam into the air.

"Why'd they build it here?" Clem asked.

"The pilings are rotted through and through. The entire pier can collapse into the Bay at any instant. Newer docks take the cargo skiffs when the ship stays out in the Bay. This place might be rent-free for the owner."

"Who'd claim it?" Clem wrinkled his nose. The smells wafting from inside combined the worst of a harbor and a saloon. Dead fish. Spilled, stale beer. Vomit. Spittoons never emptied. Blood. Lots of blood.

Charlie looked inside and grinned. He saw the source of the stench, and there was more. A parrot screeched as it dived wildly on patrons. It cussed in at least four languages he recognized and a couple he didn't. Only when one bar patron bought the parrot a shot of whiskey did it settle down, waddling along the bar to grab the shot class in its cruel beak. With a well-practiced twist of its neck, it downed the entire shot. Nearby patrons applauded. The now-drunk bird staggered away and sank down at the end of the bar, cursing anyone who came near it.

"Cobwebs," Clem said.

The cobwebs dangling from rafters overhead formed an eye-confusing pattern. The smoky oil lamps scattered around the filthy interior shined through the cobwebs and created eerie shadows above that gyrated with the air currents every time the door opened. Charlie wondered what lurked up there. The rafters weren't anywhere a sober man ventured. He doubted the cursing parrot was alone in exploring the upper reaches in such a place as the Cobweb Palace.

They stepped in and stopped to stare at the walls. Cobwebs draped over pictures of nude women on all four walls. Charlie edged closer and started to brush the sticky strands away to get a better look.

"Wouldn't do that, mister," a sailor at a nearby table said. "Warner likes it like that."

"Warner?"

"Abe Warner owns the place. That's him behind the bar."

A burly man without a shirt and who wore a battered brown leather apron moved from one end of the bar to the other without causing so much as a whisper among the cobwebs. As he reached the end closest to the parrot, the feathered menace screeched, "Grandfather!"

"That's what the bird calls him. It's the only one who does. I seen him bust a man's back for callin' him that."

"He doesn't even clean the webs off the bottles on the back bar."

"Ole Warner took a likin' to spiders. Never interrupts them when they start spinnin'. Most all of them don't do anything but spin." The sailor took another long drink of the beer in front of him, belched, and sank forward. He laid his head on the table. In seconds, he snored louder than the cursing parrot's calumnies on all and sundry.

Charlie looked around and tried to guess how many spiders it took to fill a huge room like this. Not only were the walls decorated with the racy pictures of naked women, here and there on display were racks of scrimshaw. Walrus tusks and sperm whale bones had been intricately decorated.

"You here to stare at the gewgaws or to get drunk?"

"This looks like a place where the owner's not interested in drugging us. He'll get a whale of a lot more money by serving us whiskey."

"I want brandy," Clem said.

"Brandy it is." Charlie and his partner wended their way through the maze of tables. They leaned against the bar.

The bare-to-the-waist barkeep ambled over.

"What'll it be? Speak up. Them monkeys are causin' quite the ruckus."

Charlie ordered over the chattering monkeys locked in cages at the far end of the bar. Warner expertly slid two glasses along the bar and started to pour. Clem caught the man's brawny wrist.

"We'll work on the whole danged bottle."

Warner's eyes widened just a little when Charlie

peeled off enough bills to pay for the brandy. Seeing the bar owner's reaction, he looked around. Men on either side of them noticed the thick wad of greenbacks. This had gotten them into trouble before. He scooped up the bottle and said, "There's a table."

"Somebody's already there," Clem pointed out.

"He won't bother us. He's passed out."

They sat and Clem poured shots of brandy. Before he set the bottle on the table, their unconscious companion showed some life.

"Me, too. Gimme some."

The partners exchanged a glance, then came to a mutual decision. Clem poured a shot.

"To our newfound brotherhood," the man said. He clinked his shot glass with theirs and downed the brandy in a single loud gulp, followed by a belch.

Charlie and Clem matched him.

"Much obliged for the drink. Lemme inner-deuce m'self. I'm none other than Thomas Collins."

"Tom," Charlie said, saluting with his glass.

"Wait, no, thass not me. Thass my pa. I'm J. Washington Collins. His son."

"What's the _J_ stand for?" Charlie asked. Clem poured more brandy.

The young man frowned. He tossed his head and sent a shock of blond hair back. His bloodshot eyes were blue whenever they drained. He sported an almost invisible mustache and either started a beard or hadn't shaved in a couple days. If his eyes hadn't been sunken and his cheeks hollow from too much booze and not enough nutrition, he'd have been handsome.

From the remnants of his clothing, he had started out wearing fancy duds. A watch chain dangled in front of his paisley vest. The fob swung about but the watch was absent.

"The *J*?" he asked, trying to focus.

"In your name."

"Don't remember. Not important. Folks call me Wash. Friends, that is. You're my friends. Call me Wash."

"Pleased to make your acquaintance, Wash."

Charlie and Clem made sport of the young man. He liked it and joined in, making jokes at his own expense.

"What do you do for a living?" Charlie asked.

"I spend money," he said confidentially. "My pa's money. He's got plenny. Ole Wash, his boy, thass me, I can't spend it faster 'n he makes it. He's that rich. Believe me, I spend quicker 'n, quicker 'n *that*." He tried and failed to snap his fingers.

"You buy a round," Clem said. "The bottle's running dry."

"Buy? You want Wash to buy a round? Sir, my good friend, whass yer name? I, sir, am tapped out. Not unlike when you tap a beer keg and it spews foam all over the place." He threw his arms wide and leaned back to demonstrate. Charlie grabbed him before he fell onto the floor and landed among the unidentifiable debris there. Some of it was sawdust, some the outcome of giving the parrot too much to drink or feeding the monkeys ripe bananas.

"We've got enough," Charlie said before Clem protested. "We're businessmen."

"Whatcha do if I might ask?" Wash Collins closed

one eye to focus the other. "You look like miners. You mine up on Sutro Peak?" He snickered at the joke only he understood.

Charlie studied the young man a bit more. Drunker than a lord, he still had an eye for apprising others.

"We find things for people."

"Bounty hunters?"

"No, dammit," Clem said. "We aren't bounty hunters."

"If somebody loses something, we find it for a price."

"Then I wanna hire you." Wash rested his hand on Charlie's arm.

"What've you lost?"

"My sobriety!" He reared back and gave a belly laugh. Again Charlie had to prevent Wash from falling out of his chair.

"The best way to find it is to lose ours," Charlie said. He silently pointed to the bar. Clem got the hint and went to buy another bottle.

Charlie tried to stand and found his legs had turned to rubber. The smoke in the room no longer bothered him, and he thought he understood the parrot's shrill ranting. That couldn't be a good sign.

"Come on over, parrot," he called. "I'll stand you to a drink."

"Mister, he don't like brandy. He prefers whiskey," a burly sailor at the bar said. "Let me show you." The sailor came over with a bottle a quarter filled. He hooked a foot around a chair leg and pulled it under him in a well-practiced move.

The sailor poured an entire round. He whistled and the parrot launched itself from the bar, swooped low, and landed on the edge of the table. It strutted forward and pecked at the whiskey.

"See? He can hold his liquor."

Charlie paused, the whiskey in his hand halfway to his mouth.

"Go on. The parrot'll be insulted if you don't drink with 'im."

Charlie looked across the table at his partner. Clem had frozen, too.

"Drink." The sailor's tone turned nasty. "The parrot won't like it. If you don't drink my whiskey, I will be mighty riled."

"To you," Charlie said. He turned his head away and pretended to empty the glass. Most of it spilled on his shoulder. The few drops that touched his lips burned like fire.

Clem had moved even quicker in dumping his drink to the floor. Wash belched, hoisted his glass, and drained it. Then he ran his finger around the rim to catch the last drop and licked it off. His eyes were barely focusing before the drink. Now they crossed.

"Surely was s-s-strong," he said. He grinned foolishly, then he passed out.

Clem and Charlie both moved as fast as they could after polishing off a bottle of brandy. Their six-guns slid into their fists, they kicked free of their chairs and stepped away from the table.

"Whoa, gents, don't go throwin' lead all around. This is a peaceable gin mill," the sailor said. He held out his hands, palms up, to show he wasn't holding a weapon.

Two others moved to stand by his shoulders. Charlie

tried to decide which he'd shoot first. Three of them? Or six? His vision was doubled.

"Shoot the one in the middle," Clem advised.

"We're goin'," the sailor said. "Us and our friend." They hoisted Wash between them and dragged him to the back of the Cobweb Palace. A trapdoor opened and they lowered the blond dandy down. With a nimbleness born of working the high rigging on sailing ships, the three sailors dropped through the trapdoor.

It slammed hard, causing Charlie to jump.

"We can stay for some more drinking," Clem said.

"Let's find a place to sleep off what we already swilled," Charlie suggested. He patted the roll of green-backs in his pocket to be sure he still carried it. Only then did he make his way through the maze of tables.

He hardly brought down a cobweb on his way out into the chill San Francisco night. The parrot berated him as he went.

# CHAPTER 7

"My head feels like it'll blow up," Charlie said. He held his temples as they walked toward the restaurant. "Makes me think of the time we blowed apart all those pumpkins with a ten-gauge." He clapped his hands together and then separated them to show the extent of the destruction. He regretted sharing the memory. It sent new waves of pain into his head.

"Would have felt worse if we'd drunk that popskull the sailor dished out."

"I know, I know, Clem. Wonder what happened to our friend?"

"The parrot?"

Charlie had to chuckle. It cost him a surge of dizziness. He settled down and so did the spinning world. He answered, "Wash. Wash Collins."

"Don't know, don't care."

"He was shanghaied. We would have been, too." He turned toward the Bay. A half dozen tall-masted ships heaved up and down as the ocean waves rippled in from the Pacific. Getting sailors willing to sign on for a two-year trip to the Orient and back was hard.

Finding experienced sailors was even harder. The shanghaiers depended on taking the incautious, holding them until the ship was too far out at sea for their impressed victims to swim back, then training their unwilling sailors in the harshest way possible.

Work the rigging or not get fed.

Charlie shivered. That was no life for a man. For a miner like him and Clem.

"He'll see land again in a few months."

"All I want to see," said Charlie, "are bacon and eggs. Maybe some fried potatoes."

They turned into a café. Clem pushed through the tightly spaced tables to one by the window. Charlie hesitated long enough to stare back the way they'd come. When he was satisfied, he joined his partner.

"You spotted him," Clem said.

"You already did?" Charlie was disappointed. He thought he was the only one who had picked out the smallish man trailing them.

Clem nodded once.

Clem scooted around in the chair so the Colt thrust into his waistband was closer at hand. The man stopped outside the window and openly stared at them. He was hardly five-foot-three and thin as a rail. Frail came close. His face would have been considered handsome on a rat, if he'd had whiskers long enough. His brown mustache was trimmed down to look like a dirty smear on his upper lip. Large ears held up a too-large bowler. When he took out pince-nez glasses and wiped them with a white linen handkerchief, the image of a mousy man was complete.

"Doesn't have a gun," Clem said.

"He might have something up his sleeve. You've seen those spring-loaded rigs gamblers wear that shove a derringer out into their hand? He looks like the type to have something like that."

"A derringer, maybe. Not the spring contraption."

"He's coming in," Charlie said. He caught his breath, then released it slowly. "To join us, it seems."

The man walked over, each step precise as if he expected to slip and fall. He adjusted his eyeglasses and said, "May I join you? I have a business proposition."

"That anything like a job?" Clem asked.

Charlie shoved out a chair and waited. The man hesitated, then sat, perched on the edge as if ready to take flight at any instant. He cleared his throat and looked from one man to the other.

"Spit it out," Clem said. "We got real business to do."

"Breakfast?" The man raised a thin eyebrow. He smiled weakly.

"I am Hiram Hickman. My employer has need of someone to find, uh, to find . . . someone."

"We ain't pimps." Clem signaled for the waiter to come over.

"Sir!" Hickman sat straighter. "I assure you it is not like that. No, not at all."

"So what is it like?" Charlie and Clem were served cups of coffee, gave their orders, and pointedly ignored the interloper on their meal. When the waiter left, Charlie sipped his coffee. It was bitter. No amount of sugar would cure that. In spite of what Clem said, he made better coffee than this. Sometimes it took longer to boil, but he threw in eggshells. That cut the acid taste and made his coffee drinkable.

Hickman looked around, bent over the table, and spoke in a low tone. "My employer's son has been . . . misplaced."

"Kidnapped? Run off?"

"You know, Clem, some folks are lucky and find themselves a good woman. That's enough for a man to light out for parts unknown, just to appreciate what fortune has delivered." Charlie sipped more of the bitter brew. It grew on him. His headache slowly retreated, too.

"While Jerome has a wild side, I have reason to believe he was kidnapped. And you two were the last ones to see him."

This got their attention.

"How's that? We slept in a stable last night. Unless this Jerome fellow's got four legs and eats hay, we never laid eyes on him."

"In the Cobweb Palace," Hickman said. "You were seen drinking with him."

"There was a parrot," Clem said. "Never caught its name."

"Jerome? Like in Jerome Washington Collins?"

Hickman nodded.

"Do tell. We shared a drink or two. The boy was all tapped out, he said. We took pity on him and stood him a shot of peach brandy," Charlie said.

"'Til he found a new friend." Clem touched the plate

set in front of him. The china was hot enough to make him recoil and suck his burned finger.

"A sailor came over and tried to drug us," Charlie said. "We left. I don't know what happened then." He scowled. By then he had one drink too many and things jumbled in his head.

"But not quite," Hickman pressed. "What about this sailor?"

"Friends," Charlie said. He began work on his own breakfast. He mechanically forked food to his mouth, but he didn't taste it. His mind raced. "The sailor had a couple friends and they—"

"Dumped Wash down a trapdoor at the back of the bar," Clem finished. He looked at Hickman. "That's what he told us his name was. Wash."

"Such a foolish lad. You're sure he was shanghaied?"

"Could have been," Clem said. He dived back into his food. Any interest he had was gone now in favor of filling his belly.

"I have it on good authority you two are most adept at returning lost items."

"Where'd you hear that?"

"My employer's lawyer is . . ."

"Lecroix," Charlie said. "He put in a good word for us?"

"No, quite the contrary. He ranted for ten minutes about how you stole a horse and caused him a considerable amount of trouble talking the police out of arresting him for it."

"We got his horse back," Charlie said. Then he remembered how Clem had handed the reins of the other horse they'd stolen from Sarkasian's stable to Lecroix. The horse trader knew he had no claim to Black Knight but had tried to make trouble claiming the other horse was stolen.

"He's a lawyer. He can defend himself."

"It never came to that, of course. From what he said, the police only required a donation to their Mutual Assurance Fund of several hundred dollars to decide the horse had wandered off by itself."

"I'm sure they collected a nice reward from Sarkasian for finding the horse," Clem said. He polished off the last of his breakfast, running a biscuit around the plate to sop up the last egg yolk.

"That hardly sounds like he'd recommend us for anything but a lynching," Charlie said.

"Your unusual methods are what my employer requires to deal with his wayward son. He needs discretion first and foremost."

"Thought he wanted his boy back," Clem said.

"Yes, of course, that's first. But he cannot have any sort of scandal. He is a pillar of the community and must not be sullied by the hint of illegality. Such might cost him millions."

"Millions?" Clem looked hard at Hickman.

"We've got plenty of money. There's no need for us to—"

"Mister Dawson? One thousand dollars. Retrieve the young Mister Collins, alive, as unmussed as possible, and your reward will be one thousand dollars."

"Gold?" Clem asked.

"Any way you want."

"That kind of money, in this town, we'd want it all deposited in a bank," Charlie said.

Hickman laughed now. It was genuine, and he shook all over. When he brought himself under control, he said, "That isn't a problem. Mister Collins's bank is second only to, well, let's say it's large. It's a very large bank with prominent customers."

"Our poke won't last forever," Charlie said to his partner. "With that kind of money, we can get Betty Sue back."

"Or buy into a better mine," Clem said. He grumbled a little. "One with gold."

"There's plenty of pay dirt in the Betty Sue. I—"

"Gentlemen, will you retrieve Jerome? I fear time is running out for him."

"They don't shanghai men to keep them around for long," Charlie said. "The ship must be about ready to sail, if it hasn't already."

Hickman looked from one to the other. His lips moved silently as he mouthed, "One thousand dollars."

That sealed the deal.

"You got yourself the two best, most honest gents anywhere in San Francisco to work for you, Mister Hickman," Charlie said. He shoved out his hand. Hickman looked at it skeptically, then shook. His grip was surprisingly strong matched against Charlie's hand toughened by daily work in a mine. Charlie wondered if the man's strength came from counting money all day long.

"Bring him to the main office of the California Security Bank at Market and Geary. Please be quick." Hiram

Hickman pushed back and left, again picking his way through the café as carefully as an alley cat stepping over debris.

"You think he's on the up and up?" Clem drained his coffee and leaned back.

"I can see Wash being a rich man's son. Can't you, Clem?"

"I can't see how we're going to find him. He's halfway to China by now."

"Maybe not. There are a half dozen ships out in the Bay. We've got a chance to kidnap him back."

"Why not?" Clem said. "I don't have anything else to do today."

"We're the team that finds things and returns them to their owner."

Clem snorted.

"I'd do most anything for a thousand dollars, but we're not putting the money in his pa's bank."

"Nope, not at all. I agree," Charlie said, his mind already turning to how they could find where Wash Collins was and how to free him.

# CHAPTER 8

"That's the table where we sat?" Clem frowned. "Don't recollect that much."

Everything inside the Cobweb Palace looked different in the bright late afternoon light seeping through cracks in the walls and roof. The monkeys were asleep in their cages, and the parrot was nowhere to be seen. The only thing that hadn't changed was the half-naked owner prowling back and forth behind the bar like a tiger in a cage.

Charlie Dawson stared at his partner. He scratched his stubbled chin. Finally, he asked, "Do you remember what Wash looked like?"

"I should. There was two of the varmints."

"But you don't. Not really."

Charlie ducked as the parrot showed up from wherever it had been hiding, dived low, and grabbed at his flat-brimmed felt hat. The claws ripped a tiny hole in the crown. He got some satisfaction in that the parrot, unbalanced, careened away and smashed into the side of the bar. Claws grasping frantically, it caught a protruding pine knot and hung on. Squawking angrily, it pulled its way back to the top of the bar. It staggered along. When it craned its neck around, it wobbled and then fell on its side.

"Finally," Clem said. "Somebody in worse shape after a night of debauchery." He belched loudly. The parrot cursed him but wasn't able to stand right away.

"Abe!" Charlie called. "Abe Warner!"

"That's my name." The bartender rubbed his eyes, then came over. "You want the same rotgut as you was drinkin' last night."

"Minus the knockout drops," Charlie said.

"Yeah, but that wasn't brandy. That was something the sailor boy tried to push off on you. Think it was my special whiskey, but not brandy. That's my good stuff."

"You remember what we drank?" Clem's eyes widened in appreciation.

"That's my business. If you tried to drink anything else right now, I wouldn't have a ghost of a chance of rememberin' you." He dropped two shot glasses on the bar and poured healthy levels of the potent liquor in both.

Charlie sipped, tasted nothing but brandy, then knocked his back.

"I remember the taste now. This stuff kicks like a mule."

"I distill it myself. Cuts down on the cost. Besides, you don't know how hard it is gettin' good tarantula juice here. You'd think, what with all the ships comin' 'round the Cape 'nd all . . ." He shook his head sadly. "Two more?"

Clem tapped the bar for another round.

Charlie nursed his.

"We're looking for our drinking companion. He was drinking our brandy."

"You mean Wash? He's a regular. Or he used to be."

"Used to be? It was last night when we was in here," Clem said.

"Why the questions, gents? Anyone askin' too many questions ends up floatin' face down in the Bay."

Charlie and Clem exchanged looks. They hadn't concocted a reason to hunt for Wash Collins that'd satisfy a suspicious resident of the Barbary Coast. Charlie thought fast.

"Money. He owes us money."

"Wash owes damned near everyone money. He's a rich kid—or his pa is—but he's always poor as a church mouse." Warner put a third glass on the bar. Charlie thought the barkeep intended to join them. Instead, he tapped the rim. The parrot staggered over and stared balefully into the empty glass.

"Your friend's dry," Charlie said. "Maybe we can buy our feathered friend a drink." He dropped a five-dollar bill on the bar. Abe Warner never twitched a muscle. A second and third bill finally brought out the brandy. He poured the fiery liquor, and the bird drank it almost as fast as he filled the glass.

"I thought the bird didn't like brandy," Charlie said.

"Mister, he'll drink anything twice that doesn't kill him outright once. And with his iron gut, that's 'bout anything that pours."

"Mighty expensive drink, that one," Clem said. He

eyed the pouch in the leather apron where Warner had tucked the five-dollar bills.

"But it's worth every penny, isn't it, Abe?" Charlie nudged his partner in the ribs. This was the barkeep's bribe to loosen his tongue. Turning cheap now only drew out the time it took to find where the banker's son had been taken.

He dropped several more five-dollar bills onto the bar to loosen Warner's tongue.

"Too many of them sailors to know which boat they crew." The barkeep's eyes flickered. That was all the hint he gave.

Warner was quick, Charlie Dawson was faster. He slammed his hand down over the bills on the bar. The barkeep tried to pry his hand loose but long hours scrabbling rock from a tough mountainside kept his hand flat and Warner frustrated.

"There's six ships gettin' ready to sail. The shanghaiers can belong to any of them." Warner tried to slide the greenbacks toward his side of the bar.

Charlie didn't budge.

"But there's one that's more likely, right? Right?" He released the money on the bar and added another five.

Warner moved hesitantly. He looked Charlie square in the eye and said, "I'd be guessin'."

"Make it a good one."

"The *Pacific Princess*, bound for Hong Kong. It sails with tomorrow morning's tide. But I can't be sure."

"Do you think you can entice the sailors to come after one more recruit?"

Clem looked at him in surprise. He started to speak, then clamped his mouth shut.

"Kin I keep the bounty?"

"How much?" Clem asked. Then he shook his head. "Don't want to know." Warner slid the twenty dollars off the bar.

"Set yonder, the table nearest the far end of the pier. There's a trapdoor in the floor. I'll give them a signal, but you better know what you're gettin' into. Them's not like the run-of-the-mill toughs along the Coast. They're sailors. They're rough and tough. The more fools they shanghai, the less work they have to do once they put to sea."

"We have to leave for a spell," Charlie said. "We'll be back in an hour."

"Make it later. They like to take their new crew 'round 'bout midnight. The tides then make it easier to row back to the *Princess*. Even shanghaiers are lazy louts."

Charlie left after giving the parrot a final look. The shot of brandy they'd bought the bird had laid it out on the bar, too drunk to even sit on its perch. He ducked cobwebs and stepped into the early evening.

"What in the name of all that's holy are you thinking? That we decoy them sailors, get the drop on them, then what?" Clem was almost livid.

"We need to be sure which crew stole away our wayward son."

"I can't be sure I'd know any of 'em."

"That's right, Clem, you can't. I can, so that's why I am the bait. You'll need to keep me safe since I'll likely be all woozy in the head to make them think they've got a new recruit."

"I can't swim."

Charlie hesitated, then slapped his partner on the back.

"Then you'd better steal a boat that won't sink. Let's go fetch some supplies that'll come in real handy."

"Not fair," Clem grumbled.

"It's too late to switch now," Charlie said. He looked around, eyes sharp and clear. Slurring his words, "Whass that? You cain't s-say that to me!" With a clumsy swing at his partner, he flopped across the table.

Clem pushed him back into his chair. He kicked his chair back and glared at Charlie.

"Drink up," he said. With a sweep of his hand, he knocked the glasses off the table. Storming from the Cobweb Palace, he cast one last look back.

It hadn't taken the sailor long to swoop down on Charlie.

"He sure treated you bad," the sailor said, picking up the chair Clem had kicked away. He sat opposite Charlie.

"S-spilled my drink."

"Don't you worry about that." He produced a bottle and two glasses. With practiced ease, he filled both. "Let's drink to our friendship!"

"Yeah, thanks, friend." Charlie put his hand over the mouth of the glass and contrived to spill as much as he could before lifting it to his lips. Most of the drugged liquor spilled onto the floor. The dirty sawdust sucked up the knockout-drop-laden whiskey. He still knocked back a few drops. He almost gagged. The taste was terrible.

"Another. To us. May we see the world together."

"See it all," Charlie agreed. This time he had to swill most of the knockout-drop-laden liquor. It hit him like a sledgehammer to the gut. "Oh." He got that much out before he toppled to the floor.

He never quite passed out. Eyelids at half-mast, he watched boots moving in front of his face. He grunted as two men hoisted him enough to drag him along on his knees. The sailor who had given him the drugged drink opened the trapdoor in the floor. Charlie was glad he had chosen a table near the back. His knees were scraped raw and splinters tore into his flesh.

Blinking hard, he saw the open door. Bobbing below the pier, a rowboat with another sailor waited for him. He let out a cry as they dumped him headfirst into the boat. The sailor waiting below broke his fall. Otherwise, he would have snapped his neck landing headfirst.

"Get him out to the ship right away. The Cap'n wants to sail with the dawn."

"You fixin' to snare anymore?"

"Row, damn your eyes. We'll signal if we get another drunk."

"Don't forget to bring a bottle or two of whiskey. I'm tired of the rum the Cap'n stocks for us."

Charlie lay in the bottom of the boat. Bilge rose and fell around him as the sailors talked. The trapdoor slammed shut. For a minute all was dark. Then the sailor grabbed the oars, grunted with every stroke, and sent the small boat skimming along the choppy Bay. All he could do was stare up at the night sky. Clouds moved in. There'd be a storm by morning.

The up-and-down bobbing of the boat made him sick. He tried to turn his head to the side and almost made it.

"Damn you! Don't puke on my boots. They're new." The sailor landed a kick to his ribs. Charlie groaned. He tried to move away when the sailor rubbed his sullied boot against Charlie's coat. "What you carryin'? I thought they'd searched you already. Might be you still have somethin' of value for ole Peter One-eye?"

The movement of the boat rolled Charlie around enough to look up at his captor. The man's left eye socket was hidden by a filthy black leather patch. The brief glimpse went away as the boat rolled about, forcing the sailor to row faster. Charlie tried to relax and not drown in the water sloshing around the bottom of the boat. Bit by bit, he regained feeling in his toes and fingers. By the time the rowboat crunched against the side of a much larger ship, he thought he was strong enough to land a punch that'd mean something.

He restrained himself as Peter hoisted him up. Strong hands above grabbed him and dragged him over the railing to land in a pile on the deck of the rolling ship.

"Get on back to shore," someone from high in the rigging called. "They're signalin' they got another one."

"I wanted to—" Peter fell silent, then dropped back into the rowboat. His chance to search Charlie was lost.

"Is he all doped up?"

"Ain't movin' a muscle," came the reply from the sailor dragging Charlie along the deck.

"Dump him into the hold with the others. The Cap'n wants them sails mended before we set course in the morning."

Charlie let out a cry as he tumbled below decks. No one paid him any heed. He landed hard on a coil of rope. Barely daring to stir, he recovered his strength and finally rolled away. All around him were men in chains. Some sat with heads bowed, still lost in the fog of the knockout drug. A few others listlessly yanked at their chains but paid him no attention.

"Wash?" He whispered the name. "Wash Collins?"

When a man at the far end of the hold rattled his chains in reply, Charlie made his way to kneel by the prisoner. Finger under the man's stubbled chin, he lifted and stared into eyes clouded over with narcotic. Charlie had expected this and had prepared. He searched his pockets until he found the bottle of smelling salts.

The first pass under Wash's nose caused almost no response. The second made him flinch. The third brought him around, protesting and trying to push away the bottle with the spirit of hartshorn. The powerful ammonia stench caused Charlie to recoil, but he passed the bottle once more under the captive's nose.

"Stop, stop, you're choking me to death."

"Are you awake now?"

"Who are you?" Wash Collins leaned forward and squinted in the darkness. "I know you. You bought me a drink at Cobweb Palace. You're one of them who shanghaied me!"

"I'm one of them who'll get you off this ship before you end up a eunuch in some Middle Kingdom harem." Charlie tossed aside the now empty bottle and fished some more in his pockets. He drew out a metal ring holding a half dozen keys. "The locksmith guaranteed one of these would work on about any lock used on a prisoner's chains."

"Gimme. Let me do it." Wash reached clumsily and knocked the keys from Charlie's hand. He swore, then hunted for the keys, finally lifting them from a pool of filth. He had been chained in one spot long enough to create quite a mess.

"Go on," Charlie said with some distaste. He wasn't fastidious, but if the prisoner wanted to free himself now with the filthy keys, he was willing to let him.

Four keys failed to turn the lock. Charlie silently thought of tortures for the lying locksmith. The metallic click of the hasp falling away turned the curse into high praise. Then he realized the locksmith had probably sold these locks to the shanghaiers and cursed him again.

"Get to your feet. We're getting off the ship right now."

"I can't swim. Are we at a dock?"

"Come on." Charlie pulled him along. The few prisoners who had recovered from their drugging called to them for help.

"Go on," Charlie told Wash. "Open their locks. All of them. Then get up to the deck."

"They're all pirates," Wash said. "Every man jack of them has a pistol or knife. They'll slit your throat and toss you into the Bay to feed the sharks and never think twice."

While Wash worked on one lock after another, Charlie looked around for a way to climb to the deck. A dangling cargo net let him move up slowly to peer around. None of the crew was in sight. Like a snake, he slithered onto the deck and crawled, belly down, to the rail facing the shore. He found another package wrapped in oilskin. He unwrapped it and spread the contents along the railing.

"What are you doin'?" Wash crouched beside him.

"Signaling." Charlie struck a lucifer. The match flared, then ignited the gunpowder he'd spread out in a thin layer. The rail blazed along a two-foot stretch. The wet wood failed to catch fire, so Charlie added a length of rope from a piece at his feet. This produced a signal beacon a blind man could see.

"Your partner's coming for us?"

Charlie nodded, then he cursed. The other prisoners finally made their way to the deck. None of them was cautious or quiet. The lookout high in the crow's nest spotted them and let out a long, loud warning cry.

The ship came alive. The officer on the foredeck began ringing an alarm bell and sailors boiled out from below.

"We're under attack! They've boarded us!" the officer bellowed.

"Over the side," Charlie said. He grabbed Wash's collar and lifted him to his feet.

"Sharks! There! I see fins! I can't swim. I—"

Charlie got his arms around Wash's waist and heaved him overboard.

He fell for what seemed an eternity and then smashed hard into the waters of San Francisco Bay. Cold, choking, the water filled his nose and mouth. Charlie exhaled hard and shot to the surface. Moving his arms and kicking slowly, he tread water until he got his senses back. Above reared the dark side of the China clipper. A dozen fights ranged from the prow to the stern. From what he heard, the escaped shanghaied prisoners weren't faring well against the armed crew.

He had other worries. He hadn't been hired to find and release any of those poor fools.

Wash Collins flailed about a few yards away. He dog-paddled to him and reached around the struggling man's shoulders.

"Stop fighting me. We can float together," he said.

Wash settled down for a moment. Then he renewed his frantic thrashing.

"Sharks!"

A fin cut through the dark water, heading for them fast.

# CHAPTER 9

Charlie Dawson fought down panic—and Washington Collins. The blond man lashed out and landed a fist on the top of his savior's head. Charlie went underwater. He saw the dark shape arrowing toward him.

He acted instinctively, doubled up and kicked out. He felt his foot hit something rubbery. It yielded and then disappeared.

"It . . . it's going away!"

Charlie sputtered and fought his way back to the choppy surface. A wave broke over his head and almost carried him back under. Only a strong hand on his collar kept him afloat. Then he was pulled upward and dumped belly down across the side of a battered rowboat.

"Get yourself in the rest of the way."

"Clem?"

"It's not Davy Jones, or whoever those salts talk about all the time." Clem grunted and heaved Wash into the boat.

Charlie tried to get in but found himself too weak from all he'd been through. Then he found an added incentive. Sailors aboard the ship began firing at him.

Tiny splashes all around him showed how bad their aim was in the dark. From the number shooting at him, one would get lucky sooner than later. The idea of a bleeding wound in a bay filled with hungry sharks spurred him to even greater effort.

"They put a hole in the bottom. Damn them!" Clem caught Charlie by the wrist and yanked hard. He flopped like a caught fish in the bottom of the rowboat. "Stick it in."

"What?" Charlie wasn't sure what his partner meant until the hand gripped his wrist even tighter and guided his finger into the bullet hole in the bottom of the boat. He kept the rowboat from sinking while Clem and Wash grabbed oars and began rowing.

He shook himself and sat up, keeping his finger in the hole. At first, water leaked around his finger. Then it began to swell and the hole was completely plugged. He wondered if he'd have to chop off his finger to get free.

"You're rowing in a circle," he warned. "Wash isn't pulling his oar as fast."

Clem cussed a blue streak, pushed the rescued man aside, and gripped both oars. He put his back to it, and the rowboat shot across the water in the direction of the city.

"Here, you plug the hole for a while." Charlie held back a moan of pain as he pulled free. He guided Wash's finger to the hole. The man's finger was too slender. He replaced it with his thumb, then swung around and sat beside his partner. When he took the second oar, they fell into an easy rhythm that quickly carried them away from the ship of shanghaiers.

"I'm glad you saw my signal. I wasn't sure that'd work."

"What signal?"

"The gunpowder. The flash. I lit it!"

"Never saw it."

"How'd you find us?"

Clem laughed harshly.

"I followed the boat that took you out."

"You didn't have time. Dang," he said, when he realized Clem had followed the boat the second time when Peter One-eye had returned for another drunk. If the sailors hadn't found another victim, he'd be on his way to China.

"I appreciate what you gents have done for me, rescuing me and all, but I've got another request."

"What's that?" Charlie put his back into yet another pull on the oars. Wash sat cross-legged in the bottom of the boat, leaning forward.

"My thumb's 'bout gonna fall off. I think fishes are nibbling at it, and I worry that the shark will be back."

"Heard about sharks," Clem said. "They drink a man's blood."

Wash shuddered and said, "If he's lucky. Otherwise, they eat him one huge chunk at a time." Wash rocked forward and yanked his thumb out of the hole. "You hit a rock."

"We beached the boat," Charlie said. His arms ached and his head threatened to split wide open. He hoped it was from the drug the sailors had forced on him. The only other time he'd felt this bad was when a support beam in the Betty Sue fell on his head. He'd been unconscious for a day, and the severe headaches refused to go away, no matter how drunk he got.

Right now he was particularly parched.

He climbed out of the rowboat, sloshing through ankle-deep water to the rocky shoreline. A rock tripped him up—and saved his life.

A shot tore through the night air where his head had been a fraction of a second before.

"They're after us," Clem called. He unlimbered his Colt and began shooting across the water.

Charlie moved around until he found a spot where the approaching boat caught reflections from the water.

"There must be ten of them!" He scrambled up toward a road running along the shoreline. They had beached above the Barbary Coast. The gin mills and brothels were all farther south toward the center of town.

Even if they got there, they'd not find any sanctuary. If anything, the men who frequented the saloons and whorehouses—and the opium dens—were more likely to take a few dollars reward from the sailors than, out of the goodness of their hearts, help fugitives.

"Run for it," Wash cried.

Charlie and Clem followed. Clem's six-gun came up empty. He didn't have time to reload.

"Where's my six-shooter?"

"Back with our gear. There wasn't any way I was carrying it out on the water. I can't swim. Three pounds of iron shoved into my waistband would have sent me straight to the bottom."

"You can't swim, either?" Wash stopped to thrust out his hand. "Put it there, friend!"

A few more bullets sang past. Charlie caught the faint command issued by the officer in the prow of the longboat. "Don't shoot them; we need more hands for the upper sails."

He shuddered. It had taken a spell for him to get used to being in a dark mine twelve hours a day. Climbing the tall masts and edging along the spray-slickened upper spars would take as long to learn. He'd end up in the ocean long before that happened.

"Run," Wash gasped out. Even as he spoke the obvious, he slowed and then stumbled along, slowing his rescuers.

"What's wrong?" Charlie nudged him.

"Legs," gasped out Wash. "They're all banged up from being tossed into the hold."

"They'll swing you from a yardarm when they catch you." The admonition did nothing to speed the blond man.

Charlie tried to herd him. Wash wasn't having any of it.

"You gents go on. Leave me. I can't take another step." He bent over, hands on his knees, panting like a hound dog on a hot summer's day.

"They've got us," Clem said. He shoved his emptied six-gun into its holster and balled his hands into rock-hard fists.

Charlie saw they had to make their stand now. If they tired themselves out anymore trying to run, the sailors had them. Ten men in the longboat meant they were all fresh for the fight. Clem and Charlie had exhausted themselves rowing. Ten men pulling on the oars spread the effort among them all.

"I can fight," Wash said. He duplicated Clem's belligerent stance, hands held up and cocked for a quick punch.

To Charlie's surprise, Wash got in a good blow when a sailor ran toward him. The jab to the salt's chin rocked him back. He stumbled into two behind him.

Then Charlie had his hands full. He punched and jabbed, kicked, and found himself pushed back. When a sailor tackled him, he went down hard. Two others swarmed on top of him, pinning him with their weight.

He was strong from working in a mine. They were stronger, younger, and fit from working long hours dragging heavy canvas sails up and down tall masts. Try as he might, he couldn't wiggle free of the pair. He heard Wash cry out as a sailor got him in a headlock and spun him around and around. From the scuffle going on, Clem more than held his own, but his curses became less frequent as he lost his breath in the struggle.

They were lost.

And then they weren't.

Charlie saw a pair of huge hands come from above, seize one of his opponents by the shoulders, and bodily throw him aside. Another hulking man used a slungshot on the sailor's head. Blood exploded and the sailor disappeared.

Charlie sat up, ready to join the fight again. There wasn't any reason. All ten of the sailors lay stretched out on the cold ground. Two weren't moving. The rest moaned and stirred but weren't able to run. Circling them were four men the size of mountains.

In the distance, he heard Wash say, "You took your time getting here, Hiram."

The mousy Hiram Hickman stood with arms crossed, looking reprovingly at his employer's son.

Charlie wobbled a bit as he walked to where the two stood. He saw that Hickman's knuckles were bruised. Then he saw the brass knuckles the man had used on one of the sailors. From the way white bone jutted from the unconscious sailor's jaw, Hickman had broken important bones with a single punch.

"You know my father's right-hand man?" Wash started to perform the introduction.

"He hired us," Charlie said.

"You mean you didn't come after me because it was the right thing to do? My father *paid* you to fetch me?" Wash looked sour as that worked its way into his head.

"Mister Collins, your father is waiting for you. It will be past his bedtime soon. He will want to speak with you tonight."

"Let him go to bed. I'll talk to the old man in the morning. I need a drink." Wash found himself lifted by his elbows and carted off between two of the burly brutes Hiram Hickman had brought along. He kicked futilely as they lugged him to a carriage and tossed him in.

Clem stood beside his partner as they watched the carriage rattle off into the night.

"You pulled our fat from the fire," Clem said. He thrust out his hand.

"You are employees. Mister Collins does not like his

employees to . . . fail." Hickman looked around at the felled sailors with some distaste. "He should do something about shanghaiers."

"But he won't, will he?" Charlie knew the reason the rich and powerful in San Francisco allowed the slavery to continue. They depended on the cargo ships sailing between China and the nearby docks for their wealth. It was, for them, a small price to pay for immense riches from the Orient.

"You show a deeper understanding of economics than I expected." He eyed Charlie closely.

"How about showering the rest of that economics on us?" Clem held out his bloodied hand, palm up.

"Of course." Hickman drew out an envelope and laid it across Clem's palm. He immediately clamped down, as if he expected Hickman to snatch it back.

Hiram Hickman turned to leave, then stopped and turned.

"I have a question, if you will answer." He paused, then asked, "I hadn't wanted to hire you, but you came highly recommended. How often are you successful in finding lost things?"

"So far, we've never failed," Charlie said. He elbowed Clem in the ribs to keep him from protesting that they'd only taken on two jobs.

"Never?"

"Never," Charlie said loudly.

"One further question, if you will. Are you blabbermouths or can you keep quiet about the . . . items you recover?"

"I do all the talking and I can keep my yap shut, if the price is right."

"What Charlie said." Clem opened the envelope and slowly flipped through the greenbacks inside. Satisfied with the count, he stuffed the money into his coat pocket.

"I see that you are tight-lipped," Hickman said, giving Clem a once-over from head to toe. "And you don't seem to brag on yourself much. That's good."

"You have another job for us?" Charlie asked. He spoke to Hickman's back. The man stepped up onto a horse. One of his henchmen held the reins and then passed them up to him.

"We won't say a word about Wash—Jerome! We don't even know anybody who'd ask."

"Shut up, Charlie. He can't hear you over the horse's hooves."

Hiram Hickman had already galloped into the night.

Charlie Dawson sagged. He had hoped for another job that paid as well as getting the banker's son away from the shanghaiers. Now they had to find a new mission, but they didn't have to do it very soon. They had just earned a king's ransom.

He stepped over a moaning sailor and hurried to walk alongside his partner. They had to find a saloon and wet their whistles. And not take any drinks from friendly sailors.

# CHAPTER 10

"Let's head back to Potluck," Charlie Dawson said out of the blue. He held a fork holding a hunk of steak, then used it to stab toward his partner for emphasis. "We have plenty of money to fight Jimmy Norton and his pa."

Clem looked up from his plate where he sopped up the remainder of a runny yoke with a sourdough biscuit. Working slowly, he trapped the last dollop and popped it into his mouth before saying a word.

"Nope."

"The Betty Sue is *our* mine. We can't let them skunks steal it from us."

"You saw the assay. No gold."

"There is," Charlie said, anger rising. "I feel it in my gut. The Betty Sue will make us both rich. We go back, we fight them in court."

"Let me guess. The money's burning a hole in your pocket?" Clem shook his head. "I like San Francisco."

"That's because you found a lady last night that wasn't completely disgusted with the way you smell."

"Everyone in this town smells like fish." He ran his

finger across the bottom of the plate to remove the last bit of breakfast. He licked it off. "You forget how I came to smell like that."

"You rowed halfway across the Bay to pull me out of the water."

"Never seen a shark before. Don't fancy ever being that close to another one."

"All the more reason to get on back to Potluck. You don't have to worry about not being able to swim there. The river running past town's hardly a foot deep and you can step across it in places. And there aren't any man-eating sharks there."

"Like there is in here," Clem said. He looked out the café window in the direction of the Bay. From here the masts on the sailing ships were just visible.

Charlie looked from his impaled steak to his partner.

"What do you mean?" He turned slightly to catch the reflection in the café's plate glass window. Behind him stood a man dressed in a plain brown suit that fit his personality. Twisting around, he asked, "Are you following us, Hickman?"

The mousy man took an empty chair from the next table and sat down unbidden. He rested his forearms against the edge of the table, careful not to place his elbows on the top. He showed that much etiquette, even if he had joined them unbidden.

"There is no need for me to follow you, sir. You leave a wide, noticeable wake in your path."

"Sir?" Clem stiffened. His hand moved toward his Colt stashed in his holster. "Nobody calls either of us 'sir' unless he wants to dupe us into doing something 'gainst our will."

"Your quick success in finding and retrieving Jerome did not go unnoticed."

"By his pa?" Charlie guessed. His heart raced now. As much as he wanted to return to Potluck and again take possession of his mine, Hiram Hickman wouldn't be here unless another job needed doing. The last one had paid well. Charlie wondered how much more they could charge after rescuing Wash Collins had been so successful.

"Indeed," Hickman said. "I've questioned Jerome at length. He vouches for your discretion."

"What you want from us is illegal?" Clem shook his head. "I don't mind retrieving property that's been lost, but I won't steal something that's not owned."

"Two thousand dollars."

Charlie put his fork down, breakfast forgotten. He tried to get a hint of what Hickman's game was.

"We don't kill people for money, either," he said.

"There might be gunplay, but it is not the goal. If you can retrieve a lost . . . object . . . without shooting anyone, that is something Mister Collins would celebrate."

"What's lost?" Clem got right to the point. He pushed his licked-clean plate away and turned to study Hickman like he was a bug under a magnifying glass.

Hickman looked around as if someone crowded close to eavesdrop. The nearest customers chattered away, ignoring anyone but their companions.

"This cannot be discussed in public. Come to Mister Collins's office."

"Now?" Clem's belligerent tone caused Charlie to shoot his partner a hard look. Hickman had dangled a considerable amount of money in front of them. He was willing to hear about the elder Collins's job for a chance at two thousand dollars.

"Now."

"Say please."

Charlie thought this would be it. Hickman would stomp off in a huff, and they could kiss two thousand dollars goodbye. He caught his breath when the man nodded once and said, "Please accompany me, sir."

The addition of "sir" rocked Clem anew. Charlie was thunderstruck. Nobody talked to hard rock miners like that, with any hint of respect. Hickman's request didn't carry a hint of disdain or mockery. They might have been important businessmen, robber barons even.

They followed Hickman outside.

"Your horses will be tended to." For a moment Charlie thought Hickman would bow. He made only a slight nod in the direction of the same carriage that had whisked Wash off the night before.

Clem climbed in. Charlie settled beside him on the plush red velvet cushions. He pressed his callused fingers down and said, "I could get used to this."

"So could my hindquarters," Clem said, leaning back as the carriage lurched away.

They rode through the business district and came to a halt in front of a bank occupying a three-story building. Before Charlie had a chance to open the door, the driver had hopped down and pulled it open for them. The liveried man's eyes worked over both of his passengers. A flicker of disdain showed. Otherwise, he kept a poker face. The door was held as they climbed down.

Clem rubbed his rear end.

"Going to miss the cushion."

"If Wash's pa pays us as much as Hickman claimed, you can buy your own pillow."

"And a pretty waiter girl to push it under me before I set myself down all the way." Clem walked like a king through the front door and into the bank lobby.

Charlie wondered how much gold leaf had been used to decorate the statues and frames around the paintings on the wall.

"That's more 'n we ever took out of the Betty Sue," Clem said, reading his mind.

"This way, please." Hiram Hickman somehow had arrived before them and motioned them to a flight of marble stairs leading to the next floor.

Charlie and Clem tramped up. Charlie wasn't surprised when they kept climbing to the third floor. He caught his breath at the sheer opulence all around. The furnishings were better than he'd ever seen in his life, even in Miss Lucy's House of Pleasure in Sacramento. He had to rush to keep up with Hickman as he headed for huge maple double doors decorated with intricate carvings that made him blush when he made them out. Miss Lucy needed to hire whoever had fashioned these doors.

And in a bank. He marveled at that.

The doors swung open. A cherrywood desk as big as the main deck of a sailing ship curved around a rotund man. Piles of papers on the desk had been disturbed. The anxious secretary standing to one side looked eager to sort everything.

The nameplate with what had to be solid gold lettering told Charlie all he needed to know. This was Thomas Collins, bank president.

The man shoved aside papers. The secretary scooped them up, then looked expectantly at his boss.

"Out, Mister Arthur. I need to speak with these gentlemen in private."

"But, sir . . ."

"Out!" Collins sounded less angry than he did frightened.

His secretary gave the two miners a cold look, clutched papers to his chest, and marched out, head haughty and high.

Charlie saw that Hickman made no move to leave. Whatever had to be said was already known to the bank president's assistant.

"Thank you for dragging my worthless son back."

"Not so worthless, Mister Collins . . ." Charlie started. The man cut him off with a sharp hand motion like he chopped wood. Or someone's neck.

"Jerome is a ne'er-do-well. I know it. His mother knows it. *He* knows it." Thomas Collins sank into his comfortable leather chair and crossed his arms. His beetle brows crept closer to his eyes as he frowned, then he looked up.

Anger had been replaced with that hint of fear again.

"Your discretion is paramount, gentlemen. Not a word of what I say can leave this room."

Charlie glanced at Hickman. For all the man's mousy look, a feral, red-eyed brown wharf rat dwelled somewhere in his brain. Breaking confidence provoked a hailstorm of death he didn't want to consider.

"What are we supposed to find?" Clem had no time for small talk.

"There was a railroad accident recently somewhere in the Sierra Nevadas. We don't know exactly where."

"You want us to track down survivors? That's more the job of the railroad, isn't it? Or the local sheriff."

"Mister Dawson, the railroad must not know anything about the freight that was lost. It was shipped by my bank for, well, let's say it needs to remain a secret."

"Some cargo the bank sent was lost in a train wreck, and you want us to find it?" Charlie frowned. "If we don't know what we're looking for, how do we know when we find it?"

The banker cast a sidelong glance at Hickman.

"It's a case. A crate. About six inches square and something over two feet long."

"It's a wood crate, nailed shut," Hickman added. "It's marked as hardware, but it's not very heavy. Only a few pounds."

"If you know what it looks like, why don't you go find it?" Clem fixed his cold stare on Hickman.

"Hiram is able to do much to aid me, but he isn't up

to ferreting out such things. He is of immense value in what he does, but this is not his kind of job. You men have shown yourselves to be adept at this."

"Finding lost items," Charlie said.

"Can we ask the railroad about the accident? How much freight they lost?" Clem shifted his weight back and forth. Charlie had seen him anxious like this before. He erupted into a fight more often than not.

"They only know that such a crate was shipped, but the bank's name was not on it." Hickman coughed. "You have all the information we can give."

"When it was shipped is important. Today, last month, when?"

"A few days ago," Thomas Collins said. "Pay them, Hiram. Enough to get them on the job. A hundred dollars should get them on the trail. You'll receive the balance when you deliver the crate and its contents to me personally."

"Not to him?" Clem stared hard at Hickman.

"To me," the bank president insisted. "This is to remain a complete secret. Tell no one what you're looking for—"

"Not hard since we don't know," Clem said.

Charlie waited for the banker to order them out. Such insolence had to be alien to a man as rich and powerful as Thomas Collins. It came as a surprise when the banker spoke.

"Get after that crate. Right away. Please." Collins's voice broke with strain and sweat beaded his high-domed forehead.

Hiram Hickman came over and counted out a hundred dollars onto the banker's huge desk. He stepped away. Charlie almost left. He felt as if they stuck their necks into a noose. Taking the money meant standing on the trapdoor. And they didn't even know who the executioner was. Nothing about the job appealed to him.

He picked up the money and tucked it into his coat pocket.

"We'll get right on it."

He and Clem started to leave. Thomas called after them.

"There's one more thing."

They faced the banker. He was as white as a bleached muslin sheet, and his hands shook as he ran his fingers through his thinning blond hair.

"You've got to find the crate and its contents in ten days. Less, if at all possible."

"If we don't?" Clem asked.

Thomas Collins turned even whiter. That was as good an answer as Charlie needed. He steered his partner from the office. Hickman closed the heavy wood doors, but they heard the two men shouting at each other through it.

"We've just bought a pig in a poke, partner," Clem said.

"Here's some of the bacon." Charlie counted out half the money and gave it to him. If they had a lick of sense, they'd hightail it for the high country and never show their faces in San Francisco again.

If they had the sense God gave a goose.

A total of two thousand more dollars awaited them when they found the crate and its mysterious contents. The money was good, but the mystery appealed even more to Charlie.

What made a rich and powerful banker like Thomas Collins so scared?

# CHAPTER 11

"Let's just clear out," Clem said. He pointed east across the Bay.

"We took the man's money. We're obligated."

"Collins lied to us."

"How, Clem? How'd he lie to us? The greenbacks he paid us are legitimate. We cashed them in for gold at his own bank." Charlie clinked the gold coins in his pocket to let his partner know what had to be done.

"He didn't tell us everything."

"What wasn't he saying?"

"That's the problem. He didn't tell us so we don't know what trouble we're sticking our snouts into."

Charlie thought on this. It bothered him that Thomas Collins had not come right out and told them what was in the small crate. The money he paid had to be worth more than the contents, otherwise, even an honest man might be tempted to take the contents and hightail it. Not Charlie Dawson, and he hoped not his partner, but the remaining reward money was more than a small fortune.

It was a big fortune.

"I wonder why he didn't set those thugs of his onto the chore," Charlie said.

"Didn't trust 'em."

"You might be right about that, Clem, but why does he trust us? Because we found a man's thoroughbred and then got Thomas's drunkard son back before he was impressed into a ship's crew?"

"That makes us sound danged reliable," Clem said.

"But if he doesn't trust his own men . . ." Charlie thought on that. Then an idea came. "He trusts them to find whatever's in the crate. He doesn't trust them not to tell everyone what's inside."

"He did chase that sour-looking secretary out before hiring us."

"More than that," Charlie went on, hardly hearing his partner, "he doesn't think the one man he does trust—Hiram Hickman—can find the crate."

"He's a cold one, Hickman. He looks like a teeny old mouse, but we saw him fight using those brass knuckles. The man's dangerous. I don't trust him."

"We don't have to. Collins does, but he knows his right-hand man isn't up to poking around in the mountains and tracking down the crate. He's dangerous in the city. He's not any good when it comes to tracking or living off the land."

"If the crate's so important, why didn't he send out Hickman along with a company of guards? There's not a one of the men I saw working for him that's not up for living in the wilderness. Better 'n us, if you want the truth."

"Secrecy. He didn't want anyone to know it was being shipped."

"We should have asked where *it* was sent." Clem spat. "This whole deal will get us killed. We don't know what we're doing, and we don't know nothing about what we've been sent to find."

"Two thousand more dollars," Charlie teased.

"We got a thousand. Five hundred each. We split up the money, then go our separate ways."

"This is more than we ever got out of the Betty Sue, but do you want to ride off without me?"

Clem thought a minute, then said, "Being partners with you's the best thing that's happened to me. I wanted to see if splitting was something you'd want."

Charlie doubted that, but in spite of the possible rift in their partnership over taking this job, he trusted Clem more than he had any other man. More than once in the mine, Clem had saved him from serious injury or even death at the risk of his own neck. He had done the same. That made them even, and that was how a partnership should be.

"The money's waiting for us," Charlie said. "More 'n that, aren't you just a little curious what's in the crate?"

Clem laughed and slapped his partner on the back.

"Danged right, I wonder what's in it. Let's find out."

"You see him?" Charlie asked. "The fellow in the tan duster who's followed us around all morning?"

"He's got a partner. He's wearing a black frock coat and looks like a tinhorn gambler."

"I missed him," Charlie admitted. Clem had more trail experience and picked up spoor better than he did. "What are we going to do about them?"

"Get rid of them."

"I'd like to find out why they're trailing us. Who hired them?"

"Collins might be having second thoughts about giving us so much money."

Charlie laughed. They'd only been given a hundred dollars of the two thousand. For a man like Collins, that was walking-around money and hardly worth telling his bookkeeper about.

"That doesn't explain why he'd hire more cutthroats to follow us. Send them out to find the crate. After all, if we find it, they'll know and can take it from us."

"They can try."

Clem had a bloodthirsty streak in him that Charlie ignored. Mostly. Now he wanted to see more of it. He wasn't above shooting a man in self-defense, but going after someone for only dogging their heels was something to leave to Clem.

"What'll we do? Try to ambush them?"

"Not in the city. We've got our supplies. Let's board the ferry to Oakland and ask them real polite-like what they're up to after we're in the middle of the Bay."

He looked at Clem. His partner wasn't the kind to carry on long conversations. Right now that suited Charlie. The men on their trail were up to no good. All day they had trailed them, going from store to store as they bought supplies, then crowding closer to be sure they were on the same ferry.

Charlie made sure their horses and supplies were secured. The horses protested the rocking boat but didn't require more than a bit of gentling to calm them when the ferry pushed away from the dock. A quick nod sent Clem to the far side of the deck. He edged toward the stern where the man in the duster leaned over the rail. Charlie wasn't much of a sailor. The man he approached was even less accustomed to being on the choppy water. He made small retching sounds as he leaned out over the Bay.

"You should have stayed on solid ground," Charlie said.

"Can't abide the boat rockin' this way," the man said. He stiffened when he realized his quarry was giving him the advice. He tried to turn.

Charlie stepped up and pressed his body into the man, pinning him to the rail. A quick hand clamped around a brawny wrist when the man went for his six-shooter.

"Why'd you follow us all around San Francisco? We're not greenhorns looking to be robbed."

The man twisted away, once more shoving his belly against the rail. This gave him a little space to move. He dragged out his six-gun. Charlie was ready for it. He slammed the man's forearm against the railing.

"Not only are you a terrible tracker, you don't have the sense God gave a goose. Who hired you to follow us?"

The man cursed and began to struggle.

"Was it Collins?"

The man found the gun trigger and pulled it. Charlie jumped back as the bullet grazed his boot. He stumbled but the boat rolled just enough to keep his assailant off-balance. Another round went high and wide.

Charlie bent low and charged like a bull. His shoulder caught the man in the bread basket. As he hit the man's belly, the ferry rolled again. His impact lifted the man off his feet. For a terrifying second, the gunman perched on the railing. A screech ripped from his throat as he fell backward off the ship. He splashed into San Francisco Bay and was quickly left behind in the froth caused by the rapidly rotating stern wheel.

Charlie grabbed the railing and looked into the churning fantail. He thought he saw the man's hand, still holding his six-gun, rise from the water. Then it vanished.

Panting, Charlie bent over the railing and fought to catch his breath. He'd learned nothing but had gotten rid of one of their trackers. Memories of sharks and cold water twisted his gut. The man was likely dead or close to it in a few minutes.

With that thought burning in his brain, he spun around and made his way to the far side of the ferry. Clem and the gambler stood nose to nose, about to come to blows. He had no need to sneak up on the gambler. The noise of the engine, the slapping waves against the ferry, a symphony of other sounds all drowned out the click of his boots on the wet deck. His Walker Colt slid from his waistband, and he held it low in case some of the other passengers might notice.

He need not have bothered. They were all focused on the dock ahead on the Oakland side of the Bay.

"You're plumb loco! We weren't following you. We just wanted to go to Oakland when you did. Pure chance. Nothing more than that!" The gambler stood with his hands open but held between him and Clem. If he carried a derringer in a fancy spring-powered rig that shot the gun into his fist, he'd have his two-shot out and firing before Clem so much as touched the butt of his Army Colt.

"We? You and that other fellow in the duster? All day long you've watched me and my partner. Why's that?"

"Where are you going to look for it?"

The question dumbfounded Clem. He stared at the man.

This gave the gambler the chance to twist his wrist just enough to send the derringer out. He caught it, wrapped his finger around the trigger, and jammed the weapon into Clem's gut.

"Tell me. Where is it?"

Clem glanced behind and saw Charlie approaching. The small eye movement and a facial tic were all the gambler needed to know something had gone wrong. He tried to spin and ventilate Charlie. The Walker Colt rose and fell on the man's forearm. Steel Colt barrel struck fragile spring mechanism. The blow wasn't enough to force the small two-shot out of the gambler's hand, but it bent the mechanism. From the yelp the gambler let out, a rod might have busted and poked into his arm.

Clem acted then. His arm circled the man's throat and pulled him back into a chokehold. Charlie grappled with the gambler to wrest the derringer from him. It came loose. A quick move sent it flying through the air to splash in the Bay. The man choked from the grip on his throat, but Charlie added to his misery. He shoved the gun muzzle up under the man's quivering chin.

"One small twitch'll send a slug into your brain," he said. "Who are you working for?"

"Hell with that," Clem said. "What's in the crate we're supposed to find?"

The gambler gagged. Clem made the mistake of loosening his grip. The man moved like a snake and twisted free. From somewhere in his coat's hidden recesses he drew a knife with his left hand. Charlie reacted rather than thought. His six-gun discharged into the man's elbow. Things came loose. The lower part of his arm flopped around free, and the knife clattered to the deck. His joint had been completely smashed by the bullet.

He cried out in pain. Both Clem and Charlie reacted instinctively. They grabbed hold of the fancy coat and heaved.

The gambler joined his partner in the turbulent water. Like his companion, he quickly fell astern of the ferry and disappeared from sight in seconds.

Charlie gripped the railing. He shook all over. Clem leaned next to him. He wasn't shaken, he was furious.

"We coulda found out what he knew. I suppose you tossed the other owlhoot overboard, too?"

Charlie nodded.

"I knew we should have taken the money and headed for the hills," Clem said. "We've got men chasing us and we don't know why."

"Whatever's in the crate is valuable. We know that."

"Whatever it is," Clem said hotly.

"The only way to find out is to find it."

His partner glared at him, but Charlie's curiosity outran his greed for the money Thomas Collins promised. That crate had to hold a king's ransom. Or something even more valuable to the right people.

# CHAPTER 12

"You're as jumpy as a long-tailed cat in a rocking chair factory," Clem said. "You're making me nervous. I don't like that."

"Why shouldn't I be all het up after what happened back on the ferry?" He shuddered, remembering how he had tossed two men over the railing. For all he knew, both men were dead. And deservedly so. The gambler and the galoot in the duster hadn't been the kind to give their victims any mercy.

They hadn't wasted any time getting to the Oakland Wharf Station, the depot for the Central Pacific Railroad, and boarding a train to Sacramento. They'd been lucky in their timing and hadn't waited, either to secure a freight car for their horses or to board themselves.

"That's done with. Think about what's in front of us."

"The train left from yonder depot," Charlie said. "What good's that?"

"It's the Central Pacific Railroad Sacramento Depot, that's what's good. We got here fast."

"Danged near killed our horses," Charlie said. "They didn't take to riding in a rail car."

"We got here faster 'n if we rode the trail. That'd have been a good two days of hard riding. This way nobody was after us along the trail."

"There's that," Charlie said.

"No telling who'd trotted after us if we'd ridden."

"And Miss Lucy's brothel isn't too far away." Charlie craned his neck as if he could see the brothel from the railroad station. He knew better but the thought of spending some time with Miss Lucy now that he had a few dollars in his pocket appealed to him. She'd treat him special.

"Time's a'wasting."

Charlie sighed. He was usually the one to worry about such things. This time his partner was right. Thomas Collins had given them very little time to find the crate.

"I suppose we should ask around about the train wreck. If anybody knows anything about it, it'll be the station master." He hitched up his pants, made sure the Colt was tucked away safely, then set off with intent. It was time for him to take over again and be the responsible one.

He climbed the steps to the depot platform and went to the ticket window. The man inside looked up.

"How far do you intend to go?"

"What's that?"

"Wait a couple weeks, and I can sell you a ticket all the way to New York City. Eight days for the entire trip, give or take."

"The railroad'll go all the way across the country? Well, I never."

"You need to read the newspaper, mister. That's all they've been writing on for the past month. The Central Pacific will meet up with the Union Pacific. Or you only want to go somewhere closer? Utah, maybe? That's where the line ends right now."

"The wreck," Clem said, pushing past Charlie. "What happened?"

"What wreck?" The station master turned cagey. "Ain't paid to talk 'bout such things. Travel by train's the safest way to go these days. A ship rounding the Horn takes months and the storms do a fair amount of 'em in. Cross at Panama? Die from some tropic disease. Nothing but bugs there. And don't even think of ridin' them horses of yours all the way. It's downright cruel to inflict such a trip on a horse when you can ride in comfort. The Central Pacific has a dining car on some trips, it does."

"Did it have a dining car on the train that wrecked?"

The station master glared at Clem.

"Mister, you got a one-track mind." He leaned forward on the other side of the iron bars and put his fists on the counter. "The boss, he said not to talk about it. And he got the word from Mister Judah himself. That's not like God speakin', but it's so close it don't matter."

"That's a shame since we have some money for one of the men who walked away," Charlie said.

"Money?"

"Insurance money."

The agent thought a moment, then said, "I can pass it along. Gimme what you've got and—"

"Doesn't work that way. Sorry," Charlie said. He turned to go, then paused. Over his shoulder, he called out, "We heard that the man at the rear of the train . . ." He let his words trail off.

"Berenson? Bernie Berenson? He lost his arm in the derailment."

"Do tell," Charlie said. He had wormed the information from the station master. "You keep on selling your tickets."

"Wait, wait, Bernie'd want me to take it for him. He's got a bad gambling problem. He'd lose it all on the first turn of the cards."

Charlie and Clem left the man ranting about how unfair it was that he got nothing, but a lowdown, no-account caboose man got money from doing nothing more than being in an accident.

"Where do we find him?" Charlie asked.

"Miss Lucy?"

Charlie laughed. It was his partner's turn to want the lady of the evening's company. He pointed down the street at a saloon already overflowing with patrons.

"That one looks popular, and unless I miss my guess, the gents crowding in are all railroad men."

"Sooty and dressed for it," Clem agreed.

Charlie doubted they'd be lucky, and they weren't. Not exactly. After several rounds of drinks and talking to a couple dozen of the railroad crews, they found one who knew Berenson.

"Spends all his time at the church down the street. His close call with death put the fear into him," the brakeman said. For his clue to the other railroad man's location, Charlie bought him a half bottle. It was mostly gone by the time he and Clem pushed their way from the saloon.

"That one? With the steeple?"

"Well, Clem, it's certainly a church. Let's mosey on over and see if it's the one that Bernie Berenson frequents now instead of a gin mill."

Clem slowed more and more as they approached. He was downright antsy by the time they reached the whitewashed fence circling the church.

"You go on in and poke around," he said. "I'll scout outside."

"You want to check the graveyard?" Charlie asked.

"Better 'n going in," Clem said, surprising his partner.

Clem had never shown much in the way of being superstitious but always avoided bone yards. Choosing to look over this one rather than go into the church showed more about Clem than he'd known before.

He jumped the low fence and walked to the front doors. They were well-kept. Both had been polished to a sheen that'd turn blinding if the sun ever hit them.

"It won't," came a ragged voice from inside. "The church faces north. The sun never shines on those doors, but I got 'em all spick-and-span."

Charlie peered into the dark interior. He couldn't see who spoke.

"You the padre?"

A raspy laugh greeted him.

"Not me. I'm the handyman, though I ain't so handy these days." A smallish man stepped from the shadows so Charlie got a good look. The man's right sleeve was pinned up.

"You must be Bernie Berenson," he said. "The station master told us about you."

"You and the other fellow? The one who looks like he fears for his mortal soul if he steps onto hallowed ground? He's your partner?"

"His name's Clement. Everybody calls him Clem." Charlie introduced himself and made small talk for a while until he finally got to the heart of the matter. "What happened to cause the wreck?"

"Derailment, up in Dos Robles Canyon. A nasty grade, steep and enough to tax the most powerful engine." He shook his shaggy head. The hair was receding over his forehead but he more than made up for that with the long hair dangling all around like some furry brown halo. "Only there was a leak in the boiler. Blew out a rivet or two and the engineer had to vent steam or risk the engine boiler explodin'."

"That doesn't sound like a derailment."

"Was," Berenson insisted. "When we lost upward speed, a rail twisted as we rounded a bend over a steep canyon. Dos Robles is *real* steep there. Close to two hundred feet straight down. A freight car went first. Took the mail car and the caboose with it."

"You were in the caboose?"

"I was the lantern man. Was. Can't swing a lantern to warn other trains and hang onto the handrail no more." He twisted back and forth, causing the empty sleeve to spiral outward and then fall back.

"Did you go over with the cars?"

"Suppose you could say I was lucky. I jumped. My buddy Fred went over. I caught my arm on a rock and smashed it up so bad they had to lop it off."

"So Fred's at the bottom of the canyon?"

"Must be. Nobody went down to see. Too dangerous."

"Who else went over?"

"Can't say. I heard tell that the clerk jumped out before the mail car took a tumble. If anybody got away, it'd be him. Laramie was always a slippery cuss. Never quite did his work but always got away with his sloth. Yes, sloth. That's one of the deadly sins, and Laramie perfected it, if you can perfect a sin."

"Some people can."

Berenson chuckled. "If anybody could, it'd be Laramie Reynolds. Lazy cuss." He shook his head as he remembered.

"What was in the mail car?"

"Can't say. Don't know about the freight car, neither. All me and Fred ever did was keep the back of the train from gettin' smashed by another train. Mostly our jobs meant something when we got to a rail yard."

"Nobody's tried to get to either the freight car or the mail car?"

"If they have, they never told me. But then, why'd anybody do that? I got fired when I lost my arm. The padre here's good enough to give me a place to sleep and food if I do what chores I can."

"How far along the tracks is this canyon?"

"Dos Robles? There's a long flat stretch to the east of Sacramento, then the steep climb that tests an engine's worth right there. The first big canyon? That's Dos Robles."

Charlie started to shake the man's hand, then realized the hand was missing. He covered himself by lifting his hand and pretending to cough.

"The poor box is by the door if you've a mind," Berenson said. "The padre's good about helpin' a passel of folks."

Charlie fished around in his pocket and took out a five-dollar gold piece. He ran his finger around the rim, then dropped it in.

"Much obliged," Berenson called after him.

He walked outside into the sunlight. The information he'd gotten was worth five dollars. It was likely worth another two thousand dollars. He waved to his partner who joined him. A look of relief passed over Clem's usually emotionless features. He was downright jubilant when Charlie told him about the derailment and where to find the cars.

They might be riding into hell, but they were leaving behind the graveyard. For Clem that was an improvement.

# CHAPTER 13

"We shoulda taken a train," Clem said. "The steep slope is killing my horse."

"We passed a couple handcars on sidings," Charlie Dawson replied. "Why not use them?"

"Pump our way *up* this grade? You're loco."

Charlie felt his horse faltering. He dismounted and walked alongside. The railroad tracks were laid on a ledge that had been chipped out of solid rock, with little room to spare on either side. If a train came along, they'd all be killed, man and beast alike. There wasn't room to avoid such a passage along stretches of track. The crew that had carved away the ledge on the side of the mountain had cut small depressions every few miles where a few men might take cover to let a train pass. None was large enough for two men and their mounts.

"The station agent said no trains were running right now. The next one won't come from the east for another day."

"We need to make better time or find a place to get off the tracks pronto."

"You feeling edgy, Clem?"

"This is one hellacious stretch of track. How they blasted it puzzles me."

"They dangled the Chinese down from above in baskets. They chipped it out one stone at a time."

"No blasting?"

"It doesn't look like it," Charlie said. He lengthened his stride and found himself tugging on his horse's reins. He walked faster. The horse refused to speed up against the altitude and steep grade.

"Any sign where the train derailed?"

"Nope, and I've been looking. I'm not even sure this is the right canyon."

"We're not being paid enough." Clem spat. The gob caught on an updraft and spiraled around, threatening to come back after him. A vagrant current finally smashed it against the sheer rock face alongside the tracks.

"Dos Robles," Charlie said. "This has to be the place." He paused, then pointed where the tobacco gob had spattered.

"All cut up," Clem said. "The track's been replaced, too."

"We're about three-quarters of the way to the summit."

"More 'n one place in this godforsaken stretch might have been replaced."

"That's what I like about you, Clem. You always find the cheerful side of any problem." Charlie inched to the verge and peered over. He felt at home in a mine, with tons of mountain rock all above him waiting to come crashing down. Some complained that being a miner wasn't much different from digging your own grave.

Being in tight, dark places filled with dust and damp was no bother for him. Looking over the edge down a sheer two-hundred-foot embankment gave him the collywobbles. His stomach tightened and his head spun. After closing his eyes for a few seconds, he dared to look again.

"I see something, Clem. Not twenty feet down there."

Clem pulled out field glasses and trained them on the tree growing precariously from the side of the mountain. He moved around until he got a better view.

"Body."

"They didn't even try to rescue him?"

"Fell onto a dead tree branch. Skewered him good and proper from what I can tell," Clem said.

"It must be Berenson's partner, Fred. Or maybe the mail clerk, Laramie. They never found either of their bodies."

"Tie a rope around your middle and chuck yourself against the tracks," Clem said. He spun several turns of rope around his waist and walked to the edge. A quick, impatient gesture hurried Charlie along.

Charlie sat down, feet pressed hard against the inside of the steel rail. He tugged on the rope, then signaled his partner to go over the verge. Even ready, the sudden weight half lifted him to his feet. Charlie tugged harder and pushed with all the strength in his legs to check Clem's descent. He held on for dear life until he heard his partner call to him. He couldn't make out what Clem said.

"I'll pull you up. You got the body?" A muffled reply did nothing to tell him what to do next. Taking that as his signal, he began pulling on the rope. Inch by inch, he drew it up until Clem's face appeared over the side of the drop-off.

"Keep pulling," Clem ordered. "I tied the body to the end of the rope." He fell forward. Charlie kept the tension on the rope. Clem turned and began dragging on the rope until the body flopped to the tracks.

"He is very, very dead," Charlie said. The man's face had been smashed in by the fall. Dozens of cuts showed that the fall down the side of the cliff had been deadly. Even if being impaled on the dead branch hadn't killed him, he'd have bled to death without the larger cuts getting patched up soon after the tumble down the mountainside.

The two miners looked at each other and frowned.

"Are you thinking what I am?" Charlie asked.

"This isn't a railroad man," Clem replied.

They began searching the man's pockets. The pocket watch from his vest had been crushed. Charlie held it up and let it spin on its chain.

"No respectable railroad man would have a cheap watch like this," he said.

"Got his wallet." Clem took out sheets of paper and dropped them onto the railroad ties after giving each a quick look. He stared at his partner. "Nothing here shows that he worked for the railroad. Not a single scrap of paper with the Central Pacific insignia."

Charlie read several of the pages more carefully.

"This is a telegram telling him to find the mail car.

It's not signed. And the other pages make him out to be a bounty hunter. A receipt for turning in a prisoner in Sacramento. A pair of warrants, no wanted posters, instructions on how to get here."

"He was a hired hand, just like us."

"Maybe. The one thing for sure is that he wasn't working for the railroad."

Clem returned to the edge of the cliff and used his field glasses for another twenty minutes before handing them to Charlie.

"Halfway down the mountain. It looks like a patch of red flannel."

"A shirt?" Charlie took his time and studied what his partner had found. He finally lowered the field glasses. "That's another body, even more torn up than this one."

"From the look of it, they tried to go down the cliff without ropes around them."

"There's no sign anyone up here tried to lower them." Charlie heaved a sigh. "I can't see the bottom of the canyon because the mountainside juts out halfway down. Cuts in the stone and torn-up vegetation most of the way down show where the cars fell, but I can't see them at the bottom."

"Stop whining," Clem said. "We need to think of another way down. It's more 'n two hundred feet. We didn't bring enough rope for one of us to go down, much less both of us."

"These two showed mountain goats would have a hard time going down here. Did you see another place along the tracks that'd be easier to go down?"

"Maybe. Remember the fissure a couple miles back?"

"Do you think it goes all the way to the canyon floor?"

Clem shrugged.

"The loose gravel would make it hard for the horses to go down."

"Going down's easy. Just start sliding until you get to the bottom. There's no chance of getting back up."

Charlie tried to study the canyon as carefully as he could. The sheer sides hid the canyon floor.

"There must be ends to the canyon. When we're down there, all we have to do is either go up or down along the floor. A canyon this deep must have a stream running along it, too. We'll have water." Charlie wiped his dried lips. "We've got water for us but the horses need to drink."

Clem considered the narrow ravine with the loose gravel. Then he let out a loud shout, whipped his hat off, and waved it around over his head. His horse hit the edge of the loose gravel. It dug in its heels, but the slide wasn't controlled. The horse shrieked as loudly as its rider.

"You crazy . . ." Charlie watched his partner disappear down the crevice. Clem's loud cries echoed between the steep canyon walls. That they didn't end abruptly told that he was still alive. Charlie had no idea what condition his partner was in after such a tumultuous fall.

There was only one way to find out.

He heeled his horse until it inched forward. When it began sliding, he let out a cry matching Clem's. The rocky crevice walls rushed past. Gravel flew all over the place like bullets ricocheting from the sides. And he fell and fell and fell. As suddenly as his descent began, he popped out just above a tree line. For a heart-stopping second, he thought he'd crash into the trees. Then they flew past. Somehow he followed the rock fall downward through the trees and finally burst out at the bank of a deep stream.

His horse hit the water and splashed around. It took all his skill to keep the horse from breaking a leg. They made it to the far side of the broad stream and jumped up onto the rocky embankment.

"Took you long enough." Clem sat astride his horse a few yards away.

"I never want to do that again." Charlie paused, smiled slowly, and then said, "Maybe one more time."

"Nothing got broke."

He looked up where he and his partner had descended. That was nothing less than a miracle. Maybe they were the ones to find the mysterious crate. Whoever the others were that tried to climb down the sheer sides had lost their lives. He saw no reason others trying to reach the derailed cars wouldn't suffer the same fate.

"There's where the rail cars came crashing down." He pointed to a huge gap in the trees torn apart by the derailed caboose.

"No reason to look in that car," Clem said. "The mail car's just ahead. The freight car must be farther down the canyon."

"We might find Berenson's partner. He'd appreciate knowing for sure what happened, if we find the body."

"Body? Ha." Clem snorted in contempt. "If there was a body, the animals got it by now. Coyotes or wolves.

Maybe even a bear." He pointed to the ground where a pile of fresh bear scat drew flies.

"We've come this far. It can't hurt."

"The walls give me the willies. They look like they're falling in on me."

"You rode down that slope, risked your life every inch of the way, and yelled and shouted like you enjoyed it, but you're a'scared of solid walls that won't go anywhere?"

Charlie yelped when a rock fell from the cliff on the far side of the canyon. He chanced a quick look at Clem, but his partner wasn't going to mock him for jumping in fright. His own nerves were giving him the panics, too. The derailment had turned the canyon floor into a vast graveyard.

Or it'd be a graveyard if they found bodies.

"Let's get to work. That's what we're being paid for, after all, not standing around trying to spook each other." He rode behind Clem, but he kept looking up at the walls just in case a new rockfall started an avalanche.

Being buried alive at the bottom of this canyon wasn't the kind of grave he wanted for his eternal resting spot.

# CHAPTER 14

When his horse shied, Charlie Dawson held up his hand to stop his partner. It took a bit of gentling to calm his horse. The animal's nostrils flared, and its eyes were ringed in white from fear.

"The nag's afraid of being smashed by more falling rocks," Clem said. He looked around to see how accurate his prediction of more tumbling rocks was.

"There's something else bothering her. There. Higher on the slope behind the caboose."

The railcar had slid downhill and lost its undercarriage. Where the wheels ended up wasn't something Charlie had much interest in finding out. They might have caught on rocks higher on the slope and been ripped off by the falling weight. The wooden frame had been twisted and slats popped out from the fall. What caught his eye was a hand poking up above what remained of the peaked roof.

"That the friend? Fred?"

"Must be," Charlie allowed. He dismounted and secured the reins to a rock before making his way up the rocky slope to where the caboose had come to rest.

The first thing he noticed was a lantern dangling from an iron hook at the rear. Somehow the glass had survived the tumble down the mountainside. Iron handrails and the rear platform had been bent beyond recognition, but the glass in the lantern wasn't even cracked. He shook his head at how such things happened.

If the dead man had enjoyed similar luck, he'd have lived. From what he saw, the crewman had taken all the destruction that should have been meted out to the lantern plus a considerable amount more that smashed up the body.

"You need help?"

"I can do it," Charlie said. His partner let out a loud sigh of relief. Clem got squeamish at the strangest times. Charlie clambered over rocks and grabbed a length of iron jutting from the caboose. He pulled himself up, got his feet under him, and jumped to flop belly down on the roof.

The body—what remained of it—lay a dozen feet in front of him. He got to his knees and stared.

"You leaving the body there, aren't you?"

Charlie ignored Clem's question and made his way slowly along the treacherous roof. He grabbed a handful of the dead man's bloody shirt and rolled him over. Pushing aside his distaste, he searched the pockets, found a wallet, and tucked it into his waistband alongside his Colt. He backed off, reached the side of the caboose, and dropped a few feet to a spot between the car and the stream.

Clem rode up, looking anxious.

"Why'd you take his wallet? Robbing a dead man's not a good idea."

"That's another one like we saw higher on the hill. There's been a small army coming after the cars. He wasn't a railroad crewman, either."

He and Clem exchanged a look. Both said at the same time, "Coming after the crate."

He swallowed hard and pulled out the wallet. It had a few greenbacks in it. He handed those to Clem. The papers were more interesting.

"This galoot worked for Collins. It looks as if he lived in Sacramento. Here's a telegram telling him to fetch back the crate."

"He was Johnny-on-the-spot," Clem said. "Only had to travel a few miles. We had to come all the way from San Francisco." Clem scowled in thought. "You reckon this one made it down first, ahead of the others?"

"Must have. He got the word to get the crate right away from Collins."

"The others didn't. They were bounty hunters. All on their own."

"Do you reckon we're the third gang hunting for the crate?"

"Maybe, maybe not. There might be something worth more in the mail car. Gold? Silver? A bank shipment? Just because we're looking for Collins's shipment doesn't mean all the others are, too. They might be nothing more than scavengers."

"The others were bounty hunters," Clem said. "But this dead man worked for Collins. We weren't his first pick."

"Not his first choice, but a convenient choice. And we got here pretty quick, considering we had to come from San Francisco."

He looked around, expecting to see even more bodies littering the landscape. The utter silence wore on him. The wind had died and the sun warmed the walls, turning the canyon bottom into a heat bath. The only sound was the gentle ripple of the stream as it made its way south.

"Let's find the other cars." Again, Clem cut to the heart of the matter. It didn't matter if Thomas Collins had sent out one or a hundred men ahead of them. They were here and the others looked to be very, very dead.

Charlie and Clem rode in silence. The freight car was a hundred yards away, also at the bottom of a swath of destruction caused when it tumbled down the cliff. It was partially hidden by a huge boulder that had stopped its fall. Pieces of the car were strewn around, making it appear as if it had been blown apart by a ton of dynamite.

"Don't think the Central Pacific is going to salvage that one."

Charlie saw what his partner meant. The steel wheels were folded under as if they were no more than foolscap. At least, unlike the caboose, the undercarriage had remained attached to the freight car. They both went to the freight car and put their backs into opening the door. It had popped off the track.

"Pry off a slat or two," Clem suggested when they couldn't budge the door. "Destroying railroad property's not going to be noticed."

"The railroad didn't hire us. Collins did. If Judah and Stanford and the rest object, Collins can buy them off."

He slid his fingers under one side panel. He pulled hard. The wood broke. A second plank fell off in his hand, giving enough space for him to squirm into the car. Clem followed. They slid about on the slanted floor but quickly checked the cargo.

"Not much freight," Clem said.

Charlie grunted as he moved heavier boxes around. All the crates were much larger than the one they sought.

"We should see what they were hauling. Nobody'll care if we help ourselves."

"They won't care, but how are we supposed to carry out anything bigger than the crate we're hunting for? We've got two horses. This is a box of nails." Charlie kicked it over, sending the ten-penny nails clattering around on the freight car floor.

"Don't need nails."

"Nothing in these boxes will be useful when we get the Betty Sue back," Charlie said. "We ought to be glad there wasn't blasting powder in the freight. The entire car would have been blown to smithereens."

They searched for another hour without finding Collins's crate. Exiting through the hole they'd broken in the wall, they stood in shadows and shivered. The sun shone down on the bottom of the canyon for only a short time each day due to the towering walls. It was only early afternoon, and already the sun had passed overhead and was hidden by the western wall.

"Hunting in the dark's not a good idea," Charlie said.

"What if we miss it? What if we step in a hole and break a leg? Or get snake-bit? Snakes come out this time of night. That's why the Apaches never attack at night. They're all scared of snakes." He looked at the dark ground around for any trace of slithery movement.

"The caboose lantern wasn't all busted up. We can see if there's coal oil in it."

"Time's against us," Charlie agreed. He kicked his feet a bit to scare away any snakes creeping up on him. "I'm hungry and about tuckered out. You think we ought to both keep looking until we pass out from exhaustion or take turns sleeping? One can hunt while the other eats and catches some shuteye."

"I'll get the lantern. You see if that jerky's got worms in it yet."

"The worms'll be better tasting," Charlie said. He returned to where their horses grazed on the grass along the riverbank. After rummaging through their saddle-bags, he got enough food to gnaw on while they searched.

Clem fired up the lantern and held it high, casting a bright yellow light against the twilight. Together they finished going through the freight car and finally gave up.

"It'd better be in the mail car," Charlie said. "I'm so beat I can hardly raise my arms." He looked up at the pitch-black cliffs on either side. It was only really about sunset. The canyon stayed warm, but the unlit rocks would cool fast now.

"Other 'n the gents who tried to climb down from above, we haven't found any of the crew."

"You don't suppose they had the same luck as that

lantern?" Charlie shook his head at the notion anyone survived the downward plunge that wrecked the cars.

"Why do we think the crate and whatever's in it that the banker wants so bad isn't destroyed?"

"He didn't seem bothered by that idea. Maybe it was the triumph of hope over experience."

"He might be a lucky son of a gun. We got his son back. If I'd had a chance to bet on that, I'd have lost every cent I had betting against us."

"Your confidence is just what we need right now. You think we won't find the crate. Chances go up that we won't if you believe that." Charlie vowed to stay positive, even if his gut feeling was that they were on a wild goose chase.

"I believed there was gold in the Betty Sue. Look where that got me."

"Rolling in the clover, that's where. We'd never have returned that thoroughbred or plucked Wash Collins from the hold of that ship if it hadn't been for the Betty Sue Mine."

"You got a twisted way of looking at things," Clem said.

Charlie tromped along, lantern high over his head. They both searched the deep shadows for where the mail car had landed.

"If we wait for morning, we'll have wasted half a day," Charlie said, thinking out loud. "But we aren't seeing anything in the dark, even using the lantern."

"Hush." Clem lowered the lantern and hid its glow with his coat.

"What's wrong?"

"Don't know. Listen up." Clem craned his neck around and turned slowly.

Charlie strained to hear anything, but the stream rushing along a few feet away muffled most noise. In the far distance, a lovelorn coyote howled. That plea for companionship lasted only a few seconds before dying. Deathly silence fell. Not even insects droned along the stream. He turned slowly, hand cupping his ear to better catch any sound. He was a tad deaf from being too close to too many blastings in the mine. That didn't keep him from hearing what might have been whispers coming from upstream.

"You make out what that is?"

Clem shook his head. He pressed his finger against his lips to quiet his partner.

They continued to listen, but the unnatural stillness ate away at his resolve. More and more he wanted out of the canyon and back where he could hear men laughing and women singing and whiskey-filled shot glasses clicking down on a bar. Being a miner meant long hours alone. Or with no one but his partner.

Now he wanted shoulders crowding him and too many men he didn't know by their first names urging him to join poker games or play just one round of faro.

"Don't hear it any longer," Clem said.

"There." Charlie took a step toward the stream. "There it is."

Clem lifted the lantern. On the far side of the stream rested the mail car. It had come rolling downhill so fast it hadn't stopped at the base of the cliff. It had jumped over the stream and tried to climb the far canyon wall.

"Time's a'wasting," Charlie said.

As he waded across the stream, he looked back up the canyon. A shiver passed through him. Then he forgot all about it when Clem called out in victory as he pried open the door so they could enter the car.

# CHAPTER 15

"Give me a boost."

"Why?" Charlie demanded. "I can get up and look through the car. You give me a foot up."

Clem stood as silent and still as a stone statue. His partner finally relented, grumbling as he moved to the side of the mail car, cupped his hands, and waited. A heavy, rough boot rubbed against his callused hands. He bent and then lifted with all his strength. Clem shot through the air, arms windmilling around.

"Why'd you go and do that? You coulda killed me."

"Are you in the car?"

"Take my hand. I'll pull you up."

Charlie caught his partner's fingers, then grabbed with his left hand. He closed on Clem's wrist. Kicking to find a foothold but not finding one, he let the other man draw him up. He finally found footing on the edge of the car and flailed around to get a better grip. He flopped on the slanting floor next to a large safe.

"Been opened," Clem said. He swung the door back and forth to show the vault had already been opened. "Whatever was inside is gone."

"Not gone. Scattered all over the car," Charlie said. "From the look, it might have sprung open by itself because of the fall."

"Don't think so," Clem said. He ran his fingers over the sliding bolts. "Too clean. Not enough metal torn out of its seating."

"So? It's been opened?" Charlie's heart missed a beat. They might be too late to retrieve the crate.

He braced himself to keep from slipping on the slanted floor and began pawing through the papers that had spilled from the safe. As he hunted, he saw what had happened. Somewhere during the descent, the corner of the safe had struck a rock. The impact twisted the heavy metal enough to pop open the thick steel door.

"If I'd blown it open with dynamite, I couldn't have done a better job," Charlie said. He threw the mail he found onto a pile. By the time he'd sorted every piece, he was sure nothing important had been sealed in the safe.

Nothing important meaning the crate they sought.

"The boxes are tossed all around. The car must have turned over and over a dozen times."

"Like a rock polisher," Clem said. "Only I don't see any blood."

"The mail clerk must have been in the car when the car was on the tracks. Was he thrown out? Before the car came down the cliff? Or was he left somewhere along the fall?"

"No way to know." Clem scooted along the floor and kicked hard at a piece of wall that had collapsed into the car. "Well, now lookee here. Our luck just changed."

"Another safe!" Charlie's heart ran away with itself. They hadn't found Collins's crate. It had to be in the second safe.

He slid down the tilted floor and caught himself on a jagged edge of a plank. He turned around and got his knees under him to study the safe more closely.

"It didn't break open like the big one. If anything, getting into it will be danged hard. Somewhere between the top of the mountain and here, its handle was busted off." He ran his finger around the cavity. The safe opened with a key. The keyhole had been pushed in. He ran his finger around the keyhole, then teased out a piece of metal.

If they had the key now, there'd be some small hope of opening the door. If they had the key . . .

"The box has to be inside. We've looked everywhere else."

"Too small."

"Clem, you're always looking at the dark side of things. Where else could the crate be?"

"Say what you want, the safe is too small. Collins said the box was a bit more 'n two feet long."

"Two and a half, maybe," Charlie allowed.

"More 'n three was the impression I got. It's not in this safe."

He measured the safe carefully, wanting to catch Clem in a mistake. After measuring the safe in all direc-tions, he sat back and shook his head. Even wedged in diagonally, that long a wood box wouldn't fit. This was a safe intended only for valuable documents and likely greenbacks or specie being shipped from one bank to another.

"The crate must have been tossed out when the car rolled down here."

"The mail clerk might have swiped it."

"Clem!" Charlie was angry at not finding their box. He was tired to the point of exhaustion, hungry, and wishing he'd stayed in Sacramento. Miss Lucy ran a fine house of ill repute. She served top-notch liquor to her best customers and had always treated him like he was the owner of a fabulous gold mine, even when she knew he was barely scraping by.

"No reason to get all het up. I'm just saying the box isn't in the teeny safe."

"We'll have to work our way up the hill and search for it. Maybe we'll get lucky and find it at the base of the cliff. Hanging onto rocks by the tips of my fingers doesn't appeal to me. Besides, it'll take days and we don't have that long. We—"

"Charlie."

"What?" He was cranky and in the middle of a rant. Being interrupted by his usually taciturn partner was more irritating than it should have been. He looked up from the safe that taunted him with its destroyed front and heavy sides. Even using a chisel and sledgehammer would take effort to knock off the hinges to reveal the contents. And it'd be a waste of time since the box probably wasn't inside.

"You reckon this box fits the description?" Clem held up a box three feet long and six inches square on the end.

Charlie tried to speak. Words failed him. He reached out and laid his fingers on the rough wood, stroking along its length as he might Miss Lucy's bare leg. The crate had been banged up but hadn't been crushed. The end panel had been ripped off and crudely replaced. Nails poked out where they hadn't been hammered back in properly.

"What's it say on the side?"

Clem held the lantern closer so Charlie got a good look at the lettering.

"This is it. That's the number Collins said was painted on."

He sagged back in relief, then sat straighter, anger returning.

"Why didn't you show it to me right off?"

"It was jammed under the safe. I had to clear away debris around it so I could pull it out."

"You wanted to make me think it was lost. You were tormenting me! You!" He lunged for his partner. Clem clutched the box to his chest and kicked free, losing his balance. He slid down the sloping floor to crash into the wall of the car pressed into the ground.

"Let's see what's inside. From the way the bottom's been nailed on, somebody already looked at it."

"Or it might have been damaged and poorly repaired. There's no telling how good Collins's shipping department is. We'd have to ask the mail clerk about its condition when he signed for it in Sacramento."

"Maybe he didn't. Collins said he sent this so nobody'd ask questions. If the clerk had to sign for it, that'd cause some curiosity. I found it under the safe, it mighta been rattling around free, no special handling on it."

Charlie looked around. "You see anything showing what happened to the clerk?"

"There's a dark stain on the floor, but I can't tell if it's blood."

Charlie wiggled toward the spot his partner pointed out. He pressed his face down close. The black stain might have been blood or coal oil or a dozen other things. Nobody swept up mail cars like they did a passenger car. The spot was dry. He sniffed, wondering if there might be a copper tang of blood. Nothing.

"You'll get splinters in your nose if you keep that up." Clem wormed around a pile of debris, kicked away letters and legal documents from the big safe, then got his feet under him. He stood, wobbled around, and then held up the box.

"We've got it," Charlie said. "Let's get back to San Francisco and hand it over to Collins."

"We should see what's in it," Clem said. "We've risked our necks for it."

"We'll be paid another two thousand bucks, minus the hundred Hickman fronted us. Don't mess with it. Collins might go back on his word if he thinks we saw what's inside."

"He won't know. Aren't you even a teeny bit interested in seeing what's inside? You're the one always poking his snout where it doesn't belong because you're curious about danged near everything."

"You claim you're never curious. Why the change?"

"What's worth that much money to get back?"

"On a deadline," Charlie said. He heaved a deep breath. His partner knew him too well. His curiosity bump was throbbing. "Come on, let me have the box."

"You don't want to find out what's in it?" Clem held it away, juggling the box in one hand and the lantern in the other.

"You're right. I got this far. Let's see what's in it."

Charlie reached for the box, then froze.

"Listen. Do you hear it?"

"Our horses!" Clem scooted past his partner and dropped out the partially open mail car door.

All Charlie could think was a wolf finding an easy meal. Their horses were old and easy prey for a hungry critter. He went headfirst out the door, caught the edge, and somersaulted around. He crashed into the side of the car, then let go. He landed hard ten feet below. His hand went for his gun.

"Come on," Clem called. "I don't want to walk back to San Francisco."

Charlie ran as fast as his aching legs could move. He matched Clem and then passed him. Splashing through the water, he rounded a bend in the stream.

"They're gone. Where are they?" He looked around frantically.

"No wolves," Clem said. He sniffed the air. Then he bent low and studied the soft earth where they'd left their horses tethered. "No trace of any wild animals. Except for this." He stepped away from the stream and placed his foot alongside an imprint in the soft earth.

"Horse thieves," he said.

Charlie looked around frantically.

"Clem, down!"

He swung his Walker around and got off a shot into the bushes along the stream. He fired once. A dozen bullets ripped through the night in reply.

# CHAPTER 16

"They stole our horses," cried Charlie Dawson.

"Thievin' horse thieves." Clem started cursing even as he fired into the bushes where the outlaws had been. Charlie realized his few slugs tearing through that brush had incited the return fire, but the shifting shadows told him they were moving through the edge of the forested area. They were hightailing it and weren't going to give their victims a chance to recover their horses.

"How many?"

"I can't tell," Charlie called back. He emptied his Walker, then began the tedious chore of reloading it. Clem kept up a steady fire until the hammer on his Colt fell on an empty chamber.

He cocked his once-again-ready six-gun. His hearing was never too good, but his vision, especially his night vision, was about perfect. So many days spent in a darkened mine had honed his eyes to where he saw the slightest glimmer of a gold fleck. Now he watched for a horse thief to show himself.

After a full minute of utter silence, he moved to the stream. Clem lay flat on his belly along the muddy bank. His muzzle roved endlessly, looking for a target. He didn't have any better luck finding someone to plug than Charlie.

"How many do you reckon there were?"

"Only takes one to steal a horse."

Charlie looked around. The sheer dark canyon walls looked as if they arched above and threatened to fall down on him. Smells of pine and fish mingled with gunsmoke. He waited for the outlaws to show themselves.

"They've run off," he finally said. "They stole our horses and ran like cravens. Yellow-bellied cowards!"

"Keep your voice down."

"I won't! I'm mad! They took our horses. Those weren't the best horses in the world. Not like the one we got back for that lawyer fellow, but they got us here without breaking down. They *stole* our horses!"

"Never heard hoofbeats. They must be camped nearby."

This cooled Charlie's wrath a mite. If the horse thieves hadn't just ridden away and kept going, that meant there was a chance to get the horses back.

"You hear them?" he asked Clem.

His partner shook his head. Neither of them caught the smallest clue that anyone else existed in the canyon.

"You think they might be Injuns? The Pomos are around here somewhere."

"Not that tribe. They're out along the Coast," Clem said. "Them's white men. Here's another boot print. An Injun'd wear moccasins." He traced the outline with his finger, then inched forward to the next one. "Tall galoot. Maybe six-foot from his stride."

"He was hurrying along. He didn't want to tangle with us," Charlie said. All the answer he got was a contemptuous snort. "We're dangerous men. We took on the best—the worst—along the Barbary Coast and lived to brag on it."

Clem said nothing.

"We found the crate Collins wanted. All the men decorating the side of the cliff died trying to get it."

"Don't know this is what they wanted." Clem patted the box at his side.

"Of course we do. The papers on one man said he was hired by Collins. Why else would he be out here?"

"So the banker man sent others ahead of us. The only reason he hired us was that they never reported back."

"That makes us better. It does!"

"Think on it, Charlie. These owlhoots took our horses. They coulda ambushed us for this." He patted the crate.

"They can't know we found it." Charlie stomped and snorted like a bull. He felt full of piss and vinegar. They had found the crate and others, men who looked like gunslicks, had failed and died before them. He and Clem had found the lost crate, and no gang of horse thieves would take their horses!

"Wait here. I'll be back with our horses before you know it." Charlie got his feet under him, slipped some in the mud, then duckwalked along the stream. The rushing water hid any sound he made. He hoped the darkness cloaking everything on the canyon floor kept the outlaws from spotting him.

Clem grumbled but made no effort to join him. That suited Charlie just fine. He'd sneak up on the outlaws, steal back their horses, and then they'd gallop off. He clutched his Colt tighter. If he had to shoot his way in, he'd do it. The thieves had no call to take his horse.

He waded across the stream and edged up to the bushes where the thieves had shot at him. The pall of gunsmoke still hanging in the air choked him. He turned his head and tried to breathe through his coat sleeve. That helped some, but he coughed again. The coat needed cleaning in the worst way. It reeked so badly he worried the horse thieves could smell him coming after them.

A quick glance back convinced him that Clem hadn't stirred from his position on the far side of the creek. He sucked in his breath, then pushed through the sticker bush. On the far side, he found where the gunmen had crouched, shooting at him. He wasn't as good as Clem at deciphering such things but thought he made out three sets of footprints. This might be the entire gang.

Or it might be a paltry few. He had no idea how many he faced. Charlie moved ahead in a crouch now, bent low to keep his silhouette near the ground. The woods were so dense and dark he blundered into one tree after another. It finally occurred to him that if he couldn't see but a foot or two ahead, neither could the thieves. Walking upright let him make better time. He kept his left arm out straight to use as a guide while he gripped the wood handle of his Walker Colt in his right hand.

He stepped out into a clearing before he realized he had done so. He stiffened when he realized that eight men sat around the fire not twenty feet from him. The darkness again came to his aid. Each step slow and quiet, he melted back into the forest. Moving around until he sneaked even closer to the campfire let him eavesdrop on them without being seen.

"Are you sure you killed them, Roy?"

A man with a florid face and a white scar that ran across his forehead, past the bridge of his nose, and onto his cheek, nodded. Every movement of his head made the white scar glow like it was on fire as the dancing flames lit him.

"Sure as rain," Roy said. "Both of 'em! I never miss."

"You fixin' to put notches on your gun handle?" asked another. This caused a snicker to go around the circle.

"What are you sayin', Garcia? You sayin' I lied about the other three men I killed?"

"You didn't take their scalps. You didn't take these men's hair, either. How do we know you didn't just run 'em off?"

"They're dead. I saw their bodies in the creek. They wasn't movin'."

"You have such an imagination, Roy. But we can use the extra horses." The man's raspy, low voice was almost hidden by the crackle of the fire and the distant gurgling stream.

"Thanks, Swine." Roy puffed out his chest and looked pleased as punch at the compliment.

Charlie strained to get a better look at the one Roy

had called Swine. He sat all hunched over. The duster was pulled around his body like a shroud, hiding any detail that might show. Charlie couldn't tell what kind of gun Swine carried or if it hung at his side or in a cross-draw holster. For all he knew the man was like Quantrill, riding along festooned with a half dozen guns to match the firepower of an entire Yankee squad.

Or Swine might have been one of the men with Roy who'd emptied his six-shooter and then run off with the stolen horses.

Whatever it was, Swine commanded some respect. The leader? Charlie guessed that was so.

"You think they mighta found the box?" Roy poked at the fire with a stick. Embers stirred and went curling upward into the night sky like drunken lightning bugs.

The question caused Charlie to take an involuntary step forward, revealing himself—if any of the thieves had been looking his way. He moved back into hiding, anxious to hear the answer.

"We only got here, Roy. Those two cowboys were coming from up the canyon. Did you have any call to think they were searching the train cars?"

"Just saw the horses and took 'em."

"So," said Swine, "you don't know. They staked out their horses to go prowling around. Is that the way you saw it?"

"I suppose, Swine."

"It'd have been smarter to ride up to them, all grins and how-are-yous, and find what they were up to. Instead, you saw their horses and stole them."

"They're good horses. And I tell you, me and Shorty and Kent killed them when they shot at us."

"That true, Shorty?" Swine turned slightly and pulled the pitch-black duster even tighter around his body. Charlie saw the man was smallish. That did nothing to cut down on the respect he commanded around this campfire.

"Can't say. Roy rode over, grabbed the horses, and lit out. We never got a good look at the men, before or after we shot it out."

"They might be alive, eh?"

Shorty nodded like his head was mounted on a spring.

"That box is real important. I want it more 'n I do a couple swayback, brokedown nags."

The murmur passed around the campfire. Eight men. All hardened criminals if Charlie was any judge. They ranged from impulsive and stupid like Roy to being a careful leader like Swine.

"Let's get some grub and then go find these gents," Swine said. "If they found the box Reynolds said was so all fired valuable, I need to take it from them." From the folds of the duster came a flash of a blued-steel gun barrel. The pistol was held in Swine's gloved hand.

Charlie slid back into the depths of the forest. He bounced from tree to tree in his hurry to return to his partner. Covered in sap and bleeding from a half dozen small cuts caused by twigs and branches, Charlie blundered down to the stream where he had left his partner.

"Clem?" He kept his voice low. The outlaws would

be finished with their meal before he knew it and on their way to retrieve the box. "Where are you?"

"Over here."

A shadow moved, then separated from a tumble of rocks.

"I found them," Charlie said breathlessly. "The thieves. Not a hundred yards that way." He pointed over his shoulder, downstream. "Maybe a couple hundred yards. I can't tell since I lost my bearings in the forest."

"How many?"

"Eight," Charlie said, swallowing hard. "They look like they're on the run. Hard cases. Maybe they all have rewards on their head."

"And?"

He was always amazed at how Clem understood when there was more. It was as if he saw his thoughts. Or maybe his face betrayed his thoughts. Clem played poker. Charlie knew better.

"I overheard them say they're looking for the crate, too. I don't know if the dead men up there"—he pointed up the cliff in the direction of tracks where the train had derailed—"or if they're another gang out hunting for it, but they know what they're after."

"Eight gunmen?"

"Look, Clem, we can't fight that many if they come after us. We need our horses back. If we barter the box for our horses and to be allowed to ride off, then we . . ."

Clem laughed harshly.

"Did any of them sound like they have a touch of mercy in their souls?"

"Well, no. One named Roy shot at us. He lied about

killing us. And their leader, somebody named Swine, said—"

"Swine?" Clem spoke so sharply Charlie stopped talking and blinked in surprise. "The leader's name is Swine? Like in Swinburne?"

"I don't know. Nobody ever called him that."

"Him? You're sure Swine is a man?"

"That's crazy talk." He scowled as he considered the question. "Are you asking if that was a woman?"

Clem said nothing.

"I suppose it could be," Charlie admitted. "The voice was low and raspy."

"From too much whiskey and smoking."

"It could have been. And·Swine kept a duster pulled tight around him—her."

"A coal-black duster?"

Charlie's mouth turned to cotton. He licked dried lips and hesitated to ask the question that choked him up. He finally spit out the words.

"Do you know Swine? Swinburne?"

"Yeah, I do."

"How?"

"She's my wife."

# CHAPTER 17

Charlie Dawson stared at his partner, mouth agape. He shook himself and finally croaked out, "You never told me you were married."

"Never came up."

"You should have told me."

"What would you have done about it?"

"She's an outlaw! Her gang stole our horses! And . . . and they want that." He pointed at the box resting against a boulder where Clem had taken refuge.

"It figures. She always was a conniving, sneaky, old—"

"Clem!" Charlie snapped now. "You know her. She's your wife! Talk to her and get our horses back so we can ride out of here."

"We're divorced," he said. "Went to Fargo up on the Red River and made it official and everything."

"Your former wife, then. You ask her to let us go. You *tell* her to!"

"Greta's not the sort to give in so easy. She'll shoot us both."

"Kill us?"

"And she'd enjoy every second of it, especially if I suffer a lot. She's like that. She took up with Dupree. The two of them together's a bad pair. They feed off each other's orneriness. He's worse, in a way. He shoots first and thinks later, if ever. Greta, now, thinks before she shoots and then never has regrets."

"Let's trade her the box for our horses. She wants that. We can hide it and when we get our horses can tell her where it is."

"She'd shoot us down 'fore that."

"You make her out to be a stone-cold killer."

"She didn't get the name Swine for being all sweetness and light." He heaved a deep sigh. "The first time I laid eyes on her, though, she was dressed all in crinoline and lace. She looked like one of them fancy belles of the ball you're always hearing about."

Charlie turned and lifted his six-gun. Sounds of horses approaching put him on guard.

"The gang's coming for us. One with a scar named Roy is—"

"Roy Dupree? That snake! He's the one I mentioned. He was having his way with Greta while we were married. I know it, though she denied it. And Roy'd lie about the sun coming up. I cut him good."

"Across the face and nose and cheek?" Charlie ran his finger down his face to show where Roy's scar stretched.

"I'm glad I left that mark. Maybe he'll think twice about chasing after another man's woman."

"He's still with her. You're not," Charlie said. If his partner had given Roy Dupree that facial scar, chances were good the outlaw'd never consider letting them go. That meant he had to deal only with Greta Swinburne.

He stared at Clem in wonder. His partner ever being married was a wonder. Even worse, it came as a complete shock to him that he'd once been married to a treacherous outlaw like Swine.

"There're eight of them," Clem said, craning his neck to look downstream. "Unless you're a better shot than you've shown before, we'd better hide out."

Charlie touched the wood handle of his Colt. Clem was right. Between them, they had twelve rounds before they had to reload. That was an arduous process, and he was running low on powder and shot for his pistol. Even if they both hit one target with one round, that didn't mean they'd slow down the outlaws. Getting hit with a slug never slowed some determined men down.

Worse, all his spare ammo was in his saddlebags. Which Swine's gang had stolen.

He pointed past the rock where Clem stood. They silently crept to the far side of the large boulder, then made their way toward the rugged cliff face. Below them, they heard Greta and her gang splashing along in the stream. The outlaws argued constantly. That gave Charlie a chance to judge how far upstream they'd gone.

"Let's go," he said, turning to head back in the direction where the gang had camped. If the outlaws kept riding, that put plenty of distance between them.

They made as good a progress as they could in the dark. He wished Clem had kept the lantern, though that would have betrayed them right away.

"Their camp's on the other side of the stream, in that glade." He took a step and froze when he heard a six-shooter cock.

"Yup, that's right where we pitched camp."

"You were left behind to guard it," Charlie guessed.

"Not exactly. Nobody got left behind. The others just decoyed you."

"Shorty's right about that," came a gravelly voice. "I decided it was easier to flush you like birds from a blind. Scrounging around in the dark'd only make us testy."

"You always were real testy, Greta."

"What's that?" A rider trotted forward. The figure astride the horse threw back the folds of the black duster to lean forward. "As I live and breathe, it's my husband, Clement. I haven't laid eyes on you in a month of Sundays."

"Too bad it wasn't longer," Clem said.

"You never change. But now you'll never get a chance to." She drew a six-shooter and aimed it at her former husband. Clem stood tall and didn't flinch.

"Wait, wait, Greta!"

"Nobody calls me that, nobody 'cept Clement. And he won't be doin' it for long." She cocked her six-gun.

"Swine! Miss Swinburne!" Charlie was frantic now. "Let's make a swap."

"What can you trade? I'm always up for some give and take."

"Is that what you call it now, Greta?"

"Shut up, Clement. I always said you talked too much. Let your partner here have his say. It sounds more

interestin' to me than anything you'd have to offer."
She laughed harshly. "After all those nights we spent
together, I can say that as the Gospel truth."

"I want to trade the crate for our lives. Our lives and
our horses. You take the box and we ride out. We never
have to cross paths again."

Charlie made a grab and snatched it from Clem's
fingers.

"I got it right here."

"She'll kill us anyway, you fool." Clem spat. "That's
about the only thing she likes to do."

"That's not so, Clement!" she flared. "I like doin'
things with real men."

"Like Roy?" Clem spat again. "That's not a real man.
He's hardly a rabbit."

Roy Dupree galloped up and kicked at Clem. He
missed.

The sudden confusion was too good an opportunity
to pass up. Charlie swung the box like a sledgehammer
and struck Dupree's horse in the front leg. It shrieked
and went down on that leg, throwing its rider. Charlie
drew and fired his pistol, not caring if he hit anyone.
The outlaws' horses all reared. They fought to keep
them under control as Charlie ducked and dodged to
keep from being kicked in the head.

Roy Dupree fought to stand. Charlie had brought
down the outlaw's horse using the box. He gripped it
tightly and swung again. The end of the box crashed
into Dupree's forehead. Blood spurted everywhere. If it
ever healed, he'd have a new scar on the other side of
his forehead. Somehow the idea that he had given

Dupree a scar to match the one Clem already had gave him new courage.

He jumped, grabbed a handful of shirt, and yanked Shorty from the saddle. Wrestling the crate, he stepped up. Holding his prize in his left hand, he shot and fired the single-action Walker Colt in his right hand.

Greta Swinburne shouted orders to the others. This added to the confusion. The horses all kicked and turned and began to buck. Two riders were thrown hard. Charlie called to his partner, but Clem didn't need to be told this was their only chance to escape.

He jumped onto Greta Swinburne's horse and put his arms around the woman's waist. With a cry of triumph, he hoisted her up, turned, and threw her to the ground. She landed in a heap, stirred, and moaned.

"Is she all right?" Charlie asked, fighting to get his horse under control.

"You've got your gun out. Shoot her. I can't reach my iron." Clem's horse spun in circles and then sun-fished. All four hooves left the ground as the maverick horse arched its back and tried to buck off its rider.

"I'm not going to shoot a woman."

"She's no woman. She's my ex-wife." Clem brought the horse under control and reached for his six-gun.

"Come on!" Charlie emptied his pistol at the rest of the gang. He sowed confusion but didn't hit anyone. The horses rearing and pawing at the air with their front hooves gave them a good enough start.

They splashed as they raced downstream in the dark. Charlie was afraid his horse would step in a hole or slip on a wet rock, but there wasn't nothing he could do about it. If they didn't put as much distance between them and the gang, they'd be goners. Clem had been right about Greta Swinburne's bloodthirsty ways. She would have killed them and taken the box.

She would have killed them even if she hadn't gotten the box.

"They'll be after us in a nonce," Clem said. "How long can our horses gallop along?"

Charlie's mount already tired. He drew back on the reins. The grateful horse slowed to a canter and then a trot. It took some goading to keep it from breaking into a walk.

"We have to put more distance between us. You still have the box?"

Charlie lifted it to show he clung to it as fiercely as he did the reins.

"Cut away from the stream. Go on upslope toward the canyon wall."

"What good will that do us? They're sure to track us down. If not in the dark, then at sunup."

"I see dark holes up there. Caves? We might get into one and hold them off."

"I'm almost out of ammunition. No, that's not true. I am *out* of bullets. I never thought we'd get into a long gunfight. What about you, Clem? Do you have much ammo left?"

"Not much. We have to go to ground. Outrunning them's not going to work."

They threaded their way between the rocks and entered another stand of trees. The pines and firs were farther apart here, giving them an easier ride to the far side of the woods. Their horses were quivering from strain under them. They stopped to give their stolen mounts a rest.

"What else haven't you told me?" Charlie demanded. "You're married to a murderous outlaw."

"Was, not is. We got married in Pembina."

"North Dakota?"

"And we rode from town to town. Towns up there are mighty far apart so we had plenty of time to get to know each other. After six months, we were close to killing each other. She was about the purtiest filly I ever did see, but she's got . . . habits."

"Like killing people? What else? How'd she get to be the leader of a gang of cutthroats like Roy and Shorty and the rest?"

"I'm surprised to see Roy's still with her. He never had a lick of sense. Only a mean streak a mile wide." Clem sighed. "But she can be real persuasive when she sets her mind to it."

Charlie held up his hand to silence his partner. The sound of horses back toward the stream echoed upslope.

"They found our trail," Clem said softly. He turned his horse toward the canyon wall. "If we get to the wall, we can follow it out of here."

Charlie wasn't going to argue that. He felt as if he had stepped into a grave, a grave with mile-high rock walls. Every time he looked up the walls seemed to bend over to fall on him. The small segment of the night sky showed few stars, making him feel even more hemmed in.

"We can't keep the horses," Charlie said when he

heard pursuit getting closer by the minute. "We have to hide."

"Those caves I saw. Head for the cliff. We'll have to hide there."

Charlie put his heels to the tired horse's flanks. It clopped along faster, but it also made more noise. The whoops and hollers from the outlaws after them grew closer by the minute.

"There," Clem said. "Inside."

Charlie hesitated. Going into the cave was dangerous. The opening was too narrow for them to lead the horses in.

"What if there's a bear in there? Or a mountain lion?"

"There's a pack of jackals on our trail. Which do you want to tangle with?"

Charlie jumped down and hoisted the box onto his shoulder. He turned to see Clem swat his horse on the rump to get it to run off. The horse he'd just ridden lit out after Clem's.

"Get in. Now." Clem drew his six-gun.

Charlie heard the gang break from the edge of the forest. When they spotted their quarry, the outlaws opened fire. Clem ducked into the cave, wiggling through its narrow opening. Charlie went to follow when a bullet cut past his ear. He flinched, stumbled, and dropped the crate. Going to his knees, he tried to pick up the dropped treasure.

Roy Dupree let out a whoop and charged. Bullets flew all around Charlie. The crate slipped from his fingers. As he tried to pick it up, Clem grabbed his arm and swung him around.

"In. Leave the box." He leveled his six-gun and fired until it came up empty.

From inside the cave, Charlie asked, "Did you hit any of them? That was Roy Dupree who rode me down."

"Missed. Every single bullet missed." Clem broke open the gun and began reloading. The faint light at the mouth of the cave suddenly vanished. Clem snapped the last round in and said, almost to himself, "This is the last of my ammo." He turned toward the cave mouth and pointed his gun, ready to make what'd be their last stand.

One of the broad-shouldered, massive outlaws blocked even the starlight entering the cave.

"We've got the box. And we've got you where we want you."

"Come on in, Dupree. Let's see how brave you are," Clem shouted.

The answer wasn't what he expected. Rock creaked, moaned ominously, and then broke. The outlaws levered rocks above the cave mouth into a small avalanche.

The rockslide blocked the cave entrance and left them inside the pitch blackness. Trapped and left to die under tons of rock.

# CHAPTER 18

"It's dark."

"You think so? I thought I'd gone blind." Charlie snorted in disgust. "They collapsed the mine mouth and trapped us."

"Cave, not a mine."

"I've spent half my life underground. What's it matter?" Charlie reached out and touched a rocky wall. He inched along, stumbling over the rocks on the cave floor. "Oww!"

"You found the rock holding us in this prison," Clem said. He had remained where they'd stood when the outlaws closed the cave mouth.

Charlie began feeling the rock for loose shale, gravel, a spot where he could begin pulling rocks away to get them free of the shaft. He grunted and cursed and ended up kicking at the rock. Nothing budged. They were securely trapped.

"The plug is too thick to shove aside a few stones and get out," Charlie said. He made his way back to where he heard Clem breathing heavily in the dusty air. A fleeting touch assured him his partner was sitting. He dropped down beside him.

"If this was an abandoned mine, there'd be picks and shovels. And a few miners' candles. I surely could use some light in here about now." Clem grunted and shifted about on the rocky floor.

"We're lucky there's not a bear in here with us," Charlie said. He shivered at the notion of a bear, awakened from a short nap, deciding it was time to sharpen his six-inch claws on human skulls.

"If you call that luck. I'd rather be a meal for a bear than a feast for maggots after I'm dead."

"You lit the lantern back at the train wreck. Do you have more lucifers?"

"A couple." Clem fumbled around. The bright flare of the match dazzled both of them.

Charlie blinked hard and took a quick look around before the match burned out. He had hoped to see something other than rock walls. A quick glance toward the plug of rock bottling them up further discouraged him. Two huge chunks of rock had fallen straight down. Dynamite would blow them to smaller rocks which could be shoveled out or dug with a pickax.

They didn't have a pick. And they didn't have dynamite. Even if they had much ammunition left, the pitiful few grains of powder used in their guns wouldn't scratch the hard rock.

"I've got two matches left."

"Save them," Charlie said. He had no idea what need they'd have in the future that they didn't have now, but the matches being there and unburnt made him feel better. Hands on his bent knees he tried to think. His mind churned and he finally blurted, "I don't know if my eyes are open or not. It's too damned dark!"

"This is what it's like to be blind," Clem said. "I don't like it." He struck another match. The sulfur fumes rose and made Charlie sneeze. By the time he got his eyes open again, the match had sputtered down to Clem's fingers. He dropped the match to keep from being burned.

They sat in the darkness for hours. Or minutes. Charlie wasn't able to tell. For all the time he had spent working in a mine, he'd always had a miner's candle or one of the newfangled carbide lamps.

"What do you think was in the box?" he finally asked. No answer.

"Clem? You there?" He reached out in panic. He found his partner's arm. Clem pulled away.

"Don't do that. And I don't know what was in the box. You wouldn't let me look."

"We hardly had time. Your wife came along to kill us before we had a chance."

"Greta's my ex-wife, and how'd she know about the box?"

"Do you think she knows what's in it?" Charlie chewed his lower lip in thought. "How valuable can it be? I lugged it around. It can't weigh more than ten pounds. Fifteen? And some of that's the wood crate."

"It rattled around loose inside. Whatever it was didn't have packing around it, so it must not be fragile."

"Gold?" Charlie asked.

"That doesn't make a lick of sense. Thomas Collins

is a banker and throws around thousands of dollars every day. Lights his cigars with dollar bills. Doesn't bend over to pick up a penny on the ground. There couldn't be enough gold in that box to make him spend stacks of greenbacks with the likes of us."

"And the other men, the ones who died on the cliff trying to get to the wreckage."

Silence fell. The only sound occasionally destroying the quiet was the drip of water somewhere deeper in the cave.

"We won't die of thirst if we find that water," Charlie said.

"With the luck we've had, a dam will break and drown us like rats."

"All this talking's made me thirsty. Light another match?"

Clem grumbled some. The sound of him pulling out the tin case with his matches momentarily disturbed the quiet.

"Only got one left. Is this what we use it for?"

"Reckon not, though what we save it for is beyond me." Charlie got to his feet and placed his hand against the wall. He began moving slowly, going deeper into the cave. Once he stumbled when the passageway widened and his hand slipped away.

"I found the water," he called. "There's even a small puddle on the floor." Bending down, he slapped his hand on the shallow water. He licked it off his hand, then tried to scoop some up in his palm. All he did was dampen his lips.

Panic flared when he realized they were going to die in this cave.

"You were right, Clem," he said softly. "We should have taken the money Collins gave us and headed north. Or south. Somewhere that wasn't here."

"You'd never have done it," came Clem's voice much closer than he expected.

"We took the money to find the box," he said. "We were obligated."

"We got halfway there. We found the crate Collins wanted."

"But we didn't return it to him." Charlie sighed. "What was in the box? I wish I'd found out before I die."

The sudden flare of the match made his eyes water. He turned toward Clem. His partner held the match high overhead.

They were in a fair-sized cavern. There might have been deeper pools of water a few yards away but Charlie didn't get the chance to study them before the match flickered out.

"There's water," he said. "I'll try to find it." Yellow and blue dots danced in front of him. They slowly faded as he took cautious steps into the middle of the cave.

"You looked down. Did you see what the match did?"

"It burned out."

"It flickered."

Charlie wondered what his partner was getting at. The prospect of dying in the dark, in the cave, must have driven him a little bit loco.

"So what?"

"Take a deep whiff of the air."

Charlie did. He shrugged but Clem couldn't see it.

"I don't smell anything."

"There's the smell of pine trees. No sulfur stench from the match."

"Pines? That's not possible."

But it was. If air seeped into the cave from outside it was very possible.

"Do you think the match flickered because of air blowing through some vent to the outside?"

"Look across the cave, up high."

For a minute Charlie saw nothing. Then he caught his breath. A sliver of light sneaked past the rocks. Before he cried out in joy, the faint light vanished, then returned. Clem had stepped in front of the light as he made his way to examine the rocks.

In spite of his eagerness to see what that flash of light meant, Charlie stepped carefully on the damp, smooth rock floor. He bumped into his partner and recoiled when he reached the far side of the cave.

"There's enough air coming in so we won't suffocate," Clem said.

"There's got to be more than that if we're going to survive," Charlie said. He pushed past Clem and ran his fingers over the rock under the tiny speck of light high on the wall.

Finding footholds large enough to use as a step, he worked up the wall. He curled his fingers around a large rock that was cool with the breeze blowing down a small chimney.

"Stand back," he called. "I'm going to do some ore removal!" He laughed as he tugged hard on the big rock. It crashed to the floor. Charlie began burrowing like a badger, stones flying as he enlarged the hole.

Panting, he finally wore out. His fingers cramped from the effort and his legs wobbled. And he had a large space that let in a steady breeze. Now and then, a particularly strong gust erased the sweat from his face. Eyes closed, he turned to get the full draft.

"What do you have up there?"

"Clem, my partner, it's big enough for me to see the sky. The sun's shining!"

Charlie kicked hard and wiggled into the shaft. He scrabbled along the crevice until he was almost upright. The rock broke free, letting him widen the shaft enough to keep moving upward. By the time his callused fingers bled from tearing at the rock, escape was within his reach. Straining, he reached high, caught a lip of rock, and pulled himself up.

He popped up into open air. The vent opened a dozen yards above the ground on the sheer cliff face. Charlie kept hammering away at the rock and enlarged the opening so he had room to swing his feet out. He sat on a narrow ledge and looked down.

Free!

He looked back into the vent shaft. The top of Clem's head filled the hole. Then his partner was out and sitting beside him.

"The canyon was about the ugliest thing I ever saw," Clem said. "I've changed my mind." He blew a kiss into the wind.

"We got out of a tight spot," Charlie said thoughtfully. "Now what do we do?"

Clem stared at him but said nothing.

"Look, Clem, we risked our lives and got the box. We can't return it to Collins."

"You're giving up?"

"I'm saying we're going to get ourselves killed if we try to run down your wife—your ex-wife—and get that crate back for Collins."

"I never thought I'd hear you say that your word wasn't worth anything."

"I took the money, we had a contract with Collins and his bank," Charlie said. "We need to realize we're not up to fighting off a gang like Greta Swinburne is leading. We're not gunslicks. They're killers. They tried to murder us. The box isn't worth our lives."

"Nope, it isn't," Clem said.

Charlie wondered why he felt so lousy that his partner agreed with him. His honor was tarnished, but he was alive. Returning what remained of the hundred dollars Collins had given them to get on the trail of that damned box was the honorable thing to do. That'd mean they were almost killed for nothing. But honor demanded he return the bank's money.

Even if there wasn't more than a few dollars remaining. Supplies and railroad tickets and bribes had chewed up almost all the money Collins had fronted them.

"It's an affront." Clem blurted that out, then spat.

"What do you mean?"

Clem stared out across the canyon.

"Greta insulted me. Us. And she's turned you into a spineless worm. You're giving up your honor because it's too dangerous to get that consarned box back."

"Clem," he started. "Our lives! We'd be risking our necks. For what?"

"Yeah, Charlie. *Your* life. Don't you go putting that on the line again." Clem scooted to the edge of the rock, then pushed free. He hit the steep slope and skidded all the way down to the canyon floor.

What upset Charlie the most was that his partner never looked back, not even a glance, as he stomped off and disappeared into a wooded area.

# CHAPTER 19

Clement jumped off the ledge and careened downhill. He hit a large rock, spun around, fell, and then came to his feet. He brushed himself off. Ahead lay a small stand of trees. He touched the Colt at his side to be sure it was at hand, then started walking.

Every step he took steamed him even more. Greta should have been a bad memory, perhaps an occasional nightmare to torment his sleep, but now she intruded on his life again. Their divorce in Fargo had been the final nail in the coffin of their romance. For a brief while, Clement had been excited by her wildness. She was everything he wasn't, and he had been content to follow her and revel in everything she dared.

They had been eating breakfast one morning when she'd looked up at him and said, smiling her sweet smile, "We need money."

She had patted her lips with a white linen napkin, stood, and walked across the street to a bank. Hidden away in the folds of her skirt had been a derringer. Cocking it as she went into the bank, she called out, "This is a robbery!"

No one had paid her any attention. She shot the nearest teller. That got everyone's attention. Greta had walked out of the bank with almost three hundred dollars. Clement's biggest mistake, after marrying her was dealt into the wild game of her life, was following her then and there. Finishing breakfast, mounting, and riding in the opposite direction would have served him better.

They'd been fugitives for a month. The town marshal had a bee in his bonnet because the teller Greta had shot had been his cousin. Dodging a posse of the lawman's relatives had kept their necks out of a noose.

Even then Clement wasn't convinced about leaving her. When life got too dull, she held up a stagecoach and wounded the shotgun messenger "because he looked cross-eyed at me." That robbery had brought her less than a hundred dollars and gave Clement the best night between the sheets he'd ever had. Greta needed the thrill of robbery and, he suspected, the excitement of shooting her victims.

Fargo's easy divorce laws got him out of the marriage and left her bitter toward him. As far as she was concerned, their life together had been improving with each robbery, with every shooting . . . or killing.

"She won't get away with stealing what I found," Clem said softly. He slid his six-gun from its holster and thrust it in front of him, though he didn't have a target. Light filtered through the upper branches of pine and juniper and cast eerie, dancing shadows all around.

He ignored the sense that he wandered through some alien world with critters and bushes unknown. By keeping up a steady pace, he reached the stream and stared downstream. If he had to choose a direction, that was the way he'd go. Greta was nothing if not predictable. She'd consider that direction the same as staying downwind from a hunter. Whatever floated on the river had to be a warning, just as a scent carried on the air and blown downwind gave an alert man a chance to prepare for attack.

An alert man. An alert woman.

He found tracks alongside the stream and judged he wasn't more than a couple hours behind them. He lengthened his stride and wished they hadn't taken his horse. By now he'd have overtaken them since they weren't in any particular hurry.

As he tramped along, his mind turned over all possible outcomes. One against eight? He could creep up on them when they camped. Taking Greta captive was one way to come out ahead. Finding the box and snatching it from under her nose appealed to him more, but if he did that, the entire gang would be on his trail when they discovered the loss.

Steal the box, take the contents, and replace whatever was inside with rocks. That was the best he could do. Let Greta take the box and try to sell it back to Thomas Collins or whoever offered the highest price for it. That had to be her plan. The contents were more valuable to someone other than her, and the only players dealt into this game were Collins and his bank and Leland Stanford and the Central Pacific Railroad.

So much depended on what the box held. Clem walked faster, taking time to sip some water or grab a berry or two when he spotted wild raspberries or blackberries. Time weighed heavily on him. Letting Greta escape the canyon meant he'd have lost. His resolve hardened. That wasn't going to happen. Not again.

Twilight fell and still he pressed on. A half moon lit the water and gave him enough light to keep from falling and breaking a leg in the darkness. He was almost ready to quit when he caught the sharp odor of beans cooking. Mingled with it came pine. And then coffee.

He was close to the outlaws' camp.

He checked his six-gun once more, then moved away from the stream, working his way toward the canyon wall. A flash of orange flame through the trees warned him he was getting close to his goal. Clem slowed and then crept forward, bent low until he spied on Greta's camp. The gang sat around a large fire. A kettle of beans produced the most aroma. His belly growled so loud he was sure they'd hear. But they were too busy arguing.

He wasn't close enough to overhear, and what caused such a heated exchange was of no concern. Working through the woods, he circled the campfire. He counted the heads bobbing about, darkly silhouetted by the fire.

"One's missing," he said low and to himself. "A guard? Where'd he be? Where?" Clement continued his circle around the campfire until he came to their horses. A rope stretched between two trees provided a line where the horses were tethered.

Ten horses. They had not only their own but the ones he and Charlie had ridden. He almost stepped out to take the entire string of horses when a hint of tobacco smoke reached him.

Not ten feet away, sitting on a stump and smoking his cigarette, the final gang member stared off into the night. He puffed until the coal burned a bright orange, then exhaled. The curl of smoke rose into the moonlight.

Greta had posted him to keep the wolves away from their horses. This deep in a canyon even hungry coyotes would bring down a horse for dinner. That meant the guard would be armed with more than his six-shooter. Clement moved around another few feet and spotted the rifle leaning against a nearby tree trunk.

Charlie would fret and stew and try to come up with the perfect plan. That was his partner's curse, thinking too much. Clement stood and walked straight over to the rifle. He picked it up and took two more steps to the guard's right side.

"You shouldn't leave your rifle out of reach," he said.

"Aw, don't go raggin' on me. I was just smokin' a—" The guard dropped the still-lighted cigarette and went for his six-gun when he recognized Clement. He was too late.

Clement gripped the rifle by the barrel and swung as hard as he could. The stock crashed into the side of the man's face. A sick crunch told of a broken bone in the cheek. The guard flopped onto the ground, but he still had fight in him. Clement took care of that with a second swing that connected with the top of his victim's head.

The outlaw lay stretched on the ground, knocked out cold.

Clement plucked the man's six-shooter from his holster and tucked it into his own gun belt. He took a step toward the camp, then stopped. He needed a better plan than barging in and demanding to be given the box. Unfastening two horses, he led them off into the woods, out of sight of the others. He fixed the spot in his mind, then gripped the rifle and returned to spy on the camp.

By now they'd finished their meal and lay about. A few slept. Roy Dupree and Greta sat close to each other and spoke in whispers. One by one, the others all pulled their blankets up and drifted to sleep. Clement waited impatiently for Dupree and his former wife to similarly go to sleep. In a perverse way, he hoped they would find something other than sleep to occupy them. It would give him reason to hate Dupree more and to scorn Greta.

But they joined the rest of the gang in sleep. Each had a separate blanket, and they turned so their backs were to one another. Dupree's loud snores were almost drowned out by Greta's.

Clement waited a few minutes longer to be sure all of the gang slept, then advanced slowly, carefully picking his spots to step to not break a twig or cause any other commotion. When he got close enough to feel the heat from the dying fire on his face, he stopped and studied every lump and bump.

His heart raced when he saw the end of the box sticking out from under a saddle. As quiet as a stalking mountain lion, he stepped to the saddle. The leather creaked as he lifted it to free the box. When Dupree stirred, Clement froze. The sleeping man snorted, rolled over, and pulled the blanket up over his head.

Moving carefully, Clement pushed the saddle aside and picked up the box. It was none the worse for wear and tear since Greta had taken it from Charlie. Box tucked under his right arm and the rifle gripped firmly, he backed away from the fire. The heat faded and then disappeared against his face. The cold breeze felt like a slap.

It brought a gasp to his lips.

The small noise was all it took to bring Greta up and looking around.

"Clement," she said. It was as if she had some sixth sense that allowed her to find him in the dark. Her dark eyes fixed on him as she reached for her six-gun.

"Don't," he said, lowering the rifle and pointing it straight at her.

"Now, my dear husband, you wouldn't shoot li'l ole me, would you?"

"You're not my wife."

"But you still love me. I can tell. I see it in your eyes."

"That's not love. And I will plug you."

By now the others mumbled and thrashed about. All but Roy Dupree went back to their dreams.

"It's him! How'd he get out of that cave? He was well and surely buried."

"You always were a bungler, Roy. Didn't I tell you Clement would find a way to get out of that cave?"

"It was his grave!"

"You should listen to her, Dupree." Clement backed up another step. "You're a bungler and a fool."

Greta laughed. It came out like a hen's cackle. Her raspy voice left rough edges on everything she said and every sound she made.

"Listen to him, Roy. Clement was always a good judge of character."

"Except where you're involved, Greta. Drop the gun. I will shoot."

"You'll be dead before I am. You don't think the rest of my gang will let you live?"

"He's got the box!" Dupree saw the reason for Clement sneaking into the camp the way he had. "Everybody, he stole the box!"

"Roy is like an impulsive little boy," Greta said. "But this time it worked in his favor. We're wise to you now. You can't fight all eight of us."

"Seven," Clement said. He squeezed the trigger. Although the rifle was pointed squarely at Greta Swinburne, he rushed the shot, jerked back, and caused the slug to go wide.

She returned fire, but Clement dodged to the left and avoided her deadly bullets. He struggled to cock the rifle and get off another shot. By now the entire gang fired at him. Whether they were still more asleep than awake or simple good luck favored him, Clement reached the nearest tree without taking any lead.

They targeted him fast. The tree took one bullet after another. Splinters and sap flew all around. Clement knelt, rested the recovered box against the tree, and lifted the rifle to his shoulder. He sent one round after another in Greta's direction. The outlaws scattered, hunting for cover. He thought he hit Dupree, but it proved to be wishful thinking.

The outlaw shouted at him, "You'll pay for this, Clement. I'll skin you alive. I'll have your scalp hanging on my belt. I'll—"

Clement wasn't able to see the screaming Dupree, but he tracked him by the cursing. He saw a bush shiver at the far side of the clearing. This time he squeezed off a well-aimed shot. He was rewarded with Dupree's cry of pain. If he'd had a clear shot, a second round would have ended Roy Dupree's miserable life.

A hail of bullets drove him back behind the tree. He realized the outlaws spread out and worked to get him in a crossfire. If they flanked him, he was a goner. Clement grabbed the box and retreated in the direction of the two horses he'd cut from the outlaw remuda. Outfighting Greta's gang wasn't in the cards. That left him only one way to freedom.

Mount up and ride off before they realized what he'd done.

He emptied the rifle's magazine as he moved deeper into the woods. For a moment, he got turned around. Then he was headed back toward the outlaws' horses when two of them charged. He cleared leather and fanned off three shots. His Army Colt fired straight and true. He took down one of them coming for him.

Then he stopped. He dropped his six-shooter and raised his hands.

"That's real smart, givin' up like that. You snuck up on me and stole my rifle. You took my pistol. But you left me with my knife. Now I'm gonna gut you like a fish."

Clement winced as the tip of the guard's knife drove into his back.

# CHAPTER 20

Charlie Dawson called to his partner, but Clem had already reached the woods and ducked between the towering pines. A feeling of betrayal caused him to spit and snarl like a stepped-on cat. Then he settled down and stared across the canyon. The warm sun and the gentle breeze soothed his ruffled feathers. His partner had left him without so much as a backward look, but they were both still alive and kicking.

For the moment. Charlie knew Clem had no chance against his former wife's gang. They were cold-blooded killers. Greta was, from Clem's account, no better. She was probably worse because he had never heard of a woman leading an outlaw gang before. She had to be twice as ruthless to keep control of those cutthroats. Just eavesdropping on them convinced him that Roy Dupree was the kind who'd shoot his parents and then complain that he was an orphan.

Greta Swinburne was no better.

"What are you getting yourself into, Clem? What?" Charlie closed his eyes and basked in the sun, thinking it would bring him solace. If anything, it made him more aware of a gnawing loneliness. Clem hadn't been gone five minutes and he already missed him.

"You're a fool, Charlie Dawson. A complete and total fool." He slid forward on the rocky ledge, then jumped. He tried to keep his feet under him and got caught up on a rock. He began somersaulting down the slope until he slid into a grassy area.

Stunned, he lay on his back staring up at the blue sky until he got his breath back. Sitting up caused pain in places he didn't know he had places. At least he wasn't buried in a cave waiting to die of starvation or filled with lead.

Groaning, he got to his feet and stumbled along a few paces. Each step was agony, but he discovered that moving along eased the aches. He flopped into the running stream. He gasped as the frigid water bathed him and stole away even more of his pain. Shivering, he got out of the water and shook himself like a dog.

"What'll I do? What *can* I do?" He looked around, hoping to see his partner.

Disheartened when he didn't see Clem, he left the stream and sat on a rock. He squeezed out as much water as he could and emptied his boots. The warm sun made him drowsy, but he snapped awake. He had a big decision to make. It'd be easy to tromp off and leave Clem to his own devices. But he felt guilty thinking about what his partner intended.

They had promised Thomas Collins to get the box. It had been in their hands and had let it slip away.

*He* had lost it.

Giving up to save his own neck was the smart thing

to do. It was easy. Recovering the box and putting it into the banker's hands was the right thing to do. Charlie felt more than guilt that Clem had gone off alone. Betraying their friendship piled onto the guilt of not keeping his promise.

"You'll get us both killed," Charlie said, heaving to his feet. He headed downstream since that was the likely direction the other miner had taken.

Finding the trail proved easy. Not only did Clem leave muddy footprints in the soft stream bank, the outlaws' horses chopped up the ground. Trying to figure out if there were more than the owlhoots he'd seen ride with Greta Swinburne wasn't necessary. One, two, too many. He touched the six-gun tucked into his waistband. No ammunition. He patted his pockets. He found plenty of gold coins from rescuing Wash Collins. There was even a five-dollar gold coin left from what the banker had advanced them to find the crate. But what good did gold do him now? There wasn't anyone to sell him a single damned thing. He couldn't eat gold. And even hurting the way one back molar did, there wasn't any way he could use that gold to fill the cavity.

His ire rising, he started walking. Faster and faster until he was almost running. Charlie fell into a rhythm that made all the aches and pains go away. He stared ahead but saw nothing. This spurred him on to greater effort. His feet moved and his mind turned blank.

He ran and ran and ran and . . .

Twilight swallowed him. Charlie slowed and then stopped, bent over with hands on his knees so he could catch his breath. He had no idea how long he'd run, but it left him dizzy and weak. When he recovered enough to look up, he took a deep breath. A grim smile came to his lips.

He hadn't seen a living soul since he began his pursuit. Now he smelled food cooking. The sharp tang of pine being burned. And he even heard horses protesting. Neighs. Hooves stamping.

Working his way into the woods, he came upon the horses. A quick count showed eight. He had found the outlaws' camp. Cautiously exploring, he hunted for a guard. Greta Swinburne didn't strike him as a trusting person. Even if she doubted anyone would steal their horses out here in the deserted canyon, she'd post a guard to keep the night-prowling predators away from the tethered animals.

No guard. That worried Charlie. He considered letting the horses go free to stir up some trouble when he heard gunfire. His first instinct was to run. Then he heard Clem's outcry and knew what had to be done. Without any firepower left, he had to find a way to get his partner to safety.

"Eight against one," he said. "Those are odds even Clem can't overcome."

He made his way through the trees. A slug blasted out a chunk of tree above his head. It had to be a stray bullet. He wasn't visible in the dark. Moving faster in the direction of the voices, he saw two indistinct shapes ahead.

Some uncanny sense told him one was Clem. The other must be the guard left to watch the horses.

"I'm gonna gut you like a pig," the broad-shouldered man directly in front of him said as he reared back.

Charlie moved fast. His gun came into his fist. He shoved it hard into the outlaw's back.

"I'll blow you in half if you don't drop the knife."

"Both of you? You both got outta that cave-in?" The outlaw half turned.

Charlie swung his pistol in a short, vicious arc that ended on the man's wrist. The knife fell to the forest floor. As the man howled in pain and grabbed for his injured arm, Clem dropped the crate, circled the man's neck with his brawny forearm, and clamped down hard. All cries turned to gurgles. Then nothing. Clem dropped the man and scooped up the fallen knife.

"You took your sweet time getting here." Clem turned back to the approaching outlaws. They'd stopped shooting wildly and now sought out their prey.

"Where's his gun?" Charlie frantically searched the fallen outlaw.

"Used it up already. His rifle, too."

"The horses are back there," Charlie said. "Let's hightail it." He turned, but Clem grabbed his shoulder and spun him around.

"I'm not leaving without the box. She's not making a monkey out of me again."

"We don't have a gun." Charlie looked at the knife in his partner's hand. That wasn't much good against seven cutthroats intent on filling them full of lead.

"Here. Go cut the rope holding their horses. Spook 'em good."

"I'll cut out two for us," Charlie said, not sure how that would work.

"Don't bother. I've already hidden two. Get them varmints chasing down their horses. Make as big a commotion as you can."

Charlie hesitated, then found the knife pressed into the palm of his hand. Clem lit out and disappeared into the darkness. Rather than wait for the tide of killers to wash over him, he retraced his steps to where the eight horses were tied. A quick slash severed the rope. For a moment, the horses just stood, confused. When he hooted and hollered at them, they raced off into the night. The pounding hooves brought all the outlaws at a dead run.

Ducking behind a tree, Charlie held his breath. He recognized Roy Dupree's voice.

"After them, you lamebrained fools. We can't let our horses run off!"

"Roy, the rope's been cut."

"It sure wasn't Shorty's doin'. Somebody broke his neck and left his body back there in the forest."

Charlie slipped away as the cutthroats argued about what had happened. Several passed within a few feet as they trooped off to run down their frightened horses.

He passed Shorty's body and trailed Clem. The burning pine scent from the campfire guided him to the clearing. Clem rummaged through the gear strewn around.

"There it is," Charlie called, pointing.

"I saw it. I'm getting us some supplies." Clem held up boxes of ammunition. He stuffed them into his pockets.

A spare six-shooter joined another already thrust under his gun belt.

As his partner scavenged, Charlie picked up the crate. Again he tried to judge what was inside. Too light for precious metal. Too heavy to be packed with greenbacks. All the arguments about Thomas Collins having a bank filled with money rushed back to further confound him. Charlie started to pry loose the end to take a peek when Clem called to him.

"They're coming back. Let's skedaddle."

He joined his partner. Clem thrust a spare six-gun into his hands. Cautioning him to silence, he led Charlie into the woods. Two outlaws returned to their camp, cursing whoever had released their horses.

"Let the others run down our horses," Roy Dupree said. "They let Shorty get his neck broke. They need to be taught to tend to chores around camp, too. I need a drink."

"You need a kick in the butt," Greta Swinburne roared, coming from the woods. "You're gettin' lazy, Roy. You oughta be out there runnin' down the horses. This whole forsaken gang's gettin' to be fainthearted and downright heavy-footed."

Charlie tugged at his partner's arm. When Greta Swinburne walked into the camp, Clem had frozen like a statue. He stared at her. Deep in his throat, he growled like a dog ready to attack.

"The horses. You were taking us to the horses." Charlie considered shaking his partner. It didn't come to that. Clem continued growling but turned away and plunged into the woods.

Charlie followed slowly, wary of making too much noise when Greta Swinburne and her henchmen were so close. They wove in and out between the closely growing trees until he worried Clem had lost his way. Then the two horses suddenly appeared, as if out of nowhere. He saw their reins secured to a single fallen tree limb. Clem had prepared well, stealing the horses and then securing them.

"Not stolen," Charlie said, realizing these were the horses they'd bought in San Francisco. Getting their own mounts back from horse thieves wasn't stealing. It was recovering. He grinned foolishly.

"This is what we do. We recover lost property."

Clem handed over the reins. With a quick vault, they both mounted. It took a few seconds to orient themselves before heading away up the canyon. The gang had gone after their spooked horses downstream. For Charlie, either direction worked just fine as long as it was away from the array of guns that'd be aimed at them because of what he carried.

He patted the crate pinned between his left arm and his body.

"Yes, sir, we're doing business the right way. We find things folks have lost."

"It'll be a long hunt," Clem said.

"What're you talking about?"

"You've lost your mind. Good luck finding it." Clem hunched over and snapped the reins to get his horse trotting down to the stream.

Charlie splashed after him. He felt good. All they had

to do was shepherd the box back to San Francisco and put it in the banker's hands to collect what remained of the two thousand promised dollars.

They'd be rolling in the clover before either of them knew it.

# CHAPTER 21

"He should have come to us," Clem said.

Charlie Dawson laughed. He felt good. They had reached Sacramento after two days of following Dos Robles Canyon and then the tracks to the capital. Once in Sacramento, Charlie had sent a telegram to Collins. The red carpet had been rolled out for them. Collins arranged for first-class railroad tickets down to the Oakland Wharf Station, and now they braced themselves against the railing of the *Berkeley* as the ferry boat bobbed across San Francisco Bay toward the city. Again they had their way paid. Tickets had awaited them.

Charlie reflected on how they could learn to like this treatment. When they collected their due, such travel would be easy. And well deserved. He puffed out his chest thinking that not just anyone could have found the crate and returned it so fast. Bodies of others Thomas Collins had sent out littered the slopes under the derailment.

Those were failures. He and his partner were the successes.

"You never would have ridden in a Pullman car that fancy," Charlie said. His words echoed his thoughts.

"The engineer highballed it all the way. I liked that." Clem had ridden partway with his head thrust out the window, the racing wind in his face until his parchment-skinned face turned to leather.

"I wish he'd sent a launch for us for the rest of the trip. That would have cut the time it's taking for us to cross the Bay." His stomach turned and twisted as the ferry's rolling motion worked its evil on him.

"We got him waiting for us." Clem pointed.

Charlie wiped saltwater from his eyes and squinted. The tight knot of men standing at the dock came into focus for him.

"Hickman," he said.

"If this box is so danged important to Collins, he should be here to take it in person."

Charlie ignored his partner's disdain. He wanted the job over and done as quickly as possible. He didn't like Hickman. The mousy man looked more like a rat than a teeny mouse all decked out in his plain brown suit and derby. If it took Hickman escorting them straight to the bank president, that was fine with him. The sooner the money bulged in his pocket, the sooner they could get back to Potluck and settle accounts over the Betty Sue.

The ferry bumped hard as it docked, almost throwing him over the railing. Clem caught him by the collar and dragged him back.

"Don't drop that box now."

"I promise," Charlie said. He clutched it to his chest as if it were a lifeline and he was a drowning man.

They walked down the swaying gangplank. Once he touched solid land, he felt all the strain disappear. All that remained from his churning emotions was anticipation.

"You have it? Give it to me." Hiram Hickman grabbed for the box.

Charlie turned away. The fury on Hickman's face matched the worst he'd ever seen on a drunkard's face in the lowest dive along the Barbary Coast.

"We were hired to give it to Mister Collins."

"I'm his assistant. I'll take it to him." Hickman lurched forward and once more tried to pull it from Charlie's arms. This time he found himself lifted off the dock and held at arm's length. Clem was much stronger than he looked, and he was six inches taller than the mousy man.

"No," was all he said.

Hickman sputtered and tried to push free. Clem's grip proved too powerful to break. When Hickman stopped kicking and cussing, Clem dropped him to the dock.

"Is that our carriage? Or do we waste more time getting one to take us to your boss?"

"You know, Charlie, it might be we should walk and take in the sights. San Francisco is all civilized. We need a dose of that after all we've been through."

He saw right away what his partner did. Charlie approved with a huge smile.

"You're right, my friend. Why, we might stop off

and have a drink or two before we hand this over." He held up the box. Hickman tried to take it again, but he anticipated the move. He turned at the last instant. Hickman almost fell off the dock into the Bay.

His face was fiery red with anger when he recovered his balance.

Charlie asked, "Do we ride in style? Or walk? It's good having to decide, isn't it?"

Hickman snapped his fingers. The driver of a carriage hopped to the dock and hurried to them.

"Escort our guests to Mister Collins," he said. "As fast as you can."

The driver nodded. He reached to take the box, but Charlie wasn't having any of it. He and Clem pushed past and climbed into the fancy carriage. They sat back on the leather-covered seats and felt the nippy salt air against their smiling faces. This was the way to travel.

This was the way to live.

"You got your gun handy?" Clem asked.

"Of course. Why do you ask that?"

Clem shook his head. He had not only his Colt at his side but a brace of pistols thrust into his gun belt. From the way he squirmed, there might be a fourth gun tucked into the middle of his back. All Charlie had was his Walker Colt. He felt underdressed now. Then he pushed such concerns aside and enjoyed riding along like a king. He grinned, waved to the ladies strolling along Montgomery Street, and took great delight in the way some of them returned both smiles and waves. They had no idea who he was, but he rode in a splendid carriage with a liveried driver. That made him someone.

Beside him, his partner muttered to himself. As much as Charlie enjoyed the ride, Clem hated it. He fingered his six-guns and looked ready to begin shooting at any instant.

The carriage rattled to a halt in front of the bank far too soon. If he'd had a lick of sense, he'd have ordered the driver to drive around first, just to spite Hickman. More than that, Charlie enjoyed pretending to be rich.

He climbed down, Clem pressing close behind.

"Let's finish this fast."

"Enjoy it, Clem."

"What?"

"The feeling of being in charge. We've got what Collins wants and until we give it to him, we're being treated like robber barons. Leland Stanford himself wouldn't get better service."

"Box. Money. We need to clear out fast."

Charlie ignored his partner's glum words. He strutted through the lobby and up the marble staircase to the third floor. Thomas Collins had two of his burly guards blocking entry into his office.

"Announce us," Charlie said. "Misters Dawson and Clement."

From inside the office came a lion's roar. Both guards jumped and opened the double doors into the banker's inner sanctum.

He looked at Clem, grinning ear to ear. This was how it was supposed to be. He said softly, "I can get used to this."

"Don't," was all Clem said, looking glummer by the second.

They walked to stand in front of the huge desk.

Collins, flustered and anxious, hurried around and held out his hands as if asking to hold a swaddled infant.

"Give it to me. Now!"

Charlie wanted to play it out just a little longer, but his partner yanked the box from his grip, ignored the banker's outstretched hands, and dumped it on the desk with a loud bang. Collins pounced like an eagle grabbing a rabbit in its claws. He yanked off the poorly nailed end and left a bloody trail behind. The rough wood and sharp nails cut his soft, manicured hands. With a quick move, he upended the box and shook.

A railroad spike fell to the table.

For a brief instant, a look of relief crossed the banker's face. Then he turned livid. He picked up the spike and pressed his thumbnail into the side. He looked at them, daggers in his eyes.

"What kind of cheap trick is this?"

"No trick, Mister Collins. That's the right box. The number on the side says so. You wouldn't believe the trouble we—"

Charlie Dawson almost lost his head as the banker swung the steel bar. Only quick reflexes kept the spike from crushing his skull. As it was, he barely dodged the blow. The sharp tip of the spike left a shallow cut on his cheek.

He touched the cut and stared at the blood on his fingers.

"You got no call treating me like that."

"This isn't what I paid you to recover!"

"That's what was in the mail car. The number matches what you said, and that's the box just like you said. You got what you wanted. Now hand over our money. Two thousand dollars."

"You are idiots! I won't pay for a steel railroad spike. I wanted *it*!"

Collins swung the spike at Charlie again. He was prepared now and stepped away. The dangerous weapon missed him by inches this time. At his side, Clem put his hands on the two six-guns tucked into his belt.

"If that's not what you expected, it's on your head. You should have told us. You said you wanted the box. That's the right box," Charlie said. He rested his hand on his own pistol. This was turning ugly fast.

"To hell with the box. I need what's in it. Time's almost run out!"

"So's my patience," Charlie said. "You owe us the rest of what you promised."

"No!"

"We shook on it. Are you going back on our deal? Our contract?" He expected the banker to react better to using terms he was familiar with. The handshake had sealed a deal. A contract and its terms were agreed upon. Promises had been made and kept. So far.

"Hickman!"

Clem looked sidelong at his partner, then drew both his guns. Before he leveled them on the banker, a metallic click froze him in place. Charlie glanced behind them. Hiram Hickman covered them with a sawed-off shotgun. The expression on the man's face told the story. He'd take real pleasure in turning them both into bloody pulp. If his boss happened to be in the way, he'd hardly notice. Or maybe he would, and take real glee in that death, too.

"This close, he'd kill both of us. And you, too," he pointed out, hoping to have Collins call off his bulldog.

"I don't care. I may as well be dead since I don't have *it*."

The guards stationed outside the office rushed in when he bellowed for them, followed by four more bruisers. Charlie had seen bouncers in waterfront dives who weren't this big or strong or menacing. They all had blood in their eye.

"It doesn't look like we're going to get paid," Clem said. He let Hickman pluck the guns from his hands. Then his holstered pistol was dropped on the desk with his other two.

Charlie was similarly disarmed by one of the guards. His Walker Colt clanked onto the pile.

"I won't be cheated. You won't get a dime more of my money for this . . . for this *swindle*! You won't get a dime!" Collins sputtered and spittle ran down his chin.

"Don't bite yourself," Clem said. "You'll give yourself rabies."

"Where is it?"

"You've got what you paid for," Charlie said.

"Get them out of here. Out of my sight now! And take those guns with you."

Charlie grunted when Hickman shoved the double-barrels into his back. A metal spur tore at his coat. Whoever had sawed off the barrels should have done a better job filing the ragged sawed edge.

"Take them to the warehouse," Hiram Hickman

ordered once they were out of Collins's office. "I'll be along in a while."

The two miners were herded out, not going back through the lobby but down backstairs. They acquired a small army of guards like barnacles on a ship's hull. Charlie caught sight of five surrounding them and a sixth trailed, a rifle carried in the crook of his arm. Even if they fought off their captors, the man with the rifle would fill them full of lead before they got half a block.

Taking alleys and poorly traveled streets, they made their way across town north to the Barbary Coast. This was an area so tough the police patrolled in platoons. More than one tight knot of specials saw them being taken along against their will. The policemen never so much as twitched a muscle to free them, much less to ask what was happening.

"There," the guard immediately behind Charlie said. He was shoved forward. He crashed into a door. It slammed open, and he fell face-first to the filthy floor.

They were dragged along until they came to an overhead support where chains dropped from the beam. Charlie almost fainted when he saw bloody meat hooks on several of the chains.

It hardly came as a relief when those hooks weren't used. He had flashes of fear they were going to be hoisted up like they were in a Sioux Indian Sun Vow ceremony. Instead, metal cuffs clicked around their wrists. A crank turned a hoist, and they were stretched out until they dangled inches off the floor, swinging slowly every time they moved.

The pain grew in Charlie's shoulders. As he twisted

slowly, he saw that the small army of Collins's cutthroats had left. Only one guard remained. He cleaned his fingernails with a huge, thick-bladed knife. The smirk on his face told how much he anticipated using that weapon on their helpless bodies.

"You reckon he's not going to pay us?"

Charlie spun around, in spite of the pain in his arms and chest to glare at his partner.

"You didn't stick that spike into the box, did you?"

"Did you? You're the one with the curiosity bump."

"Whatever Collins expected to find, that wasn't it. And no, I never looked. It wouldn't have changed anything since I had no idea what ought to be inside." Charlie licked dried lips. "You're sure you didn't replace whatever was inside with the railroad spike?"

Clem grunted. From the man's drawn, gaunt look, he suffered more than his partner.

"Where is it?"

Rough hands spun him around and around. Every time he completed one complete revolution he caught sight of Hiram Hickman.

"I will take you apart one inch of your worthless hide at a time. I will make you scream until you tell me. Save yourself the pain. Where is it?"

"We don't know what was supposed to be in the box." Charlie began to feel woozy. Whirling around pulled at his shoulder joints to the point the pain washed over him in waves. His vision blurred and every thought scrambled like morning eggs.

"I'll be back. Tell me what you did with it then, or

you'll end up floating facedown in the Bay when the morning tide comes in."

"I think he means it," Charlie said.

"I can't swim," Clem said as he ground his teeth. Then he passed out.

Charlie Dawson had never felt more alone.

# CHAPTER 22

"I never thought we'd end up like this," Charlie Dawson said. "Buried alive? Probably. Working ourselves to death in the Betty Sue? Yup. But strung up like sides of beef? Not us. We're more mutton than prime beef."

Charlie rotated slowly, his toes barely scraping the floor. Clem wasn't listening. He had passed out. Or if he hadn't conked out entirely, he was doing a good job of not listening.

Swinging back and forth gained Charlie nothing but joints that threatened to pop free of his body. He stopped his feeble struggles and hung, panting harshly. Sweat poured down his face. The salt burned his eyes. Never had he thought this was the way he'd end his days. Dying with his boots off had been a distant hope.

Hardly knowing what he did, he tried to kick off his boots. They refused to budge. Somewhere in the back of his mind, he thought this would rob Hickman of his victory. If only they had found the real box.

He turned slowly and stared at his partner. Even now he wondered if Clem had taken the real contents from the box and hidden them when he wasn't looking. He finally decided that was wrong. Clem was a stubborn cuss, but it meant their lives if he knew where the box Collins wanted so badly was and didn't tell Hickman.

Then his pain-numbed brain figured it out. Even if Clem fessed up, Hickman would kill them. He read that in every line of the man's face. Before he had seen only a docile man rushing about to do his boss's bidding. Now he saw a river of pure cruelty that gushed out and threatened to drown both him and Clem.

"Why have so many died for that railroad spike?"

"Because it's worth a fortune, that's why."

The voice came from a distance. Familiar, threatening, but not threatening. Not like Hickman. Or Thomas Collins. He tried to blink the sweat from his eyes to get a clear look. He failed. What he noticed was that the torture was beginning all over.

The windlass squeaked and squealed. He laughed. It needed oil. The chains tugged at his arms and then his legs gave way under him. It took a few seconds to realize he lay in a heap on the floor. He lifted his manacled hands and stared at them stupidly. He had been dropped to the floor.

"Let me get those consarned things off."

He cried out when the manacles fell away. His wrists bled, and somehow being freed hurt more than being strung up. With a sweep of his sleeve, he blotted the sweat off his face and out of his eyes.

"Swine!" The name exploded from his lips.

"Not so loud. Everyone'll want me. You know how men are." Greta Swinburne stared at him, then laughed. It came out more like a cackle. "Maybe you don't know."

She turned from him to free Clem's wrists. He lay unconscious on the floor. She nudged him with her boot. When he didn't stir, she kicked him hard. This forced a groan from him. "Great. The lazy son of a buck is only pretendin' to ignore me. Some things never change. He was like this when we was hitched."

"Where'd you come from?" Charlie's voice sounded weak, distant. His lips were swollen and his throat tight from lack of water.

"Passed through Sacramento. Saw you on that fancy train so I snuck into a freight car. You two are terrible at hidin' your trail."

"We weren't trying," Charlie said. He got to his knees, then managed to stand. Dizziness hit him like a sledgehammer. He held onto a dangling chain to steady himself until the vertigo passed.

"You weren't tryin'," she said angrily. "This lout tried hard enough to steal the spike."

"We gave it to Collins." He took a few steps to get his strength back. "He strung us up rather than pay us."

"A little bird told me that you gave him a real spike."

"I'll drive it all the way up his . . ."

"Clement, you're back among the livin'," she said as he spoke. She kicked him again and got him to his feet. "We'll be in a world of trouble if we don't clear out muy pronto."

"Door," Charlie croaked out. He tried to point but his arm wouldn't lift.

Greta Swinburne cursed and dragged out her six-gun. She poked Clem and got him moving. Charlie followed, feet shuffling, and tried to overhear what she said to her former husband. The scraping sounds from the door leading from the warehouse caught his attention. Clem strained to hear someone coming. He gripped Greta's arm and warned her.

"Don't try to teach this dog how to suck eggs. I heard." Greta shoved him away from the door and trailed him.

They sank behind a large crate. Charlie moved too slowly to join them. That worked to his benefit. He saw his Walker and Clem's Army Colt on the top of a crate. He snatched up the two six-shooters and stared at them. It felt good to have his pistol in his fist again.

He waited too long celebrating this minor victory. The two cutthroats coming in from the street spotted him.

They didn't bother shouting for him to drop the pair of six-shooters or raise his hands. They opened fire. Charlie winced as a bullet dug out a chunk of flesh from his right calf. He stumbled and fell. That saved his life because the air where he had stood an instant before filled with enough lead to bring down a rampaging bull.

He lay flat, his blood leaking from his wound. Then both Greta and Clem opened fire. He twisted around to see Collins's two henchmen walk straight into the bullets. They didn't even gasp before they died.

"You're as good a shot as ever, Clement." Greta Swinburne slapped Clem on the shoulder, staggering him.

Clem had somehow managed to keep the gun tucked into his waistband behind his back. He had used it to good effect.

"There's the way out," Charlie said. Light leaked around a dark doorway ahead of them.

Greta and Clem beat him there. He hobbled along. When he stepped out of the warehouse, he was startled to see that it was night. What light there was came from gas lamps. They were a dozen yards away from the shoreline. He got his bearings. Meiggs Pier with the Cobweb Palace at the end was only a few hundred yards distant.

"We need to hide," he said.

"Need whiskey," Clem insisted.

"Clement's hardly ever right. This time he is. I need to dip my beak in some rotgut." Greta laughed raucously, putting any crow to shame. They started for the saloon. Charlie hesitated. If he had any sense left, he'd put as much distance between him and the warehouse as possible.

If he had a lick of sense, he'd clear the hell out of San Francisco, away from both Clem and Greta.

He limped after them, pushed aside a strand of sticky cobweb, and entered a different world. A sailor pumped away at a concertina to accompany two others singing a bawdy sea chanty. The parrot lay on its side on the bar, a puddle of whiskey soaking its colorful feathers. Abe Warner, the owner, worked the bar, hurrying from one end to the other and back, never missing a chance to refill an empty shot glass or foaming beer mug.

Charlie tried to shout a warning to Greta when a drunken sailor came up behind her. The salt reached out and grabbed her behind. She never broke stride as she whipped her pistol around and cold-cocked him. She and Clem reached a table at the side, under a drapery of cobwebs. She shoved one unconscious patron to the floor.

The other at the table started to protest. She punched him in the gut. As he turned to retch, she planted her boot on his backside and gave him a shove that landed him facedown on the floor. He didn't stir. She and Clem sank into the vacated chairs, side by side.

Charlie snatched a spare chair on his way to the table. He sat with his back to the room. That made him uneasy, but with his partner and the woman pressing their heads together, he had no chance to overhear what they said no matter where he sat.

Somehow, a half bottle of whiskey and three glasses appeared. Charlie fumbled through his pockets and was startled to find that he still had several double eagles in his vest pocket. Hickman hadn't searched him and his thugs hadn't robbed him.

"Here's to you, Thomas Collins," he toasted, lifting the shot glass high. He knocked back the popskull, choked, and poured himself another. "You cheated us, but we still got some of your money."

Greta Swinburne glared at him.

"Money? Clement says all he gave you was a thousand dollars to get his kid back. And for the spike? He offered two thousand. The spike is worth ten times that to the right people. Twenty!"

"The spike? The railroad spike in the box? We saw it. What's so danged important about it? It's nothing but an ordinary piece of track."

"They'll pay any amount to get it." Greta Swinburne stared hard at him. Surprise wrinkled her face, then she laughed. "You don't know what it is, do you?" Charlie shook his head and downed another shot of whiskey. He was feeling better now. The liquor erased the worst of the pain, even if he still felt blood running down his leg from the gunshot wound. Before long the wound would either clot over or his boot would fill with his own blood. Either was a signal for him to call it quits for the day.

"I smell blackmail," Clem said.

Greta laughed, leaned over, and planted a kiss on his cheek. He wiped it off and looked sour. But Charlie thought he saw a touch of something more. His partner liked the attention his former wife lavished on him.

"You've still got a sharp noodle, Clement. That's exactly why they're so desperate to get it back."

"It, it, you keep saying 'it.' What was supposed to be in the box?" Charlie almost knocked back another shot. He felt a tad dizzy and held off pouring another drink. The pain from his bullet wound and all the torture faded like an old hound dog running off to bark at the moon. He knew it was there but distance and alcohol dulled it.

Greta Swinburne leaned forward, a conspirator in a deep, dark plot. She looked from Clem to Charlie and finally said, "It's a *golden* spike. They are going to drive it into the tracks where the Central Pacific and the Union Pacific are joining up."

"The transcontinental railroad," Charlie said.

"They've made a big deal out of driving that stake. Politicians of all stripes're gonna be there. They've bribed reporters for good press to cover up a whale of a lot of scandal. There's been a ton of money stolen from building the 'roads."

"The reporters will report on the fraud if there's no golden spike?" Charlie shook his head.

"It's been promised for months. Questions about more 'n where the gold spike is will send a lot of railroad big shots and politicians to jail. And bankers," she added. "More 'n one banker's skimmed money."

"The railroad was granted alternate sections of land along the tracks. Any cheating on that would be worth millions." Charlie frowned.

"I know what you're thinkin', Charles. You're wonderin' how to get a slice of that tasty pie." Greta Swinburne shook her head. "That's all wound up tighter 'n a two-dollar watch."

"If the story comes out, the spring will unwind real quick," Clem said. He grinned wolfishly.

"They can get another spike," Charlie said.

"They have to use the one specially commissioned by Leland Stanford. He put Thomas Collins in charge of getting the spike cast and etched with a message that's been spread far and wide."

"So the public would know right away if they switched spikes." Clem knocked back a drink and poured another.

"They can't just paint a regular one gold. They have to use *the* spike."

Charlie thought about it as he sipped at another drink. This went down smooth. His mouth was numb and so was most of his body. In spite of what the tarantula juice did to his body, his mind was sharp and clear.

"They can buy off the reporters."

"Too many of them want to grab headlines. What better than to get fraud charges against the heads of the two biggest railroads in the country? And the politicians? And bankers on both coasts?"

"I suppose Hickman took care of the etching on the golden spike for the bank," Charlie said.

"Naw, it was his son. Dunno what his name is, but he's fixin' to marry the engraver's daughter."

Charlie burst out laughing. The vision of Wash Collins staggering down the aisle to marry a prim little woman standing all expectant and dewy-eyed at the altar was too much.

"Hickman came up with the idea of shipping it to the Utah ceremony without any fuss."

"In a plain unmarked wood box so nobody'd know what they had. That sure got his boss in a world of trouble." Charlie poured another drink. His eyes blurred now. If he imbibed much more, he'd pass out.

He turned over and over what he'd heard.

"Hickman'll kill us dead if he catches us. There's nothing more we can do. Let's clear out of town, Clem."

He squinted enough to focus on his partner. He had seen that look before. When the going got tough, Clem dug in his heels and refused to budge. There wasn't a mule west of the Mississippi more stubborn.

"We get the real spike and we take them for all it's worth."

"What'll they all pay to stay out of the public eye? To stay out of prison?" Greta Swinburne clutched Clem's hand in her own. "You agree with me, don't you, Clement? This is more than the money they'd pony up. This is revenge."

"Revenge," Clem said. The word carried an ugly edge to it.

Charlie Dawson stared at the two. They were cut from the same cloth. The money for ransoming back the spike was important but now taking revenge on the banker and his henchmen added more than simple greed.

He held up his glass. A bit of the liquor sloshed over and burned his fingers. The nitric acid-laced whiskey had quite a kick. He needed it to say what he had to.

"Revenge," he agreed. He immediately regretted his decision, having anything to do with Greta Swinburne.

Or his partner.

# CHAPTER 23

"The engineer," Clem said. "He has to know."

"Maybe," said Greta Swinburne, "he wrecked the train to steal the spike. Those engine jockeys are notoriously crooked. Suckin' up all that coal dust and blowin' the steam whistle makes them go daft."

"That doesn't make any sense. Why wait so long to sell it back to Collins?" Charlie asked. "The sooner he made the offer, the quicker he gets his money."

"I wouldn't do it that way," the woman said. She bit off a bit of chaw. She worked on it for a while as she thought, then she spat out a gob. "How much they'd pay for the spike goes up the nearer it is to the ceremony."

"A week or so," Charlie said.

"Make 'em sweat. They might go more 'n ten thousand for it. Them politicians and banker thieves stand to do a lot of time in prison if details of their swindlin' gets out."

"Might be he doesn't know what he has, if he stole it," Charlie said. "The sight of a gold spike's mighty tempting. Keeping it or melting it down into a smaller bar's the first thing I'd do if it never occurred to me to sell it back."

"He might have come across it and just tucked it away." Clem looked at Greta with a curious fire in his eyes.

"Nobody don't know gold. You ever see anybody who touched it, hefted it, petted it like an old hound dog that didn't know what was in their hand? And with all the words etched into it, he'd have to know it was real special."

"What if he's on another run? He can be on the far side of the Sierras now."

"Then, Charles, we find his home and search it. You don't think he's carryin' it around with him, do you? People would ask questions. 'Pardon me, sir, why you got a gold railroad spike tucked under your arm?'"

He fell silent. Greta and, so it seemed, his partner knew more about thievery than he did, and how a crook behaved.

"There's the headquarters for the Central Pacific. We can waltz on in and ask after him." Charlie took a deep breath and then let it out slowly. He was the one most likely to find where the engineer was. Greta spat a gob of tobacco and Clem growled deep in his throat like a rabid dog. Either of them asking anything of anyone would bring the companies of roving specials down on their heads.

He pointed to a park across the street, waited until the two left, hitched up his pants, moved his six-gun to his coat pocket, and went inside the fancy building. The bulge in his pocket bothered him. He was certain everyone watched him like a hawk. The lobby had marble floors and all the wood gleamed with polish. This was more like a bank than most banks he'd been in, excepting for Thomas Collins's over in San Francisco. The workers were decked out in clothing that cost a fortune, and they were only clerks. The executives behind their massive desks dressed like they were going to the theater.

"May I help you, sir?" A mountain of a man intercepting him before he crossed the lobby blocked his way.

Charlie had half-baked ideas about what to say.

"An engineer," he said. "A train engineer." He pushed away his nervousness. This got him nowhere other than a speedy ejection into the street. "I have money for him."

"Who might that be, sir?"

"The engineer that was recently derailed." Charlie held his breath. If he was asked for the name, he was a goner.

"What's his name?"

A chill ran down Charlie's spine. The question he couldn't answer, the name he wanted to find out.

He stepped closer to the huge man and whispered. The guard bent down to hear what he said.

"He owes too many people money. I'm hesitant to say it out loud. This money's for him and him alone."

"Whittaker never borrowed a penny from anyone. He's about the stingiest man I know who's not a banker."

"That'd be Henry Whittaker, would it?"

"Frank Whittaker."

"I must have the wrong man. But I have money owed him. Maybe Frank knows where I can find Henry. He's still sleeping at the railroad depot, isn't he?"

"Most of them do." Before the guard spoke again, one of the well-attired executives called to him. As he turned, Charlie stepped away and retreated into the street. He waved for Clem and Greta to join him. The pair stood with their heads together, and it took a few seconds for them to notice him.

He hesitated to think it, but they seemed thicker than thieves. At first, he'd doubted Clem's claim about being married to the outlaw, but when they were together, they finished each other's sentences. In Clem's case, that didn't mean a whole lot since he never spoke too much.

A touch of resentment washed over Charlie. They were partners. It was his privilege to finish Clem's sentences, not Greta Swinburne.

"I know where the Central Pacific terminal is. I robbed that train more 'n once." Greta laughed. Clem joined her.

They trooped off. Charlie hung back to give them time together, though he wasn't sure why he bothered. He was odd man out. Black thoughts filled him as he walked. He wasn't even paying attention to where they went and plowed into Clem when he stopped unexpectedly.

"There's the depot. The rail yard is on the other side."

"What are the chances Frank Whittaker's here?" he asked. Charlie didn't expect an answer and didn't get one. Greta and Clem whispered between themselves as they climbed the steps to the ticket office.

"The agent's not here," Clem said. He rattled a door

to the side of the ticket window. It slipped its spring lock. He moved quickly, going into the office. Charlie started to join his partner, but Greta held him back.

"Keep watch." She went into the office and closed the door.

Fuming at being cut out of the herd like that, he went to the window and watched as they rummaged through the agent's desk. From the corner of his eye, he caught movement. The agent returned from some other business. Charlie stepped up and blocked the bustling man's approach.

"'Scuse me," he said. "I'm looking for Frank Whittaker. Got money for him."

The agent looked him over from head to toe. Charlie looked like he had been pulled through a knothole backward. Worst was his torn pant leg all soaked in blood.

"Ain't likely."

Charlie said nothing. He took a double eagle from his pocket and held it between thumb and forefinger. A quick move kept it from the railroad agent's grasp when he reached for it.

"Tell him the debt's paid since he's not around."

"I can give it to him."

Charlie laughed. He cast a quick look over his shoulder. Clem peered out of the office through a slit between door and jamb. Moving like he was on a dance floor doing a Texas Star, he linked his arm with the agent's and spun him around.

"I might pay a finder's fee, but I can't give you the money I owe Frank."

"Frank? Who are you? Nobody calls him that."

"Whittaker, then."

"Wheels. Wheels Whittaker."

Charlie slid the gold coin back into his pocket and fished out a silver cartwheel. He said nothing but laid it flat on his palm for the agent to see.

"You run down that mangy dog?" Greta said, coming up behind him.

"Wheels?" Charlie said. "Wheels Whittaker? I thought so, but . . ." No striking rattler moved faster. The coin vanished.

"He's in the bunkhouse on the far side of the round-house. We put the crews up there between trips 'cross the hills." The agent snorted in contempt. "One of these days, Wheels will make the round trip without derailin' or bustin' a boiler. Once he even forgot to oil the wheels. That's how he got his name. The pistons froze up. He costs the Central Pacific more 'n he's worth."

"Sounds like a real company man," Charlie said. He led the way down the steps and across the rail yard. It took a few minutes to find the bunkhouse where the crews put up, but for the first time all day, Charlie felt confident they were getting somewhere. A quick touch on the butt of his Colt reassured him. He was ready for anything, good or bad.

"Wait here. We don't want to spook him."

"Charles, you ain't thinkin' on cuttin' us out, are you?" Greta Swinburne pushed ahead of him. Clem added his bulk to the barrier Charlie faced going inside first.

He motioned them to precede him. It riled him they acted like he intended to steal the spike for his own. He hardly trusted the woman, but Clem ought to know him better.

Rows of bunk beds stretched along both sides of the room, leaving an aisle down the middle. Two men snored away, ignoring any disturbance around them. Somehow, Charlie spotted a man at the rear with his feet hiked up and reading a dime novel and knew this was Wheels Whittaker. He stepped past his two companions and stood at the foot of the bed.

The man looked up.

"You Frank Whittaker? Wheels?"

"Whatever you're accusin' me of, I didn't do. That louse over in the ticket office thinks I'm a walkin' pile of bad luck. How'd I know the oil can was—"

"We're not here about damage to your engine." Charlie held the other two back. They'd have started torturing the engineer right away to pry what they needed to know from him. If he'd taken the gold spike, why would he hang around the railroad barracks? Whittaker would be offering it for sale or have melted it down and lit out for parts unknown.

"What were you carryin'?" Greta Swinburne demanded. "And what happened to it?"

Whittaker backed up but found himself pinned against the wall when both Clem and Charlie moved to either side. Their victim stared straight ahead at Greta, which was enough to frighten anyone, even when she wasn't trying to look hard as nails.

"Some passengers. Not many. Two freight cars. A mail car and the caboose. That was all. Oh, and the tender car. That's a steep climb and the dispatcher wanted us to get over the pass as quick as a rabbit."

"The mail car," Charlie said. "What was in it?"

"You're not Pinkerton agents. Not unless they're hiring the dregs of the earth. What's this—"

The air gusted from Whittaker's lungs when Clem punched him in the gut. Charlie held him upright. He whispered in the engineer's ear, "This'll be over quicker if you don't make them mad." Whittaker pleadingly looked at Charlie.

Charlie smiled. The engineer turned white. The smile looked different from the friendly way he intended.

"The home office wanted a fast trip. That's all I know."

"The mail car," Greta prompted.

He shrugged.

"Nothing unusual. There were two safes. A big one for the mail and a smaller one for specie. Maybe some greenbacks stuffed into it. I never know what's bein' shipped. They don't trust anybody but the clerk."

"Where can we find the clerk?" Charlie kept Greta from punching the engineer. "It's real important to us."

"I can see that." Whittaker swallowed hard. "You think he swiped something? Is that it?"

Charlie slammed the flat of his hand into the wall beside the engineer. He jumped and turned a shade paler.

"Look, I don't know what they were shippin'. If it was gold, it'd be in the small safe. The big one had shelves. Nothin' too big'd fit into it other than letters."

"The mail clerk had the combination to the big safe," Clem said.

"He struck me as a sneaky guy. A weasel. A jackal. You know the type. Never kills anything but waits for it to die. A vulture! That's what he was."

"What was his name?" Greta moved closer. She slammed her body against Whittaker. "Where can we find him?"

"He . . . his name's Reynolds. That's all I ever heard. Honest. You want more, ask the station master. Or the dispatcher. They know everybody that gets paid."

Charlie kept Clem from menacing the engineer more.

"He's squeezed dry."

"We don't know where to find Reynolds," Greta groused. She gave Whittaker the evil eye. He wilted like a flower out of water.

"The station agent," Charlie said. He turned to the engineer and tried to flash a feral smile to intimidate him into silence. Whatever had scared Whittaker before now made him grin sickly. "Don't go telling anybody we've been here."

Whittaker shook his head.

They left him at the rear of the barracks. The others hadn't stirred. As the trio walked out, Charlie wondered if any of the other railroad employees knew Reynolds. Then he decided the best way to find where the mail clerk had gone was to share some of the interrogation tactics Greta and Clem enjoyed so with the man.

As they rounded the building on their way back to

the depot, Charlie stopped suddenly. The other two crashed into him.

The station agent pointed at them. The four men with him were familiar. Charlie had seen them at one time or another around Thomas Collins's bank. All four went for their six-shooters. They were very fast. And their aim was remarkable considering the range.

# CHAPTER 24

Charlie Dawson stumbled. His injured leg saved him. The instant he saw the four gunmen going for their pistols, he tried to run. His bad leg gave way under him and sent him sprawling. The lead flew through the air where his head had been an instant before.

He cringed when Greta and Clem returned fire. They had been as quick responding as the gunmen had been to open fire. Charlie crawled along and got cinders in his elbows and knees. A hand grabbed him by the collar and lifted him bodily.

"Do better," Clem said. Then his partner leaned around him and continued to fire at the men trying to ventilate them.

Charlie got his legs under him. His calf felt like fiery needles were thrust into it, but he'd feel a damned sight worse if he didn't ignore the pain and run. He saw an open door in a warehouse and headed for it. The other two backed up behind him until their six-guns were empty.

They ducked into the building behind him. Charlie covered them now, taking careful aim as their attackers rushed up. He hit one squarely. When he went down he wasn't going to get up again. Charlie winged a second man, hitting him high in the shoulder. The impact spun the gun around and put the fear into the other two.

"Where're we goin'?" Greta Swinburne demanded. "We stay here, they'll get more cutthroats and wait us out. Or shoot us out."

"That," Clem said. "That's what they'll do. These gents aren't the wait around and see what happens types."

Charlie agreed with his partner. Collins's men were just as easily mistaken for outlaws as they were law-abiding bodyguards for a bank president. He reloaded and looked around. Greta and Clem argued what to do. It was up to him to figure it out.

"There," he said. "This is a repair shed."

"That's a teeny engine used to move freight around the yard. What're we going to do? Hijack it?"

"Why not?" Charlie hobbled a few steps then gritted his teeth and ran, ignoring the pain shooting up into his thigh. He pulled himself up on the small engine and stepped into the cab.

"What'll I do now?" he asked, more to himself than the others. The gauges bobbed back and forth. Levers and handles poked up from strange places.

"What's the difference?" Greta said. "Those gunslicks are coming into the warehouse. Told you they was impatient cusses."

Even as she spoke a bullet ricocheted off the metal plate above one steam pressure gauge. Charlie ducked involuntarily. He grunted as Greta shoved him to the side and yanked hard on a handle. The small freight-hauling engine lurched and strained. Metal tearing filled the warehouse.

"Brakes," Clem said. He shoved Charlie in the other direction and used both hands to release another lever. The engine blasted away amid screams and screeches and steam venting hard.

The fog created by the released steam filled the warehouse and blinded their pursuers.

"Take that, you miserable dogs," Greta cried. She emptied her six-gun into the billowing clouds. Whether she hit anything didn't matter. It had to cause Collins's men to hesitate. Every minute they hesitated, Charlie and the others got a bit farther away.

"How do you steer?" Charlie shouted over the racket caused by the engine. He peered out the side. The engine careened along through the rail yard. Ahead loomed a huge engine.

"You don't steer. You follow the tracks," Clem said.

"Then switch us onto another track!"

Charlie closed his eyes and waited for the crash. He felt hot wind rip past his face. When he chanced to open his eyes he saw with great relief that they ran along a track parallel to the full-sized engine. Luck had smiled on them. The switches were open to the right tracks that kept them from colliding.

Greta leaned out the far side and shouted. Then she shot a couple times until her pistol clicked on a spent round. Charlie looked out the other side and caught his breath. A yard crew frantically worked to throw a switch to get them off the track they rattled along on. Greta's orders and bullets had sent them scurrying to keep the freight-moving engine from causing a massive pileup by crashing into the back of a freight car.

"Thanks!" Greta shouted to the crew as they sped past. She let out a loud war whoop and sank down on a drop seat. "Look at me. I'm the engineer on this hunk of tin." Pulling and pushing levers, thumping pressure gauges and otherwise pretending to be an engineer caused Charlie's temper to flare.

"You'll get us killed!"

"Ain't done that so far. Not like you provokin' them cutthroats back at the depot."

"They saw us and opened fire. I didn't do anything."

Greta laughed and looked at him with crazy eyes. She aimed at his midriff. He knew that if she hadn't emptied the cylinder, he'd have a couple ounces of lead in his gut. The wildness died down, a little, and she went back to poking and prodding levers.

"We're on a stretch of track leading south," Clem said. "This must round the end of the Bay and hook up somewhere beyond Oakland."

"A line goes to Sacramento," Charlie said, shaking. He worked to get his six-shooter reloaded. The wind whipping past made his eyes water. His hands shook and he wanted nothing more than to ride the engine to the ends of the earth to get away from San Francisco and all the trouble brewing there.

Too much of it was his own doing.

"We're slowin' down," Greta said. "One of you boys get to stokin' the firebox. The wood's back there, what there is of it."

Charlie saw a small stack of logs cut to size to fit into

the furnace. When Clem made no move to feed the fire, he began shoving one length of wood after another into the firebox. The heat blasted back in his face. Between the wind tearing at his face and the waves of heat radiating from the furnace, he felt his strength vanishing. He could work twelve hours a day in a mine and hardly feel the effort. Just a few minutes in the engine's cab wore him to a frazzle.

"That's more like it. I like this highballin'. That's what they call it. Hellbent for wherever we're headin'. Might be you and me, Clement, can take up train robbin'. Only instead of robbin' passengers and takin' whatever's in the mail car safe, we can steal the whole danged train. I like this. I like this a lot!"

Greta Swinburne opened the valves. Pressure built in the boiler until the needles entered the red side. Charlie wasn't sure but he made a good guess what that meant.

"Pressure's going up fast. The boiler will blow."

"Then we're not goin' fast enough," Greta said. She played the levers. The engine lurched as it sped along even faster.

Charlie wasn't about to disturb her. The pressure needles edged down from the red zones even if the boiler rivets began creaking so loud he heard them over the whine of steel wheels against the rails.

"You're not taking up with her, are you, Clem? We're partners. Me and you. Not her and you."

The expression on Clem's face made him feel worse than the threat of the engine blowing up. His answer was as plain as if it had been written in bright red ink on his forehead. He was thinking about going with his former wife.

Greta Swinburne cursed, stood, and swung around. She hung on the side of the engine for a moment, then jumped.

"Greta, what are you doing?" Clem took a step after her, then stopped. "Charlie, we're gonna crash!"

Charlie pulled himself over to the side and looked out. Another train rattled along. They were overtaking it at a speed that'd cause such a collision that they'd never find even tiny body parts when they hit.

Charlie reached up and grabbed the steam whistle cord. He sank down as the shriek filled the air.

"You idiot! They're not getting out of our way!"

"But the boiler on this engine's a tiny little thing. Release the steam, slow down. There isn't much in the way of brakes. It's not supposed to go this fast."

He held the cord and watched the pressure in the boiler fall off fast.

"Jump!" Clem cried.

"Hold on!" Charlie corrected.

Their small engine crashed into the caboose of the bigger train. For a moment, Charlie thought they should have jumped and risked having the derailed engine skid along and crush them. If its boiler had ruptured, it would have shot rivets all over like bullets from a Gatling gun. Or the ruptured boiler would spew boiling water and scald them to death. A dozen ways of dying came to him because he'd wrecked the engine.

The impact rattled their teeth but didn't derail the

smaller engine. Their speed fell off to almost nothing. Charlie hung onto the whistle until his arms gave out. When he released it, the sudden quiet was almost painful.

Their engine sat immobile on the tracks. Steam hissed from the boiler and metal groaned as it cooled. The smell of burnt steel filled their nostrils.

"She saved her own skin," Clem said. "She never gave me a warning. She jumped."

"That's the way it looks." Charlie sat on the engineer's seat where Greta had watched the forward tracks. The other train was almost a dot in the distance. It hadn't slowed. If anything, other than the damage done to its caboose, the engineer probably never noticed anything was wrong.

"That's the way she always was."

"She would have let you die," Charlie said. He took no satisfaction in telling his partner such an obvious truth.

Clem stared from the cab back along the tracks.

"You want to go hunt for her?"

"No need," Clem said softly. "She's gone."

Charlie vented a sigh as loud as the steam leaking from their damaged boiler. He finally said, "We need to hightail it ourselves. There's no reason to keep hunting for the mail clerk and the golden spike."

Clem stared at him.

"You fixing to give up on selling the spike back to Collins?"

"Partner, we're out of roads to travel. We have the

clerk's name and not a clue where he got off to. If we went back to the depot and asked the station master, we'd end up on the wrong end of a muzzle. Collins might expect us to go back, and even if he didn't, the gunmen who survived our fight looked like they were the kind to carry grudges. We shot 'em up pretty good."

"Killed one, maybe two," Clem supplied.

"We need to give up our hunt for the spike. We've got plenty of money left from what Collins gave us. It might last us a few months. Longer if we don't get drunk every night."

"You mad at me for thinking on teaming with Greta again?"

Charlie considered his answer. It came easily enough.

"We're partners. Partners don't abandon partners."

"I know where Reynolds is." He looked sheepish. "Well, maybe I do."

Charlie shook his head, thinking he'd misheard. Sometimes his ears played tricks on him.

"How?"

Clem dragged out a handful of letters from his coat pocket and handed them to his partner.

"I took these off the station agent's desk. Mail addressed for a dozen folks."

Charlie tossed one letter after another into the firebox. He stopped when he came to one addressed to Laramie Reynolds. He looked up.

"You reckon this is the man we want? The clerk?"

Clem grinned and said, "No harm in delivering the letter ourselves and finding out."

Charlie stared at the name and address on the letter. It was his lucky day. They had avoided being killed by Collins's gunmen. They hadn't wrecked the engine. Entirely by luck, Clem had found a way to track down the elusive mail car clerk. Best of all, Greta Swinburne was gone.

# CHAPTER 25

"You saying that letter's addressed to Reynolds at the railroad depot?" Clem snorted and shook his head. "That doesn't do us any good."

"The return address is in a town just north of Oakland, on the route to Sacramento," Charlie said. "Whoever sent a letter might know where he is."

"Not if they only addressed it in care of the Central Pacific."

"Maybe the reason the letter wasn't picked up is because Reynolds and whoever wrote the letter got together." Charlie lifted the envelope to his nose and sniffed. "No hard rock miner ever used perfume like that."

Clem tried it. He smiled crookedly, held the letter up, and tried to read it through the envelope. He held it upside down.

"Give that to me." Charlie snatched it from his partner and tore it open.

"That's US Mail. You can't open it. That's a crime."

Charlie stared at his friend in amazement. Clem had

a curious sense of what was right and what was wrong. Taking up again with Greta Swinburne wasn't wrong, in spite of her boasting on how they'd rob trains and steal from banks. But opening someone else's letter was close to a hanging offense.

"If he's dead, it won't matter."

Clem thought on that, then said, "We owe it to the lady writing the letter to tell her what happened. If Reynolds is dead, that is."

"Or to find out if he stole the gold spike, like I— we—think he did."

"Where else could it be?"

"Nobody but Reynolds had the chance to replace the real one with a steel spike," Charlie said. Even as the words came out, he wondered if that was true. Who had crated it and put it in the mail car? Hiram Hickman was hardly an honest man. Or Washington Collins? The bank president's son had to know about the gold spike if he was sparking the engraver's daughter.

Any of them might have known and let details slip. Thomas Collins was a powerful banker surrounded by clever people. One tiny hint could have set into motion a scheme to steal the spike. His secretary—Arthur—had the look of a man who knew everything, or found out if he wasn't told.

He came back to the same problem. If any of them had the spike before the shipment, why hadn't they ransomed it already? Greta Swinburne insisted the price was ten thousand. The closer the ceremony for connecting the two railroads came, the greater the value for the spike.

Until . . .

Until the date passed. If the newspaper reporters got their ire up and began printing all they knew of the politicians and railroad executives—and bank presidents like Collins—the spike's value would only be whatever the melted gold brought.

"Time," Charlie said softly. He unfolded the letter. It was written in a flowing hand he found hard to read. He deciphered the flowery words and grew concerned until he came to the bottom. He looked at his partner. "She signed it 'With all my love, Lily.' That's plenty to start with in a small town like Bonaventure."

"How do we get there?"

"Buy a ticket. We've still got money." Charlie patted his pocket where the remaining gold coins from Thomas Collins rested. For a moment, he thought the small double eagles had shifted around behind a seam. His search became frantic. He looked up, stricken.

"She took it," Clem said. He laughed. Whether it was rueful or appreciative, Charlie couldn't tell.

"Swine? She stole our money? When?"

"She was always good at pickpocketing."

Charlie tried to remember. When Greta Swinburne had pushed past him and jumped, then she might have dipped into his pocket and stolen their poke. Or at a dozen other times when they'd crowded close. Dodging bullets proved more than enough distraction for a good pickpocket.

"I might have dropped the lot of them while I was

flailing about," Charlie said. "Killers shooting at me, me diving for cover, getting hit—" He held out his injured calf. The blood caked the pant leg to his skin. Every movement sent new thrills of pain up into his thigh and down into his foot. That was enough distraction for him to have lost the money without Greta's stubby fingers robbing him.

"She got them," Clem said with assurance. "Once a thief, always a thief."

"Or a killer," Charlie muttered. Louder, "What'll we do? We have to get to Bonaventure and find Reynolds's 'darling Lily' fast. We can't buy horses. All I've got left is a handful of small coins." He turned out his pocket to show nothing but lint, two dimes, and a nickel. "We don't have anywhere near enough money for a ticket on the train."

Clem laughed and shook his head.

"Train. We'll ride. It just won't be in style."

"You're saying we don't have money for a Pullman car," Charlie said glumly. "What do we have the money for?"

"Riding the tie rods under the Pullman car. All we have to do is avoid the railroad bulls if they come checking for freeloaders."

"Like us."

"Like us," Clem agreed.


Charlie Dawson dropped to the tracks and landed across a railroad tie. The creosote-soaked wood cut into his back. For a moment he thought he had broken his spine. He stared up at the rusty rods crisscrossing the bottom of the freight car. They had barely escaped the railroad dicks when they'd crawled into a freight car. Only luck had let them slip out and duck underneath. The train had pulled out as they were getting situated. Slowly at first, then with gathering speed, the cradle of rods had moved above him.

Clem had grabbed on, then jerked Charlie up. He had been clumsy because of his bullet-holed leg. It took some scrambling, but he situated himself in time to glance to the side. The legs of the railroad detectives flashed by and then the freight yard vanished. The train chugged south through farmland, curled around the end of San Francisco Bay, and headed north.

In spite of the noise and uncomfortable position, Charlie had slept a little. Or perhaps he passed out. All he knew of the trip past Oakland to Bonaventure was his partner nudging him to leave their berth.

They had arrived. Finally. Alive.

He closed his eyes to keep cinders and spatters of oil from blinding him. When he blinked and stared straight up, he saw the pure azure California sky and Clem towering over him.

"We've got to get out of the rail yard. There's a bull here with quite a reputation. He'll beat up anyone he thinks is catching a free ride."

"How do you know?" Before his partner answered, Charlie waved him to silence. "Never mind. Help me up."

A strong hand gripped his and lifted him to his feet. Walking proved more painful than he expected, but the possibility of a railroad detective using a slungshot on his already aching head moved him along faster than he'd thought possible just a minute earlier. They went to the railroad depot and sat on the platform as if they waited for a train rather than having just arrived.

"How do we find Lily?"

"Thanks to your light-fingered ways, we've got the address." Charlie took out the envelope and held it up for Clem to see. "The return address in the corner."

"Oh."

Charlie frowned. He'd never asked during the two years they'd been partners if Clem could read and write. Whenever something requiring those skills came along, he'd taken care of it and felt good about being in control. Clem signed his name, but he did it as if he drew a picture rather than scrawled a signature. His partner had never even commented when he spent time reading a penny dreadful or poring over a *Police Gazette* at the barber shop on the rare times when they'd gotten a shave and a bath. It may have been that Clem wasn't inclined to draw attention to his own lack of education.

"Let's go find Miss Lily and see if she's taken in a boarder who used to be the mail clerk for Central Pacific."

The Bonaventure depot was dinky compared to the ones in San Francisco or Sacramento. The sleepy clerk stirred when they walked up.

"You gents got a wait. Ain't a regular passenger train due through 'til way late today."

A sudden flash of inspiration hit Charlie.

"It's not that. We haven't been reading the papers lately. When is the ceremony joining the two railroads?"

"Connecting the Central Pacific and the Union Pacific?" The clerk stretched. "You fixin' on catchin' a train to see that? Best way's to get on over to Sacramento, but the high and mighty've chartered all the trains to get from there over to Utah."

"When?" Charlie pressed.

"It's supposed to be May tenth, but there's a rumor that the ceremony might be tied up in details."

"Like not having the gold spike to complete the roads?"

The clerk looked curiously at Clem. He shook his head and said, "Ain't that so much as the politicians from back in Washington takin' their sweet time arrivin'. Can't do nuthin' on time, if you ask me."

"Next Monday," Charlie mused. He looked at Clem. They had exactly one week to find the spike and convince Thomas Collins to give them a pile of money for it.

"Reckon that's right," the agent said, pushing his eyeglasses down to look at a calendar nailed to the wall. "Yup, a week from today. Now, what can I do for you boys? Tickets to Sacramento so you can get on out to Promontory Summit for the ceremony? Next train coming up from Oakland will whistle into the station around sundown."

"We're looking for a friend who just moved to Bonaventure. Here's the address." He held out the envelope and showed only the return address. If the agent knew Reynolds, he might be inclined to warn him that men were hunting for him.

"Who might this be?" The agent looked suspicious.

"Miss Lily," Clem said.

The agent relaxed.

"She's over at the schoolhouse. She's the schoolmarm now. Did you know her down in Oakland?"

Charlie made a noncommittal noise. The agent rambled on.

"Lovely young thing. She worked at the Oakland Long Wharf for the boss."

"The fellow in charge of mail?" Charlie asked, taking a shot at a connection between Lily and Reynolds.

"I believe that's so. You had me going for a second. I thought you was up to somethin' . . . quirky. Sounds like you do know her. But how'd you come by that letter and not know about her situation?"

"Much obliged," Charlie said. He steered Clem from the depot into the street before the agent thought too much about them and their relationship with Lily.

"A schoolmarm," Clem said thoughtfully. "You think she and the mail clerk are in cahoots to steal that gold?"

"They worked together in Oakland. Both for the railroad. It sounds more likely now than it did before that Reynolds had an accomplice." He lifted the letter to his nose and sniffed in appreciation. She used mighty fine perfume on her letters. No lady did that for someone she had only met.

"Let's go get eddy-cated," Clem said.

# CHAPTER 26

The clerk in the mercantile store laughed at them. He started to speak, then laughed even harder.

"What's so funny about asking where the schoolhouse is?" Clem pulled himself up to his full height and thrust out his chest. His hands formed fists and then relaxed when his partner put a restraining hand on his shoulder.

"It's not like we're looking to become students," Charlie said. The mercantile clerk wiped away tears. He struggled to control his laughter.

"No, you're way too old to learn anything. Can't teach an old dog new tricks."

"I'll teach you—" Clem stepped forward. Again Charlie held him back. The clerk never saw how close he came to getting punched out.

"We've got news for Miss Lily and were told she's the new teacher."

"It'd better be good news. She'll chew you up and spit you out if you cross her. She's a pistol. Has to be with rowdy kids like those in her school."

Charlie said nothing and cautioned Clem to stay

quiet. When the clerk settled down, he said, "Go on out of town, maybe a mile. The schoolhouse is on the south side of the road." He grinned widely and added, "You want to take the teacher an apple? Got a barrel right here."

Clem plucked an apple from the barrel and took a big bite. Before the clerk protested, he spat out the apple and tossed the rest back into the barrel.

"Worm," he said.

They left the store. The clerk sputtered and shouted after them.

"He thought we wanted educating," Clem said. "If you hadn't held me back, I'd've educated him real good."

"No reason to create a fuss," Charlie said. He looked around the sleepy town as they hoofed it along the road. Stirring up the locals and getting the town marshal riled at them wasn't helpful. They only had a week to find the spike and ransom it back to Collins.

They hiked in silence until Charlie spotted the schoolhouse. At one time it had been a church. The steeple had been lightning-struck and never replaced. A burnt stub dominated the entryway. The rest of the building needed whitewash, and one window pane had been broken.

"A kid with good aim should have taken out the rest of the glass," Clem said. He eyed a rock alongside the road, as if estimating distances and how hard he'd have to throw it.

Charlie hoped his partner wasn't inclined to be that kid. He hurried along the dirt path to the front door, which stood ajar. Inside sat twenty children, all trying to pay attention. Not many of them succeeded. Charlie saw two passing notes back and forth.

He pushed the door open further. The hefty woman at the front of the class was dressed in a pale green floral print skirt and a stiffly starched white blouse with a high collar. Her midnight black hair was pulled up into a severe bun. Her close-set, dark eyes darted about the classroom, fixing on miscreants passing notes or whispering. With lips pursed disapprovingly, she pointed at Charlie.

"You may wait outside until class is dismissed."

When Charlie hesitated, she snapped, "Now!"

A few in the class snickered. Charlie decided this was a town appreciating a joke at someone else's expense. He touched the brim of his hat and stepped away from the door. Clem said nothing. They stood to one side of the doorway for almost a half hour until a bell rang inside. That was the signal for a room full of children to rush out, shouting, shoving, and laughing.

"At least they aren't laughing at us this time," Clem said. His eyes snapped around to the doorway.

Miss Lily filled it with broad shoulders and hefty hips. She looked as if she had sucked on a lemon before coming out to meet them.

"You disrupted my class."

"Ma'am," Charlie said, pinching the brim of his hat again. "We believe you sent this letter to Mister Reynolds?" He held up her letter.

"Laramie? You know where he is?"

The large, dominant woman melted before their eyes at the mention of the mail clerk.

"We hoped you had some idea. We're trying to find him."

"I haven't heard from him since the . . . since the accident. His train derailed, you know."

"We do," Charlie said. "We found some of the others and talked with the ones who survived."

"Survived? You think he's dead?"

"We never found his body," Clem said, speaking up now. "The railroad never ordered anyone to find it."

"He's dead, then?"

"We don't think so, Miss Lily."

She looked down her long Roman nose at him with some disdain. A quick "harumph" to clear her throat and she said, "The name is Miss Denton."

"Ma'am, Miss Denton," Charlie said. "If you don't know where he is, there's no call for us to upset you further."

"Wait," she called when they turned to leave. "Why are you looking for him?"

"Insurance," Charlie said, that being the first thing that came to him.

"On his life?"

"The Central Pacific hates to see any loss, whether it's their trains or their employees." He motioned Clem to silence. He had no idea what that meant, but it soothed Lily Denton's ruffled feathers.

"You aren't giving up finding him, are you?"

"Miss Denton, we've got other work to do, and we've come to the end of the road now that you can't say where to find him."

Charlie had never been much of a fisherman, but he

knew how to bait a hook. Her disappointment that they didn't have any idea where to find Reynolds was written on her face, as surely as if she'd done it in her neat cursive letters across her forehead.

"You won't tell me where he is?"

"We're like you," Charlie said. "We don't know what happened after the derailment. We found the mail car and blood. There wasn't a body, though."

"I'll pay you!" she blurted.

"Pay us for what, Miss Denton?"

"To find Laramie. He's the love of my life. And he loves me, too. He said so. We were going to be married when he got a few dollars ahead."

"The gold spike," Clem said softly.

Charlie thought so, too. The mail clerk found the gold spike, had no idea that Collins, Stanford, and dozens of politicians wanted it for reasons that had nothing to do with the joining of the two railroads. Reynolds might not have even known the spike's purpose, only that it was made from gold. Gold that'd let him marry his sweetheart.

Collins's secrecy worked against him and the railroad officials intending to drive the golden spike. If more had known the unique spike was on the train, they'd have lined up to return it after the wreck.

"How much?" Charlie asked.

"All I have is four dollars in scrip." She began fishing around in a small handbag and pulled out the crumpled greenbacks.

Charlie almost didn't take it when Clem hissed at

him. Without that money, they were dead broke, thanks to Greta Swinburne's quick pickpocketing fingers.

He tucked the four bills away in the same pocket where a small fortune in gold coins was once hidden. The dollar bills now kept company with the two dimes and nickel.

"We need something more to go on. Anything. The train wreck was in Dos Robles Canyon. Is there anywhere between here and there that Reynolds—Laramie—might hole up?"

"There was a shack outside Sacramento where his uncle and he stayed. His uncle's name was, I don't remember. Oh, oh, yes! Rafe Carroll. But he died, I'm sure. Laramie was quite morose when his uncle tangled with a black bear near the cabin. That was a few months ago. The bear was ornery and had just come out of hibernation. Laramie's uncle Rafe wasn't the kind to tolerate any creature intruding on his supplies."

"Sounds as if he made a bad choice who to tangle with," Clem said.

Lily Denton shot him a cold look.

"We'll let you know what we find," Charlie said hurriedly, aiming to avoid a clash between the schoolmarm and his partner. "And"—he hated himself for this—"if there's any insurance money due, we'll see that the Central Pacific pays it to you, almost married to him and all."

Lily Denton teared up. She dabbed at the trickles down her chubby cheeks with a man's handkerchief. Charlie wondered if that had belonged to Laramie

Reynolds. He made a hasty departure. Seeing a woman cry like this tore at his heartstrings.

His thoughts flashed from Lily Denton crying for her lost love and how Charlie'd like to make Greta Swinburne cry as he exacted his revenge for the way she'd stolen his money.

His and Clem's. They were partners.

"We've got money for train tickets," Clem said.

"The agent said it'd be a spell before the train for Sacramento came through. Sundown?" He licked his chapped lips. "It's been too long since we've tasted a drop or two of whiskey."

"Brandy," Clem insisted. "Make it brandy. And not much. We've got to watch what we spend the money on since this is all we have."

Charlie didn't remind his partner of the reason they were almost paupers again. He read Clem's anguish over the knowledge of how they'd lost Thomas Collins's payment when he hired them.

Bonaventure had only one saloon, but that was plenty. The brandy tasted good, damned good.

# CHAPTER 27

"Sacramento's not as big as San Francisco," Clem said. "That doesn't help us one little bit finding the cabin."

"A cabin which might not even exist," Charlie went on. They had no idea how honest Laramie Reynolds was, or if he had another woman in Sacramento. Using a fake uncle and cabin as an excuse for not spending more time with Lily Denton was possible. Charlie had to assume a man who'd steal the golden spike was dishonest about other things in his life.

He twisted this way and that to avoid the rush of passengers boarding the train. Most of them were well-dressed, even elegant. They must be on their way to the ceremony celebrating the joining of the road in distant Utah.

"Or an uncle that may not exist, either."

Charlie heard the defeat in his partner's words. Clem had come to the same conclusion about Reynolds that he had. The man could be a bald-faced liar as well as a thief. Or not.

He refused to give up. They had seven days—closer

to six but still a week, in his mind—to find the memorial spike.

"Going up to people on the street asking if they've heard of Rafe Carroll isn't likely to work in a city this size." He wondered what he might learn asking the ticket agent or any of the railroad crews about Laramie Reynolds. If Reynolds had passed through this depot often enough, someone must know him. All they had to do was avoid Collins's thugs and, by now, the railroad bulls who must have their descriptions.

Still, there was no way around it. Charlie looked around the passenger platform and saw a potential source of information.

"You, porter," he said, grabbing the uniformed man's sleeve to stop him. "I'm looking for a mail clerk on a train named Reynolds. Laramie Reynolds."

The man's dark forehead turned into furrows. Bright eyes shone as he shook his head.

"He got hisse'f kilt in a wreck."

"That's too bad," Charlie said. "How can I pay my respects? At a funeral home? Has he been buried?"

"You ast questions like that other fella."

"Other? Who's that?" All he got was a shrug as an answer. "When was this other fellow asking after Reynolds?"

"This mornin' 'bout six a.m."

"So he wasn't on a train? He rode over to the station?" Again he got an eloquent shrug showing ignorance.

"Gotta work. The boss man he gits all het up when I

stop movin'. That's cuz I don't move so fast, so I keep movin'. Slow's better 'n not movin' no how."

"That makes sense," Charlie said. It was his turn to frown. He went to Clem and said softly, "Someone else asked after Reynolds this morning. We're trailing someone else."

"They're ahead of us," Clem said. "What do we do?"

"Ask more people working here about Reynolds." Charlie pointed toward the rail yard. Clem was more likely to get the freight handlers to talk. He was built like them, tall, solid, square of face, and using few words.

He worked through as many of the depot workers as possible before he aroused too much suspicion. The station master was a busy galoot who ordered his men around like a field general. From what Charlie saw, the station ran smoothly enough. That might have been recent, though, because of the important men with their fancy ladies traveling through to Utah. From the excited words he heard, this was going to be a gala unmatched since the nonstop parties celebrating the end of the War.

He sank to a bench after an hour of questioning everyone he thought might help. His leg hurt something fierce, but it was his spirit that proved most injured. He had expected someone to know Laramie Reynolds. Charlie jumped when Clem collapsed beside him. He had been sinking too low into his own black mood to notice his partner's approach.

"Anyone mention Reynolds?" He read Clem's face well. "What do we do now?"

"We ride on out to Rafe Carroll's cabin."

"How'd you find it?"

Clem pulled a scrap of yellow telegraph foolscap out to catch the last rays of the setting sun. He spread it on the bench between them. Faint pencil lines had torn through the thin paper. Clem pressed them flat.

"The telegraph operator knew Carroll. He'd sent more 'n one telegram out to him."

"The telegrapher drew this map?"

"Which way's it go? Yeah, this way's north." Clem turned the map ninety degrees. "We're here and the cabin is five miles east of town."

"That'll take us forever to get there," Charlie said. He rubbed his leg. It had been punished so much he worried if he had another mile in him, much less five—and that was five after they left town. Getting through a city the size of Sacramento might take another mile or two of hiking.

"Not if you're up to another train ride. The cabin is within sight of the tracks as they start the climb into the mountains."

Charlie's spirits rose. He pushed himself to his feet and asked, "What're you waiting for? We've got another train to jump."

"They're not still chasing us, are they?" Charlie Dawson hunkered down in the ditch running parallel to the railroad tracks. His head swiveled around as he looked for the railroad bulls. The sun was going down fast, casting long shadows that hid them even more.

"They stayed on the train. I heard one of them say they're working as bodyguards for some high muck-a-muck from the Central Pacific. It might have been Stanford or Judah."

"Maybe the train coppers weren't after us," Charlie said, thinking over the matter. "I mean us by name. They only wanted to keep any scavenger from sneaking onto the train. It would look bad if the owners found out anyone was cheating them out of the price of a ticket."

"There were enough bulls checking every car," Clem said. "We were lucky to slip up under that Pullman."

Lucky wasn't the word Charlie would have used. After they situated themselves on the tie rods, the aromas from finely prepared food had drifted down and mingled with the burning steel and hot oil from the undercarriage. His belly growled thinking of the food so near and yet so far. He wasn't inclined to be a highwayman. Sticking up people to steal their valuables rankled, but for a plate of food, he'd have compromised his principles. It had been too long since he'd had a decent meal.

"Time's a'wasting," Charlie said, resolve hardening. He got to his feet and rubbed his leg. It had gone numb. Slowly, circulation returned to it. With the blood flow came pain. He had learned to ignore it after going through so much.

He saw a trail leading from the tracks. A quick look on the far side of the rails told him this was a trail cut by a man. If the railroad had cut across a game trail, both sides would show where animals trotted. After a ten-minute hike into a wooded area, he slowed and then held out his hand to stop his partner.

"Something's not right."

Clem just looked at him.

"I feel it in my bones. Let's scout the area before we go barging in."

"Good idea," Clem said. "If Reynolds is hiding, he wouldn't take kindly to strangers knocking on his door." He looked pointedly at Charlie's injured leg. "You get any more shot up and I'll have to carry you."

"No, thanks," Charlie said. He cut off the trail and worked his way through the forested area. After ten minutes, he began edging in toward where the cabin must be. He came to a grassy knoll before he reached the cabin.

He caught his breath. On the top, a small wooden cross stood outlined against the darkening sky. Walking carefully, he made his way to the grave. It wasn't fresh but hadn't been dug too long earlier.

"A couple months," he said when Clem joined him. "The dirt's been compacted on top of the body." He ran his hand over the slight depression. An inch-high growth of grass covered the grave.

"Can't make out the name," Clem said, peering at the cross.

Charlie stood behind his partner and had no trouble reading the name.

"It's the uncle. Rafael Carroll. No date." He ran his finger over the carved name. Wind and weather had rounded the edges just a little, giving further proof the grave had been here for a few months.

"No other grave," Clem said, making a complete circuit around the hilltop.

Charlie cocked his head to one side and turned slowly. His ears weren't particularly sharp, but the sound of a nervous horse worked through the woods from the direction where the cabin had to be. He slid down the hill, made sure his Colt was ready, tucked it into his waistband, then pushed through undergrowth until he found a game trail. Deer hoofprints showed he was right about how this was blazed through the trees.

He reached the edge of the woods. A small cabin stood in the middle of a clearing. A small shed doubling as a stable was barely visible around the side. A well, a cord of firewood, a few odds and ends. Some tools scattered about. All showed the signs of recent habitation.

But was it that recent?

"I'll check to see if there's a horse out back," Clem said.

Before he had gone ten feet a shot sang toward him. Clem fell forward and began wiggling. More slugs kicked up the dirt all around.

"To your right. A ditch," Charlie called. He dragged out his Walker Colt and fired through a cabin window. Glass shattered.

He caught faint moonlight reflecting off a gun barrel. Two more shots directed at the gun failed to stop return fire. The gunman in the cabin changed his target from Clem to the man hobbling along, trying to foolishly draw his fire.

A bullet hit a rock directly in front of Charlie. A stone chip blasted off. It cut through the side of his boot.

The impact knocked his weakened leg from under him. Crashing down, he rolled over and over until he ended up in the same gully where Clem had taken cover. The ravine wasn't more than a foot deep but ran the length of the property. In the spring during runoff, it probably overflowed its narrow banks. Now only mud remained.

"Stop shooting, Reynolds! We're not robbers. We have a message for you."

"Message?" came a barely distinguishable answer.

"From Lily Denton."

Silence.

"How come he's not jumping for joy?" Clem asked. He rested his Colt on the edge of the gully. "She's supposed to be the love of his life."

Charlie called, "She wants to marry you. Don't shoot. I'll tell you all she said." He eased up to his knees.

Clem yanked his arm and pulled him to the side when a new fusillade ripped through the air. The gunman in the cabin emptied a six-gun worth of lead at him.

"Doesn't sound like he's accepting her proposal," Clem said.

"Reynolds! Laramie! Don't shoot. We're not going to hurt you. We want to talk."

"You daft? Don't give him a target again." Clem glared at his partner in frustration.

Charlie slowly rose again, staying on his knees. Something warned him. He didn't need Clem pulling him down. He lurched to the side and got off another shot that tore through the window. As he had done before, the gunman emptied his six-shooter at Charlie.

"Rush him! Get him before he reloads!" Charlie shouted the command. He got to his feet and stumbled. He fanned off a couple more shots before his gun came up empty. Clem tore at top speed toward the cabin under Charlie's feeble fire. They had gambled on the shooter reloading after emptying his cylinder.

Clem pressed into the cabin wall. He worked to reload. Charlie did the same and then slithered down the muddy trench until he was on the other side of the door from his partner. He took a deep breath and ran for the door. Two quick shots through the window kept the shooter inside honest.

Panting harshly, he pressed his back against the wall on one side of the door. Clem hunkered down opposite him. He lifted the latch, then nodded. Charlie moved fast. He kicked in the unlatched door and sprayed bullets all around. Clem crowded in behind him and added to the din filling the small cabin. One bullet hit the cast-iron stove and sent a ricochet bouncing back in their direction.

"Drop your gun!" Charlie yelled. His ears rang. He wasn't sure he'd hear anyone surrendering. But Clem's reaction told him the danger had passed. His partner lowered his pistol and stared.

Charlie stood up straight and edged around a table in the middle of the room. He silently pointed.

"You reckon this is Reynolds?"

A body sprawled in the corner facedown, arms and legs outstretched. Charlie pressed his thumb into the man's neck and looked up.

"He's dead. From what I can tell, he's been shot in the back."

"We did that?"

"I don't see a gun." Charlie lifted blankets and pillows and paper hunting for a weapon. "I don't see a hogleg anywhere."

"Then who . . . ?"

Both of them ducked behind the table, then peeked out from either side. A window at the rear of the cabin had been shoved out.

"A horse!" Clem vaulted over the table and raced to the window. He fired several times and then sagged down. "Missed. Whoever it was had a horse out back. I never saw it when I checked the shed."

Charlie sat heavily on the cot. He began rummaging around and found saddlebags. Piece by piece, he went through the contents.

"That's probably Laramie Reynolds."

"And this is his uncle's cabin." Clem pursed his lips. "And Unk's buried out there on the hill."

"One thing's for certain," Clem said, nudging the body with the toe of his boot. "No bear got this one. Not unless he's a backshooter bear."

Charlie searched the cabin more thoroughly. Not only wasn't there a gun, he didn't find the golden spike. Once more they had played a punk hand.

# CHAPTER 28

"Did we kill him?" Charlie stared at the body. "We put a dozen rounds through the window."

"We didn't kill him," Clem said. "Look where the bullet hole is. He was shot from someone holding a gun down low. Like this." Clem bent, turned his six-gun upward. "The bullet went in at an angle and tunneled all the way up through to his shoulder."

"He might have bent forward to avoid our fire and we shot him down and through," Charlie said. He contorted his body to demonstrate how it might have been possible. Clem didn't see it.

"That's an exit wound on his shoulder. We didn't kill him. He was shot from down low and behind."

"And he wasn't armed. Or if he was, whoever was in here with him took his gun."

"Look here," Clem said. He pulled the man's pant leg up. A splint had been applied to his right leg.

"Busted. His leg was broken. That explains why he was holed up here and wasn't able to get into Sacramento." He rubbed his own wounded leg, wondering if a splint would help. He doubted it. He didn't have a broken bone. The muscle of his calf had been shot off. A plaster patch would serve him better, replacing the muscle blown away by a bullet.

They continued their search of the cabin. Charlie found a small tin box thrust under the cot. He pried open the lid and leafed through the papers inside.

"Most of the letters are Rafe Carroll's," he said, "but a couple have Reynolds's name on them. He was Carroll's sole heir and the title to this place was transferred to him. I reckon this is a legal will." He held it up and tried to make out the writing in the darkness.

"So the body's Reynolds. Where's the spike?"

"That, Clem, is a question not likely to be answered other than to say that whoever we shot it out with is the likely thief."

"If Reynolds had the spike at all."

Charlie hiked his foot up onto the cot to rest it as he thought.

"If Reynolds had it, it got him killed." He stared at the body on the cabin floor. He heaved a big sigh. "We need to bury him."

Clem silently left and came back in a few minutes with a shovel.

"It was in the shed. There's a brace of mules there. They looked hungry so I fed them."

"You've got loyal friends for life," Charlie said. "If you fed me, you'd have another."

"You're already mule-headed. Come on, give me a hand."

They found a wheelbarrow and loaded the body into

it. They found a section of the hill near Rafe Carroll and dug a decent grave in the soft earth.

"He needs a grave marker, but we need to get moving," Charlie said.

"Say a few words over him. That'll do." Clem shifted uneasily as he made the suggestion.

Charlie did the best he could for a man he had never met and didn't know, except for a single letter from the man's lady friend. In the back of his mind, he knew they had to let Lily Denton know of her paramour's death. Their hunt for the spike was over, so Bonaventure was on its way to . . . where?

They had to decide.

He tossed the shovel back into the wheelbarrow after the last of the dirt had been mounded over Laramie Reynolds. They returned to the cabin in gloomy silence. As Charlie opened the cabin door he heard a mule braying.

"We've got a ride back to Sacramento," he said. "Or should we go straight to Potluck? The Betty Sue's been in unfriendly hands for too long."

"There's not a whale of a lot we can do about the mine," Clem said. "We don't have any money and Jimmy Norton still has it in for us."

"And Marshal Thompson's not forgotten us, either. Count on that," Charlie said tiredly.

Silence fell. Night sounds began as the moon rose higher in the sky, lighting the land with a bright silver intense enough to read by. They put the shovel and wheelbarrow into the cabin, then went to the shed where the two mules stomped and kicked at their stalls. As

Clem worked to quiet the unruly beasts, Charlie walked around, hunting for something they could sell for a few dollars. He intended to return the four dollars to Lily Denton, even if they had found Reynolds. It seemed wrong to keep the woman's money, even if they had succeeded in doing what she had paid them for.

"There're tracks leading away," he said. Easing down, he examined the hoofprints pressed into the soft ground. He looked up. The tracks led to a game trail.

"So?" Clem looked at them over his shoulder. "We're not trackers."

"We don't have to be, Clem. The killer's tracks are as plain as the nose on your face." He looked up at his partner. "And that's a big nose. Use it to sniff out the trail. Don't you smell gold? A golden spike?"

"We don't know that."

"Nope, we surely do not," Charlie said. "That's why we owe it to ourselves to follow the tracks and see if the owlhoot has the spike. If Reynolds had it, whoever killed him took it."

"Why not bury it? Maybe it's in his uncle's grave."

"Reynolds was too banged up for anything like that. He buried his uncle before the derailment and him busting his leg. If you broke your leg like he had, and you took the spike, you'd keep it close so you could feel good about something. Knowing he had the spike'd give a sense of winning. He'd tell himself once he healed he and Lily'd get hitched and live happily ever after."

"Seems farfetched." Clem started walking along the hoofprints. He nodded slowly and mumbled to himself.

Charlie knew he had convinced his partner. He turned his attention to the mules. A sack of dried carrots won over the larger mule, but the smaller refused to have anything to do with him. Whenever he came close, snapping teeth threatened to take another hunk of his flesh.

"We can do it," Clem said.

Charlie took a second to follow his partner's thoughts. Then he pointed to the cabin and said, "We can take what supplies are there. Should we fix a meal before hitting the trail?"

"No time to waste."

Charlie led the mules out of the shed while Clem wrapped up the victuals from the cabin in two burlap bags and slung them over his mule's rump.

"Not riding in style," Clem said, "but it's better than walking."

They set out, Charlie watching the tracks disappear into the dark forest. He had despaired of finding the golden spike before. He felt holding it in his own hands now was possible.


"Sacramento's just over the next pass," Clem said.

"If you say so." Charlie had lost track of where they were. All he cared about was the trail they followed. Even though he wasn't much of a woodsman, he had no trouble keeping the hoofprints in sight. The rider never strayed from the trail. More than once, their quarry had stopped to rest his horse. Or he had taken a rest.

Their mules weren't near as fast as a horse, but they

were determined and persistent. They kept moving and moving and moving until Charlie wanted to take a rest. He forced himself to ignore his own exhaustion. The golden spike was just ahead. He felt it. Not more than a mile. A few yards. Within his reach.

"Wake up!" Clem reached over and shook him.

"Sorry, I was dozing."

"We're being followed."

This brought Charlie instantly awake. Not once had he thought that was possible. The tracks kept to the trail. He'd never spotted a place where the rider left the trail and circled to come up on them from behind. He told Clem this.

"Not him." Clem looked over his shoulder. "I don't see them now but there's at least three. Maybe four and they're trying not to be seen. With sunup in a few minutes, there's plenty of light to reveal them."

That wasn't good. A solitary rider might not want to risk showing himself to a pair of men riding along on mules. But three or four mounted on horses? They had nothing to fear. They outnumbered the men ahead of them, and if they weren't inclined to outshoot them, their horses easily outpaced a mule.

"What do you think we should do?"

"We can ambush them."

"Are you joshing me, Clem?" He saw his partner's grim expression. "We can't do that. We're not killers. And we're certainly not road agents willing to gun down anyone at the drop of a hat."

Clem's visage turned darker. Charlie wondered if he

needed to reconsider that. *He* wasn't a cold-blooded killer. The past week had been nothing but one surprise after another as Clem's true nature bubbled up. Clem might very well be a stone killer.

"No," he said firmly. He heeled the flanks of the mule and got it moving just a little faster. Not much, but some. That gave hope he'd outrun the men following them.

It only took a few minutes for him to catch sight of the four riders behind them. He and Clem worked their way up a steep slope toward the pass that led down to the road into Sacramento.

"Wait, Clem. Hear that?"

"A train. We're close to the mainline for the Central Pacific."

"They might be heading for the railroad. There's no reason to believe they have it in for us."

"We can hide and see if they ride on by. They'd do that if they intended to catch a train. Or even go right on into Sacramento."

Charlie felt a cold knot form in his stomach. As queasy as he got, he knew they had to try such a subterfuge. Outlegging the four men wasn't possible. Outshooting them wasn't, either.

"Head for the rocks over yonder," he said. "We'll have half a mountain at our back and be able to watch the trail."

Clem shifted his weight, convinced his mule to leave the easy trail and pick its way through a rocky field. Charlie followed, wary of those on their back trail. They reached a sandy pit with a wall of boulders all around. He dropped to the ground and immediately regretted it. Pressure on his legs sent new jabs of pain into his hips. Rubbing his rump, he got circulation back. Riding as long as he had took the starch out of him.

"You got too used to the easy life in San Francisco," Clem said.

"Easy? What do you mean by that? We were shot and almost shanghaied and beaten up. And the drunk parrot! What good's a drunk bird? You—"

Clem shushed him. He went to the crevice in the rock where they'd squeezed through just minutes earlier. From here, he had a narrow view of the trail below. The first rider crossed his line of sight. Then the second. He gasped out when he recognized the third rider.

"That's Roy Dupree!"

"Quiet," Clem said. "Wait."

Charlie forced himself to settle down. He squinted to get a better look at the trail. Dupree vanished from sight. He waited. Then he waited some more. His heart raced when the fourth rider never passed.

When he couldn't stand it any longer, he said in a low voice, "Are you sure there were four of them on our tail?"

"You saw them, too."

Charlie had a premonition. He ducked low and pulled out his smoke wagon. As he did a bullet scored the rock by his head. The bright silver streak was all he saw for a moment. His body responded long before his brain did. He dodged in the opposite direction, avoided a second round, whipped his gun around, and fired without a target in sight.

His bullet spanged! It slid along a weathered boulder and sang its deadly song away uphill. By now, Clem was firing, too.

"Where is he? I don't see him! Where is he?" Charlie sank to his knees and scoured the higher ground for any hint of their attacker. The fourth rider had left the party some distance back along on the trail and circled behind them.

How he had gotten above in such rough country didn't matter. He had. When a flash of light glinted off a pistol barrel high on the rock directly behind them, Charlie got off three more shots. He missed but drove their back shooter away. Working furiously, he reloaded. While they'd been on the trail, he rode with the hammer on an empty chamber. Now he wished he'd risked an accidental discharge. Another shot now meant the difference between life and death.

Clem covered for him, then let his partner reload. Any hint of motion from above caught his attention. The gunman had turned cautious and wasn't showing even a hat to draw their fire.

Then Charlie yelped. Six fast shots filled the rocky arena where they'd thought to hide from the gang. Bullets ricocheted around, forcing him to duck.

"The trail!" Clem's warning came just in time.

Charlie spun around on his knees and rested his six-shooter on a rock to steady it. The other three riders had returned and tried to make it up the path he and Clem had found so difficult on surefooted mules.

Dupree led the way, but his horses stumbled and slid back downhill a few feet, protesting loudly the whole way.

With a coldness he hadn't known was in him, Charlie aimed and fired. Roy Dupree screamed in pain, threw up his hands, and fell off his horse. The man rolled downhill until his cries stopped.

"You get him?"

"I don't know if I killed him, but I surely did ruin his day." Charlie hated the way he felt. Gunning down Dupree felt good. They were in a life-and-death shootout, and he defended himself. But knowing he had put a bullet into Roy Dupree felt right. It felt *good*.

"Can't see whoever's above us," Clem said. "I'm going after him."

"No, wait!" Charlie's warning came too late. His partner already slipped between two tightly spaced rocks and worked his way to the right of the arena where the two mules brayed and kicked up a fuss at such a commotion.

Charlie waited nervously. He had to be careful not to shoot Clem if he came back. But he also had to be alert for the back shooter still somewhere in the rocks above him. The tactic of firing so many rounds into the space by Charlie and hoping the ricochets would take him out had almost worked. He touched his arm. A sliver of lead had grazed him. Bright silver streaks on other rocks nearby showed how effective bouncing the slugs around had been. If his attacker had used a rifle with a full magazine, he'd be bleeding to death on the sandy floor.

Or he'd be dead with a bullet in him.

Charlie's finger drew halfway back on the trigger. He relaxed when Clem slid down the rock and landed heavily beside him.

"We've got to get out of here." Clem pointed. "That way."

"Where's it lead?"

"Away from the three men on the trail waiting for us to sashay on down into their gun sights."

"What happened to the sniper?" He pointed to the top of the boulder.

Clem shook his head. He grabbed his mule's reins and got the balky beast moving. Charlie wasn't going to stand around and argue. His mule was more amenable to getting out of the trap where they'd almost died.

He hoped they weren't going from the frying pan into the fire.

# CHAPTER 29

"We'll never outleg them. We're traveling through rocks and they have horses down on the trail."

"Do you want to give up? I don't." Charlie Dawson settled down on his mule and grimly plowed ahead. The sparse juniper trees provided less cover than the piles of rock that had tumbled down from higher on the mountain. But the trees hid Dupree and the rest of the gang.

He reluctantly admitted they also hid them from Dupree.

"We have to fight. They tried to ambush us. We can do that to them."

Charlie didn't see any way, but his partner was right. If they didn't reduce the odds against them somehow, they'd be goners. He drew his pistol and kept it aimed directly ahead. If he saw so much as an eyelash move, he'd fire.

"Here's our chance," Clem said when they rode into a clearing. The trail downhill was empty, but Charlie saw a few places where they could lie in ambush. He pointed them out to Clem at the same instant his partner identified the same places.

They stared at one another. Then they laughed. This wasn't any different from finishing each other's sentences.

"They'll come from between those trees. If we get on either side, we have them in a crossfire," Charlie said.

"Good idea, only we're out of time." Clem slipped out his six-gun, dropped to the ground, and then flopped belly down to take aim. He got off the first shot as one of the outlaws broke out of the forested area.

His shot took the man from the saddle, but Charlie saw him wiggle to cover after he landed hard on the ground. His horse reared and galloped away.

"You winged him, but you didn't kill him." Charlie spat dirt from his mouth and wiped his lips. "You didn't even put him out of action. He's got a rifle now."

A slug whined over them. Clem cursed a blue streak as he dashed for cover behind a fallen log. Charlie wanted to warn him the rotted log wouldn't provide much cover, but he figured that Clem knew that. If it hadn't occurred to him when he took cover, he knew it right away. The dozen lead hornets whining in his direction all penetrated the rotted wood.

"You all right?" Charlie bit his lip. He shouldn't give away his own position. Nor should Clem answer, even if he was still in one piece. Let the outlaws guess who they faced.

A few more rifle reports warned of a continued attack from the shelter of the forest. Charlie kept his head down in the gully where he had taken refuge. He held his fire, waiting for a decent target. It never came. The gang used their rifles to good effect. On his best day, Charlie's marksmanship wasn't up to hitting any of his enemies with a six-gun. The range was too great, and his skill had been dulled by long days chipping away at rock in the Betty Sue.

Worse, his hands shook from exhaustion and his wounded leg sapped his strength. He was in no condition to fight, but if he didn't, he'd die then and there. That put steel into his spine.

"They're on the move." Clem pointed to a spot on Charlie's right. Two of them tried to flank him.

When Roy Dupree showed his ugly face, Charlie fired. The outlaw grunted and grabbed his belly. A huge red spot already stained his shirt. He had been wounded earlier. Try as he might, though, Charlie wasn't able to put Dupree into his grave. The outlaw caved in and fell to the ground. The crown of his hat was barely visible, then it vanished as the man retreated.

Charlie remembered seeing a deep ravine about where Dupree disappeared. There wasn't anything he could do to head him off and prevent him from escaping into the woods. If only he had an inkling how badly wounded the outlaw was!

He took a few shots into the forested area. Lacking a target, all he hoped to do was keep them hiding. Eventually, they'd get antsy and charge. That'd be the best—the only—time to strike. Otherwise, the outlaws had them pinned down out in the open and without their mules.

Where the balky beasts had gone, he wasn't able to say. The gunfire might have spooked them, but the mules weren't as skittish as a horse. They also weren't dumb animals. On some level, they knew that standing in a field while outlaws shot at the men who had ridden them all night was dangerous.

"What are we going to do, Clem?"

"Damned if I know," came the answer.

He thought for a second, then said, "Keep on the move. Get around and find where they tethered their horses."

"You mean steal them?" Clem laughed harshly. "You're turning into a thief, Charlie. I'd never have believed you had it in you, not a single minute we worked the mine."

Charlie held back a surge of anger. It wasn't like that at all. This was a tactic to save their lives, not to steal horses for profit.

He let Clem get a decent lead, then started ahead on foot. His leg throbbed, but the pain was going away as his heart tried to run away with itself. He had barely gone fifty yards when a distant sound caused him to drop flat and wait. Through the trees, he saw a column of rising black smoke. His heart leaped into his throat.

Forest fire!

Then he calmed down and realized he spotted the billows of black smoke from a railroad engine working its way up the steep slope. The train curled back and forth on the steep grade. It was just beginning its ascent and would be near the gang's rendezvous point in several minutes.

He stayed on the ground and began crawling to get a better look at what they faced. From a small rise, he got a clear view of the outlaws clustered together and arguing.

Roy Dupree was covered in blood. More than one slug had punctured his worthless carcass. From the splotches on his shirt, he'd been hit in both the shoulder and the belly. Wounds like that would kill a man—eventually.

Charlie took careful aim. The range was too long for him to be sure of a killing shot, but if he came close, he'd give Dupree something more to worry about.

And if luck favored him with decent marksmanship, he'd eliminate one of them. For his money, maybe the worst of the gang.

"I wouldn't go doin' a thing like what you're contemplatin'."

His finger almost drew back on the trigger, in spite of the warning.

"I never thought our paths would cross again, Greta."

"I didn't get that gold spike like I wanted. You shoulda knowed I wasn't givin' up."

"You stole what gold coins I had."

"You got careless, Charles Dawson. That wasn't my fault. They just popped from your pocket into mine. It's like I have a magic touch when it comes to such things."

"As you bumped into me before you jumped from the engine cab."

Greta Swinburne laughed harshly.

"Welcome to the world of bein' a thief. Where's the spike? You ain't got it on you. I'd know."

"I don't have it."

"Where'd Clem stash it?"

"*We* don't have it. Somebody gunned down the mail clerk."

"Now ain't that a convenient story to spin? Who're you sayin' made off with it?"

His trigger finger turned slippery with sweat. He considered his chances of rolling over and firing. He'd get shot again. There wasn't any way Greta Swinburne didn't have her sights lined up on him.

"Don't go tensin' up, there, Charles," she said. "You doin' somethin' as dumb as tryin' to shoot me, and that'll be the last thing you ever do."

He jumped when she fired. The bullet tore up a piece of sod next to his head.

"I'm a real good shot. Clement mentioned that to you, I'd wager. I always outshot him."

"You'd lose. He never said a word about you."

Again came her raspy laughter. She kicked at him with her boot.

"Lose the smoke wagon. Then roll the other way onto your back."

He did as she ordered. The sunlight filtering through the tall trees shined in his face, blinding him. He shielded his eyes and saw that he'd been right. Greta had her six-gun pointed straight at him. The look on her face showed how close to losing her patience she was.

"The spike. I want it."

"You're not the only one. You should have been following whoever killed Laramie Reynolds. We were."

Greta stepped around so she had an even better view of the gun in his gnarled fingers.

"I think you're lyin'. Clement's got the spike. If he ever wants to see you alive, he'll fork it over."

"The way we figure, somebody who works for Thomas Collins killed Reynolds and took the spike. His son, Wash, maybe, or his right-hand man, Hickman, both are likely suspects. Wash is courting the daughter of the man who etched the spike. He might have told her, or her pa could have bragged on what a great job he did."

"You're accusin' David Hewes's daughter? Now I know you're joshin' me. You might as well accuse that drunk parrot in the bar where we had a drink. You're pickin' names out of the sky, Charles. That's tryin' my patience somethin' fierce." She stepped closer so he stared down the bore of her six-shooter. It looked like a railroad tunnel it was so big. "Where's the spike?"

A sudden commotion behind her caused Greta to whirl about and fire. Charlie kicked out with his good leg and caught the woman behind her knee. She tried to keep her balance. He kicked again. This time she toppled backward.

"Run," came Clem's unnecessary command.

Charlie snatched up his gun. He wasn't going to run. With his leg, he wasn't able to do more than stumble along. He intended to put a bullet in Greta Swinburne.

His shot went wide. She thrashed around on the ground and sprayed lead in all directions. Clem rode his mule past, cutting between his partner and his former wife. Charlie shouted for him to get out of the way. By the time Clem's mule moved far enough for a clear shot, Greta had hightailed it into the woods. She screamed for the rest of her gang every inch of the way.

"She shot my mule," Charlie said. He stared at the mule feebly kicking on the ground. Her bullet had gone smack into the mule's broad chest. From the blood and pink foam bubbling from the wound, she had punctured a lung.

"Get in back of me." Clem scooted forward on his mule.

Charlie hesitated, then went to his dying mule. A swift shot dispatched it from its pain. He looked around, wanting to do the same thing for Greta Swinburne. She had disappeared, but the sound of Dupree and his cronies charging up the hill kept him from going after her. He awkwardly climbed behind Clem.

"What now?"

Clem bent low and got his mule trotting along at a decent gait. Bullets filled the air all around them, but none came close enough for Charlie to bother ducking. He got off a shot, but it went wide. Swine's gang never noticed.

Rather than keeping on the course away from the outlaws, Clem veered back downhill. The trio shouted at each other. Then a fourth voice added to the confusion. Greta emerged from the trees and fired at them. Her rounds went high.

"What're you doing?" Charlie demanded.

"You wanted to spook their horses. Here's our chance." Clem rode straight for the spot where the outlaws had been arguing a few seconds earlier. Their horses weren't securely tied. One jerked free and raced off as Clem trotted past.

Charlie hit the ground and stumbled along. He fell to one knee. With a wild grab, he snared all the remaining horses' reins and yanked them free. He got to his feet and tried to mount. The horse bucked. He worked to the side to grab the pommel. The horse spun away. For an instant, his fingers slid under the skirt. Then the horse kicked out and sent him spinning.

"Get the horse, Charlie! It's your only chance!" Clem had stopped ten feet away.

There wasn't any way the mule could ever overtake the outlaws' galloping horses. The gunfire turned more accurate. He jumped as a slug grazed his boot and caused him to stumble again.

Greta screamed. Dupree shouted orders. The other two in the gang ran hard to get within range. They all fired as they ran. One of them would get lucky if the two miners didn't clear out fast.

Clem rode back and pulled his partner up. The mule had been amenable to carrying their combined weight before. Not now. It balked. Clem flew over the mule's head and landed hard on the ground. Charlie tried to grab the reins and missed by inches. When the mule jerked its head around and snapped at him, he tumbled to the ground, too.

"Run," Charlie said.

"We'll never outrun them. Not with your gimpy leg. We fight."

"We *run!*" Charlie shoved Clem hard.

He saw the billows of smoke from the train straining on the uphill grade. They fired over their shoulders as they ran. They came to an embankment that ended at the railroad tracks a dozen feet below. Without even thinking what they did, both men jumped and landed on the seats of their britches. They rattled and clanked and slid down the steep slope. When they hit the cinders on the railroad bed, they jerked to their feet.

Greta and the other three had reached the top of the slope. They hesitated, arguing about the risky fall down the embankment.

Charlie got off the last round in his six-shooter. That brought a curse to Roy Dupree's lips. Charlie doubted he had hit the owlhoot. It wasn't necessary. It sowed confusion and started a new argument between Greta and Dupree.

"The train," Charlie panted. "Jump on board."

He and Clem crossed the tracks before Greta got off another shot. Then it was too late for her. The engine puffed past, along with three passenger cars. The freight cars behind gave Charlie and Clem the break they needed. One freight car door had slid open.

They ran a few steps alongside the straining train, grabbed, and pulled themselves into the car where they lay on their backs, panting harshly.

"Where's the train going? To or from Sacramento?" Clem asked.

Charlie didn't know. Right about then, he didn't care. They had barely escaped by the skin of their teeth.

# CHAPTER 30

"We should have jumped off at Sacramento." Clem sat with his legs dangling out the freight car door. The countryside flashed past.

"We've been arguing over this for the last hour." Charlie was fed up with his partner. "The only people likely to have the spike are in San Francisco. If they're not, we'll never find it. And if someone else killed Reynolds and took the spike, the only place where he can get money for it is in the city."

"That's Collins or someone at the railroad," Clem said. "It's a fool's errand. We're too late."

Charlie gritted his teeth. After all he'd been through, he was not giving up. More than that, like Thomas Collins or not, the banker had paid good money for him and Clem to find the spike. Charlie Dawson never went back on his promise. Even if he'd foolishly lost the money already given them.

And Collins had tried to kill them after they'd turned over the steel spike to him.

He touched the pocket where the four folded single dollar bills crinkled as he pressed down. Greta Swinburne had stolen money they'd earned all fair and square. They'd risked their lives to rescue Wash Collins from the shanghaiers. Getting it back looked like a good way to buy a one-way ticket to the cemetery. Whether he owed his partner or not was another matter they had to thrash out. It was his former wife who had stolen the gold coins.

Charlie tried not to blame Clem for what Greta had done, but he found it hard.

"If we find the spike, we'll know who killed Laramie Reynolds."

"So? You reckon there's a reward on the killer's head?"

"We're working for Lily Denton, too. She deserves to know who killed her man."

"That's going to be a mighty expensive four dollars for us. Already is, the way we're going back to San Francisco and not even stopping at Bonaventure."

Charlie nodded. He was more inclined to find Reynolds's killer for the schoolmarm than do anything to save the bank president from embarrassment. A small smile crept to his lips. Small? From the sound of it, Collins might end up in jail if the news hounds were unleashed.

"He'll have plenty of company," Charlie said.

Clem looked at him and frowned. Then he pointed. They neared the Central Pacific terminal in Oakland. He held up five fingers. Four. Then the rest dropped one by one. Clem jumped off when his fingers tightened into a fist, hit the ground, and rolled alongside the still rapidly moving train.

The jump wasn't easy at the best of times. Charlie closed his eyes and shoved himself out of the freight car anticipating what lay ahead for him. He crashed into the ground. The shock tore at his senses. Pain flooded his entire leg and then he lay still, staring up at the sky. Storm clouds moved in. He thought lightning danced behind the darkest of the clouds. Then Clem shook him.

"The two in the caboose saw us. They'll tell the railroad bulls. I'm not in a mood to shoot it out."

"Help me up." Charlie winced as Clem pulled him to his feet. He took a few tentative steps, then trotted away. It hurt as badly if he ran as if he walked. Better to get away from the tracks as soon as possible if it hurt no matter what he did.

They made their way through the maze of tracks and switches and finally reached the main road running past the Oakland Long Wharf. It took another hour for the ferry to dock and almost that to cross the Bay to the Embarcadero. Only when his feet touched solid ground did Charlie feel safer. Cutthroats and pickpockets abounded along the docks. Roving gangs shanghaied the unwary. But the railroad bulls were on the other side of the choppy Bay. They hunted for him and Clem in particular. The Sydney Ducks and the Tongs and the shanghaiers hunted for victims in general.

If he had his Colt close at hand, Charlie felt confident he walked along safe enough in San Francisco.

"I can use a drink. You've still got the four greenbacks, don't you?"

"Greta didn't have a chance to steal them," he said acidly. "But as thirsty as I am, time is against us. We should go to the bank and see if we can find Wash Collins or Hickman."

"Then what?"

"We follow them to see if they're acting suspicious," Charlie said. He shook his head. It felt as if bolts had come loose inside. He held his temples until the throbbing died down. "Wait. Not that. That won't do because it'll chew up time we need. We grab the first one we see and force him to talk."

"So if we nab one and he won't talk, that means it's the other one we want?"

Clem spat and then started down Montgomery Street, walking at a pace meant to force Charlie to always trail behind. Charlie had a hard time keeping up. He knew his partner was angry. He just wasn't saying as much. The more he thought about Clem being mad, the angrier he got. They had a job to do. Acting this way didn't serve either of them well.

"There's the bank," Clem said, stopping so suddenly Charlie plowed into him. It was like hitting the side of a mountain. "Now what? We can wait a long time. What if they use a different exit?"

"I'm not going to ask to see Thomas Collins again, not until we retrieve the real spike."

"He's a sidewinder," Clem said with acid tinging his words. "We need to think of other folks willing to pay for the spike."

"If we're smart about it, Collins won't dare to double-cross us if it means not getting the spike out to Utah in time for the ceremony."

"What's the plan? Hickman doesn't seem the type

who'd come and go through the front door. He'd want a private door."

"There are several doors all around," Charlie said, thinking hard. Clem had a point. They couldn't watch all the exits. "What was the name of the engraver?"

"I don't know."

"Greta mentioned it. The father of the girl Wash Collins is sweet on."

Clem stared off down the street. "I never listened much to Greta when we were married. And now?" He shook his head.

"David Hewes." Charlie felt a tiny glow of satisfaction that he had remembered. "That's where we start."

It took a half hour to find someone able to direct them to the engraver's store. Charlie worried no one would be in the store since it was so late in the day, but the light burned in the shop and a man wearing a jeweler's loupe worked in the front window for passersby to watch.

Charlie boldly went up and stared at the man. David Hewes had a receding hairline. A bushy mustache seemed out of place for a jeweler, but he worked around it as he thrust his face down to get close to his project. Nimble fingers pressed gears together and careful use of a tiny screwdriver connected everything in the watch. Hewes twisted the stem once, then held it up. The second hand marched around.

Pleased with his handiwork, he displayed it for Charlie.

"Do we beat it out of him?" Clem asked.

"Whoever stole the spike isn't likely to have told the

man who created it. Even if it's his own son." Clem stepped back. Hewes turned away when a young woman came from the rear of the store, putting on a floppy-brimmed hat festooned with fake flowers. She chattered away at the jeweler. He never showed any sign of hearing her as he carefully laid the repaired watch on a velvet pad until she reached the front door and opened it.

Charlie overheard, "Don't you go chasing after him now. He's no good for you, dear."

"Oh, Papa." She adjusted her hat to a jaunty angle, stepped out, and closed the door just a little too hard. Charlie saw that she was peeved. But at her pa? Or the man her pa declared was "no good"?

"Miss Hewes? A moment, please?" Charlie tried to sound official without scaring her off.

She reached into her clutch handbag as she faced him. He didn't doubt that she gripped a small gun. Her eyes darted back toward her father working diligently on a new job, a mantel clock.

"I don't want your pa to overhear this."

She half drew the pistol. She made sure he saw what she held to deter him.

"It's about Wash. My partner and I are looking for him. It's real important that we find him in a hurry."

"I don't know where he is."

"If you have any idea where he, uh, where he chooses to imbibe, we can look for him there."

"What's your business with Mister Collins?"

"Wash and us, me and my partner, are friends. Business friends, that is."

"We saved him from a long trip to China," Clem said.

"When he was shanghaied? You rescued him?"

"Yes, ma'am, we did. It's important we talk with him. And it's not got anything to do with his pa, either."

"Such a vexing man," she said. She dropped her pistol back into her purse.

"That's one way to describe him," Charlie said. "He hired us to rescue Wash, but we were never too high in his estimation, even after Wash was all safe and sound."

"I don't know where he is," the woman said. "I'm worried about him, even if *he* isn't." She turned and stared at her father.

"Is there any place he might go?"

She looked as if she'd bitten into a lemon.

"All those places aren't fit for a lady."

"Ma'am, in case you didn't notice, me and my partner aren't ladies. We don't mind going where Wash is likely to be." Charlie tried to smile as winningly as possible. He knew he looked like he'd crawled out from a grave. His pant leg was caked with dried blood, there was hardly a square foot of clothing that wasn't torn or dirty, and he had a gaunt look that hinted at starvation. Clem was hardly in better condition, only the blood soaked into his clothing wasn't his.

"You rescued him before?" She sounded as if this was hardly possible.

Charlie nodded. He didn't trust himself to say the right thing. His own pa had always said it was better to keep your mouth shut and let them think you were a fool than to speak and remove all doubt.

"I cannot pay what Mister Collins did." She fumbled in her purse. Charlie tensed, expecting her to come out with the gun in her small hand. Instead, she held two silver dollars. "This is all I can spare." She grinned weakly. "Truth be told, it's all I have." She held it out.

"You're hiring us to find Wash? Again?"

"And extricate him from whatever mess he's gotten himself into. I worry that he's gone back on his promise not to imbibe Demon Rum."

"He did that? I mean, he promised to give up drink?"

She nodded sadly. Then she said, "There's one bar of poor reputation along the Barbary Coast he has taken a fancy to. Or so I am led to believe. It's called the Bilge Bucket or something truly awful like that."

"I know the place," Clem said. "It makes the Cobweb Palace look like . . . a palace."

Charlie fingered the two silver dollars. He still had three dollars left from Lily Denton's stake. If he found enough lovelorn women hunting for their beaus, he could make quite a living off this. Six dollars was more than he took from the Betty Sue in a poor week.

It was close to what he took from the mine in a good week.

"We'll do our best, ma'am."

"When you do find him . . ." she said. Her resolve hardened. "Throw him in the Bay until he sobers up. Then . . ."

"Then bring him to you?"

"Either that or let him drown. Oh!" She stamped her foot, took Charlie's hand, and shook hard. Then she hurried off without so much as a backward look at them.

Charlie saw they'd drawn her father's attention. The man laid aside his jeweler's loupe and reached under the counter. If he'd pulled out what he sought there, little doubt that it'd be a six-shooter existed in Charlie's mind. He grabbed Clem by the arm and steered him away in the direction opposite from that taken by Miss Hewes.

"Let's find the Bilge Bucket. That sounds like a good place for the drink you were hankering to swill."

"Maybe not. Customers disappear through trapdoors in the floor faster than about any other bar along the Coast."

"One drink, no knockout drops, and we'll watch each other." Charlie hitched up his pants and settled the Walker Colt in his waistband. "And we'll both keep an eye peeled for Jerome Washington Collins. He's got to tell us where that spike is."

"Always hoping, that's you, Charlie. Always hoping." Clem set off at his brisk pace that was difficult to match.

# CHAPTER 31

"This is the kind of place where you could catch your death," Charlie Dawson said.

"Of cold?"

"No, just catch your death." He pointed out the three men lurking just inside the saloon door. They stood quietly. Most of the patrons were drunk. Not this trio. Their sharp eyes missed nothing. If anything, their eyes were too sharp and almost glowing.

"They've been chasing the dragon," Clem said.

"What do you mean?"

"Opium smokers. It makes them aggressive when it starts wearing off after an hour or two."

"You surely do know a lot about such things," Charlie said. He wondered if Clem only invented the experiences or if he actually had lived them. The past two years hadn't given any hint of what sounded like a wild and woolly life before the Betty Sue. Opium and Greta Swinburne? Robberies and killings and who knew what other crimes?

"They're not getting what little money we have."

"They're hunting for other game," Clem said. "We're

not rich enough, but they might just enjoy killing. The opium makes them bold and cruel." He shuffled around, hand resting on his Army Colt in its holster. "Then again, someone might have hired them to look for the same person we are."

"Why do you say that?"

Then Charlie saw what his partner already had. The trio stared at the street behind him. Wobbling along uncertainly came Wash Collins. He'd take a step, regain his balance, then let loose with a snippet of a song. He sang so poorly Charlie had no idea what song the man tried to warble.

The three inside the Bilge Bucket stepped out. Charlie thrust out his leg as the first of the men passed him. The impact jolted his leg all the way up into his hip and half spun him around. But the move accomplished what he'd hoped. The man crashed to the ground. From his lack of coordination trying to stand, he had been taking some illicit substance that ruined his attack.

Again, Clem's knowledge of such things proved true.

The other two ignored their fallen compatriot. Clem took care of them by walking between them, then shoving out his arms at shoulder level. He caught both of them across the neck. They gagged and tried to turn away. A quick hammer blow on the top of one man's head drove him to the ground. Clem took out the other with a punch to the throat.

"Let's get Wash and clear out," Charlie said.

He'd barely taken a step when a heavy hand landed on his shoulder. With a quick turn, he struck the man trying to stop him by driving the palm of his hand into the man's face. He felt the bulbous nose crush. Blood spurted everywhere. The anguished cry of anger and pain came an instant later.

"Get him, get him," the injured man shouted.

Charlie caught the glint of light off the man's badge. He stepped back, but the man rushed him. Without any thought, he thrust out his leg again. Once more the tactic worked. This time the policeman fell heavily to the ground. Charlie saw an immediate difference. Three other officers from down the street came rushing to their fallen comrade's aid.

With his injured leg, Charlie wasn't up to outrunning the specials. They caught him right away. He fought and then regretted it. They used saps and nightsticks to beat him to the ground. He knelt, arms curled over his head to keep his skull from being broken by their blows.

"Let him be!"

Clem lit into the three men. His fists bounced off them as if they wore armor. They were used to brawling and taking worse punishment than either of the miners could mete out. Worse, they felt no pain because of the opium in their bodies.

The last thing Charlie saw before a nightstick clobbered him was Wash Collins staring at him. He rubbed his eyes, then bent forward, as if the extra inch or two closer gave him a better look.

"Lock them in the paddy wagon," one policeman wearing a sergeant stripe said. He took a sadistic glee in hammering away at Charlie. "Show 'em they can't break a special's nose."

"If the nose is busted, it'll improve O'Niel's look,"

one cop said. "He always was an ugly spud. Now he'll have a nose to match his nickname!"

This brought a round of laughter to the cops. Charlie relished the momentary cessation of blows landing on him. When the cops finished laughing at their partner, they laid into him again until he groaned. Somehow they knew how to hammer away at him so he never passed out. They wanted him to appreciate how severely they punished him.

Two of them dragged him away. His toes cut into the ground as they pulled him along. Behind him came Clem being given the same treatment. Their captors dropped them face down on the ground and unlocked the door of an armored carriage.

Like sacks of potatoes, they were heaved into the back of the carriage. Shackles were applied to their ankles, then the door was slammed.

"We got six more to arrest if we want to keep the lieutenant happy."

"You think the two in the wagon have enough money to pay a big fine? They look well-heeled. We can get by with only a couple others and make our quota."

The four went off arguing about how big a fine their two prisoners could pay.

Clem pulled Charlie up to the hard bench seat beside him. He bent over and rattled the chains.

"Not a speck of rust on those manacles," he said. "The locks are as heavy as any I've ever seen." The chains rang to a sturdy ring bolted to the carriage floor.

"So we're not going anywhere," Charlie said. He ached all over from the beating. Bruises were turning his skin splotchy. His muscles hadn't started to scream in agony. Yet.

Clem fought against their chains. He grabbed with both hands, braced his feet, and yanked as hard as he could. The bolts holding the chains to the floor never budged. He gave up when he began to pant from exhaustion.

"We're gonna die if they take us to the police station."

"All I've got is five dollars. Even if they sell our guns, that's not enough to bribe this bunch."

"Corrupt," Clem muttered. He added other descriptions about their ancestors. Charlie agreed but no amount of cussing freed them.

He leaned back and closed his eyes. A throbbing in his head warned he had taken more than one blow to the skull. When he opened his eyes, he knew he was seeing a mirage. A face floated on the other side of the barred window at the back of the prison wagon.

"You want out?"

"Wash?" Charlie grabbed the bars and shook until the carriage rocked on its wheels. "Get us out of here. They're gonna kill us!"

"Why'd you let them varmints stick you in there?"

If Wash Collins hadn't been drunker than a skunk, Charlie would have launched into a tirade that'd put Clem's to shame.

"We wanted to buy you a drink," he said.

"You do?" He brightened. "Gotta get you out if you're bein' my . . . my . . ."

"Friends," Clem spoke up. "We're your friends."

"Got me off that rotten ship. Friends. No, more 'n

that. You're my guardian angels. That's it. Angels." He held up a key ring. "I was gonna return these to the coppers. One of 'em dropped it."

Charlie slid his hand through the bars and caught the ring weighed down with a dozen keys.

"You go on and g-get yourselves out. I'll be in there takin' care of my th-thirst." Wash turned to point, lost his balance, and staggered away, mumbling to himself about being lost in a bone-dry desert.

Charlie tossed the keys to Clem. His partner cursed constantly as he tried one key after another. Their leg irons refused to open.

"It's the wrong set of keys," Charlie said in panic.

"Got it!"

Charlie hated himself for having so little faith. The last key opened their shackles. He searched the door for a keyhole.

"It's barred on the outside and there's a padlock we can't reach," Clem said. "I saw that when they locked us up." He slammed his fist against the sides to no avail and then turned to the front of the enclosure.

With a bull roar, he slammed his fist into the partition between the prisoners and the driver. He went berserk when his fist tore a big hole. When he had a big enough opening, he grabbed the edges and pulled with all his might. The entire panel came loose and then fell down at their feet.

They were free!

Charlie followed Clem to the driver's seat. For an instant, he considered taking the reins and galloping off. Stealing the specials' paddy wagon would show them.

Then he remembered why they'd come to this section of the Barbary Coast.

"I saw him go into the saloon," Charlie said.

Clem held the reins. He had thought the same thing about stealing the wagon and its team.

"Damn," was all Clem said. He crowded Charlie along until they both stood beside the paddy wagon.

"They're coming back." Charlie's hand went to his waistband. No six-gun. He looked around for a place to run. There wasn't any way to sneak away without the policemen seeing them.

"Here." Clem fished around in the foot well of the wagon. He found their six-shooters. A quick toss and the Walker rested in Charlie's shaky hand.

His muscles began to rebel after all the beating he'd taken. Using both hands to steady his six-gun, he waited for the coppers to round the wagon. He'd hang for it, as sure as the sun came up every morning, but it'd be worth getting revenge on the brutal specials.

"Don't," Clem cautioned. He pushed his partner to the side of the street where they were still hidden from the approaching police officers by the wagon. With a quick swat, he got the team pulling hard. He delivered another smack to the nearest horse's rump and this set them off at a frightened gallop.

Charlie didn't have to be told what to do. He stepped away, turned, and bent almost double. Clem pressed close beside him. The specials let out a cry of anger and ran after the wagon. They never saw two more derelicts standing in the shadows. For all they knew, their prisoners were safely shackled inside the paddy wagon.

As they rushed past, the officers slowed. Catching the runaway wagon wasn't possible. Charlie edged away, then straightened and walked the best he could. Even knowing his life depended on it, he wasn't able to move very fast. Clem crowded him from behind and tried to hurry him. All he could do was lurch along and try not to cry out in torment.

They went a few yards along a pier before he wasn't able to take another step.

"I'll hold them off. They won't chase you if—"

He let out a cry as Clem picked him up and heaved. Charlie flew through the air. With a loud splash, he landed in the freezing cold waters of San Francisco Bay. Thrashing about, he finally righted himself and dog-paddled toward the pier supports. Before he could make his way to a ladder a few yards distant, he heard the policemen charging out onto the wood planking.

"They've got to be here somewhere."

"Don't see nobody, Sarge."

"You're not lookin'. Look, damn your eyes! And keep lookin' 'til you find them. The lieutenant don't like it if we let drunks get away."

Charlie twisted around. He saw a head wearing a policeman's helmet poke over the edge of the pier just above him. The officer didn't look down. He looked out across the Bay.

"There ain't no trace of anybody, Sarge. There is a shark's fin a hundred feet away."

This panicked Charlie. He came halfway up out of the water and clung to the rough pier piling. From his vantage, he saw the shadow of the shark's fin cast across the water. The moon was at the precise angle where the fin looked like it was ten feet tall. The shark silently swam to and fro, then the fin vanished.

Charlie closed his eyes and clamped his legs together, sure he'd feel powerful jaws and ripping teeth tear off his legs at any instant. He'd heard stories about the vicious ocean predators. When he began shivering from the cold water, he slid down the piling a foot. Two. Then only his head bobbed above the choppy waves.

He clung to the wood support for what seemed like hours. A glance back across the Bay to see where the shark had gone showed him the moon had only crept a little higher in the sky. He'd been immersed for less than fifteen minutes. But he knew what eternity felt like.

He never wanted an eternity filled with sharks and killer coppers again.

"You drown yourself yet?"

He paddled out a few feet. Clem stood on the pier at the head of the ladder he had tried to reach.

"F-freezing," he said, his teeth chattering.

"You'll have to climb up on your own. I'm not coming down there to fish you out."

"W-wouldn't w-want you to m-melt." Charlie pulled himself up a few rungs on the ladder, then rested to regain his strength. "What happened to the coppers?"

"They moved on. If they don't bring in enough criminals, their captain gets all fussy."

Charlie didn't ask how his partner knew that. Clem had a remarkable past to draw on—a remarkable past he never mentioned for two years.

Working his way up the slime-slippery ladder,

Charlie finally flopped onto the pier. Water poured off him and ran back into the Bay through the cracks between the planking. He sat up and wrung out more water. He shuddered as he worked until he was only damp, not soaked. Standing, he moved around. He noticed something surprising.

"The dip in the cold water's taken away all my aches and pains." He tried to look at his arms to see if the bruises were there. In the dim light of the moon, he wasn't able to tell.

"Don't matter if you see bruises as long as you move easy. Try going for that six-gun," Clem urged.

Charlie did. His gun came into a steady hand. Firing the pistol after being dunked in the Bay wasn't a good idea, but he felt better than he had since he'd had a chunk of his calf shot off. He took a few tentative steps. Even that injury faded away.

He shivered as a light breeze slipped across the Bay. He worried his aches and pains were destined to return when the cold no longer numbed him. For now, he was willing to put up with feeling as if he was better suited to mining in the Yukon, midwinter, without a parka.

"Let's find Wash," he said. "He was so drunk, he's probably passed out by now. Let's hope he doesn't get himself shanghaied again."

They trooped off the pier and cautiously returned to the Bilge Bucket. The three-man welcoming committee was gone. They had either moved to greener pastures or they had joined the other coppers from the paddy wagon. Charlie stepped into the smoke-filled room and looked around.

"I don't see him."

"Neither do I," Clem said. He pushed through the closely spaced tables, grabbing one man by the nape of the neck and lifting his face. He let him fall back.

Charlie tried not to tell his partner what to do, but he worried they were drawing unwanted attention as they crossed the room.

"Not him." Clem shook another unconscious man. With a careless gesture, he slammed the man's forehead so loudly on the table that it brought the barkeep over. He carried a slungshot in his hand hidden under his leather apron.

"You can't go robbin' my customers. We got a reputation."

"We're looking for a friend. Wash. Wash Collins." Charlie saw the distaste cross the bartender's face.

"Ain't here. He was earlier."

"When did he leave?" Charlie doubted Wash could be too far ahead of them, not in the condition he was in when he entered the Bilge Bucket Drinking Emporium.

"They left ten, fifteen minutes ago." The barkeep turned to go back to work.

Charlie grabbed his brawny arm and spun him around. He drew his six-shooter and held it between them to keep the barkeep from using his slungshot on his exposed head. The sight of the gun aimed at his belly slowed the bartender down. He stepped back.

"You said 'they' left. Who was with him?"

The barkeep spat toward a cuspidor. He missed by a foot. Most earlier tries had missed, too, from the gooey stains on the side of the bar.

"Him and a whore. That's all I know."

Charlie and Clem stared at each other. Wash Collins had been in their grasp and had slithered away to who knew where.

# CHAPTER 32

"We might as well give up," Clem said. "A whore? There are as many along the Barbary Coast as there are sailors. More."

Charlie stared across the room. His eyes burned from the smoke and his mouth turned to cotton. He needed a drink. His partner was right. Wash Collins had walked off into the night with a Cyprian. Finding who that was presented a mountainous problem.

"I need a drink," he said. Clem protested but followed.

"Barkeep," he called. "What'd she look like?"

"Who? Oh, the one who hooked your pal?" He shrugged. "What do any of them look like?"

"Rough-looking, sure," Charlie said, "but she wasn't all gussied up, was she?"

"Wore trousers. Thought at first she was a man, but her voice?" He shook his head. "Screechy like a hooty owl. All deep and gravelly like she'd been smokin' 'nd on a drinkin' binge."

"Her name's Greta, isn't it?" Charlie felt Clem tense beside him. He ignored his partner and stared at the barkeep. The man wasn't spinning a tall tale. What he described was what he'd seen.

"Yeah, heard him say somethin' like that. He musta knowed her. Or maybe she told him what her name was. It's not my place to interfere in a working girl's job."

"How much did she pay you?" Charlie saw this hit home. The bartender involuntarily reached for a pocket in his pants.

"Don't know what you mean."

"She wasn't one of the usual flock of soiled doves that flutter through here. She was a greenhorn."

"There wasn't nothin' green 'bout that one. She swore like a swabbie and looked like she'd been rode hard and put away wet. She carried an iron in her holster like she knew how to use it. Nope, nuthin' green about that one." He eyed a still-damp Charlie. He refrained from making any further comment.

"Did you rent her a crib? Just for the night?"

"I ain't in that kinda busi—"

He gasped for air when Clem reached across the bar and grabbed his throat. A squeeze and a lift got the man onto his toes. His face turned redder as the tendons on Clem's forearm increasingly stood out.

"You won't need to worry about breathing any more in a second or two." Charlie waited. Clem released the barkeep just enough for him to gag. Then the powerful fingers clamped around the man's greasy throat again.

Charlie drew his six-gun and smashed it down on the barkeep's wrist when he tried to use the slungshot he carried under the leather apron.

"I bet he can't last another minute, Clem."

"Less. Ten cents says he's a goner in fifteen seconds."

"Ten cents?" Charlie shook his head. "Are you giving me odds?"

The barkeep gurgled and tried to speak. When his tongue protruded and began to turn purple, Clem let up. Just a little.

"A street over. Above Zhang Yi's store. I only rented the room to her for an hour."

"If we want to join the party, we've got to hurry." Charlie tapped Clem on the wrist holding the barkeep's throat. "We've got to hurry *now*."

"You're always spoiling my fun."

The bartender collapsed to the sawdust-covered floor, gasping for air.

"We'll be back if we can't find the place," Clem said in a flat tone that was scarier than if he'd barked it out at the top of his lungs.

"A street over," Charlie said, stepping into the chill night. The cold wind off the Bay renewed his strength. He hoped he didn't have to move here to enjoy being pain-free. The rough and tumble section of San Francisco wasn't for him. He preferred being in the Betty Sue Mine, chiseling away rock in the hope of finding pay dirt.

Tamping a bottle of nitro into a blast hole was safer than walking these streets.

"That's the place." Clem started to go into the store. Charlie held him back.

"We don't want to walk into a trap. There's likely a guard to keep out the riffraff."

"That's us," Clem said. "Riffraff." He made it sound like a badge of honor.

"Back me up," Charlie said. He tucked his six-gun into his waistband, then lifted his chin and walked confidently to a flight of stairs leading to rooms above the store. As he climbed the steep stairs, a dark figure loomed above. He kept climbing until he was a couple steps lower. "This where Greta brings her special gentlemen?"

"Don't know nobody name of Greta. Go on, boy. Run along. Find yourself some other place."

Charlie put one foot on the step just under the landing and shifted his weight.

"Can you tell me where I can find another Cyprian, if not here?"

The man growled and reached to grab Charlie. He caught a hairy wrist and tugged. Just a little. The man stepped forward, his foot landed on the same step that Charlie had already claimed. He hooked his foot behind the guard's heel and swept out. Charlie moved fast to get out of the man's disastrous tumble down the steps. At the bottom, he groaned, rubbed his head—then went out like a light when Clem slugged him.

Charlie didn't wait for his partner to join him. The commotion would have alerted a wary woman like Greta Swinburne. He threw open the first door. An empty room. The second door brought aggrieved cries from a half-naked pair stretched out and entwined on a narrow bed. He closed the door and went to the third door. Hand on the knob, he turned slowly and then opened the door with a rush.

Unoiled hinges screeched and the brass knob came off in his hand. He dropped it and went for his six-shooter. There was no call to.

Washington Collins sprawled on the bed, staring up at the ceiling with its peeling paint and water stains.

"Is he dead?" Clem looked over Charlie's shoulder.

"Who's dead? Not me," whispered Wash. He kicked feebly, trying to sit up. He didn't succeed. Charlie put his arm around the man's shoulders and lifted him upright.

"Are you hurt?"

"Mortally hurt. Com-completely d-devastated." His words slurred. "She brought me here and th-then l-left me."

"Greta Swinburne?"

Wash turned bloodshot eyes toward Charlie. There was no sign of recognition there.

"What'd she want from you?"

"I told her 'bout the spike Mister Hewes made." He tried to show its length and toppled to his side. Charlie righted him again. "I told her all about what it looked like. Not that I ever saw it. Just heard. Dinah tole me all 'bout it. She even helped her father."

"Dinah?"

"My betrothed. Or will be. Gotta ask her. If I remember."

"She hired us to find you."

Wash Collins's eyes focused. He licked his lips and for a moment appeared sober.

"She *hired* you. To *find* me?"

"We'd done it before. She figured we'd be the ones to do it again."

"I'm so humiliated." Wash began tearing up. He rubbed his nose on his sleeve. "Don't 'serve her. Deserve her. Don't."

Charlie shook him until his teeth rattled.

"We found you. We'll get you sobered up for her so you won't disgrace yourself."

"Too much," Clem muttered.

Charlie glared at his partner. He hoisted Wash to his feet and forced him to take a step or two. The drunken stupor faded just enough for Wash to stand on his own without support.

"We'll help you, but you have to help us. Greta. What did you tell her?"

"The lovely lady who helped me up the stairs?" Wash waved his hand around and almost keeled over. He caught himself on the bed. Clem would have let him crash to the floor.

"Her name's Greta Swinburne. She wants the gold spike."

"So many do. It'll be their death if they don't get it. Questions will be asked," he said sternly. He tried to poke his finger into Charlie's chest. "Too many of them promised too much. Now they can't deliver."

"We know all that. The newspaper reporters will start digging if they catch so much as a whiff of scandal. Not having the spike will set off that scandal."

"Why can't Collins and Stanford and the others back East just paint a spike gold and claim that's what they intended?" Clem sat on the bed and pushed Wash away.

"Because, good sir," Wash said, spinning around and striking an orator's pose, "my dearly beloved's father has released a complete description of the golden spike to the *Alta California*. Big scoop for them. Picked up everywhere. Even in New York and Washington."

"So the cat's out of the bag," Charlie said. "What did you tell Greta? About the spike?"

"Where is it?" Clem cut in. "Tell us!"

"Don't rightly know. Told the lovely lady that, too." Wash rubbed his eyes to clear them. "Wasn't too lovely, was she? Kinda ugly, but she listened to me."

Clem shot to his feet. His hands balled into fists at the insult Wash had laid on his former wife. Charlie moved between the two to keep his partner from ruining any chance they had of finding Greta from something Wash Collins might tell them.

"You haven't given the spike to your pa?"

"Charlie Dawson, my good friend, how can I when I don't know where it is? Might not, even if I had it. My father's not a good man. The things I know. He's a real scoundrel. Not like me. I'm a drunk."

"You haven't tried ransoming it to the Central Pacific, either?" Clem pushed past Charlie and planted himself squarely in front of Wash.

Wash looked up at him and put his palm against Clem's chest. "You are one huge fellow, aren't you? Tall. Strong. Wish I was. I'm nothing but a coward. How can I ever be the man Dinah deserves?" He sniffled, then began to cry.

Clem threw up his hands in disgust and turned away.

"He hasn't tried selling it back to either his pa or the

railroad owners. Since Greta was asking him where the spike was, she doesn't have it, either."

"We're running out of people who might have it," Clem said.

"Whoever killed Laramie Reynolds must have it. Greta's gang hunted for it. They don't have it. We don't. He claims he doesn't know." Charlie stared at Wash. The man sobbed uncontrollably.

"That leaves Hiram Hickman."

"Hiram?" Wash perked up. "He's my father's right-hand man. A low-life, scum-sucking yellowbelly, but he's good at his job."

"Not too good, unless he's given it back to his boss."

Charlie and Clem looked at each other. Greta hunted for it. They did, too. And Thomas Collins was still in a panic the last they saw of him.

Hiram Hickman double-crossed his employer. If they wanted to get the spike back into the hands of the rightful owner, and claim the rest of their money, they had to track him down and pry the spike from his greasy hands.

"Come on, Wash. We'll clean you up and get you back to Dinah."

Charlie helped the drunk down the stairs. Clem would have pushed him down.

# CHAPTER 33

"No, stop, can't t-take any more of this torture!" J. Washington Collins thrashed about. He struck Charlie on the cheek with a fist. The punch mustered all the force of a newborn kitten. Without its claws.

Charlie put both hands on the man's shoulders and pushed down hard. Wash gurgled and blew bubbles as his head disappeared underwater. Again San Francisco Bay proved to have healing qualities. The man sobered up fast as the cold water ran into his mouth and nose.

"Keep him under. He's not good for anything but feeding the fish." Clem sat on a piling, arms crossed, looking bored.

While letting the banker's son drown was possible since he fought so feebly, Charlie didn't hold a grudge against him.

"He got us out of the paddy wagon," he pointed out.

"Wouldn't have been there if it wasn't for him."

Charlie gripped the bony shoulders and pulled hard enough to half lift him from the water. Wash sputtered and wiped water from his face. He shook his head and sent water spraying all about, like some retriever who'd plunged into the water to fetch a downed duck.

"Sober," Wash got out. "D-don't d-do that again."

"Do it again," Clem advised.

Charlie turned and hauled Wash onto the rocky shoreline. He sat beside him.

"Do you have any notion where Greta got off to?"

"Greta? The woman who took me to that room?" Wash shuddered, and it wasn't from the cold. He closed his eyes and bit his lips. Charlie shook him until he brought a new complaint to the man's lips. He tried to push Charlie away but failed.

"She doesn't have the spike. You don't. Who does, Wash? You can tell us. We're your friends."

"Can't say. All I know is that it's too late for Mister Hewes to make another. He put his best work into it. More than two weeks, and that was after he received the gold spike."

"What does your pa have to gain if he's stolen his own spike?"

Wash looked at Clem. He shook his head slowly. Water ran in tiny rivulets from his hair. He brushed a stream away from his eyes.

"Can't see that he gains anything, except maybe . . ."

Charlie perked up. He thought Clem was grabbing at straws. Wash's reaction made him change his mind, just a little.

"What do you mean?" Charlie held his breath. Wash might not have sobered up all the way after his therapeutic dunking in the cold water. He had shown quite a knack for spinning wild tales.

"The Central Pacific's borrowed a boatload of money from my father's bank. Most of the other banks in town, too. Building through the Sierras was hellaciously expensive. Leland and my pa got into an argument a while back when he said the railroad was likely to repay everyone else first, banks could go fish. I don't know what my pa said or did, but he's got a temper. He made Leland real mad at him, and they shouted at each other before Leland left in a snit." Wash idly rubbed his upper arm, as if remembering some past assault.

"The bank would go under if the railroad refused to pay?"

"Even if it delayed a payment or two, the bank's cash flow would be hit hard. We're just hanging on by the skin of our teeth now. Pa gambled everything on building the railroad and getting a huge interest on the funds loaned."

"So your pa might use the spike to insure the railroad pays back his loan before the others?" Charlie scratched himself as he turned this over in his head. "When did Leland—that's Leland Stanford—and your pa argue? Before or after the spike was shipped?"

"After, I think. It's hard to remember when my head feels like a rotted melon about to split open." He held his head in his hands and rocked back and forth.

"If they'd argued over repayment before the spike was shipped, all Thomas Collins had to do was stick it in his lower desk drawer," Charlie said.

"What makes you think he shipped it at all? That bogus spike in the box might have been what he sent."

"You saw his reaction when he opened the box," Charlie said. "He was surprised." He sucked in his breath. Thomas Collins had been more than surprised. He had been madder than a wet hen. And then he was scared. Considering what Wash said about the bank's risky loan to the railroad, he had every right to be frightened.

His shareholders would lynch him. Compared to what the ordinary depositors who entrusted him with their pennies for safekeeping, a necktie party might be merciful.

"He could be an actor worthy of the stage at the Bella Union."

"You giving him too much credit," Charlie said. It was still a possibility.

"I'm at the end of my rope. I don't want any more to do with this." Clem heaved to his feet.

"Wait, you can't—"

"Can and will, Charlie. Give me half of what you've collected to find him." He pointed at Wash. "And that other fellow. Reynolds."

"Here's three dollars," Charlie said, peeling it away from his vest pocket. His dunking in the Bay had soaked the greenbacks. "That's more than half."

Clem said nothing. He took the money, turned, and walked off without a backward look.

"You and your partner have a feud going on?" Wash asked. He came close to getting both sets of Charlie's knuckles pounding his face because he sounded halfway cheerful.

"I'll get you back to your sweetheart. She paid for you, after all." Charlie struggled to get Wash on his feet and stumbling along.

He felt better than he had in days but supporting the other man taxed him. They worked their way through town. Wash muttered the whole way about being afraid of the Sydney Ducks. Charlie wasn't exactly sure what the young man meant. The Aussie gang might have it in for Wash because of something he'd done or said. Mostly Charlie didn't care. Other problems piled up on him. Having Clem walk away like he did rankled. They'd been partners for two solid years. That should have meant more than failing to find a gold spike.

"There she is. In her pappy's store. I don't see anyone else around."

"Lodge night," Wash said. "Mister Hewes is off at his lodge meeting. He's a Mason. He holds it against me that I'm not. He probably holds it against me that my father's an Elk."

Rather than listen to Wash's list of failures and shortcomings, Charlie stepped into shadows and let the young man tap on the window. Dinah Hewes looked up, then brightened. She rushed to the door and let him into the shop. Charlie watched with some envy. In spite of being a wastrel, Wash Collins had found himself a woman willing to put up with his shortcomings. They embraced and engaged in a very public, and very immoral kiss.

He turned and wandered back in the direction of

Portsmouth Square. As he walked, he went over the hills and valleys of his life. Things hadn't been too bad, but losing Clem as a partner hurt the most. With only a couple dollars left in his pocket to show for being shot and battered—and failing to find the gold spike—he considered chucking it all.

"No." He muttered under his breath. Then, louder, "No, I will not give up." And then he bellowed this at the top of his lungs. Passersby stared at him, moved away from the crazy man, and hurried on their way.

Charlie Dawson had accepted money to find the spike. He wasn't one to give up, no matter how Collins had treated him. More than this, he had given his word. A slow smile came to his lips. Returning the spike and being paid the remainder of the promised reward would be icing on the cake.

He cut across the square and took a street toward Thomas Collins's bank. Finding a shadowy doorway let him settle in to watch the main entrance. The three-story building was imposing, fronted with limestone and windows all around. The cost of those glass windows would have kept him and Clem in clover for a year working the Betty Sue.

That thought turned Charlie morose. He tried to push his former partner from his mind. He had to find the spike on his own. Distractions like Clement only got in the way. He sank down to his haunches and kept staring at the mostly dark building. After an hour, his eyelids drooped. The rigors of the day wore on him and his battered body.

He slept.

And came awake with a start when a loud argument echoed across the street. He rubbed his eyes. Thomas Collins yelled at his assistant. Hiram Hickman wasn't having any of it. He shouted back. Try as he might, Charlie was unable to follow the argument. They had come from the bank. When Collins turned to lock the door, Hickman stormed off.

Charlie waited to see what the bank president did. If he followed, he should find out if Collins engaged in any shenanigans. Collins paced back and forth in front of the bank, then shouted for a passing cab. Again Charlie failed to overhear what the man said to the driver.

The carriage driver snapped the reins and trotted off with Thomas Collins hunched over in the back.

He stepped from the alcove and watched the carriage clank and rattle down the street. A dozen things collided in his head. The bank president's son had wondered if stealing the spike was a way to force the Central Pacific Railroad to keep from reneging on huge loans. Non-payment was sure ruin for Collins.

"Blackmail," Charlie said. He rubbed his sweaty hands on his pants legs. A single step after the rapidly disappearing carriage was all it took for him to spin ninety degrees and hurry after Hiram Hickman.

Waiting so long to follow Collins's right-hand man meant he had to rely more on luck than skill. He came to the next intersection and looked around.

"I just drew to an inside straight," he said softly.

Hickman argued with two men on the corner of the next intersection.

Charlie used the dark to move closer, avoiding the wan

light cast by gas lamps along the far side of the street. Just as he reached a point where he might overhear what Hickman argued about or had a chance to clearly see the other men's faces, Hickman turned abruptly and stalked off. Charlie ran to the corner and looked after the two men who'd been with Hickman. They hurried north toward the melodeons and saloons of the Barbary Coast.

He made another decision and followed Hickman. This part of town was more deserted. His bootheels clicked as he walked. He tried to walk softly, as if he stalked a deer, to keep Hickman from glancing back.

Hickman turned a corner. Charlie rested his hand on his pistol and went to the corner. He chanced a quick peek around. His heart leaped into his throat. Hickman was nowhere to be seen. Sliding his Walker Colt out, he worked around the corner and pressed flat against the brick building.

His hearing wasn't the best, but he heard someone climbing stairs. The first door he tried was locked. The second opened. Stairs leading both up to a closed door on a second-floor landing and down into a cellar forced him to decide.

He worked his way up the steps. Only a single creaky step betrayed him. He caught his breath and lifted his pistol. The door at the head of the stairs opened a fraction of an inch. Someone looked out. Without thinking, he vaulted the railing and fell. He hit the stairs going down with enough force to jolt him. Pain shot up his leg and made him woozy. Charlie braced himself against the wall. The dizziness passed. No one looked over the railing.

He started back up the steps, intending to reach the second story again to spy on Hickman. It had to be Hickman in that room. It had to be.

He flopped belly down on the steps when the door leading to the street opened. He almost cried out when Greta Swinburne came into the building to stand staring up the stairs. She took two steps and paused. She looked around like a deer being stalked.

Charlie started to confront her. Then the door to the street opened again. Once more he dropped to hide.

"Clem!"

The name slipped unbidden from his lips. He couldn't help it. But his partner was too intent on . . . . Greta Swinburne.

"Is he upstairs?"

"You know he is, Clement. Ain't I the best danged tracker in all of California?"

Charlie couldn't hear Clem's reply, but it was sarcastic. Greta chided him for it.

"Go on. Get up there." Clem herded the woman up the stairs.

Charlie stayed low and watched them ascend. They pressed against the wall. Clem put his ear to the door, spying on the occupant.

"He's in there. I hear him moving around."

"Let's not waste no more time, Clement. I'm just itchin' to be rich."

Charlie held his breath. They had come to the same conclusion he had, that Hiram Hickman was the thief who had swiped the golden spike. Clem hadn't given up on the hunt. He had switched partners and once more rode the owlhoot trail with his former wife.

Anger built in him, causing a flush to turn his face purple. Charlie thought he controlled his emotions well. Most times. This wasn't one of them. He had been beaten and swindled and now his own partner had betrayed them.

Clem had betrayed *him*.

Gun lifted, he started to call to them. Clem kicked in the door and Greta surged in after him. Gunfire broke out. Charlie started to rush in—but who would he aid?

A feral grin crossed his face. He'd take the spike for himself!

He took the steps two at a time. He reached the landing and never slowed as he rushed into the room, gun swinging around.

"Hands up! Drop your guns!"

Charlie pointed his gun at an empty room.

# CHAPTER 34

Empty. The austere room was devoid of any life but his own. Charlie Dawson swung his six-gun around, thinking he had walked into an ambush. Nobody hid in the wardrobe or under the bed. He made a quick search of the room, thinking he'd find the spike hidden here.

Nothing.

Then he went to the window and chanced a look out. A balcony under the window led around the back of the building. He ran his hand over the windowsill. At least two bullets had left fresh holes in the wood. The best he could tell, Hickman had been in the room waiting to ambush Clem and Greta. They hadn't been as good or as secretive trailing Hickman as they thought. Somehow, they had alerted him he was being followed.

Charlie swallowed hard. He might have been seen by Collins's right-hand man. He was lucky they had gone after Hickman before he had a chance to.

The instant they kicked in the door, he ambushed them. Clem, and probably the outlaw woman, had returned fire. Hickman might have crouched outside the room on the balcony, his pistol aimed at the door.

Charlie found fresh cuts in the windowsill bolstering his idea of what happened. He crawled through the window clumsily and cautiously explored. Before he reached the far end of the balcony, more shots sounded. He hadn't found any bodies or blood. Clem and Greta still chased after Hickman. And Hickman still ran from them in a deadly cat and mouse hunt.

He reached the corner of the balcony and rounded it without being cautious enough. Bullets flew all around him. One winged close enough to graze his cheek. He flinched away. That saved him from taking another slug between the eyes.

He dropped to his knees and steadied his Colt with both hands. His finger drew back but stopped just short of releasing a round. Clem was the only one directly in his sights.

"What're you doing here?" Clem demanded.

"Getting killed by you, it looks."

Clem shifted his aim and spun around to look over the railing into the street. His shoulders slumped.

Charlie advanced and took a quick assessment of everything happening below. Mostly he saw what wasn't there as opposed to what was.

"Where's Hickman?" he asked.

"Where's Greta?" Clem retorted. "We cornered that rat. We had him! Or we thought we had. He was waiting for us out on the balcony. He shot into the room, then hightailed it when we started firing."

"I figured that out. You and Greta? How'd you team up again?"

"I ran into her after you left me standing in the street."

"I did what? You were the one who walked off." Charlie was outraged. Clem wasn't listening.

"We went to a melodeon and talked some. She's found out plenty. I don't know how, but she can be mighty convincing when she puts her mind to it."

"I noticed."

"She said ransom notes were sent to both the bank and the railroad. Ten thousand dollars each."

"We're pikers. We took Collins's job for nickels and dimes compared to that." Charlie heaved a sigh. He'd still take the balance of the two thousand dollars they'd been promised.

But twenty thousand dollars for the gold spike? That was a king's ransom.

"She doesn't think Collins was working any kind of swindle. He went straight to Stanford and Judah when he got the note."

"That didn't work well for him," Charlie said. "They had him over a barrel, threatening to not repay the loan with his bank."

Clem pursed his lips, then looked at his partner.

"You've been busy, too."

"Greta's not the only one who can worm information out of people."

"Anyway, they agreed to pay, Judah and Stanford did. Collins figured out his flunky was responsible. He was stupid enough to tell them. They blamed him for everything."

He remembered the two arguing outside the bank.

But what about the other argument? The one between Hickman and the pair of toughs on the street corner? That pair must be holding the spike in safekeeping until Hickman collected the ransom money from the railroad barons.

"When you broke into his room, he must have thought Collins sent killers after him."

"Or the railroad owners. From what Greta tells me, they're as ruthless as they come. Collins isn't anywhere near their equal, and they think of him as their lackey."

"The spike wasn't in Hickman's room. I looked."

"We chased after him. With him slinging lead all around, we didn't have time to search his room." Clem hesitated, then asked, "How good did you search the room?"

"I'll give it a better going-over," Charlie said. He started to complain when Clem joined him. They weren't partners any longer.

But the search went faster with the two of them working as a team. Charlie felt that they had poked into every nook and cranny. There weren't loose floorboards or wall panels. No trace of a hiding place in the ceiling caught his eye.

He sank down on the bed and looked around, taking in every detail in case they had missed somewhere. The ceiling was an acre of peeling paint, and the cracks in the walls and floor had not given up anything looking like a railroad spike. A third search still failed to turn up the spike or any possible hiding place.

"Do you think Greta ran him down?"

Clem shook his head and looked glum.

Charlie read the expression. He expected Greta to double-cross him if she did run Hickman to ground.

"If anyone can get the truth out of Hickman, it's Greta." Charlie prodded a bit more but failed to get any reply from Clem. He switched to a different tack. "Do you have any idea where Hickman ran off to?"

"He'll go to ground somewhere he feels safe." Clem looked back toward the boarding room window. "This hardly looks like a place where a rich and powerful man would hang his hat."

"Maybe not so rich and not as powerful as he wants." Charlie thought hard on the matter. "If he didn't hide the spike here, he has it where he feels safer."

Clem shrugged. He had nothing to add to the conversation.

"Greta either kept on his heels or knows where he's headed."

"Why do you say that?"

"She's not back," Charlie said.

"Hickman might have plugged her. She's tough but not made of steel. A bullet through her heart?" He shook his head.

Charlie refrained from saying a bullet aimed at the woman's heart was sure to miss. Greta Swinburne didn't have a heart. But he kept his sarcasm to himself because of the way Clem looked. Charlie wasn't sure if his partner missed the woman or just stated the obvious.

"From all I've seen of her, she's tough enough to dog his tracks and run him down."

"He'd be Collins's courier to Sacramento," Clem said suddenly. "The livery stables."

"The railroad depot," Charlie countered. "A man like him won't sit on a horse when he can ride in a Pullman car, surrounded by all kinds of luxury."

"He won't ride around the south end of the Bay. He'll take the ferry to the Oakland Long Wharf."

"He'll have a place to stay near the railroad depot across the Bay." Charlie stared hard at his partner. Or was Clem still his partner?

"Unless we swim, we need to catch a ferry," Clem said.

"Yes, we do." Charlie felt uneasy at assuming their partnership was again intact, but he wasn't going to question having Clem backing him up. Hiram Hickman had shown himself to be a slippery, dangerous cayuse.

"Can't say I've seen him recently," the Oakland ticket agent said. He yawned, covered his mouth and then stretched. "But then, I've been catchin' up on my sleep. There's been so many limiteds and expresses headin' out, it's keepin' me up and puttin' in long hours."

"Limiteds?" Charlie tried to figure out what the man meant.

"One-time trains with the likes of Mister Judah and others from the main office. They're all movin' east toward Promontory Summit."

"For the ceremony linking the east and west coasts," Clem said. "Was Hickman on one of those trains?"

"Nope."

"Or one of the regularly scheduled trains?" Charlie pressed.

"Can't say I seen him in a while, but I take real good care of him when he does go up to Sacramento. He's Mister Collins's negotiator with the governor on lots of important money matters."

"Would you know if he's heading out any time soon?"

"For Mister Collins and the bank? Well now, lemme see. Yup, he is." The agent reached up and pulled down a ticket where it had been stuck above the window.

"A man like that's not staying in a hotel, is he?"

"Not when the bank's got special quarters for their executives." The agent frowned. "What are you two goin' on about? You ain't askin' to buy tickets."

"Got money to give Mister Hickman," Charlie said. "Mister Collins sent us. Didn't we mention that?"

"Nope, you didn't. What's a man who works for a bank need with money?"

Charlie laughed, although he wanted to reach through the window and throttle the clerk.

"It's a private thing. Gambling. He was a big winner."

"Him and Mister Collins are gamblers? Why don't he just give Hickman his money when he sees him in the office?"

"This is a special payment," Charlie said. "If you know what I mean?" He hoped the ticket agent would build his own reason. He was about out of fanciful tales.

The agent thought this over for a moment, then said, "I'll give it to him. Whatever money you have for him. He'll be on the noon train."

Charlie glanced at the Regulator clock on the waiting room wall. It ticked out its ponderous seconds. They might wait for five hours. Or they could press the ticket agent and find out where Hickman was spending the night.

"We've got to get back to San Francisco. If we don't give it to him now, he'll have to wait until he gets back."

"From the Promontory Summit ceremony?" The clerk scratched himself. "I can give it to him. Like I said, he—"

His words caught in his throat. Clem had his Colt out, cocked and pointed at the man's heart.

"It's important," Charlie said, irritated that his partner had resorted to such a show of force. The clerk was likely to summon the police now unless Clem pulled the trigger to prevent the clerk from doing anything ever again. Then Charlie would have an innocent life on his conscience. He wasn't cut out to be the outlaw his partner seemed to be, with or without Greta Swinburne's influence.

"Over two blocks and down toward the ferry terminal. On Berkeley Street."

"Hiram will thank you for letting us know. Ask him when he shows up," Clem said. He released the hammer and stuffed his six-gun into the holster with a show of authority that made Charlie wonder if his partner had ever worked as a lawman. In some parts of the country, outlaw and lawman weren't much different.

Clem herded him from the railroad depot and down the steps into the street.

"He'll have the coppers on us before we're around the end of the block."

"Clem, you need to keep your impatience under your hat."

"Hat's got holes in it. Walk faster or I'll leave you behind." He set out at a pace that forced Charlie to half-run to match.

They zigzagged through the streets and as they came closer to the ferry dock they had left almost an hour earlier, gunshots rang out. They exchanged looks and sped up. Charlie outlegged Clem in spite of calling for his partner to slow down.

Charlie rounded a corner. A house stood in the middle of a small plot of land with a garden, flower beds, and a few fruit trees. Smoke curled up from its chimney, and out back a shed held a horse already kicking at its stall. The sporadic gunfire set it off again, neighing and snorting as it tried to get free.

"There," Charlie said, coming up beside Clem. "That's Greta. She's the cause of all the gunfire."

"Half of it," Clem corrected. He pointed. A rifle barrel broke through a pane of glass. Orange fire exploded from the muzzle.

Charlie twisted in time to see Greta drop behind a watering trough out on the street. The bullet drove through the outer side of the trough and caused a tiny fountain. Two more rounds sped along the trough, draining its contents onto the ground into a mud puddle.

The thin wood sides began turning to splinters as Hickman levered one round after another into his rifle and fired with deadly accuracy.

Charlie had no call to do it, but he acted in a flash. He stood and started walking toward the window where Hickman's rifle protruded. He fired slowly, as accurately as he could while walking. His gunfire drove the man back to cover.

"Run," Charlie shouted. "Take cover somewhere else!"

Greta Swinburne was not going to obey even a sensible command. She jumped over the destroyed watering trough and rushed the house, too. She fired as she went, keeping Hickman down. Charlie had hoped that the man would pop up and give him a single good shot. The woman smashed into the side of the house, rebounded, and spun so she fired through the window at anything moving inside.

"The door, Clem, break through the door!" Charlie cast a sidelong glance where he had left his partner. Clem was nowhere to be seen.

This left Charlie in an open space with an almost empty pistol. He moved as fast as he could, but the front door flew open. Hickman leveled his rifle and fired as quickly as he could lever in a new round and pull the trigger.

Charlie felt the hot breath of a bullet touch his already wounded leg. He collapsed on the spot. Hickman stepped outside for a better shot to finish him off. On his belly, Charlie tried to fire. His six-gun came up empty. He feinted to the right and rolled left. Bullets kicked up dust devils as he rolled and rolled and rolled until . . .

. . . he crashed into a hitching post.

His dodging had been effective, but when he came to such a sudden stop, it gave Hickman the chance to aim.

"Got you covered, Hickman!" Clem shouted from the side of the house. Hickman had stepped far enough out to expose his back.

For a heart-stopping instant, Hickman's eyes and Charlie's locked. The man wasn't going to throw down his rifle. He pulled it snugly into his shoulder and fired. Charlie closed his eyes and winced. Then all hell broke loose.

Both Clem and Greta fired on Hickman. Charlie lay in the dirt wondering why he wasn't dead. The shot that should have killed him went high. One of the others—Charlie thought it was Clem—targeted Hickman accurately enough to seriously wound him.

Hickman's arms rose as he arched his back and staggered forward. This opened him up to a new round of Greta's bullets. Charlie watched it all, kicking about helpless in the dirt. Again his eyes and Hickman's locked. The bank president's assistant looked daggers at him. Then the world erupted in a new hail of bullets.

Somehow, neither Clem nor Greta had killed him. Hickman dropped to one knee, then lurched forward, falling more than walking. He vanished through the door. An instant later, it slammed shut.

"Wait, don't follow him," Clem shouted at Greta. "That's what he wants. He'll kill anyone going through after him."

Greta and Clem pressed against the wall on either side of the door. A deathly, ominous silence fell. No one fired.

Charlie fumbled to reload. When he had fresh rounds in his Colt, he tested his leg. Hickman's bullet stung but hadn't torn away much skin. It certainly hadn't busted a leg bone or hit a major artery. He limped to the door and looked at the other two.

No one spoke. They knew what had to be done if they wanted to flush out Hiram Hickman.

Charlie nodded, braced himself, and then crashed into the door. His shoulder felt as if he crushed every bone. The door popped off its hinges, and Charlie, off-balance, followed it into the house.

Greta and Clem crowded in after him. Again Charlie was flat on the floor. He looked around. Shadows provided too many hiding places for the wounded Hickman to ambush them. He came to his knees. A half turn to his left let him see into the parlor.

"Where'd he go?" Greta stomped past him. Clem trailed her.

"The blood," Charlie said. "Follow the blood trail."

They were already in the back of the house and didn't hear his advice. Moving slowly, Charlie moved around the parlor, using first a table and then a settee as support for his shaky legs. He listened hard. Greta and Clem rampaged through the rest of the house. They'd never hear what he did.

Harsh breathing. With care, he sank onto the settee and homed in on the location of the increasingly ragged breathing. Curtains hung to the floor on either side of a window. The light coming through the window revealed nothing.

But the slowly spreading bloodstain on the material showed exactly where Hickman hid. Charlie rested his six-shooter on the back of the settee and pulled halfway back on the trigger. If he had to, he could fan off all six rounds before Hickman had a chance to escape.

"Come on out. We can get you patched up." The curtains rippled now. The blood spot spread where Hickman pressed into the pleated cloth. "All we want is the spike."

Everything happened at once. The curtain crashed down as Hickman fell forward. The wounded man pushed his rifle out and got off a round in Charlie's direction. The lead screamed past his ear, forcing him to jerk away. His bullet missed Hickman but added to the confusion.

Hickman swung his rifle like a club. He missed Charlie but hit the settee and shoved it back a foot. Then he fell over the back. His hands turned into claws, groping for his attacker's eyes.

Charlie fired again. Hickman grunted and recoiled. Before he got off another round, Charlie was knocked backward by the man's furious attack. They landed in a pile on the floor. Charlie was stunned by the fall. Hickman fought like a wounded wildcat.

Pinned under the man's weight, Charlie found it hard to fight. He twisted hard to the side, then drew back and slammed his elbow into Hickman's questing fingers. This unseated the man. He sprawled on the floor, kicking feebly. Charlie found his six-gun and aimed it at his opponent.

He didn't fire. There was no need. Hiram Hickman's eyes turned to glass. He was very, very dead.

# CHAPTER 35

"Unless he comes back from the grave, he's not going to tell us a danged thing," Clem said. He prodded Hiram Hickman's corpse with the toe of his boot.

"You can bury the varmint, if you think that's gonna work to make him talk," Greta Swinburne said in disgust. "We got no idea where he stashed the gold. Thanks, Charles." She glared at him.

"He's got plenty of my lead in him, but he was shooting at me. All of us," he said defensively. How she made him feel guilty for being the one to walk away from a gunfight irritated him. She made it sound as if not having the golden spike in their hands right now was his fault. "We haven't looked for it. This is a pretty fancy place. There must be plenty of places to stash the spike."

"Might be a safe somewhere," Clem said, looking around.

"There're pictures on the walls where you can hide a safe," Charlie said.

They roamed around the room, taking down the pictures hung. Charlie wanted to tell them a hidden wall safe wasn't likely in exterior walls, but then there was no harm in looking. It gave him a chance to recuperate.

"This is a fancy place," he said as the two completed their circuit of the room.

"Nothing's too good for the bank executives," Clem said. He opened the door into the dining room and looked around for a moment, then returned. "Maybe it was for railroad muckety-mucks." He pointed to a foot of track mounted on the wall like a hunting trophy.

Greta peered at a brass plate under the section of track.

"From the first rail they laid here in Oakland. I do declare, these people worship trinkets. A hunk of steel rail, a golden spike."

"Keep the track," Clem said. "I'm going to find the gold." He began rummaging around the room. Tiring of it, he moved to a different room. Greta shot Charlie a cold look, then followed Clem on his scavenger hunt.

Charlie sank into a chair and stared at the track segment on the wall. Of everything in the room, that was out of place. The pictures were all of trees and streams and women dipping bare toes in ponds. But the steel contrasted with the pastel paintings in such a way that it gnawed away at him.

He heaved to his feet and went to the trophy. The brass plate read exactly as Greta had claimed. That meant she was the one doing the reading and writing when she and Clem were married. He wondered if Clem had ever been married to her. She could have stuck any sheet of print under his nose and told him it was a marriage license. For all any of them save Greta knew, Clem had signed a worthless hunk of paper.

He shoved that from his mind. Clem claimed they had gotten a divorce in Fargo. If they both believed that, then it was true. Reaching up, he laid his fingers against the section of cool steel track. When he stepped back, he dislodged part of the plaque holding the trophy. Charlie fished around behind the track. A big brass key dropped out. He caught it before it clattered to the floor.

"So, what's this open and why'd you hide it?" He knew that Hickman might have known nothing about the key. This entire house—this mansion—belonged to his boss or even the Central Pacific Railroad. Men that powerful had reasons to hide keys to . . .

. . . what?

Turning in a complete circle, he tried to find a key-hole that'd open some secret to him. The clock on the far wall chimed. He looked at the key and then the clock. When he opened the case, the winding key was resting on the bottom of the case.

There were two openings in the clock face. Hand shaking he tried the brass key in the bottom keyhole. It didn't fit. He almost walked away in despair of ever finding the gold spike. Then he tried the upper keyhole. Not only did the key fit, it turned easily. A panel imme-diately below the clock snapped open.

Charlie almost cried out in triumph. Resting in the narrow hiding space were stacks of papers, some green-backs, and, weighing them down, an oilcloth-wrapped, slender item. Almost reverently he took the package out. Again he forced himself to silence. The dull gold sheen of the spike filled his vision. He had spent a goodly portion of his life hunting for this precious metal.

He knew gold when he saw it and felt it and . . . smelled it. This was gold. More than that, it was an engraved railroad spike.

He held it closer and made out extremely fine etching on every side.

On two sides were dozens of names. He recognized a couple as being Central Pacific Railroad officers and guessed the rest of the names belonged to Union Pacific officers. He turned it slowly and held it up to catch a ray of light from the window.

He swallowed hard as he read, "The Pacific Railroad ground broken Jan 8th, 1863, and completed May 8th, 1869." If there had been any doubt as to the authenticity of the spike, this ended it. Before he turned to the fourth side, which carried a long and intricately etched phrase of delicate cursive writing, he heard Greta and Clem returning. They tromped down the stairs.

From what they accused each other of, he knew they hadn't found anything like he had. Charlie hastily wrapped the spike in its oilcloth, closed the hidden door, and looked around the room.

Hightailing it with the spike was possible for only a few seconds. Clem stood in the hallway door, his back to Charlie.

He should have returned the spike to the hiding place under the clock. It was too late for that. Charlie spun around and went to a roll-top desk. The spike was too long to fit in any of the small cubicles. It would stick out like a sore thumb if he laid it on the desk. He tugged open the center drawer. It was the only one wide enough to take the spike. Even then he had to wedge it in diagonally. A quick shuffle of papers covered it up.

"What you have there, Charles?"

He tried not to sound panicked or guilty. He held up the handful of papers from the desktop. Waving them around he left the desk behind and shoved the papers at Greta. She took them with ill grace.

"These ain't no gold spike. What am I supposed to do with these?" She started to scatter the papers around the room, then stopped. Her eyes narrowed and her lips moved as she read one sheet. She dropped it and began examining another.

Charlie scooped up the page. His luck was fantastic. By sheer chance, he had found a stack of papers where Hickman had written several different drafts of the ransom letter. The one he held was addressed to Leland Stanford.

"What a skunk," Greta said. "He was selling the spike back to his own boss."

"Don't feel too sorry for Collins," Clem said. "Him and Hickman are like peas in a pod."

"Ten thousand dollars," she said. "That's what he was asking for return of the spike."

"This page is addressed to Stanford." Charlie leafed through other pages, smudged and each with a different demand on it. "He settled on ten thousand dollars here, too."

"Twenty thousand? He thought it was worth that

much?" Clem shook his head. "Even if it's solid 24-carat gold, it's not worth that."

"The bad publicity, the chance that reporters start digging into corruption. Twenty thousand is chicken feed to men like them. It's worth a few dollars to these men to avoid all that poking around into their accounts. Betcha they've stolen millions."

"Ain't no 'few dollars' when you're talkin' twenty thousand of them."

Charlie found another sheet on the desk that was complete. All the rest had run only a paragraph or two of demands with entire lines scratched out as Hickman chose the right words for the swindle.

"Hickman said he'd pass over the spike to them in Sacramento."

"Tomorrow, looks like," Greta said. She punched Clem in the arm. "Where's the danged spike? Find it, Clement. Find it. Then we can get ourselves to Sacramento and split twenty thousand dollars two ways."

"Two ways?" Clem frowned and counted on his fingers.

"That's ten thousand for you and Charles."

"That means you end up with half," Charlie protested.

"You're partners, you and Clement. You get one share. Me, I get one share. That's only fair."

Even Clem realized this wasn't to his benefit. He and Greta started arguing. Charlie had the feeling the kernel of their fight went back a lot of years to when they were married and had less to do with the spike and how to divvy up the money.

He glanced at the desk where he'd hidden the precious spike. How Hickman intended to collect from both bank and railroad wasn't obvious from the scraps of letters on the desk. If he wanted to work such a swindle, he'd try to give Thomas Collins a fake and Stanford the real spike. Somehow, Hickman depended on the bank president's frantic need to recover the spike and get the Central Pacific to pay off their loans. Any flash of gold on a spike might satisfy Collins. Gilt paint on a real spike?

Charlie wondered where Hickman'd hide such a thing.

"He wouldn't hide it. There wouldn't be any need." He dropped the papers and looked out the window. A carriage house behind the mansion looked like a perfect place to make a fake spike.

Leaving Greta and Clem to their spat, he stepped through the window and walked slowly to the carriage house. The ground was cut up with boot prints, coming and going. Someone had been out here several times in the past day. He knelt and ran his finger around the heel imprint. He amended his guess. Someone had come out here in the past hour or two. It didn't take much imagination to picture Hickman hiking out, determined to carry through with his ransom.

He opened the carriage house door wide enough to slip through. He left it open a few inches to let in light. A deep whiff guided him to the workbench at the rear of the room. A farrier's tools were carefully laid out on the bench. And so was a small can of gilt paint. He dipped his finger into it. Just the right color.

Letting his nose guide him again, he went to the far end of the bench and found the spike held between the jaws of a vise. If he hadn't seen David Hewes's masterpiece, he'd be fooled, especially if he only got a quick look at it. Hickman had not only painted the steel spike but had carefully added lettering in black along the top few inches. Held by the bottom, wrapped in cloth so only those top few inches showed, Hickman had a chance to fool an anxious Thomas Collins.

"Real one to Stanford, fake one to Collins. Collect from both. What a sharper!"

He lightly touched the side of the fake spike. The paint had dried. Charlie took it out of its vise and wrapped it in the cloth Hickman had already used. Tucked under his arm, he headed back to the house. How he'd use this as bait wasn't something he had worked out yet. Or if he'd try carrying through with the swindle at all. Such conduct made him a little sick to the stomach. He had been hired to find the real spike. While he doubted Collins could be persuaded to fork over the amount Hickman had demanded, a thousand or two extra as a bonus wasn't out of the question.

He entered the house through the front door. He saw how the gunfight had chewed up the door and walls around it. But this wasn't his problem. If Collins or the railroad magnates wanted to fix the damage, they had the money.

Minus what they'd pay for the return of the real spike.

Charlie stopped dead in the doorway leading to the office where the clock ticked out its solemn seconds. Clem sprawled on the floor. A small puddle of blood formed under his head and stained the fancy Oriental rug.

He pulled out his six-gun and stepped out of the doorway where he made an easy target. Edging into the room, he saw that the hidden door under the clock remained shut. But the center drawer on the desk across the room was wide open. He vaulted over his partner and searched through the drawer. Nicks in the sides of the drawer showed where the real golden spike had been yanked free.

He whirled around. Then he knelt beside Clem. The man moaned. His eyelids fluttered and his vision focused after a few seconds.

"She hit me. Don't know why. She wasn't mad or anything."

"Did she club you after she'd searched the desk?"

Clem tried to nod. He winced at the movement.

Charlie rocked back on his heels. Greta had found the real spike and had taken it. The only thing better than claiming half the ransom was to take it all.

"Come on." Charlie shook his partner until Clem growled like a bear waking from hibernation.

"Lemme alone."

"Greta has the real spike."

"What? How?"

"And she's on her way to Sacramento to sell it to

both the bank and the railroad." Charlie got his arm around Clem's shoulders and lifted him to a sitting position. Clem had to make it to his feet on his own. Charlie wasn't going to let loose of the fake spike.

He had a use for it. How many times he hit Greta Swinburne with it depended on how angry he got by the time they overtook her.

# CHAPTER 36

"Hickman's ransom notes all said for Stanford and Collins to bring the money and get the spike in Sacramento." Charlie looked at the clock ticking away. They had about eight hours to do something about Greta and her double-dealing ways.

"Why bother?" Clem stared at him. His expression defied description. Charlie worried that his partner had given up.

"We've been shot and beaten up, risked our lives, and not gotten our due." Charlie dug his heels in now. He was tired of being used and getting nothing but new bullet holes in his hide for the effort.

"We find Greta and cut ourselves in?" Clem sounded dubious.

"She's on her way to Sacramento while we stand around lollygagging."

"What do we do?"

"Go after her," Charlie said. He found the brass key that unlocked the panel beneath the clock. A few papers spilled out. He shoved them aside and found a wad of greenbacks. This wasn't close to what Thomas Collins had promised them, but it'd do as a start. With a determination that built second by second, he studied Clem closely. "Come along or not. I'm not giving in to those thieves."

"If the spike isn't delivered on time, the newshounds will be taken off their leashes. It might be best to let the reporters snap away at the heels of all those thieves," Clem amended.

"There's no satisfaction in that." He started for the door, paused, then left the house. Arguing further wouldn't change his partner's mind. Whether Clem came with him hardly mattered. Everything that had happened set him on fire.

He trooped along with the fake spike tucked under his arm, heading back to the railroad depot. Greta would take the fastest way to reach Sacramento. That was the train.

To take his mind off how his leg hurt with every step, he let his brain freewheel and come up with a dozen different improbable ideas. Most of them evaporated as being impossible. One rose up for him to work over like a dog with a bone. If Hickman hadn't changed the details of the swap, he knew the time and place for the swap. He had to hand it to the bank president's flunky. Pass over the real spike to Stanford and the fake one to his old boss. That gave him two chances to recover the golden spike.

"Will he try to keep his job?"

Charlie jumped at the unexpected intrusion on his thoughts. Clem plodded along beside him.

"Hickman didn't have the sand for that. Swindle his boss, dupe him, and keep working for the bank?" Charlie snorted in contempt. "He'd have taken the money and hightailed it."

"Reckon so," Clem allowed. "When you rob a bank, you don't stand around to count the money you stole. You surely don't ask one of the tellers to count it for you before hightailing it."

Charlie looked ahead. A huge pillar of roiling black smoke rose. The shrill whine of a steam whistle tore at his ears.

"The train's leaving. Run, Clem. We have to catch it!"

Charlie about passed out from the pain in his leg. He sprinted and then flagged to the point of gasping for air. He watched the train leave the station. By the time he pulled himself up onto the depot's passenger platform, he had a good view of the caboose dwindling in size as the train gained speed.

He went to the window and called to the ticket agent.

"What can I do for you?" The clerk rubbed his eyes.

"That train," Charlie got out. "Is it heading to Sacramento?"

"It surely is. You just missed it, but don't you fret. Another's due to leave real soon."

"Two tickets," Charlie said, taking the wad of scrip from his pocket. "When's it leave?"

"About this time tomorrow."

"Tomorrow?" Charlie tensed. "I need to get there sooner." He looked down the tracks at the now-vanished train. The chance that Greta hadn't been on it was about zero. She had lit out like a horse with its tail on fire after she stole the spike. With the information from Hickman's practice notes, she would be in Sacramento in plenty of time to collect the ransom he'd arranged.

"Well, yeah, this time tomorrow." The agent chuckled. "Less you're one of the railroad executives. They've got an express headin' out any time now."

"How do I get on it?"

The agent turned wary.

"You can't. Mister Judah himself is on that train. It's pulling his personal car."

"But there're other passengers."

"Reckon so. Heard that Mister Marsh and maybe Mark Hopkins hisself are going along. The car's all stocked with nothing but the finest for the directors of the road. Yes, sir. Makes a fellow proud knowin' important men like that are comin' through my station."

"But they aren't taking on paying passengers?"

"Tomorrow, this time, if you want to get to Sacramento."

Charlie stepped away from the window. A blanket of despair descended all over him, suffocating him.

"There it is," Clem said, pointing. On the track where the last train had steamed off for the capital huffed and puffed another engine. "Must be it. The number on the front of the engine's two."

"Stanford's engine would be one," Charlie said. He walked to the edge of the platform and looked over the short train. The engine, tender, two luxurious Pullman cars, and a caboose. With that powerful an engine and that short a train, it'd make up for the head start of the train Greta took.

"How do we get on it?" Charlie watched as a dozen railroad bulls walked around the cars, far too alert for his taste. Sneaking over and crawling up into the rods under the Pullman wasn't possible.

"Get up on the depot's roof and jumping over as it pulls out?" Clem stepped out and looked up. "That's not possible with a couple of the railroad dicks up there watching. They're carrying rifles."

"Shooting it out isn't the way to get aboard," Charlie said. He hitched up his pants and drew his six-gun. "If we want to stop Greta and get that spike, we have to do what nobody expects."

"You're sounding loco."

Charlie fumed. The special train sat a few yards away, waiting. He settled down on a bench and glared as if this brought him any closer to getting on the train. He nervously tapped the fake spike up and down until he irritated Clem enough so that he moved away and left him alone. After almost an hour, the passengers climbed into their fancy cars. The engineer blew the whistle and the wheels began turning slowly.

Seeing the train in motion got Charlie moving. A plan clicked. It was the only thing that hadn't been discarded in his long wait. He got to his feet and started for the end of the passenger platform where the train would pass in a few seconds.

"What're you doing?" Clem jumped to his feet and paced alongside his partner.

"You don't have to come." Charlie balanced on the

edge of the platform, hailed the engineer, and got a wave back. The train whistle screeched and the engine built power to leave.

As the engine moved past him, Charlie jumped over to the engine. He gripped the iron handhold and pulled himself into the engine cab. As his gun lifted, Clem pressed close behind. Both of them crowded forward into the cab.

"What're you boys doin'?" The gray-bearded engineer looked over his shoulder at them.

"We're commandeering the train."

"Boy, you're touched in the head. This train follows the tracks. We don't go tearin' off across the landscape." The engineer reached up to pull the handle that'd blow his head of steam and bring the train to a halt.

Charlie rested the gun barrel against his cheek.

"Keep on steaming along."

"You're not joshin' me, are you? This ain't some joke Lester is playin'? He never forgot how I glued his shoes to the floor when he fell asleep that time."

"Don't know anyone by the name of Lester," Clem said. He covered the stoker. The youngster had stopped shoveling coal into the firebox. A quick gesture got the boy back to work.

"You must want to get to Sacramento in a powerful hurry," the engineer said.

"The quicker we get to the depot, the sooner you're rid of us."

"You ain't thinkin' on usin' that hogleg, are you? This ole engine's set for a smooth ride 'cuz of our royalty ridin' back yonder, but that don't mean there aren't bumps. You might accidental-like tug on that trigger and you'd be on a runaway train."

"How hard can it be driving this iron horse?" Clem asked.

"You'd never get to Sacramento without me. The reason I'm engineer on this particular train is that I'm the best on the line." He puffed out his chest and hooked his thumbs under his suspenders. "You need me."

Charlie turned to the stoker.

"How long you worked for the Central Pacific?"

"Goin' on two years, sir."

"You look like a smart lad. I'd wager you know everything about this steam engine that he does."

The boy nodded, then looked at the engineer. Fright turned his face into an ugly mask.

"I didn't mean that," the stoker said hurriedly. "He's real secretive. He hides what he does so I can't see!"

The boy turned pale under the black mask of coal soot. Charlie wished they were in a poker game. He read the boy's lie without even trying.

"If he don't know it all by now, I wasted my time hirin' him. He's a bright boy." The engineer sounded the whistle as they raced past a crossing. He settled down on a drop seat and looked ahead along the track.

"But he won't help us if we throw you off the train."

"You're a bright one, too," the engineer said. "We're both good at what we do. And we're even more loyal to the Central Pacific."

The stoker's head bobbed up and down in agreement. He leaned on his coal shovel to show he had thrown in the last of the coal until the engineer gave him the order to continue.

Charlie and Clem exchanged looks. A silent agreement was reached. Neither of them had a quarrel with the engine crew and couldn't fault them for being loyal to their employer.

"We can pay for the ride," Charlie offered.

"Pay?" The engineer laughed. "The only people I let ride in my cab, those that can't fire me, are my helpers." He looked slyly at Charlie, then past him to Clem. "You can work for your ticket."

"Shoveling coal?" Clem looked at the filthy youngster, who smiled at this turn.

"Get to it. You boys are in good shape. You're used to hard work. Rafael, here, can drive the train while you do his job."

"Really?" The stoker's grin filled half his dirty, soot-covered face.

"I'll set myself down and watch. This is better than Mister Judah givin' me a day off to get drunk."

Charlie slid his six-shooter back into his waistband, set down the bogus spike where it was out of the way, and reached out for the stoker's shovel. It wasn't any harder moving coal from the tender into the firebox than it was cleaning out debris after he'd blasted a new wall in the Betty Sue. After a half hour of shoveling, he handed the chore over to Clem.

The whole while the young stoker sat in the engineer's seat, attentive to the track ahead. The engineer glanced out a few times and offered suggestions about steam pressure and how his two captive firemen needed to shovel faster. Other than this, he did nothing during the ninety-mile trip other than pull out a tobacco pound and rolling paper and build himself a cigarette.

Everything about the engineer showed he was enjoying this trip. He finally bestirred himself, pushed the stoker off the seat, and settled down. He wiped off his hands, gripped the levers, and glanced over the array of pressure gauges.

"We made good time," the engineer said. "Usually takes three hours. Did it less than that by a considerable margin. Good choice to highball it the entire way," he congratulated.

Charlie and Clem were filthy from shoveling the coal for the trip, but their work had paid off. Not a quarter mile ahead, the train Greta had taken slowed to pull into the Sacramento terminal. The engineer ordered the stoker to cut back on the coal and began working on his boiler pressure to slow down.

"Wouldn't do to crash into that train's caboose, would it?"

Charlie inclined his head. Clem nodded. They stepped to the edge of the cab and jumped. Remaining on this train when it pulled into the depot was a sure way to get arrested. If there had been a dozen bulls prowling around back in Oakland, chances were good that many and more would be on patrol here. This wasn't just a train, after all. It carried the directors of the Central Pacific Railroad.

Charlie hit the ground, stumbled over a section of tracks, and lost his balance. His leg was improved but still not up to such shenanigans. Muscles aching, he got to his feet and looked around. A railroad detective looked in his direction. Charlie waved. The bull hesitated. This wasn't what he expected from a trespasser.

The express train's whistle filled the air with an ear-splitting cry proclaiming its arrival. This drew the bull's attention. Charlie and Clem hurried away, stepping over the crisscrossing tracks until they reached the edge of the rail yard.

"We need to catch Greta," Clem said.

"That train's already unloaded," Charlie said. "It doesn't matter. We know where she's going. If we tried to catch her on the passenger platform, we'd stand out like pigs at a church social." He tried to brush off coal dust and only smeared it.

"She'll make a beeline for the swap." Clem sucked in a deep breath and let it out slowly. Charlie wondered what went through his partner's head. Whatever it was, he was right about Greta being in a rush.

They circled the depot and pressed into the crowd along the street. Charlie had been in Sacramento often enough to visit Miss Lucy and her house of ill repute to know the town's layout. He led the way, cradling the bogus spike in his arms as if it were a baby in swaddling. Clem was quieter than usual.

# CHAPTER 37

"Hickman had something in mind," Charlie Dawson said. "This can't be a good place to swap the spike for money. It's too wide open."

This part of Sacramento was deserted, in spite of it being nearly noon. Buildings had been burned to the ground. No war-torn city could have shown more destruction. From the heavy stench in the air, more than the buildings had burned recently. Men had died here. Charlie looked into the blackened husks of the buildings and shuddered when he thought he made out charred bodies. It might have been his imagination, but he didn't think so.

Sacramento suffered the blight of too many towns built in a hurry. Flimsy firetraps were crushed one against the other. Any spark spread rapidly. He looked down the littered street, wondering if an ambush had already been set up. Hickman intended to play one side against the other.

"He expected Stanford to send someone to steal the spike," Clem said. "If he hid the spike in that burned-out building, he'd be able to take the money and walk off while someone fetched the spike."

"Railroad men aren't likely to be duped," Charlie said. "Hickman had to think he'd face a gunman, not a director of the Central Pacific." This argument enforced his idea that Hickman intended to dupe Collins, then sell the real spike to Stanford. Even a railroad director knew what a spike looked like, while a bank president, already frantic to keep his establishment afloat, would only glance at the golden spike with its forged inscription. At least, that's the way Charlie saw the ransom happening.

Collins first, here, now, then Stanford or whoever the railroad magnate sent to dicker with Hickman.

"Greta is in danger."

Charlie held his tongue. She had stolen the spike from under his nose. Any trouble she found with Collins or Stanford was all hers. He looked down the street. The only movement he spied were occasional rats foraging for food among the ruins. He sneezed as the nose-wrinkling stench of burned wood—and flesh—worked its ugly spell on him. The scent was slow to blow away. He preferred the cleaner feel of coal dust in his nostrils. That didn't carry the memory of death with it.

"Anywhere along this entire street is about perfect for a sniper." He stared at the dangling balconies and upper-story windows knocked out. All were good spots for a sniper to rest a rifle on a broken windowsill and wait for whoever showed up with the golden spike.

"There. There she is." Clem lurched forward, ready to rush to Greta's side. Charlie held him back.

"Let's see if she's brought the spike with her." He clutched the fake one Hickman had painted. He longed to swap it for the one Greta carried, but there wasn't any way to do so.

"She's hiding it in that tumbledown building," Clem said. "That's smart. If she carried it for the exchange, she'd be dead." He stared at another building. A flash of sunlight glinting off a rifle barrel showed where one of the snipers had settled in.

Where there was one, there'd be more. Too much rode on this single transaction. Greta had to know that. What was her plan? Charlie wondered if her greed pushed her to make foolish mistakes. She had to know how ruthless the men she tried to cheat were.

"If we circle around and come up from the far side, the sniper won't see us," Charlie said.

"We can warn her."

Charlie wondered what ran through his partner's brain at that moment. Clem looked excited. Or apprehensive. Or . . . ? Charlie tried to guess and found himself at a loss.

They moved quickly and worked their way through the nearest gutted building. Moving more carefully as they neared where Greta crouched, waiting, was prudent. She clutched a six-shooter in each hand. Nothing moved in the street that she didn't see.

"Greta!"

Clem's call brought the woman around, both six-guns cocked and aimed. Charlie started for his own pistol in case Greta fired. The play of emotions on her face warned she considered doing just that, then she lowered her guns.

"What're you doin' here, lover?"

Clem knelt beside her. Charlie wasn't able to hear what passed between the two. He picked his way through the tumble of bricks and treacherously burned flooring. A misstep would plunge him down into a basement filled with debris that could impale him.

"You don't never give up, do you, Charles?" she called out to him. He worried that she didn't holster her guns. She kept them at her sides as if he was the one most likely to plug her rather than the sniper hiding just a few yards down the street.

"We're partners, the three of us. That's what we decided back in Oakland." Charlie doubted she'd buy that, but he had to try. Clem had given them away when hiding until the swap happened was more prudent.

She looked shifty, then a poker face hid her emotions.

"You got a good memory."

"There are snipers up high, Greta." Clem started to point them out. She swung a pistol barrel down on his wrist. He cursed and said, "You didn't have to do that."

"Don't show 'em where we are. I found two of the varmints. There's likely a third one at the far end of the street. Hickman picked this place pretty good. We got all kinds of cover and my getaway can be 'bout in any direction."

"*Our* getaway," Charlie corrected. "We're partners."

"Yeah, partners." She sucked in a deep breath and let

it out slowly. "The fellow who's supposed to bring the money ought to be here any time now."

"Hickman wanted Stanford to deliver the money," Clem said.

"Well, Clement, that ain't gonna happen. Men like that don't dirty their hands. They have men like Hickman do it for them."

Charlie chewed his lower lip. What were the chances that the Central Pacific director sent someone who knew Hickman? Or Hickman knew the man most likely to bring the money? They were all in the same social whirl and had to know each other. Or at least know of each other.

She seemed to think it'd be a Central Pacific buyer for the spike and not Thomas Collins. Charlie wondered if he had mixed up the ransom notes Hickman had tried writing.

"Wear a mask," Charlie said suddenly. "That way they'll know the spike was stolen by someone they didn't know and who didn't want their face showing up on wanted posters."

"My face is on plenny of posters," Greta said. "If they figger out who I am, that'll increase my reputation. Strike fear into their black hearts, I always say."

"There he is," Clem said. "Waiting in the middle of the street."

"He's got a carpet bag. Filled with money!"

Greta Swinburne surged to her feet and waved. The Central Pacific hired hand called out, "Come get your blood money. Let me see the . . . merchandise."

Greta grabbed the oilcloth-wrapped spike, but Charlie held her back.

"Up high. Look. The snipers are ready to cut you down the instant you show your face."

"And give them a look at the spike," Clem added.

"What'll I do?" Greta dropped back behind a pile of bricks, out of sight of the snipers.

"Go out there to see if the money's in the carpetbag." Charlie moved closer to the spike. "When you're sure all the money's there, Clem can bring out the spike. I'll cover you both."

Greta mulled over that, then nodded.

"You won't be stealin' the spike since Clement will have it, and I'll have the money."

"If I don't take care of the snipers, I lose both the spike and the money." Charlie paused, then added, "And my partner."

"Partners," said Greta, grinning wolfishly. "You got a good head on your shoulders, Charles." She slapped him on the shoulder. Agile and moving as quick as a snake, she popped up, hands held high. "I'm comin' out."

"Bring the spike," the Central Pacific gunman said. "I got the money right here."

"You get it after I see the greenbacks."

The man in the street glanced up and moved around. Charlie followed his gaze and picked out where a fourth sniper waited. Such firepower was all he expected from men used to getting whatever they wanted. Nobody stole from the railroad and lived to brag about it.

"Wait, Clem, let her go ahead of you. Follow her. Don't stand together where they can shoot both of you."

Charlie quietly showed his partner where the snipers waited.

"I can't let her stand in that nest of snakes all by her lonesome." Clem shoved away Charlie's hand and stepped out. He hovered over his six-gun. When Greta reached the man in the street and took the carpetbag from him, he stepped out to go after her.

Charlie unwrapped the golden spike and ran his fingers over its etched length. He quickly wrapped up the bogus spike he'd brought and hid the real one a few feet away. When he paid attention to the three people in the street, he went cold inside.

"Duck!" he shouted. The man who had brought the carpetbag started a tug of war with Greta. They fought over the bag. When the man suddenly released it, she staggered back and collided with Clem. They both sat heavily in the middle of the street.

This was the signal for the ambush to begin. The hidden snipers began firing.

Charlie opened fire on the nearest sniper. His first two rounds spanged off brick around the window. His third round flew straight and true. The sniper's head snapped back and his rifle tumbled out the window to crash down below in the street.

By then the other three had sighted in their targets and fired with increasing accuracy.

"Get back," Charlie shouted. "Get back!"

His words acted as a goad to the ambushers. The riflemen began pumping out more lead than anyone could dodge. Greta winced as one bullet hit her in the side. Clem blazed away. It took only seconds before his Colt ran dry. He grabbed a handful of Greta's shirt and half dragged her along the street. She kicked and fought the whole way. He finally picked her up and dumped her down beside his partner, sheltered behind a waist-high collapsed brick wall.

"There wasn't nuthin' but cut paper in the bag," she shrieked. "They tried to swindle me!"

She jumped up and blazed away. Her bullets sprayed down the street, hitting no one but causing the snipers to take cover until her six-guns ran dry. Clem pulled her down when the hidden shooters began firing too accurately for safety.

"Are you sure there wasn't any money in the bag?" Charlie asked.

"As sure as I am that they are double-crossing cayuses!" Greta had reloaded and fired wildly over the wall.

"There's no point sitting here and getting our carcasses filled with lead," Charlie told the others. He took aim and fired at a sniper some distance down the street. The riflemen had come from their high ground and advanced from building to building along the street.

"We can get them all if we fire from over there," Clem said. He pointed to a still-standing shed a dozen yards away.

Charlie saw what Clem meant and motioned for him to give him covering fire. Head down, he ran as fast as he could. By the time he ducked into the shed, his leg hurt like hellfire. This prodded him into action. Through the doorway, he had a clear line of sight for two of the snipers. Quick shots took out one. The other yelped. Charlie had winged him. Instead of driving him from the firefight, it only infuriated the sniper. He fired faster and more wildly than ever now, spraying lead from one side of the street to the other.

The man who had passed over the fake ransom yelled from down the street. The riflemen pulled back. Charlie emptied his six-shooter and then . . . then was a silence so profound he felt as if he had been buried alive.

He reloaded, then made his way back to where he'd left Clem and Greta.

When he didn't see them, he looked around. The lead had flown so fast and deadly they might have been driven to another spot out of range. He called. The deathly silence remained unbroken. Charlie sighed, went to the pile of rubble where the spike had been hidden.

Nothing.

Greta had taken the oilcloth-wrapped fake spike.

He edged over to the other hiding place where he had stashed the real spike. Like a badger, he dug, throwing bricks and debris behind him. His heart almost stopped when he thought the real golden spike was gone, too. Then his fingers brushed over the canvas wrapping it. A quick tug unearthed it.

He peeled back the covering and ran his fingers over the finely etched messages on each of the four sides of the spike. Then he pressed his thumb down on the flat end and held it up. Impressed into his callused thumb was the message: THE LAST SPIKE.

Almost reverently he wrapped the golden rod and tucked it under his arm. Charlie Dawson knew what had to be done.

# CHAPTER 38

Charlie doubted the second attempt at ransoming the spike in Sacramento had gone well, either. He never bothered to scout the spot Hickman had chosen. There was no reason. Let Greta and Clem argue that the imitation they tried to ransom back was the real item. Whether Thomas Collins tried to steal it the way the Central Pacific Railroad executive had earlier was only of small interest. The only thing he knew was that Greta had intended for the ransom to work. When it didn't, she'd try foisting off the spike onto Collins, hoping to get some money.

A deep sigh racked him. He lied to himself if he claimed that the woman had any intention of cutting him and Clem in, should she be successful. He had only disgust for Greta, but Clem was his partner. Had been his partner. He threw away two years of partnership and working the Betty Sue Mine for . . . Greta "Swine" Swinburne.

"Nobody ever said you had the sense God gave a goose," Charlie muttered.

He steeled himself. The trip back to San Francisco

had been uneventful, even if he spent the entire time looking over his shoulder. He doubted either of his former allies had any inkling what he intended, even if they suspected he had the real golden spike.

The guard at the door leading into Collins's bank stared at him. Or was it the long spike all gift wrapped in a tattered piece of canvas that held his attention?

Loudly, Charlie asked to see the bank president. The guard snickered and shook his head. Such a demand from a man who looked as if he had been pulled backward through a knothole was never to be considered. Ever.

"Tell Mister Collins I have the spike. He'll want to talk to me. If he doesn't, I'll head on out without a fuss."

The guard scowled. He didn't budge but waved to another guard who came over. They whispered for a moment, then argued. The other guard lost. He climbed the broad staircase to the third floor where the president's office sprawled across the entire end of a hallway.

Charlie tried to look as if he didn't have a care in the world, but his heart pounded. Just as he was about to walk out, the guard at the second landing waved frantically.

"The president will see you." The guard who had blocked Charlie's way hastily stepped aside. He didn't want anything to do with ushering the unkempt, probably lying, visitor into his boss's office.

Charlie kept his pace slow and took the steps carefully. Let Collins stew a mite. Besides, Charlie's leg hurt him something fierce again. He had looked at it.

There didn't seem to be any rot setting in, so he had come straight here from the ferry, after arriving from Sacramento.

He expected to see Hiram Hickman at the door, looking at him disapprovingly, but that was loco. Hickman was dead. He wondered if Collins knew, and if he didn't, what small pleasure might be gained telling him what a carrion-eating buzzard his assistant was.

Had been.

He opened the big double doors and stepped in. For a moment he didn't see Collins. Then he heard the click of the man's heels as he paced at the side of the large office.

"Well? You said it was urgent."

Charlie went to the man's desk and unrolled the golden spike. He let it clatter down, steel against wood. The spike twisted over a quarter turn and rested in its glittery glory. Somehow, a ray of sunlight caught it like a dancer on stage in a spotlight.

Thomas Collins lurched to his desk and seized the spike. He wrapped his fingers around it and clutched it to his breast. Charlie thought he saw tears in the man's eyes.

"I promised I'd get it to you. There's time to send it by courier to Sacramento, get it on a train, and have it arrive in two days. That'll be in plenty of time for the ceremony."

"Stanford said he'd ruin me because the spike was lost." Collins snorted like a pig. "It was *his* train that derailed. It wasn't any of my fault. Not a bit of it."

Collins grinned crookedly. "Serves him right, trying to bankrupt me."

"The rest of the money you promised, Mister Collins. Do you have it here or should I get it from a teller downstairs?"

Gimlet eyes fixed on him. Gone was all trace of weakness now in the banker. He continued to hold the spike close like a new lover. But his words rattled out harsh and bitter.

"You got paid a hundred dollars already. That's plenty."

"You promised two thousand. You still owe me—"

"Try to collect it." He half-turned to protect the spike when Charlie leaned forward, fists on the desk. "Don't you try anything. I've got a dozen guards!"

"I did the job you hired me for. I delivered in time for you to ship that to Promontory Summit."

"I don't know what you're talking about. This isn't anything special. It's . . . nothing."

"Plenty of men died. It's something. Hickman was the one who tried to ransom it back to you. He wanted to collect from the railroad, too. He was a real skunk and wanted to play both of you for twice the ransom money."

"I don't know what you're saying."

"You probably didn't know it was your own assistant, but you sent gunmen to cut down whoever was selling this back. He was dead. Besides, I had it. Now give me my money."

"How do I know you weren't the one who sent that note demanding money?"

"Because I'm not asking for ten thousand dollars the way Hickman did. All I want is the balance you promised when you hired my partner and me. I want one thousand nine hundred dollars."

"Guards!"

Charlie started to draw. He hadn't waded through blood and breathed clouds of gunsmoke to have the banker cheat him. He had saved Collins a stack of greenbacks. And a powerful lot of bad feelings directed at him by the Central Pacific Railroad directors.

"You've got clout now, Collins. The railroad has to repay the loans you made them. You've got their spike."

Collins turned purple in the face. And Charlie had run out of time. Two guards threw open the doors to the office. He didn't have to turn around to know they had their six-shooters aimed at him. Electric tingles ran up and down his spine. He could throw down on Collins and get off a shot before the guards killed him. He tried to decide if the pleasure of adding an ounce of lead to Collins's fat belly was worth his own life.

The guards grabbed him. One on each arm and they jerked him around as their boss shouted orders. The blood pounded like the ocean surf in his ears. He heard only snippets over the liquid roar. Someone told the guards to throw him in the street. The rest ordered up fast horses and a company of guards and a ferry trip and to telegraph Oakland Long Wharf for an express train and—

Charlie tried to keep his balance as they threw him out the back door into the alley behind the bank. He crashed into a pile of garbage and fell heavily. He started to stand but a guard clubbed him. He didn't quite pass out but was too disoriented to stop the man from rummaging through his pockets.

"Got a few bucks," the guard boasted. "Thanks! I can use this." Then they argued over how to split the money they'd just stolen. Charlie came up to his knees and reached for his pistol. This time the blow knocked him forward onto his face. For what seemed like an eternity, he lay in the garbage, staring at the filthy dirt alley just beyond his nose. A thousand improbable schemes ran through his head. Then it became a million. As he recovered to put some of them into effect, he pushed himself to his feet. At the mouth of the alley, Thomas Collins, surrounded by a company of armed guards, climbed into a carriage and trotted off.

The golden spike was on its way to Utah. This time Collins wasn't relying on secrecy. He wasn't letting it out of his clutches. And he was protected by a dozen armed men.

Charlie scraped off what garbage he could. He knew he stank to high heaven. He looked around when he got into the street. Collins and his small army were long gone. Trying to steal back the spike was impossible now. He had been foolish to think that the bank president would honor their deal. Charlie felt sick to his stomach, but not everyone was as honest as he was and kept their word. After all he'd been through, he should have known better. Sometimes, going against his deep-seated beliefs and sense of honor just wasn't possible, and it cost him.

He got his bearings and started walking.

As he made his way north across Portsmouth Square toward the Barbary Coast, he considered a quick dip in the cold water of San Francisco Bay.

He shook his head. There was plenty of time for that after he'd gotten roaring drunk.

A hand shook his shoulder. He opened one eye and tried to focus.

"Go 'way. I'm getting drunk."

"From the look of it—and the smell—you're not getting drunk. You're all the way there."

Charlie forced his eyes closed, squeezed tight, then opened them slowly. The saloon came into focus and memory crept back. He had reached the outskirts of the Barbary Coast and seen the Bella Union Melodeon with its invitingly open doors and heard the jaunty music pouring out. When he looked in, a few dancers had pranced about on the big stage, hoisting their skirts and scandalously showing their legs. It had been just the place to drown his sorrows and ogle the racy dancers. And the pretty waiter girls. But the soiled doves avoided him when he emptied his pockets and didn't have even a quarter. Collins's guards hadn't completely robbed him, though they might as well have. He had two dimes and nothing more to show for all his misadventures.

In this place, the soiled doves were high-class and charged more than that for just a peek.

But it bought him four beers.

"If you drink fast enough, you can get roaring drunk quick. That's what I'm doing," he said. Charlie put one hand over his left eye. This helped him focus. "Wash? Washington Collins?"

"None other than," the young man said, scooting his chair closer so he pressed close to Charlie. They had to shout to make themselves heard. The piano player hammered out his tunes, the dancers strutted around, and the crowd loudly cheered them on.

"Buy me a drink. I'd buy you one but . . ." Charlie turned out his coat pockets. Not even dead bugs rolled out onto the table.

"Alas, Mister Dawson, I can't. Rather, I won't. You see, Dinah has convinced me that I should join her in the ranks of those opposing Demon Rum. I have become a teetotaler." He picked up Charlie's foam-specked beer mug and ran his finger around the rim. He put it to his lips, shuddered, and set the mug back on the table. "I don't know if I am constitutionally up to be part of the temperance movement. They call themselves a league and have meetings."

"She won't marry you if you're not sober?"

"For a man in his cups, you are remarkably astute," Wash said. "That is the crux of the matter. Moreover, Mister Hewes will take me on as an apprentice to learn the trade. That makes me just a little bit more acceptable to become his son-in-law. In a few years, I can be the proprietor of a fine jewelry and engraving business."

"And married to his daughter."

"Yes," Wash said with a sigh. "Married to Dinah."

"Wh-whatya doing here if you're not drinking?" Charlie wanted to capture the last drop of beer in the mug, but Wash had beaten him to it.

"I have cut all ties with my father and to the bank. I never had it in me to foreclose mortgages on widows or engage in the shady practices my father dotes on. That doesn't mean I don't talk to those still working in the bank."

"You know I gave him the golden spike."

"That's a polite way of saying he stole it from you. From the condition of your clothing, the bullet holes and blood stains, you risked much to recover the final spike to be driven connecting the two railroads." Wash hesitated, then asked, "Am I to believe your partner was part of the cost you paid?"

Charlie could only nod.

"You lost your partner, and my father defrauded you. It's one thing to overcharge a railroad for a construction loan, it's quite another to break a contract with a working man. A man's word should be his bond."

"I can sue."

Wash laughed.

"Which lawyer will take your case? They're all on my father's payroll or beholden to him in some way or another. What will you do?"

"Go back to Potluck. Fight to get my mine back. The Betty Sue. It's got gold in it. I know it." Charlie sobered a little more as anger flooded him. Another banker and his son had robbed him of the Betty Sue. He couldn't get away from being swindled by bankers. Collins in San Francisco. Norton in Potluck.

"This might ease your misery. I found it in my father's desk." Wash dipped into a vest pocket and held up a heavy brass key. He pressed it into Charlie's hand.

Keeping one eye shut, Charlie made out the engraving. A giant dollar sign had been etched on each side of the shaft. He looked at Wash and shrugged, not knowing what this meant.

"I practiced some of my new skills. Those are my dollar signs and nicely etched, if I say so myself," Wash said proudly. He stood and looked down at Charlie. "The key might just fit something you've come across already. Good luck, Mister Dawson, and thank you for all you've done for me."

Jerome Washington Collins held his head up high and left the melodeon without downing a single drink.

Charlie leaned back in his chair, legs splayed out under the table. He ran his finger over the key, traced over the dollar signs, then brightened. The fog of alcohol burned away entirely. His luck had changed.

# CHAPTER 39

It took better than three days to hike around the southern end of San Francisco Bay. Charlie finally climbed into the back of a freight wagon and sneaked a ride until he passed a railroad station south of Oakland. He jumped off the wagon there and spent another day finding out the patrol schedules for the railroad bulls. Not having money made travel difficult. He had to find what food he could. Drinking from the Bay was impossible because it was salty ocean water, but he found watering troughs and an occasional stream to quench his thirst. He lost more weight and his leg was slow to heal, but he refused to give up.

He had found something to give him hope things would improve.

All the while he ran his finger over the outline of the brass key in his watch pocket. That gave him courage enough to duck under a freight car, avoid a detective, and then squeeze into a cargo-filled car.

When the train lurched and started its way north, he was almost crushed as the poorly secured crates shifted. He considered getting a job as a cargo handler to show these slackers how to secure boxes. The only thing that kept him aboard the car was the sight of a huge engine backing up in the Sacramento yards. The freight all around him was destined for delivery on the far side of the Sierra Nevadas—where he was bound.

Three hours into the trip, the engine began to strain. He heard steel against steel protest as wheels dug down against the rails. Charlie worked open the door and looked out. Cold night air gusted into his face and energized him for what had to be done. Again, he touched the key hidden in his pocket. He had been cheated too many times for this not to be the key to his salvation.

The train started up the steep incline. He opened the door further and sat on the edge, legs dangling. Feeling just a little daring, he leaned far out to get an idea where the train ran in its trip over the mountain pass.

From the stars, he guessed it was close to midnight when he jumped off. He hit the ground. The shoulder was narrow because the track bed had been chipped out of solid rock. Before the Chinese workers, there hadn't been even a ledge here.

Skidding and sliding downslope, he caught himself after a twenty-foot drop. He pressed back into the mountain and regained his senses. The night was clear. Not a single cloud hid the bright moon that turned the land silver and gave enough light for him to risk the arduous descent.

By morning he stood on the floor of Dos Robles Canyon. The sharp aroma of pine filled his nostrils, wind blew up the canyon, and he heard the gurgle of the stream as it hurried past. Once more, he again fingered the outline of the key in his pocket. Bone-tired but anxious to get to his goal, he shuffled along until he found the spot where the train that had originally carried the golden spike had derailed. The rising sun showed the scar down the entire mountainside where the mail car had rolled over and over. On the far side of the stream running down the canyon lay the freight car they had searched.

But it was the mail car he wanted.

Exhaustion took its toll. As much as he wanted to continue, he had to rest. When he saw the mail car, a curious mixture of anticipation and dread filled him. Wash Collins had no reason to seek him out in San Francisco and give him the key.

"Not a joke. No point," he said. He splashed frigid water from the stream on his face, washed off his hands, and then crawled up the hill to the mail car.

He wormed his way inside and sat in front of the smaller safe he and Clem had ignored before. It was too small to hold the spike. They had left it alone. The faded lettering on the side read: CALIFORNIA SECURITY BANK.

He pressed his finger against the keyhole. Charlie took a deep breath, pulled out the key and carefully guided it to the keyhole. For a moment, it refused to go in. He wiggled it about a little and a small rock came free. When he tried the key again, it fit perfectly.

The heavy safe door opened and two leather bags tumbled out amid an avalanche of papers. He pushed those aside and untied the leather thong on the first bag. He repeated it for the second.

Charlie Dawson sat back and stared at the gold coins from the safe.

"You wouldn't pay me two thousand, you skinflint. I'll keep this five thousand in your gold for my troubles."

Amid all the trouble and haste to recover the golden spike, Collins had ignored—or forgotten—that he also shipped two pouches of gold coins on the derailed mail car.

Charlie tucked the bags of gold coins into his pockets and returned to the stream. It was a long hike in either direction. He had no idea what lay downstream. Up Dos Robles Canyon lay Sacramento. On foot, Charlie arrived in the capital after a tiring six days to spend some of his gold on drinks, steaks, and Miss Lucy's finest suite. She treated him like royalty for a week.

She treated him like a bank president.

# CHAPTER 40

Charlie Dawson rode into Potluck, feeling fat and sassy. Most of the gold he'd taken from the Central Pacific mail car still bulged in his pocket. He had enjoyed all the pleasures Miss Lucy had for sale and recuperated. He had even bought a doctor's services to patch up his leg. There'd been a trace of gangrene setting it. A few quick swipes of a scalpel, some peroxide, and Miss Lucy's tender ministrations had brought him back to feeling as fit as a fiddle.

He patted his horse's neck. The Appaloosa had cost more than he'd ever consider paying for horseflesh, but what was money for if he didn't spend it? Wisely, he thought, wisely, since he deserved the finer things in life after all he'd been through. The stallion could run all day and half the night and never show a speck of lather on its powerful flanks.

"I've earned it," he said to himself.

More than this, he felt that he had done his duty telling Lily Denton what had happened to her beau. That had been hard and she had cried and he had returned her four dollars. But he had been honor bound to tell her how Laramie Reynolds had died, even if he embroidered the tale a mite to make the man into a hero.

He rode down Potluck's main street. Nobody waved to him. They didn't recognize him. He'd been gone too long. More than that, he had new clothes, a haircut, and a shave and rode a horse finer than anyone in town owned.

Including banker Norton.

He touched the Colt shoved into his waistband. He had a fancy holster tucked away in his saddlebags. After wearing it for a day in the saddle, he decided he liked his own accustomed way of carrying the six-gun. A cross-draw holster might ride better, but he remembered the days of living on nothing but beans for a month. Spending money wasn't as easy as it might be for him. In some things, the old ways were better.

Charlie drew rein in front of the bank. He started to dismount. He had business with the bank president and his good-for-nothing son. The county land office next door drew him first. He guided his horse there and hopped to the ground.

Inside the tax office toiled a youngster half Charlie's age. If the blond clerk was sixteen, it'd come as a surprise.

"Got some business, son."

"What's that?" The blond clerk half jumped out of his skin. "Sorry. You startled me. I was working real hard and . . ." He stared back at the open ledger on his desk. "What can I do for you?"

"Tell me about taxes owed on the Betty Sue Mine."

"That one came across my desk a while back. Maybe

a month or so ago. Don't recall what happened." He
went to a wood crate and began shuffling through the
papers crammed into it. "Got it." He held up his trophy
and waved the sheets around. "What's your interest?"

"Who owns it? The bank?"

Charlie took a half step back at the clerk's reaction.
He laughed until tears ran down his cheeks when the
clerk told him.

"That's a good one. The bank doesn't own a danged
thing."

"Come again?" Charlie wiped tears away and wanted
to be sure he'd heard aright.

"Norton stole all the deposits. Him and his son, the
sheriff thinks. That put the bank into bankruptcy. Imag-
ine that. A bank going bankrupt. You wouldn't have
heard about it, being new to town and all. Folks are still
steamed about it. Most everyone lost money."

Charlie considered himself lucky. He'd been so
broke he didn't have a penny in Norton's bank for the
crook to steal.

"Yes, sir, folks mighta lost cash money but a goodly
number came out ahead."

"What's that got to do with the Betty Sue?"

"All the loan records were destroyed. No way of
collecting on any of the mortgages held by the bank,
not unless folks fess up to what they owed." The clerk
grinned. "Can't believe folks are willing to do that. So,
'bout all the records left are right here. Tax records."

"What's it say about the mine?"

"The bank's listed as owner but no taxes were paid.
Norton didn't even file transfer papers or pay that fee."

"If somebody else paid all that, the mine would belong to him?"

"Nobody's going to fork over this much for a worthless mine." The clerk ran his finger down a column of numbers. "They'd have to pay close to a hundred dollars."

Charlie took out one of the leather pouches and dropped five double eagles onto the counter.

"How's that? All the costs covered?"

"And taxes," the clerk said, eyes widening at such a pile of money in front of him. "Those are what the county assessor wants collected most."

Charlie silently counted the coins one by one, then stacked them. He pushed the stack across the counter using the tip of his index finger.

"Draw up the papers making me the new owner." He grinned. "Make me the new owner again."

"How's that?" He stared at Charlie, then shook his head. "You're Charlie Dawson. You worked that worthless money pit before Norton did you out of it."

"Norton and his son. What became of Jimmy Norton?"

"Him and his pa destroyed records, took everyone's money, and haven't been seen since. It might be they were in cahoots with Marshal Thompson."

Charlie caught his breath. He had ugly memories of how the lawman had tried to arrest him.

"Some folks think Thompson lit out with the Nortons. Me, I think he wanted to avoid getting tarred and feathered for not catching them after they disappeared."

"He's not the marshal?"

"Gracious, no. The mayor hired some drifter by the name of Figueroa. Nice enough guy, but he spends a bit too much time in the saloon." The clerk made a gesture that showed the new marshal likely imbibed too much. "Sheriff Abbott has wanted posters out on all their heads, but I don't think they'll show their faces here again. And the marshal's too concerned with staring at the bottom of a shot glass to ever try collecting the reward."

Charlie didn't care if Marshal Figueroa drank himself into a stupor. He had a clean slate with him, just as he had a clear title to the Betty Sue. He tapped the desk to get the clerk back doing his duty.

The clerk flipped open the lid on his inkpot, cleaned the nibs on his pen, and began scribbling fast. Charlie watched with some satisfaction. In less than five minutes he was the sole owner of the Betty Sue.

He tucked the papers into his coat pocket.

"You have any notion where Norton and his boy went?" He rested his hand on the Colt's grip. His fingers twitched. The former bank president was one thing. His son and the way he with his worthless friends had run him off the claim had to be avenged. It was good that the sheriff wanted to hang the Nortons' scalps from his belt, but Charlie wanted to be part of the punishment.

"The marshal's got a wanted poster on them." The clerk chewed at his lower lip and said hesitantly, "You got a taste to be a bounty hunter?"

"Thanks," Charlie said, tucking the fresh deed into his coat pocket.

He stepped out into the bright sun. Finding stolen horses and rescuing men who'd been shanghaied had whetted his taste for a different life. Retrieving the golden spike, now long since hammered into the ground to connect the two railroads in one long transcontinental steel ribbon, had been dangerous. Deadly. But the price had been too high. He might be rich and once more the owner of the Betty Sue, but it had cost him dearly.

"I hope Greta doesn't slit your throat some night when she gets tired of you, Clem, old friend."

Becoming a bounty hunter until he tracked down the Nortons appealed to him. Returning to his old life as a miner appealed even more. He stepped up and turned the Appaloosa toward his claim.

The day turned dark as clouds boiled over the mountains to the east. A drop of rain or two pelted him by the time he reached his mine. The cabin looked the worse for wear and tear after being shot up and burned pretty near to the ground. For all that, it wasn't in terrible shape, and looked as if someone had used some boards to make repairs before giving up. He'd take a few days and fix it up right. Right now the roof looked tight enough for the rain to run off. He put his fine new horse in the shed and was surprised to find a small nosebag of oats. He settled that on his horse, then went to the cabin.

He hesitated entering. So many memories. And the Betty Sue's dark, yawning mouth drew him like iron gloms onto a magnet. It had been too long since he had picked up a chisel and hammer to flake off rock hunting for the telltale hint of gold.

"Got the glitter," he said, touching his bulging pockets. "But it'll be sweeter when I hit that mother lode and take out gold with my own hands. It's there. I know it."

As anxious as he was to return to the mine, he had a good meal at the café. No one recognized him. That made him feel better. He was a new man, one reborn. That meant his luck had changed, too. After finishing, he rode his fine horse to the Betty Sue.

He sat astride his Appaloosa, savoring the feel of ownership and finally having things go right. Charlie stared at the dark mouth entering the mine. He dismounted and took a few steps, then stopped. Something felt wrong. He knelt and ran his fingers over the ore cart's tracks. A layer of rust formed mighty quick if the cart wasn't rolled over the rails every day. After all this time, a thick layer should have formed.

Bright steel showed through dirt. The tracks had been used recently. And often. He looked at the pile of dross stretching down the hill from the end of the tracks. Fresh debris showed considerable chunks had been dumped within the past few days. When he had worked the mine before, it was almost as if he memorized every rock being rolled downhill. Each was an insult for not being solid gold.

He returned to the mine and drew his six-gun. Hammering sounds echoed from deep inside the mine. Someone worked the mine.

*His* mine.

Charlie went into the mine, ducking at all the right places to keep from banging his head on low support beams. He found the ledge with a miner's candle mounted on a tin holder. A leather strap secured it around his head after he lit the candle. His hands were free—or at least one was. He clutched his six-gun tightly as he went deeper into the mine.

He came to a juncture and paused. Straight ahead

was the last stope he had worked. Someone opened a new one running off to the right. The sounds of digging became louder as he inched down it.

A man hunched over a rock held in his hand.

"Is there any reason I shouldn't just plug you for trespassing?" Charlie cocked the gun to show how serious he was about the threat.

He tried not to look too surprised when Clem turned around. He held up the rock and grinned.

"It's here, Charlie, just like the assay said!"

"What're you talking about? The assayer said there wasn't any gold in these rocks. You mean I was right? There *is* gold?"

"Naw, he was right. There isn't enough gold in the Betty Sue to fill a tooth." He held up the rock. "But there *is* silver. Galena. We missed the vein because we followed that quartz deeper into the mountain. We should have gone after the black, sooty stuff." He held up the rock. "This is silver and lots of it!"

"The assay never said anything about silver."

"It did. The second page did." Clem dropped the rock and grabbed for his coat hung on the upturned handle of a shovel.

Charlie almost drilled him. He calmed down. Being too high-strung was understandable. His once-upon-a-time partner had just told him there was silver to be mined.

"See? The second page." Clem held out the wrinkled and dirty, sweat- and water-stained sheets.

Charlie tucked his pistol into his waistband. Clem

wasn't heeled. He took the familiar pages and held them up so the flickering candlelight let him read the report. The first page denied the presence of gold. The second page listed everything not in the mine until he got halfway down it.

"That's a high assay," he said. "Four or five ounces a ton."

"We can dig it out, but I looked through the dross we dumped down the mountainside. There's enough already dug there we missed because we wanted gold so bad."

"No gold," Charlie said. Then he grinned. "I'll take silver!"

Clem let out a whoop and gave Charlie a hug that threatened to crush him. When he released him, Charlie stepped back.

"What are you doing here? You and Greta took off together. I figured you'd be in Montana by now."

"She might be. Or Wyoming. She's got big plans. And she got a telegram from Roy."

"Dupree?"

Clem turned sour.

"Yeah, him. She got a telegram from him about how easy the pickings were in Wyoming. Why she'd believe a thing that buzzard'd ever say is a poser."

"You left her?"

Clem rubbed his throat and grinned ruefully.

"You might say that. I told her we were going to Montana. She tried to cut my throat while I was asleep one night."

"You always were a heavy sleeper."

"Especially after what we—" Clem rubbed his neck again. "I don't think she meant to kill me. Just to run me off because she still has feelings for me."

"What do you think of her?"

"As little as I can. That's why I came back to the mine. To take my mind off her. And I finally read the assay report I'd been carrying around all this time." He cleared his throat. "Well, not exactly. That cute new girl at the saloon read it for me. It fell out of my pocket one night after we'd, well, I was celebrating being free of Greta. May Ellen read it to me. She had no idea what any of it meant, but I did. Ruby silver ore!" He did a little dance. "Silver, Charlie, we got a whole lot of silver to mine!"

"I paid all the back taxes and money fees Norton didn't. I'm the owner. The sole owner."

"But we're partners!"

Charlie wasn't so sure about that. They had been through too much not to be partners, yet Clem had taken up with Greta Swinburne without so much as a backward look. Until she tried to cut his throat.

"I know you have a history with her, having been married and all. But what if she comes by again? Will you still call me partner if she comes back, wiggles her caboose, and shows you a little leg?"

"Oh, she showed me more than that," Clem said.

Charlie pressed his hand against the bulge in his right coat pocket. By rights, all the gold was his. Wash Collins had given him the key to the safe, and he had risked life and limb to get it from the mail car. But Clem had been cheated out of his share of the money Thomas Collins had promised.

"This is yours," Charlie said, coming to a decision. He tossed one of the pouches to Clem.

"What is it?"

Charlie explained. Clem never opened the pouch. He weighed it by bouncing the bag in the palm of his hand, but he never opened it. After a long pause, he pitched it back.

"Yours," he said. "I wasn't there to guard your back."

Charlie fished out a thousand dollars of the double eagles and held them out.

"What Collins owed *us*. Two thousand split down the middle, plus a little bonus."

Clem took a deep breath, accepted the money, and dropped the gold coins into his watch pocket.

"What about the Betty Sue?"

"That's easier. We dug out most of this crazy mountain together. There's no reason we can't dig out the other half together." Charlie thrust out his hand. "Partners?"

"Partners!" Clem about crushed his hand as they shook.

"Now that's settled, there's something more important to talk about."

Clem scowled.

"What's that?"

"Who fixes dinner? You're a terrible cook and I hate everything you fix. But if I whip up a mess of beans, you have to clean the pot."

"Me, clean it? We're rich. We got silver coming out

our ears. Let's hire one of them railroad track men who're out of a job now to do our cooking and cleaning."

"A right fine idea," Charlie said, "but what about tonight? I'll cook, you clean."

They left the mine arguing over the chores.

It was good having a partner again.

Almost overnight, Dead Broke turns into a lawless
hotbed of angry out-of-work miners
and out-for-blood merchants.
In desperation, Mayor Nugget considers a few
harebrained schemes like bringing in mail-order
brides, building ice castles to attract tourists, even
planting other minerals in the mines to fool investors.
Dead Broke needs law and order,
so Nugget sends for top gun Mick MacMicking.
But a notorious gambler named Connor Boyle
has other plans—and with his band of hired guns
will blow Dead Broke off the map completely
to get what he wants.

For this town to survive, Nugget, Mick, a drunken
lawman, and a woman gambler will have to put the
dead back in Dead Broke . . . and some cool-hand
killers in the ground.

National Bestselling Authors
William W. Johnstone
and J.A. Johnstone

## DEAD BROKE, COLORADO

**First in a New Western Series!**

**On sale now, wherever Pinnacle Books are sold.**

**JOHNSTONE COUNTRY.
WHERE DYING IS EASY
AND LIVING IS HARD.**

**Live Free. Read Hard.**
www.williamjohnstone.net
Visit us at kensingtonbooks.com

# PROLOGUE

Allane Auchinleck was drunk that morning.

But then, most wastrels on This Side Of The Slope would have pointed out that Allane Auchinleck was seldom sober any morning, any afternoon, any evening. Any day of the year. Since he had seldom found enough gold in Colorado's towering Rocky Mountains to pay for good rye, he brewed his own whiskey. It wasn't fit to drink, other miners would agree, but it was whiskey. So they drank whatever Allane Auchinleck was willing to sell or, rarely, share.

Auchinleck charged a dollar a cup—Leadville prices, the other miners would protest, but they paid.

After all, it was whiskey.

And in these towering mountains, whiskey—like anything else a man could buy or steal in Denver, Durango, Silverton, or Colorado Springs—was hard to find.

Besides, Auchinleck usually was so far in his cups that he couldn't tell the difference between a nickel and a Morgan dollar. For most miners, one cup usually did the job. Actually, two sips fried the brains of many unaccustomed to a Scotsman's idea of what went into good liquor. Two cups, a few men had learned, could prove fatal. Auchinleck held the record, four cups in four hours—and still alive to tell the story.

Although, it should be pointed out that those who had witnessed that historic drunken evening, would swear on a stack of Bibles—not that a Good Book could be found this high up—that Auchinleck's hair, from topknot to the tip of his long beard, wasn't as white, but had been much thicker, before he passed out, not to awaken for three days. That had been back in '79.

But then, Auchinleck was accustomed to forty-rod, and it was his recipe, his liquor, his cast-iron stomach, and his soul, the latter of which he said he had sold to the devil, then got it back when Lucifer himself needed a shot of the Scotsman's brew.

On this particular glorious August evening, with the first snow falling at eleven thousand feet, Auchinleck was drinking with Sluagdach. Most of the miners had already started packing their mules and heading to lower, warmer, and much healthier, elevations. Some would head south to thaw out and blow whatever they had accumulated in their pokes. Many would drift east to Denver, where the heartiest would find jobs swamping saloons or moving horse apples out of livery stables. Others would just call it quits as a miner and find an easier way to make a living.

But not Allane Auchinleck. "Mining is my life," he told Sluagdach, and topped off his cup with more of his swill.

"Aye," Sluagdach said. "And a mighty poor life it has been, Nugget."

Nugget had become Auchinleck's handle. There are some who say that the Scotsman earned that moniker because of his determination, certainly not for his lack of profitable results. More than likely, the moniker had stuck to the miner like stains of tobacco juice because Nugget was a whole lot easier to remember or say than Auchinleck.

That was the year Sluagdach came in as Auchinleck's partner. It made sense at the time (though Sluagdach was a touch more than just fairly inebriated) when such a partnership had been suggested in a tent near the headwaters of the Arkansas River.

They both came to America from Scotland, Auchinleck had pointed out. They could enter this deal as equals. Nugget still had his mule; Sluagdach had to eat his. Sluagdach had a new pickax, while Nugget had been the first to discover that Finnian Kuznetsov, that half-Irish, half-Russian gravel-snatcher, had run into a she-bear with two cubs, and had not been able to raise his Sharps carbine in time. The she-bear won that fight, and the cubs enjoyed a fine breakfast, but Nugget had given the Russian mick a burial, and taken the shovel and pack, and a poke of silver, and Kuznetsov's boots and mink hat. Although he did not let his partner know, Nugget had also found the dead miner's mule (lucky critter, having fled while the she-bear and cubs enjoyed a breakfast of Kuznetsov), which is how come Nugget brought a mule into the partnership, his own having been stolen by some thief, or had wandered off to parts unknown while its master slept off a drunk.

"I said," Sluagdach said, raising his voice after getting no response from his drunkard partner, "that a mighty poor life it . . ." But the whiskey robbed his memory, as Nugget's whiskey often did.

"Who can be poor when he lives in this wild, fabulous country?" Nugget, whose tolerance for his special malt had not fogged his memory or limited vocabulary. "Look at these mountains. Feel this snow. God's country this is."

"God," Sluagdach said, "is welcome to it."

That's when Nugget, against his better judgment, reached into the ripped-apart coat that he had also taken from the dearly departed dead miner, and pulled out the poke. By the time he realized what he was doing, the poke had flown out of Nugget's hand and landed at Sluagdach's feet.

The muleless miner stared at the leather pouch, reached between his legs—he did not recall sitting down, but that Scotsman's liquor had a way of making men forget lots of things—and heard the grinding of rocks inside. It took him a few minutes for his eyes to focus and his brain to recall how to work the strings to open the little rawhide bag, and then saw a few chunks fall into the grass, damp with snow that hadn't started to stick.

No matter how drunk a miner got, he was never too far gone not to recognize good ore.

"Silver," he whispered, and looked across the campsite at his partner.

"That's how Leadville got started," Nugget heard himself saying.

"Where was his camp?"

After a heavy sigh, Nugget shook his head.

"Best I could tell," he explained, "he was on his way down the slope when 'em cubs et him."

"To file a claim." Sluagdach sounded sober all of a sudden.

Nugget felt his head bob in agreement.

One of the nuggets came to Sluagdach's right eye. Then it was lowered to his mouth, and his tongue tasted it, then it went inside his mouth where his gold upper molar and his rotted lower molar tested it. After removing the bit of ore, he stared at his partner.

"This'll assay anywhere from twenty-two to twenty-five ounces per ton."

No miner on This Side Of The Slope and hardly a professional metallurgist from Arizona to Colorado would doubt anything Sluagdach said. No one knew how he did it. But he had never been more than an ounce off his predictions. The Russian-Irishman had never made a fortune as a miner, but his good eye, his teeth, and tongue knew what they saw, bit, and tasted.

Unable to think of anything to say, Nugget killed the bit of whiskey remaining in his cup, then belched.

"Where exactly did that ol' feller got et?" Sluagdach asked. His voice had an eerie quietness to it.

Nugget's head jerked in a vague northeasterly direction. Which he could blame on his drunkenness if Sluagdach remembered anything in the morning.

Finnian Kuznetsov had met his grisly end to a grizzly sow and her cubs about four miles southwest.

"Think this snow'll last?" Sluagdach asked.

"Nah." It was way too early, even at this altitude, and, well, twenty-two to twenty-five ounces per ton had to be worth the risk.

They set out early the next morning, finding the hole where Nugget had rolled Finnian Kuznetsov's remains and covered with pine needles and some rocks, which had been removed by some critter that had scattered bones and such all over the area. Then they backtracked over rough country, and around twelve thousand feet, they found the Irish Russian's camp.

Two months later, they had discovered . . .

"Not a thing," Sluagdach announced, although he had used practically every foul word that a good Scot knew to describe that particular thing.

By then, at that altitude, winter was coming in right quick-like, and their supplies were all but out. This morning's breakfast had been piñon nuts and Nugget's whiskey. Sleet had pelted them that morning, Sluagdach had slipped on an icy patch and almost broken his back, while Nugget's mule grew more cantankerous every minute.

"We'll have to come back next spring," Sluagdach said.

With a sad nod, Nugget went to his keg of whiskey, rocked the oak a bit, and decided there was just enough for a final night of celebration—or mourning—for the two of them.

It was a drunk to remember. Sluagdach broke Nugget's record. Shattered it, would have been a more accurate description. Five cups. Five! While Nugget had to stop drinking—*his own whiskey*—after three.

It wasn't because he couldn't handle his wretched brew. It was because he now saw everything. He saw that Sluagdach would dissolve the partnership. Sluagdach would come back to these beasts of mountains and find the Russian mick's discovery. Sluagdach would go down in history. Allane "Nugget" Auchinleck would be forgotten.

Auchinleck. What a name. What a lie. He remembered way back when he was but a lad, living near the Firth of Clyde in the county of Ayrshire on Scotland's west coast, and his grandfather, a fine man who had given Nugget his first taste of single malt when he was but four years old, had told him what the name Auchinleck meant.

"A place of field with flat stones," the old man had said.

It sounded glorious to a four-year-old pup of a boy, but now he scoffed at it all. A place of field with flat stones. Oh, the stones were here all right, massive boulders of granite that held riches in them, but would never let those riches go. And flat?

He laughed and tossed his empty cup toward the fire.

There was nothing flat on This Side Of The Slope.

That's when Allane Auchinleck decided it was time to kill himself.

He announced his intentions to Sluagdach, who laughed, agreeing that it was a fine, fine idea.

Sluagdach even laughed when Nugget withdrew a stick of dynamite in a box of dwindling supplies. Laughing? That swine of a Russian mick. No, no. Nugget had to correct his thinking. Sluagdach was a Scot. The Russian mick was Finnian Kuznetsov, dead and et by a Colorado she-grizzly's cubs.

"I'll speak lovingly of you at your funeral," Sluagdach said, and he cackled even harder when Nugget began to cap and fuse the explosive.

It wasn't until Nugget lit the fuse by holding the stick over the fire that Sluagdach acted soberly.

For a man who should, if the Lord was indeed merciful, be dead already or at least passed out, Sluagdach moved like a man who really wanted not to be blown to bits.

He came charging like that she-bear must have charged at the Russian mick, and the next thing Nugget recalled was his ears ringing and the entire ground shaking. Somehow, Sluagdach had knocked the dynamite away, and it must have rolled down the hill toward that massive rock of immovable stone.

Nugget could not recall the explosion, but his ears were ringing, and he felt stones and bits of wood and more stones raining down upon him. They would cover him in his grave. Peace on earth. God rest this merry gentleman.

"You ignorant, crazy, drunken fool."

That was not, Nugget figured out eventually, the voice of St. Peter. He sat up, brushing off the dust,

the grime, the mud, the sand, and looked into the eyes
of his equally intoxicated fellow miner. His partner.

He didn't think anyone would call him sober, but he
realized just how drunk—and how close to death, real
death, he had come.

"Oh . . . ," however, was about all Nugget could muster
at that moment.

"Oh." His partner wiped his bloody nose, then crawled
out of the rubble and staggered toward the smoking
ruins of part of the camp they had made.

"Mule!" Nugget remembered.

The brays gave him some relief, and as smoke and
dust settled, he saw the animal through rocks and forests
about three hundred yards away. It appeared that the
tether had hooked like an anchor between some rocks
and halted the beast's run for its life. Otherwise, the
mule might be in Leadville by now.

Maybe even Omaha.

He started for the animal, but Sluagdach told him to
stop. "Come up here!" his pard demanded.

Well, Nugget couldn't deny the man who had stopped
him from killing himself. He climbed up the ridge,
where he looked down into the smokiness.

He could smell the rotten egg stench of blown powder.
And he could see what one stick of dynamite could do.
It had created a chasm.

And unveiled a cave.

"Get us a light," Sluagdach said.

Somehow, the campfire still burned, and Nugget
found a stick that would serve as a torch, so they walked,

slipped, skidded, and slid down into the depression and toward the cave.

"Bear," Nugget remembered.

"If a silvertip was in there, it would be out by now," Sluagdach argued.

They stopped at the entrance, and Nugget held the torch into the opening.

The flame from the torch bounced off the left side of the cave. Slowly the two men staggered to that wall, and Nugget held the torch closer.

"The mother lode," Sluagdach said.

He didn't have to smell and taste the vein of silver to know that. What's more, when they moved fifty yards deeper into the cavern, the torch revealed something else. At first, Nugget thought it was an Egyptian mummy. He had seen an illustration in one of those newspapers he could not read.

But this wasn't a mummy. He held the torch higher, praying that it would not go out. At least there was no wind here to blow it out.

"It's . . ." Nugget could not find the words.

"The biggest . . . chunk . . . of silver . . . I ever . . . did . . . see."

*I am dead*, Nugget thought. *Or I'm dreaming*.

His partner stuck his dirty pointer finger in his mouth, getting it good and wet, then touched the gleaming mummy that was a statue of precious metal.

The biggest nugget Allane Auchinleck had ever seen. The biggest one anybody had ever seen.

Maybe he was dead after all.

Sluagdach brought his pointer finger, slobbery with

his slobber, and rubbed it on the giant nugget. It was shaped like a diamond. A diamond made of pure silver.

Sluagdach then put his finger back in his mouth.

His eyes widened.

"It . . . I . . . I . . . aye . . . aye . . . It . . ."

That's when the wind, or something—maybe Sluagdach's giant gasps at air—blew out the torch.

And Sluagdach collapsed in front of the silver diamond.

Nugget never knew how he did it, but he found his pard's shoulders and dragged him out into the fading light of the camp. The old man with a Midas tongue stared up. But his right hand gripped the coat above his breast, and the eyes did not blink.

"Your ticker," Nugget whispered.

Yes. The sight of that strike . . . it had been too much for a man, even a man who had downed five cups of that lethal brew.

That meant . . .

Nugget rose. "No partner." He ran back to the campfire, found a piece of timber, part of the suicidal destruction he had reaped, and stuck it in the coals till the end ignited. The wood must have been part pitch, because it blazed with a fury, and Nugget raced back down, past his dead pard, and into the cave where he held the blazing torch again.

It was no dream. No drunken hallucination. It was . . . real . . . silver . . . the strike of a lifetime.

He ran back, ready to mark his claim, and get his name onto a document that made this . . .

"All mine."

When he stepped outside, it was dark. He walked slowly, using the timber as his light, and stopped in front of the body of his poor, dead pard.

"I won't forget you," he whispered to the unseeing corpse. And in a moment of generosity, he proclaimed.

"You're dead, and I was broke, but, Colorado will remember us forever because I'm naming this mine and the town that'll grow up around it Dead Broke. That's it." He felt relieved.

"Dead Broke, Colorado." He nodded. The flame seemed to reflect in the dead man's eyes, and maybe it was because of the light, but he thought Sluagdach nodded in agreement.

"Dead Broke, Colorado," he said.

"Because who would want to work and live in a place called Sluagdach Auchinleck?"